Dona Gracia

The Woman Who Led
Jews to Safety
in Muslim Lands

Aaron Nommaz

Ottoman Publishing

Dona Gracia: The Woman Who Led Jews to Safety in Muslim Lands

ISBN: 978-605-82048-0-5

Author: Aaron Nommaz

Translator: Aaron Nommaz

Editor: Bonnie Britt

Illustrator: Gordon Napier

First published in the Turkish language and edited by Uğur Becerikli with the title *Dona Gracia: Kanuni'Nin Yahudi Bankeri (Dona Gracia: the Sultan's Jewish Banker) by* Instanbul publisher, Destek Yayınları,

Please address requests for bulk orders through donagraciabook.com

Ottoman Publishing, 79 Cynthia Drive, Richboro PA 18954

To contact the author: aaron@nommaz.com
On the web: aaronnommaz.com.

Dedication

My wife and angel Adel, half Izmir half Tiflis,
amazing cocktail
My daughter in law Ellen and son Vedat
perfect match/mismatch of a couple
and delightful grandson, Eytan

This story is based on historical facts.

Contents

Through the Generations   1

Escape from Lisbon   54

Wedding and Arrest   94

Eyes on Reyna   124

Betrayal   170

Entering Istanbul   204

Harem   238

Wedding   248

Sultan, The Magnificent   256

Death   261

The Doctor   267

The Inquisition, Again   304

Synagogue and Yeshiva   307

Secret News   341

Acknowledgements   375

Through the Generations

I will say it all.

Kindness, evil, conviction, bigotry, hatred, war, peace, looting, nomadism, and resistance. Centuries, thousands of years of exile.

I am Dona Gracia. To many, I am known as Signora Mendes. I was born in a land called Portugal 1500 years after Jesus.

Through the generations, I have been remembered for commissioning the synagogue and yeshiva in Haskeuy, Istanbul. My personal history is filled with events as black as the darkest night and as white as the lightest stars. I have seen all that would melt a human heart. I have witnessed the angelical as well as the diabolical side of human beings. My old eyes have seen the heavenly beauties of the world and the horrors of hell on earth. I passed to the next generation the secret confided in me, the secret that had been handed down through the generations for hundreds of decades. I protected the secret and never gave up. I did all I could to succeed. I struggled with my closest friends and direst enemies. In times when my most trusted confidantes betrayed me, I was left wondering. In other times, I received a helping hand in most unexpected ways. To protect the secret, for this purpose alone, I sacrificed my life, my femininity, and the love of my life. Was I up to the task? I never found out.

Above all, I want it to be known: I worshipped only the creator of the universe, the one God with all my being.

That ominous day —that dreadful event

Lisbon was struggling with a spreading epidemic that rendered the city unlivable. The progress of the disease was ruthless, tearing away large sections of the population from time to time, scaring away those who had heard of the disease and the death it brought. Fear overwhelmed the city; work places closed; people lost their jobs and their income. The economy was on the brink of collapse. News of affected—or lost—relatives demoralized everyone. The courageous ones who dared go out had difficulty even finding bread.

As the disease spread, it was heard that the royal family was having difficulty tolerating the depressing atmosphere. They hurriedly left the capital to a place where they could breathe with ease. They moved to the better shielded town of Abrantes. It was said that their intention was to return only after the disaster was over.

The royals succeeded in running away from the over-burdened city but difficult times awaited those left behind. The rulers were very much to blame as they were incapable of taking precautions to protect the people—even from famine.

To cover up their failings, they chose to redirect attention elsewhere—to scapegoats. The so called "Marranos" were already viewed suspiciously. Even the Spanish definition of the word Marranos is condescending in that it translates into English as "pigs." As recent converts to Christianity, they were natural targets—and they were seen as the root of all evil. Forcefully baptized Jews converted to Christianity were called

Marranos while Muslims were known as Moriscos, a word derived from the root Moors in a pejorative way. The royals accused both groups of exporting wheat with the result that locals were denied bread. As if they were the only exporters of wheat, the accusation was that "these opportunist people are the reason for the shortage." The failed leaders encouraged hatred and targeted these well-educated, good people engaged in business.

Marranos couldn't believe what they heard; it couldn't be about them. It is true—they were forcefully made Christians—but it is also true that they were good Portuguese citizens and an integral part of this country.

A Sacred Holiday on a Sunday in April

As a coincidence, a ray of light flowed from a crack in the roof of San Domingo's, a Church of the Dominican order, brightly illuminating the Virgin's face. People who were already desperately depressed from illness and famine regarded this as an important sign, a miracle. Zealous people running out of the church shared this miracle with whoever came their way. In an instant, the news of this great event spread. Everyone and anyone rushed to the church. It was such that there was no empty space left, no room to move. They needed to personally experience this miracle. The exhilarated crowd had already forgotten its burdens. The long anticipated salvation was transmitted through the sacred face of the Savior; what better proof was needed? Horrifying days were left behind, and the ray of light could be seen by all in the Virgin's face.

Dona Gracia

"Long awaited day is here! Finally, the miracle!"

Marranos had to hide their feelings. Even if they hung white sausages filled with vegetables in visible spots in their gardens to give the impression that they eat pork, they lived as good Jews inside their houses. They didn't dare air their views and, instead, had to act like good Christians. Upon my twelfth birthday, like my brothers and all other kids, I was informed of all these strange but confidential maneuvers. By the time Marranos turned 13, they would have learned much earlier how to act outside. Even when disagreeing with popular opinion, they would never challenge it openly. When insults and denigrations were hurled at them for their deeper beliefs, they didn't have the right to object to priests during New Testament lessons.

Unfortunately, all kids were not trained as well in applying the survival code. This Marrano kid was one of them. He happened to be in church that day, as was customary. He came out with his perceived reality and loudly said:

"Come on, that's no miracle! There is a hole in the ceiling! Look!"

It is also said that he might have been a little cheeky too!

A German trader claimed his daughter's crippled arm was cured; exhilarated, he was in a trance. Suddenly he pounced on the poor boy. It took only seconds for him to pull out his knife and stab the child's stomach.

"Heretic!"

The boy's warm blood gushed onto the church floor. As the flabbergasted child fell, his crimson blood puddled at his feet.

Seeing this, the crowd was amazed and stupefied.

Through the Generations

One person came to his senses, exclaiming angrily, "What have you done, Man!" How can you kill a little child? He is still a child. How would he know about God's miracles? Blood was already on the Church floor.

The smell of blood went to the heads of the enraged crowd. Wrath born of famine and death that had previously found no outlet finally found its destination in a scapegoat.

But before releasing their pent-up, collective anger, the crowd first thought it saw a miracle!

Church-goers saw light on the statue of the Virgin Mary's face during mass.

Someone yelled, "No one can make fun of our Virgin's miracle!"

Support was soon to come from some in the raging crowd. Suddenly one of them attacked a man by pounding his head. Other blows followed. Within seconds, frightful sounds from women mixed with the victorious cries of men.

The kid's body was lifted up. No, it wasn't like holding an angel. He was carried like a sack on a man's shoulders to the front of the church, and dismembered.

The dead boy's brother was there too. He was alerted but couldn't escape capture by the maddened crowd.

"Run, save yourself!"

They pulled out his arms and legs before he even fainted. They left him to die in order to follow someone with a cross in his hand.

"Let's go and finish all these Marranos!"

They made their way to the Marranos' quarters.

Senses were lost, consciences extinct. Either through fear

or euphoria, even the good ones lost their minds, and were carried by this river of craze. The ones who thrived with feelings of hate, animosity, and discrimination led the way.

Outcasts and vagabonds joined the killing party, running in a senseless torrent. Their uncontrollable hatred grew stronger.

As soon as they reached their destination, they attacked whoever came their way. Within moments, bitter sounds mixed with cries of "Damn the Marranos" were heard.

"Don't. Is there no pity?"

"Stay away for God's sake, I am baptized!"

"No, help-pp!"

"You know me, why are you doing this?"

They started slaughtering whoever they found, burning whatever was around.

By sundown, nearly all were murdered, crippled, or wounded. Blood was everywhere and houses ablaze. Rising smoke darkened the day before sunset. Night covered Lisbon like a nightmare.

That wasn't fun enough. They started carrying the wounded and crippled to the Church and threw them half-alive into the fire that was ablaze by that time. Taking advantage of the situation, bums pillaged the shops and houses.

The few who succeeded in hiding prayed fearfully "God, Please don't let them find us" while hoping for news from their men who were outside. The Lisbon Public Prosecutor tried to calm the people, asking them, in vain, to return home but it was too late. Brain-washed security forces with hatred for Marranos and Jews, stood there watching, not moving a finger.

Smoke filled the sky continuously for four days.

The smell of burnt flesh and blood filled the air. In the streets, breathing was hard. When the ones who were hiding were found, they too were killed.

The city was drowned in screams as humanity was literally trampled.

Blood stink, a revolting smell, once experienced is never forgotten. Humans are living organisms, not pieces of dead wood. However much one tries, humans do not burn completely. A streak of blood or a piece of a broken bone remains, horrifying scenes.

How can men do this to fellow men?

The square was littered with the cadavers of children, their little bodies missing arms, feet, and heads.

The fall of Granada was celebrated all over Europe with religious rituals. But further east, the conquest of Constantinople by Muslims ended nearly 1500 years of rule by the Roman Empire. It was a massive blow to Christendom. After the conquest of Constantinople, the rising Christian ideals for unity reached the realm of possibility in Europe as the fiery crusades rekindled. Despite strong protests by the Islamic world, pogroms against Muslims continued in Andalusia.

And then, there were us Jews. After Jews were expelled from Jerusalem around 600 BCE, we wandered throughout the world without a home or state. Some of us landed in Spain and Portugal.

Two years before the fall of Granada in 1490, Pope Innocent VIII, endeavored to bring European states together to organize a Crusade against the Ottomans. As leverage, the son of the "Great Turk" Zizimi was imprisoned in the Vatican. Muslims from Andalusia sent messengers to Sultan Mehmet to warn him. After the fall of Andalusia, Muslims living in North Africa were concerned for Spain had become the Ottomans' greatest enemy.

The Ottoman Empire was an escape address for Jews. For about 200 years, Jews had migrated to these lands. After the expulsion of the Jews by the Hungarian King Louis, in 1360, many Central European Jews fled to the secure lands. Ottomans proclaimed their welcoming discourse. Jews were already living in Salonica and Constantinople but after conquest, these cities were in shambles and there was need for an active population to breathe life into them. Muslim and Jewish friends sent letters to Spain and Portugal, saying"

"Come to the Ottoman lands, where everyone sits peacefully under their own fig tree. Take refuge here."

Multitudes of Jews flocked to Ottoman cities. The capital of old Byzantium was reconstructed as a thriving city of opulence and prosperity. I learned that the "The Grand Turk" settled the better off and most capable immigrants in the city, while encouraging those coming from the Balkans to live in the area between Chifit Kapı and Zindan Kapı, which had been previously occupied by Venetians. He called it the "Jewish Door." Sultan Mehmet, the Conqueror, forbade Venetians to occupy those parts of the city as he opened it to Jewish people. Those already living in Constantinople were called Romaniotes; those coming from the Iberia Peninsula were Sephardic; and the ones from central Europe were Ashkenazi. All three groups enjoyed equal freedoms. According to Muslim Law, even the Sultan had to live by the laws of the country. It is hard for a non-Jew to appreciate the consequences of this precept. My people, generation after generation, were invited by promising kings, emperors, and dukes to settle their lands in order to stabilize their economies. Jewish people enriched the lands where they relocated and revived the markets. After a while, in most cases, all commitments were forgotten, rulers put aside all laws guaranteeing their welfare, and followed their mean short-term interests. Until 1556, the Ottomans had kept all such promises and settled people coming from the Iberia Peninsula to Salonica, Patra, Edirne, Bursa and in several other cities. Newcomers formed their own congregations and built their synagogues. New quarters formed in the vicinity of synagogues.

No one gave credence to the blood libel.

The Muslim population did not believe that Jews used the blood of Christian children to make the Passover matzo.

Our business professionals, engineers, and doctors all came to the Sultan's country. Naturally we also moved to the country where "everyone sits peacefully under their own fig tree."

Life at Home

I was born to the Benveniste family in 1510 on the Gregorian calendar. My Jewish name was Hanna. I could use it only at home. Outside, I was to use the name that was deemed fit for baptism: Beatrice de Luna. I am better known as Dona Gracia.

Hanna in Hebrew means "gracious." Gracia is the equivalent in Portuguese. In all probability, that was the reason my family called me Hanna:

Through the Generations

Gracia Nasi

It is difficult to imagine how it feels to not be permitted to use your given name. We could not exist as Jews, or we would be exiled. Neither I nor my family could openly use the Jewish name for prolonged periods and, in some cases, forever.

Benveniste is a very reputable family name in the Jewish realm. The roots go to successful businessmen and academicians from Narbonne. In Catalan, the Benveniste banking house was renowned for their many subsidiaries in Spain and further East. As the myth has it, a certain Alphonso or Pedro, king of Spain, had a medical doctor as his minister of finance. The minister was also a plant specialist. During a stroll in the palace gardens, the king asked him the name of a pinkish purple plant called 'malva.' The minister replied that these plants, called 'Bienva,' had leaves that were boiled to make a certain medicine. Bienva means all is well in Spanish. An anti-Semitic person, yearning for the minister's post came to the king, told the king the plant name was 'Malva" not 'Bienva' meaning "the going is bad.

The king asked the reason for the deception. The Jewish minister explained:

"Your Majesty, it is true that the plant name is Malva." On this beautiful day when you honored us as your guests, I did not want to use the name Malva, I said Bienva and entreat your forgiveness."

"I find the malevolent words of one that is jealous of you mal-intended and shameful. Your clarification satisfies me. It saved me from losing a capable doctor and able minister. As a remembrance of this event, from now on you will be called Benveniste.

Dona Gracia

My family lived in Castile, Spain. With the "edict of expulsion" on the 31st of May 1492, all Jews and Muslims were asked to either convert to Christianity or leave Spain forever. They had 40 days to decide. The ones who refused conversion were to leave. That meant they had to sell their houses and belongings quickly, and well below market prices. According to the edict, they were not allowed to take precious metals like silver or gold but could only take whatever else they could carry. Villas were exchanged for warm clothes. The expulsion was hard on Jews and created great damage. The expulsion had long been anticipated by many. Naturally some could make use of the agents of the parallel trade mechanisms. In general, these were reliable, converted Jews who could remain and sell at more opportune times before transferring to wherever they wanted to go.

Portugal was the closest new location that was both convenient and shared language similarities with Spain. The Inquisition was not yet established in Portugal and there were no suspicions—at that time—that it would come.

My father and mother emigrated under the "New Christian" names of Alvaro and Filipa da Luna.

It was customary for the rich and the aristocratic to intermarry. The convention was neither my doing nor my undoing. The tradition, handed down through the generations, was practiced rigidly. I had to marry my uncle. The main reason, I guess, was preservation of wealth within the family.

With the Christian name, Francisco Mendes, my husband-to-be was a Semah Benveniste, who married me for the same reasons that I married him.

Through the Generations

I had two brothers, Guimar and Aires, and a sister, Brianda, who complicated my life.

I remember some aspects of my childhood very well and other aspects with some difficulty. Some memories are unforgettable memories and others rather foggy. My father, Alvaro, dealt with precious metals and other commodities. He was strongly attached to his values. Though he pretended to be a good Christian, he was still a Benveniste and, therefore, strongly attached to Judaism. As brothers and sisters, we were brought up with extreme care and without any discrimination. Our father wanted us to be well-educated with a strong and well-rounded background. He made certain we had a sound religious upbringing. Even though we seemed Christian to the outer world, we practiced our traditions and rituals as sincerely as any conservative Jewish home. My father made sure there were no diversions or mistakes.

"Darling, the outer world is full of threat for us Jews. Never forget that, even though we are guiltless, there are fanatics that would blame us even for being Jewish."

As a little girl, I sat on his lap while he told me about his business ventures and short biblical stories. He never neglected to tell me and my brothers the Bible stories. To make certain we appreciated the direness of the situation, he shared horrifying stories about the burdens imposed by the Inquisition to blessed people for being true to their faith, how they were exiled, murdered, torn to pieces. Among all the instructions I received, the one that stuck most deeply was that we had to hide our true beliefs and act differently outside. As a little girl, I figured myself as being one of the courageous heroes who would walk, head up, to death without wavering in the face of torture but yelling gloriously our true beliefs when facing the prosecutors. Naturally, at that time I had no idea of things to come.

My mother, Filipa, lit candles at sundown and made preparations to greet the Shabbat. The whole family would be joyfully present and sit at a beautiful and most attentively prepared table, have the tastiest and choicest food. Those of us who were over age thirteen drank a specially selected wine after the prayer of the termination of the sixth working day of the week. In the Purim celebration, we received many presents, though our favorite was a whiling top. We learned not to eat pork and other foods prohibited by the Torah. During Passover dinner, the half matzo (the Afikoman) was hidden. Whichever of us kids found it, would get a special present. And, we played at breaking eggs.

The Shabbat starts after sunset on Friday nights. Silently, we would all stand up while my father read the Kiddush prayer with a glass of choice wine in his hand. We recalled that God created the world in six days and rested on the seventh. We offered gratitude for being saved by Him from bondage in Egypt and for giving us the Shabbat as a precious gift. Then there would be the breaking and salting of the manna bread into several pieces. After reciting the HaMotzi prayer, my father ate the first piece of bread, leaving the rest for us.

At dinner, after the ritual was over, I always chose to sit next to my dad. Doing so gave me a warm and comforting feeling of security. I knew that my brothers and sister envied me though I didn't particularly care about Brianda's feelings.

Through the Generations

Noticing that I swung my feet in the air, my father said with a smile "You seem happy."

I bit my bread.

"I am very happy dad! Tomorrow is a free day."

He smiled again, came closer, and caressed my cheek

"Dear girl. We will rejoice in expressing our gratitude to God for all that we have."

"Dad, why is it that Christians never rest?"

He shook his head.

"Some of them believe that Sunday is a resting day. However many have to work nearly every day. Only truly civilized people like us know the meaning of a holiday. It is God's present to us. Don't forget there will be many prayers to recite."

I shook my head with the same austerity.

My mum, Filipa, said, "Brianda is neglecting her Hebrew studies."

"As to Gracia, she is working hard. At this pace she will learn the meaning of all prayers."

Brianda's threw a jealous look at me. I didn't care.

She replied: "Mom I am doing the best I can!"

Our mum moved her head disapprovingly.

"You have to try harder. It is not good enough."

My father was softer in his approach.

"Kids you know that we are not allowed to keep books written in Hebrew. If they discover these books, we could face the blame of being 'heretics.' We could be harshly punished after being accused of reverting to Judaism. As a doctor, I obtained permission by claiming that these are medical books. I want you to be more careful and take advantage of learning better Hebrew."

Mother always worried.

"I am terrified at the thought that they could raid the house or that someone can inform during a Christian inspector's visit."

My father was more courageous.

"Filipa, no inspector would know Hebrew. As I told you, if such an inspector comes, we will say that they are medical books. Be vigilant all the time! Whatever they invent to trick you, never ever reveal the truth. Otherwise they can confiscate all our property and throw us into jail. They might even kill us."

The mood at the table changed completely. Though we were kids, we understood full well what father was saying.

"I am learning Christianity well too."

"Well-done, girl. To give the impression that we are good Christians, and as I often say, we have to learn Christianity well too."

Brianda answered:

"We must appear as Christians!"

"Yes."

It was my turn to throw a glance of jealousy to her. She shrugged her shoulders.

"Must learn the New Testament too. All of you."

Mother bit her lip:

"You know, Alvaro, sometimes I get an urge to kill Father Adriano."

My mother was from a noble family and it was most unusual for her to say such things. Even father was surprised.

"Why?"

"When you told me that an instructor was needed for the

kids, I approached him. We made a hefty payment for his services but he constantly insults us Jews in front of the kids. I sometimes feel like confronting him and answering his insults, straight to his face."

Knowing full well that she would never dare, he pensively shook his head.

"Sweetheart, take care not to aggravate Father Adriano. You never know, we might someday need him desperately as a witness. His word could change much, if such a day ever comes."

"God forbid."

Frankly, I repeated the same words. The fact that we might need one day his testament that we are true and sincere Christians might save us from being judged from reverting to Judaism. Though at the time, I didn't quite appreciate what this would entail, I felt is as terrifying. Just this feeling was enough to strongly motivate me to learn Christianity, although it was foreign to me. I was small. My fear was not only for myself and not even for my brother and sisters, I was most concerned about my parents, terrified at the thought that something might happen to them. In my prayers, I always included them. This trauma would follow me to the end of my days, fears not for myself but worry for my dear ones.

After the Lisbon massacre, four years before I was born, this fright was anchored in my soul. Bloodshed, massacred Jews, burnt, dragged, torn to pieces, dismembered, subjected to horrifying tortures. Very few of those who ran, leaving behind their homes, managed to save themselves and relatives. As kids, we were told these unforgettable stories, repeatedly, as if we had been there and subjected to these horrors.

Father said, "Precious ones, the epidemic was spreading, shops were closed, people lost their jobs and livelihood. The economy was on the brink of collapsing. News of affected or lost relatives was demoralizing; the courageous ones, who dared to go out, had difficulty even finding bread. We were less affected but the condition of the poorer masses was appalling. The royal family and the rich had left for Abrantes while waiting for the disease to retreat and for the economy to be less unstable. They were really the ones to blame. The king and other administrators didn't close the doors of the city on time nor did they apply a quarantine regime to slow the spread of disease. In short, they had no idea how to cope with such a disaster. No precautions were taken to ensure that the population's minimum necessities were met. They couldn't admit to this reality and accept the blame so they reverted to the easiest and traditional way that had been used for thousands of years; they pointed at us Jews, exaggerating our wealth without mentioning that we worked hard. They pretended we were stealing what was theirs. The shortage of bread was our fault.

"They channeled hatred toward the Marranos. The crowd, enraged and agitated, attacked the Jewish quarters, spilling blood all over. Four days, children, this nightmare lasted four full days. Thousands of women and children were thrown into the huge bonfire in front of the San Domingo's Church, or murdered on the spot. The bodies of the Jews remained in the fire. They didn't allow even for the remains to be collected and buried in the proper Jewish tradition."

We already absorbed enough information. I knew the rest as

if I were there. A ray of light illuminates the Virgin's face; a Marrano kid says "That's no miracle." He is murdered there in the church, the start of the massacre of Jews that lasted four days.

"What next dad?" asked Brianda who was saddened.

"Then the king returned to Lisbon and ruled that all culprits should be brought to justice. Hundreds of gallows were built along the Tagus River. After a quick trial, those who were caught were hanged. Normally their bodies would have been left to rot but, because there were not enough gallows, the criminals were taken down to make room for others. Though many were punished, the administrators saved themselves from embarrassment. Who knows? They probably hadn't thought that so many would be killed and that things could get so much out of hand."

Mum and dad, like so many Marranos, realized that there would not be peace for them in Portugal.

"Our flaws, children, lie in the fact that we work hard and end up being successful and rich. That is the main issue. They want to steal our possessions and to make it look legal by attacking our religious beliefs."

The Secret

My uncle Francisco Mendes was one of the most handsome men on earth. Though there was an important age difference between us, we could converse liberally on many topics. He was among the richest business men in Portugal.

Softly he held my hand as a gentleman would, and asked:

"Dona Gracia, I want to marry you. You know I have been wanting this for a long time. Would you share your opinion with me?"

Dona Gracia

My heart pounded so hard, it felt like it would jump out of my chest. Nevertheless, I acted as a well-brought-up lady would. I said:

"Dear Francisco, you know very well that this decision lies with my father, I wouldn't have a say on that."

He shook his head, understandingly.

A few days later, my farther said he would like to have a private talk with me. He asked me into the library.

I knocked and waited.

"Come in."

I entered. My father had difficulty hiding his emotions. I could guess why. His eldest child had entered the age of marriage, and as a father, he shared my excitement.

"Sit down, my child. Let's talk tête à tête for a while."

I sat, silently. He was still standing. He had his hands around his hips with his back turned to me. This great man, who met so many interesting and strange people in his business life and concluded so many transactions successfully, I felt in this moment, comported himself like a novice.

"You are already grown up. You will soon be eighteen. You will have to get married soon. You understand me, don't you?"

"Yes, father."

"Like most girls with a perfect upbringing like yourself, you also have many suitors. However, my little darling, first, I would want you to marry a person of our religion and naturally an appropriate one. Your happiness is my first prerogative. Naturally, you could marry one of your choice, my dearest, but you have to be careful. When making up your mind you should consider not only yourself but also your family, co-religionists and us all.

"I understand, dad."

"My darling, as a loving father, it would make me happy to see you married to a suitable candidate that you would love or could love. We had this conversation with your mother. Your uncle Francisco wants to marry you. We have already promised your hand to him but if you object, we have the option of refusal."

He silently waited for my reaction. I was dying to say yes, but did not rush.

"Darling, your mother and I both think that Francisco is a qualifying candidate. His wealth and rank in society are well-known, and he is a relative. I cannot think of a better suitor."

He turned to face me to decipher my facial expressions. I did not want to keep him waiting any longer.

"Your acquiescence and blessings are enough for me. If you see fit, it's fine by me too."

I smiled. He smiled in return beaming with both understanding and relief.

My father's goal was to marry his children happily to proper matches that would continue his legacy. Our fortune was growing day by day and the number of proposals for his beloved girls was increasing.

"Is that all dad?"

He was silent. He turned to look out the window. A prolonged silence followed. I was naturally excited but didn't know what to make of this silence.

"Hanna, my lovely…"

Whenever he addresses me with my Jewish name, I expect

a discourse with religious connotation to follow.

"I am all ears, dad."

What I am about to tell you is of utmost importance and just as confidential. Do you follow me?"

I looked him straight in the eyes. "Sure."

"I don't want you to share this even with Brianda! This. This. is a secret shared with very few even within the family. Unfortunately, I have no surviving son. For a girl, it's a heavy burden to carry but I always fully trusted you. I have no doubt that you will cope with this mission, my darling daughter."

"Father, you are scaring me!"

"No, don't be afraid! There is nothing to fear. Always be on your guard. Even at times that you think you are cautious, revisit this in your mind over and over."

"Now, listen to me carefully. We have a secret and it is time for you to know."

My Wedding to Francisco

Francisco had a good upbringing. He was well educated. With his colossal fortune, he was the ideal prospective husband that many a young girl would dream about. With our close family tie, he was one of the few I would much like to be close to. When alone with him, just the two of us, I wouldn't need to act as a Christian. No need to act. When I reach eighteen, there would be no obstacles.

I imagined that when the wedding became a reality, I would be swept off my feet. But no, my father had altered everything. After our conversation, the excitement disappeared. I was naturally happy because of the marriage prospect but the secret that I inherited made me discover there are more important things in life than marriage, or leading a happy life with a good husband.

Brianda didn't delay in showing her curiosity.

"Are you hiding something from me?"

"Where did you get this idea into your head? What can I have to hide from you?"

"I don't know. After your talk with father, I sensed something strange about you. You have other things on your mind."

"You are talking nonsense. Don't talk like that!"

"I knew it!" She exclaimed as if she'd caught me. "There definitely is something."

"Oh, come on! Its time you grow up! You are a big girl now. Don't forget that, after me, it will be your turn to marry."

"There are no secrets about the fact that I will marry Diogo."

She was right. The most suitable candidate for her would be Francisco's younger brother Diogo, our other uncle. In fact, Diogo was more eloquent and social than Francisco. Because of our smaller age difference, we were more friendly. He also preferred chatting with me rather than with Brianda. At this stage, there was nothing I could do.

"Take care not to lose Diogo! Instead of me, you should be thinking of him. Many a Marrano family is dying for their daughter to marry him!"

"I would kill them, if ever they try."

I laughed.

Mission accomplished. Now that I got her to worry about him, she would leave me alone.

Dona Gracia

I went to the small place of worship in our house and prayed:

"Dear God, I don't know what to do. I am but your worthless servant, a little girl. I wonder if I will be worthy of this trust? Will I be able to execute my duties? Protect me and always be by my side. Never abandon me. Prevent me from faltering and betraying the secret I am entrusted with. Help me prove worthy of this duty and when the time comes, help me transfer it to the right person."

As an observant Jew, my father respected all the rituals. Francisco signed the Ketubah— a Jewish prenuptial agreement where the rights and responsibilities of the groom are enumerated and also the sum to be returned to the bride in case of a divorce is stated. After signing, my father would give Francisco a hefty fortune as my dowry. Upon the receipt of this sum, his fortune would be considerably augmented. The marriage was conducted strictly according to Jewish tradition with all the prayers and blessings, only it was performed secretly, at home.

I was the eldest and so was Francisco. He had two sisters one of whom was my mother. But the one, like him, who took responsibility for the business, was Diogo. The son of his other sister, Joseph Nasi, would play a crucial role in my life, until my last days.

Francisco's family was composed of doctors, diplomats, and high-level palace administrators. They were Benvenistes.

"I was born in Soria, my dear wife," he said. "In 1482 when I was ten, we fled the Inquisition in Spain and settled in Portugal as Jews. We are one of the rich six hundred families.

Through the Generations

But here, oppression started when I was fourteen. We had no choice but to pretend to convert as a formality and act as if we had changed our religion."

"I know, my darling."

Luckily, he was over thirteen when forced to become Christian. A Jewish boy is considered mature. Metaphorically, up to this age his sins are registered in his father's book of life but from there on, a clean book is opened in his name and the father is liberated. He is now fully responsible for his actions. Before age thirteen, kids go through a rigorous religious training where they learn Hebrew, the original language of the Torah, and some important prayers like the Shema, Amidah, Ashrei Yoshvei, Beteha, and others. By the time of the Bar Mitzvah celebrations, boys gain a sound Jewish identity and know the related code of behavior.

"You know that I am older than you."

"By exactly twenty-eight years.

"Does this worry you?"

"No, I am so happy to be married to you. The age difference is unimportant."

"At church, when I said 'Yes,' in front of the congregation, I felt that way as I did at home, during the real Jewish wedding ceremony too."

Before the wedding, I took the Mikveh bath to purify my aura among prayers. As was customary, I didn't see Francisco for a full week before the wedding. At home, the ceremony took place under the 'huppah,' a form of tent symbolizing our future home. Francisco was presented with the Ketubah and he signed it. We did the whole thing in utmost secrecy to

ensure that even our neighbors would not know. At the end of the ceremony, Francisco smashed a glass cup for all to commemorate the greatest catastrophe that had befallen Judaism, the destruction of the first and second temples in Jerusalem, and the subsequent exile.

When entering the Church, I mumbled to myself as many Marranos did:

"I only worship with all my being only the one God, creator of the universe."

Francisco constructed a little chapel in his home that was his excuse for not going to mass on Sundays.

He would keep the Shabbat together as a day of rest and fast on Yom Kippur. He did not eat pork and lived as much as possible by Jewish customs. Naturally we couldn't keep a Kosher home as 'shohets' were forbidden. This is the authorized slaughter of animals. The slaughterers would first see that the animal could walk straight, and then analyze their internals, such as kidneys and liver. If all parts of the animal were healthy, only then would the meat qualify for kosher consumption.

In spite of our efforts, I always felt that he shared the discomforted conscience of rejecting Judaism by pretention.

I know this denial has weighed on the consciences of nearly all Marranos because rejecting Judaism, even in form is a serious sin.

"I feel untrue to myself sometimes, Francisco." Laying my head on his shoulder, I feel like a sinner, doing all these things forbidden by the Ten Commandments. There is but one G-d and worshipping Christ on an object, the cross, as the son of

G-d violates the commandment, "I am the LORD thy God, no graven images or likenesses…"

"We were obliged," he said, hoping to console me. 'Dinah malhuta dina' says our tradition. You will obey the laws of the princes of the land, even if contradictory to the Torah. In spite of it all, we never abandoned our true religion, our beliefs, my love. It's all a show."

"I dream of the day when we will openly live by our tenets."

I was so overwhelmed that I nearly asked if he knew about the secret. If he didn't know, he would understand that I was hiding something. I refrained from asking. He noticed my discomfort but thought it was because of my sorrow. Suddenly he switched to a different subject.

"The sea connection to India discovered by Vasco de Gama is serving us well, my sweetheart. We will be Europe's greatest importers. The spices, precious stones and luxury goods coming from India and China will inundate Europe because of us. Particularly spices. We will have the spice monopoly."

I knew from my inspection of the kitchens that meat is hard when fresh and it stinks when kept too long. Either way, I did not find it pleasant to eat. The way to overcome these obstacles was to spice it. Moreover, it was believed that it had aphrodisiac effects, adding considerably to its attraction.

"We will import the spices. Europeans will enjoy delicious meats and, in the meantime, we will fill our coffers."

Then what's next?

~ ~

Instead of Benveniste, I was given the Mendes surname. I became Beatrice de Luna Mendes.

Through the Generations

"My beloved, you will always be Gracia Nasi to us. We will call you Hanna only in our hearts; we cannot take risks on your behalf."

"I know you always think of my wellbeing."

"Naturally, I am having beautiful dresses made for you, Venetian style with plenty of precious stones and pearls. You will wear specially selected stones we are importing from India."

"Then I will be sitting like a doll in one corner as a show piece?"

"No. You will assist me with my business. You will be by me at home and in the office."

"Really? Will you allow me to take an interest in the business too?"

"For sure! You are not the type who would be happy staying at home all the time."

That was great news. It means that my prayers were heard. Avenues were opening in front of me to enable my coping with the duties I had assumed.

Discomfort in Portugal

We couldn't call Ana, our daughter, by her given name. We had to baptize and name her "Reyna."

I wasn't happy in Portugal. Hatred towards Marranos was on the rise. We were not directly affected, so far. Our company was called the Mendes Corporation, although we were better protected in our massive house that displayed our wealth. Life for the rest of us was becoming harder with each passing day. The overall social climate was suffocating. I didn't want my daughter Reyna to grow in this atmosphere.

Due to his wealth and success, Francisco had accumulated many enemies. Although the Inquisition was not declared in Portugal, we knew it was a probable target.

"Gracia, I am well aware" was the reply I got. "I paid huge sums to the pope to prevent the arrival of the Inquisition here. I obtained a "laisser passer" with his blessing. By signing the document stating that we cannot be judged about religious issues, he also filled his coffers."

"Protection from judgment?"

"Exactly."

"That's really good news! Super!"

He was concerned lest I become careless. "Nevertheless, nothing is truly guaranteed."

"When was there ever a dependable guarantee? When did we really feel secure? I fear that a time when we will feel completely free will never come. At least you have done well by procuring an immunity document."

"Partially."

"Although we have this paper in our pocket, you know what I have in mind. The Inquisition becomes stronger and stronger each day. It will come here too and will have it at our doorsteps. We had better leave for somewhere else, a more secure place. I don't want Reyna to grow up here. I am doing what's necessary, and have started transferring part of our fortune bit by bit."

Finally, some good news!

We were sitting across each other in our large lounge but talking in whispers. Rayna was taken to bed by her nanny and, soon, was fast asleep.

Through the Generations

"Well then. Where do you plan for us to go? Are we free to leave whenever we want?"

He shook his head.

"With this document, yes! But they already noticed and are throwing obstacles."

He pointed to the sky. I knew he meant the king.

"They are mistrustful of us but want to continue enjoying the trade activity we create. They are restricting the freedoms of Marranos and are planning to forbid the transferring abroad of cash, gold and valuables."

"I am not bothered about them, Francisco. It is the Inquisition. I am terrified that this calamity will befall Portugal too. We have a beautiful house, a wonderful life, and many friends. The thought of what the future can bring frightens me. I was with my father once, in one of his business trips to Spain. You won't believe what I witnessed!"

He came close and held my hand.

"Unfortunately, I know full well. Your father shared that he witnessed the horrifying experience of seeing people burned at the stake."

I put my fingers over his lips.

"OK, I really don't want to hear. It's as if I can recall the odors."

The revolting, suffocating odor of freshly burned human flesh. I felt nauseated and nearly vomited. I turned away from the memory, trying not to think.

"Don't you worry; all will be well. Diogo opened an agency in Antwerp. We are shipping all cargo arriving from China or India directly to Antwerp. We are cautiously transferring anything of value there without alerting our enemies."

"We must act darling! I have a terrible premonition about this place."

He tried to calm me.

"Please. Rushing things might create hazards. We will execute our plan gradually. We need more time, Gracia. Patience."

I repeated the same things whenever I needed reassurance. I moved closer, laid my head on his chest while he gently stroked my hair.

We lingered for a while. Nights in Lisbon were damp and hot. I heard noises from far. Somehow there was never a time of quiet serenity.

After a while, he said, "What do you have in mind?"

"Nothing, just listening."

"What."

"The incessant humming. Can you hear it too?"

He reflected for a moment or two.

"Yes."

"The humming never stops, Francisco. Like a windmill constantly turning. Slowly, a continuous sound you would hear if you listened."

"It is perhaps the wind."

"I don't think so."

A knock on the door. Startled, I jumped up.

"What happened?"

He said "Calm down."

"Who is it?"

The answer came from the other side of the door: "It's Lisa, sir. I am sorry for disturbing you."

"Come in."

Lisa entered. She was drowsy, as if she had just awakened.

"There is a gentleman at the door. He said he is employed by you and has an urgent message."

Diogo Accused

Francisco was ready to leave. Probably there was reason to worry; he took a few of his trusted men as well as two of his lawyers.

In a small voice, I asked, "When will you be back?"

"I don't know; it depends on the business there. I might have to go to Antwerp. I will try to be back as soon as possible."

"Don't keep your daughter and me waiting for long. I will wait anxiously!"

He turned and hugged me. I knew he wanted to kiss me but with so many men around. He blinked his eye understandingly.

"During my absence, the business is in your hands."

Then they left. Brianda and I waved goodbye. Reyna was in the back, on her nanny's lap. She was not aware, as little as she was, that her father was leaving for uncertainty and faraway places. A good thing too.

The news arrived last night.

One of Francisco's employees came from Antwerp with the news that Diogo had been arrested.

"Allegations are that Mr. Diogo is continuing Jewish practices, has a spice monopoly, and is lending at exorbitant rates.

He instructed me to inform you urgently. It took me two days to reach you."

I could only say "Oh my God, this is terrible!" biting my bottom lip. "Francisco, is what I am hearing true? What are we to do?"

Instead of panic, Francisco preferred to listen to the details.

"Go and rest a little, darling. I will get the full picture and inform you afterward."

"No, I want to stay and listen."

"OK."

The employee continued his report:

"Accusations regarding Mr. Diogo are very serious. Someone denounced him. For that reason, after a proper trial, a judgment will be handed down. Mr. Diogo maintains that the accusations are false. It is believed that, because of the widening Mendes operations in the city, the process is more political than judiciary. Mr. Diogo believes they intend to impound our assets and goods. If he is found guilty, this will be inevitable."

I felt as though the sky was closing in on me. They intend to take our fortune in Antwerp and jail Diogo!

"I will not allow it to happen," said Francisco. "I have the immunity document signed by the pope himself."

"Sir, what are your plans? I have to return immediately to Antwerp and report to him."

"Tell him that I will speak to the king as well as to Charles V, the Holy Roman Emperor. I will do all I can for his immediate liberation, and will declare to his majesty that I am prepared to pay any sum he may require. Tell Diogo to be patient.

He knows what other actions to take."

Francisco rushed to the palace and asked for the king's help. And then he went to talk to Charles V. He was confident of getting support from the palace although it was most important to convince Charles V, who was, after all, the boss.

After seeing Francisco off, I followed his instructions by educating myself to take charge of the business. That meant going through thick ledgers, books, and documents that only we had the clearance to inspect. King Juan was in urgent need of cash to pay large sums to Charles V, who was preparing an army to fight the Ottomans.

We had promised the king significant sums to secure the spice trade. This was an advantage. If Diogo's goods and property were confiscated, money and receivables would also be confiscated. That would mean we would not be able to pay the king who, in turn, would not be able to pay Charles V.

Our common interest dictated Diogo's release.

I was glad to discover that there was still hope after all.

"Ohh, that's how Francisco managed to get the letter from the king—the one that is addressed to Charles V."

King Juan, in his letter, explained that Diogo, as a 'New Christian,' was his subject, and that his imprisonment would dramatically affect the economic situation of Portuguese Marranos living in Antwerp. The reduction of Marrano revenues would have an adverse effect on the king, making it impossible for him to keep his financial promises to the Holy Roman Emperor.

"For the reasons stated, I entreat you to free Mr. Diogo Mendes Benveniste. I expect you to have him released from the claws of the Dutch tribunals. The accusations are all intentional. I can assure you that such an honorable person would not attempt any wrongdoing."

Charles V's sister and Queen Catherine of Portugal had also written a similar letter and presented it to Francisco.

Our other connections and friends also intervened, and soon, Diogo was released. First it was decided that he would be judged without being imprisoned, and then he was released on bail.

"The fact that this trial can end by finding Diogo guilty bothered King Juan too," said Francisco. "Our observant king knew full well that the spice trade depended on the Mendes family. He is looking for an alternative but he will have a hard time finding a party that can manage it as well."

As usual, we ended up talking business again. That was to be expected. By and large, our lives revolved around our business.

"He is not called 'observant' in vain, Francisco!" not hiding the tremor in my voice. "I fear he will bring the Inquisition to Portugal."

"Darling, don't you see that all my efforts are to prevent him from being successful. All these years I have been struggling for this purpose! The establishment of the Inquisition will be a catastrophe for all Marranos living in these lands. The Spanish example was more than enough."

"But what can you do all alone? Shouldn't they all support you in this fight?"

The weather was warm with the smell of jasmine in the air. I was surrounded by the fragrance of flowers and could hear night birds in the garden.

He walked toward the balcony.

Naturally, my singular efforts might not be enough. The rest of the Marranos would join the struggle. They have to! Otherwise, the Inquisition would accuse them of "faking Christianity while at the same time secretly Judaizing." and impound all their property and goods.

Unconsciously, I bit my lip.

"God forbid!"

He turned around with a compassionate look.

"Gracia, don't you see that my concerns are not only for myself? God only knows, I am getting older. I have to consider many people, not the least of which is you and our daughter, Reyna. A simple letter denouncing them is enough for them to be tortured, stripped naked to the waist, and brought in front of the tribunal. They even strip women of their blouses and parade them in the streets. This way, without spilling blood, they force them to talk, and they try every trick to get them to sign. What a merciful approach! We must succeed in preventing this calamity. Otherwise it will be impossible for us to live in this damp city by the sea. I have seen this before."

"But you have your precautions, don't you? You are prepared, right? If need be we will be able to leave Portugal."

He turned toward me and held my hand.

"Don't panic, my beauty! While I am spending a fortune and entering into relationships with all sorts of unpleasant people, I have you, Reyna, Diogo, and all our co-religionists to consider. We will forge a way for all of us."

"I hope it will be that way, Francisco."

On his return home, the hope that he brought calmed me a little but sweet dreams and pink reveries were far away.

The nightmare that was 1536

Our friend, Camilo, invited himself to dinner. Light conversation and good cheer dominated the talk at our table. Once dinner was over, the maids left the room. We kissed Reyna good night and her nanny put her to bed. Camilo turned to a most serious subject.

In a burst of discomfort, he exclaimed, "The catastrophe that we anticipated is at our door step."

"What's happening?" I asked.

Francisco signaled for me to listen carefully. Camilio was one of the few who was very close to the king. Although he was a Marrano, he could freely enter the palace and was invited to join important meetings. He was considered a desirable member of some diplomatic committees.

"Juan the Observant was meeting with his ministers. The Treaty of Tordesillas that split the New World into two areas of influence has been breached by the Spanish. We expected him to be furious over these developments. The Madrid agreement granted independence to the Philippines on the condition that the Malaku Islanda were left to the Spanish. But it seems that new issues emerged with new settlements in the southern part of the New World. While developing relations with the Siamese (in latter-day Thailand) they are also sending soldiers to the new camps they developed in Macau, China. They abandoned the castles in Morocco."

Francisco was trying to guess at where the disclosures were

leading but I couldn't wait. I was impatient:

"Why are you telling us this? What are you trying to tell us?"

"My dear, the spice monopoly is controlled by Portugal, that is, by us. Costs are rising constantly, reducing profits. The palace is expanding, the number of employees is increasing, and expenses are rising. Juan has difficulty paying wages and is looking for a fast solution—sizable sums of money that he can quickly appropriate."

There was complete silence. We all knew what was coming. Camilo intervened:

"Ministers who are close to him point to the rising wealth of Marranos. They openly urge him to rob us, to take our wealth."

The news that I suspected was becoming obvious with each passing word. Francisco remained calm:

"The king has been influenced by Erasmus's speeches. I don't think he will follow suggestions coming from Rome to recreate the Spanish model."

Camilo was angered:

"Since when are we acting with our feelings? Our advantage has always been in knowing what would happen in advance, being one step ahead. Sitting down and waiting, trusting our instincts—this is not sufficient to keep us alive!"

He was right.

"Erasmus from Rotterdam writes history with his ideas. The king is drifting away from his humanistic school of thought. Unlike Protestant followers of Martin Luther, we didn't expect him to distance himself from Catholicism but we also didn't expect him to abandon the ideals of freedoms so swiftly. Francisco, my friend, the king has allowed the Inquisition to be established in Portugal."

"Wow!"

My outcry was somewhat loud. One of the maids rushed in. I asked her to leave with the wave of my hand, and I carefully watched Francisco's saddened eyes. He was dismayed.

"It is not public knowledge yet but it is a fact. Juan is getting closer to the Jesuits. He is turning a blind eye to their spreading in Portugal, even encouraging them. At this rate, Portugal will be inundated by them. He thinks he can make use of them in the New World. He hopes that they will act as missionaries but doesn't realize that, in our city where we live, hatred against Jews and Marranos will be rekindled. It might even be intentional."

I flashed back to the past when we were incessantly reminded of the massacre we had tried so hard to forget. I was thinking of the time when Jews and Marranos were savagely massacred by their Christian neighbors.

"Will there be another mass murder?" I mumbled, adding, "God protect us, not again."

"The majority of those killed had come from Spain, Gracia," said Camilo. "Perhaps we are not as unfortunate or as defenseless as they were. They had run away from the 1492 banishment when Portugal was the easiest and closest destination. When King Manual in 1496 caused the forced conversion of the Jews, he also paved the way for the 1506 lynchings. We will not engage in mass emigrations as they did. We will not run away! Nevertheless, we will take all possible precautions.

Through the Generations

Don't you agree, Francisco?"

I could tell that while Francisco was deeply disturbed, he didn't want to share his fright with me.

"They wouldn't check whether we are circumcised, would they?"

For him to ask such a question in this atmosphere was comical. For an instant, I forgot everything and smiled. However, if at that moment, I foresaw what was to come, I should have cried.

"If the Inquisition gets here, based on a simple letter of denunciation, they will storm the houses and jail the inhabitants. They will search for Torahs and Talmuds."

"We bribed them at rates they imposed, wasn't that enough?" Francisco asked.

"Why should they be satisfied with bribes when they have the power to take it all?"

"I know the king. He is not a blind enemy of Jews. I believe he will choose what is in his own best interest. Recall that he acted decisively in saving Diogo. Why should he act differently in the future?"

Camilo spoke as if sharing his life's experience:

"My friend, do whatever you want. Give as much as you want. You are a Jew! Act as a Christian as credibly as you can. In their eyes, you will always be a Jew. You will never be seen as a Christian. If they have a choice of robbing or killing someone, you will have priority over Christians. You will always be kept out of their brotherhood."

It was the first time I had seen, Francisco, my uncle, my husband, my friend for life, my one and only, shaken so strongly. I had always imagined him as an immovable mountain and I felt secure in his shadow. His presence was enough for me and all other Marranos to feel safe.

He sunk into an armchair, exhausted. I could hear his heavy breathing.

"Francisco, what's up? Are you OK?"

"Don't worry. I am fine."

A fragrant wind passed through the window overlooking our wonderful garden. Candles and chandeliers were lit and the flames danced haphazardly.

I said, "Suddenly your face grew pale!"

"Quick. Water!"

I got up and sat next to him. Camilo was also concerned. I could tell that he regretted being so candid and telling him all these realities so harshly.

"Francisco, it wasn't my intention to hurt you."

Francisco looked better already. The maid came in with a glass of water in her hand.

"I am good. You didn't hurt me, my dear friend. It has nothing to do with what you just said. I guess I am getting older. The trip also wore me out."

My anxiety was still there.

"Francisco, you don't look well—the color of your face.

He drank the water and returned the glass to the maid.

We waited for her to leave. There was an unspoken rule of not voicing sensitive issues in front of the staff. Not that we didn't trust them, they had been with us for long.

"Finally this too happened. The Inquisition will soon be here."

Through the Generations

Francisco looked considerably better:

"Don't panic. First, they are after our money, not our lives. The king knows full well that he needs us, at least until a time when he finds a replacement. In order not to disrupt the flow of business, they will not touch us. The first to suffer, I think, will be the poor ones."

"What are we to do Francisco?"

"We have to get together with all concerned to evaluate the facts in more detail. We quickly need to assess the situation, and then act swiftly. Before the pope can storm the country, we should transfer all of our business as well as our belongings and get out of this place."

We had longed for that time to come. I never imagined it would come this way.

I don't know from where but it was beyond the garden from some neighbors, we heard the sound of a song. Usually men and women, at the end of the work day, got together to sing. This time the voices were bitter and nostalgic, as if they shared my feelings.

Two tears streamed from my eyes. We had come here after running away from Spain. In growing up, we had been told heartbreaking stories of bloody massacres and escapes. Once again, it became our reality, and now, like then, we again had to run.

"Until when?"

∾ ∾

The next morning, I woke up staring at my bedroom ceiling. Part of the net was open and a mosquito had settled on my face. Windows had been opened so that the fresh morning air could come into the room before it got too hot and the whole place stank of mussels, calamari, prawns, and other fish odors from the market.

I did not sleep well because of what was said last night. At first, I couldn't get to sleep, and then I kept waking up. I was upset and felt uneasy. I stretched and yawned, and noticed Francisco in bed. This was unusual as he was always up and working before me.

"Good morning, darling. Why are you still in bed? Like me, you had difficulty falling asleep. You really are getting old." I smiled and bent over to kiss him. For a second, I was worried. He was unusually pale, ashen pale. If I hadn't seen him wink, I would have thought he was dead. I yelled in fear:

"Francisco! My good God! What happened to you?" He groaned instead of answering.

"Are you ill? Ohh, I should have guessed from last night! You are ill!"

I placed my hand on his forehead. His temperature wasn't high but it felt strange touching him, as if I were touching him over his clothes.

I yelled, "Quick, somebody! Help!"

We had night maids. Also ones who came in the morning. The two working the night shift rushed in.

As they respectfully announced their entry, I gave instructions.

"One of you, bring water and a towel. You call the doctor. Ask him to hurry. Tell him I asked that he come immediately. Quick, quick!"

As they ran around, Francisco held my hand. He had difficulty straightening. He seemed really weak.

"I am well," he tried to say.

"No, Francisco, don't strain yourself. Rest. Wait for the doctor."

"I am well," he repeated once more but with great difficulty. "Don't you worry."

At that moment, Reyna woke up. I heard her cry as her nanny tried to calm her. The first thing I did each day was to check on Reyna, but not this morning. Francisco was the most important person to tend to, at this moment.

"Hang on my darling, please! The doctor will be here any moment!" He turned his eyes to me and stared blankly.

"I am OK. I just feel a little weak. Don't exaggerate."

"OK. Now you just rest. Or even sleep if you feel like it. Is there anything I should prepare?"

He shook his head in delirium. Then he closed his eyes.

Dr. Luna's name was really Jacob; this name was thought appropriate when he was baptized. Though he was a Marrano, like us, no one bothered him as he was an excellent doctor. He also went about silently doing his job, helping quietly all patients including those close to the palace. He'd go on to the next patient, not being involved in any kind of conversation. It was as if he always managed to be invisible.

"Let him sleep as much as he wants," he said as he was leaving the room.

He closed the door gently, and turned to me.

"Dona Gracia, you don't look too well either. I would like to check you."

"I am fine. How is he? What is the matter with him? That's

what I want to know."

"He is weakened. Considering his age, that is to be expected."

"But why? He was healthy and fine yesterday. He has a strong constitution and hardly ever is ill."

"What happened yesterday?" he asked with an enquiring expression.

"Some bad news," I said, undecided as to how much I wanted to disclose. "We had a guest. He brought some bad news but Francisco was OK after that, only a bit tired."

"It must have been quite a shock. We should take good care of him and let him rest. I will prepare some medicines. One of your staff can fetch them from my cabinet. After careful treatment he will get well."

As the doctor was leaving as silently as he came, I wondered if I should warn him. Sure, even if he tries to remain unnoticed, he was a Marrano. Sooner or later he will be negatively affected, perhaps even before us.

"Doctor Luna," I said in a whisper. "The news that troubled Francisco." He turned, as if to listen attentively.

"King Juan has invited the Inquisition. After Spain, the Inquisition is coming here too. This was what disturbed Francisco so."

For a moment, I saw his lips tremble and then he was composed.

"I see. So that's why he was so saddened."

"Be careful, too! You should be, you know."

"In fact, I was expecting it," he said as if relieved of a heavy burden. "It has been coming for quite some time."

He left the leather bag that held a variety of medicines on

the large stand. Suddenly he dropped into the armchair as if exhausted.

"Would you like a glass of wine?"

"A good idea, Dona Gracia. I need to recollect myself."

I shouted: "Bring wine for the doctor!"

A cool glass of wine was placed on the stand close to him. I waited for him to drink it. When he finished, he asked:

"What are your plans?"

"First of all, he should recover. Then he will make all the right decisions."

"Sure. That's best. His decisions."

"It's good that we have a branch in Antwerp. Perhaps relocation will be easier. I would advise you to do the same, to go elsewhere."

"Where?"

"Antwerp, for example. It is said that Marranos are happy there, and under no pressure. I heard that Lyon and Venice were convenient. Perhaps even further. Being such a good doctor, you would find a similar clientele there too."

"I have to do some thinking, I am quite old. I am tired of running. Where can I run to? Wherever I go, I will take the Jewish Doctor Jacob with me, naturally as a Marrano Luna! Hiding my true name and beliefs."

Reading the desperation in his eyes, I felt sorry for him too.

He sent Francisco's medicines at dark. He had prepared a syrup for him to drink, a cream to be massaged into his back, and a few pills.

I instructed the kitchen to prepare his favorite soup and meat dishes. I selected the choicest wines from our cellar but he ate very little. We carefully adhered at home as much as possible to kashrut dietary rules.

He was a little better the next day. Doctor Luna visited. By sundown, Francisco seemed strong enough to talk comfortably.

"What is Ana up to?" he inquired.

He was not careful about who was around. He only said "Ana."

"She is good. I didn't bring her close to you thinking that your condition could be contagious. If you want to see her, however, I can bring her near."

"No, you are right," he said, pointing to the pillow.

I came close and lifted the pillow a little. Now, he could sit straight in bed.

"Gracia, I am so sad. I will not be able to see our daughter grow up!"

"Don't talk like that!"

"Unfortunately, that's reality. I can feel it. My time is nearly up. I need to save the ones that remain. I have to draw up a will."

"Francisco, why are you making me so sad? Do you want me to stop living before you?"

"My angel, I am not trying to make you unhappy. Just the opposite, I don't want to leave you, Ana, and Diogo in an ambiguous situation. Listen to me, my one and only. You are a perfectly well-brought up woman. Apart from being a perfect wife and mother, you have a business notion at least as good as any business man. You are able to manage the business comfortably."

Through the Generations

"What of the business, if you are not around? I need you and my daughter."

"Perhaps you will not always have me around. You must always be there for our daughter. She hasn't got anyone besides you. Diogo is my brother. I fully trust him. He trusts me too. We never talked about which part of the Mendes fortune rightly belongs to him. We always controlled the business. While working incessantly to grow our fortune, we never stopped to think that this day would come. We devoted ourselves to work like mad, Gracia. It has been good that we foresaw possible dangers and transferred an important part of our belongings to Antwerp. Diogo was more successful than I could imagine. I want him to control an important part of our fortune. For that purpose, I will declare in my will that half of our fortune belongs to him. Half of what remains will be under your administration. One third of Gracia's part will be my daughter's. Until she becomes a major, Gracia will control it. The residue will be spent for my funeral, donated to the poor, and to the church. If anything is left, it will be yours." I was silently listening, tears flowing down my cheeks.

"Gracia, this will conform to Portuguese laws. In this way, you will have legal protection too. Diogo's rights will be officially recognized, and yours, and our daughter's rights will be safeguarded."

"Oh, Francisco, oh! You talk as if you will die tomorrow and you are killing me with each word!"

"Gracia, my angel. This is my clear and legal will. All will know of it. I have one more wish. You will be the only one to know, and those who you think should also know. I leave that to your judgement."

I was all ears. "I am listening."

"At least I want to be buried there. At the first opportunity, have my remains taken from the family cemetery and transferred to Jerusalem."

This was the dream of every religious Jew: to wait in Jerusalem for the messiah to come for redemption.

"Francisco, I too have something to tell you."

I felt it was time for me to share the secret with him.

His fading eyes were open wide. He looked surprised to hear that his niece and wife had hidden something from him.

"Did you say a secret?"

"Yes, it's a secret you should know."

His dried lips moved but no sound came out.

"A secret with which I was entrusted: a mission."

I moved my lips close to his ear and related the story precisely, being careful not to tire him.

After telling the secret, I straightened up and saw the smile on his face. He winked.

"I can now move on feeling completely fulfilled, my dearest."

Death of Francisco

I couldn't save him.

However much I tried to make sure that he got the best possible care, it wasn't enough.

After remaining in bed for a while, Francisco spent his last breath. He left me all alone with my daughter forever, never to return.

After the church funeral, we performed the proper rituals,

according to his true beliefs at home.

I planted a kiss on his forehead and promised:

"Rest in peace. I will definitely take you to the Promised Land, to Jerusalem!"

At age 25, I was a widow and a mother in Lisbon.

There was no reason to remain in Portugal any longer. It wasn't sensible either.

Bigoted Christian priests had a free hand and increased their attacks on Jews and Marranos. Jews were openly humiliated while we could say nothing. The moment we objected, we would be accused of Judaizing, denounced as heretics, and we would meet with a thousand troubles. That was their hope anyway.

This was not the time to moan and cry. I had to make the hard decision to leave behind our wonderful residence, our friends, save whatever I could of our fortune, take the closest staff, and leave Lisbon.

The responsibilities invested in me after Francisco's death forced me to be tough. I had my informants inside the palace and I conducted my activities in utmost secrecy. They would come and find me, and promise to offer willingly their services to me with the same allegiance as they had to my husband. I told them all the same thing:

"My husband was a good Christian. We too are good Christians and we will continue to conduct our business according to laws, rules and regulations stipulated by our King Juan and the Holy Roman Emperor Charles V. We pray for our king's good health and dominion forever."

All my words were in vain. The news that King Juan had designs to take over our fortune reached me. A friend close to the king told us that Juan's hopes were revived:

"The Observant has grown an appetite for the Mendes fortune. He has instructed a committee to conduct a study to see if the gigantic Mendes fortune can be appropriated by the state. He is waiting for them to find a legal solution."

In present day reality, that was easy enough. The Inquisition was already in Portugal. All he had to do was to have the church accuse us of Judaizing—of being heretics. A simple letter by anyone claiming such a possibility was enough to start the investigation. After that, what would follow was to subject us to the cruelest of all tortures, forcing us to accept the accusations. At that point, when our lives were in danger, taking our fortune would be inevitable.

~ ~

Lazar said: "Dona Gracia arranged for a ship to take us to England and then to Antwerp."

He was Francisco's most trusted staff. Though he was not a Marrano, the good feelings he harbored for our family and his humanistic notions proved always a great help.

"How much more can we transfer?"

"We are transferring the unnoticeable larger sums; a small part will have to be left behind."

"Tell me, Lazar, will things be much better in Antwerp?"

"My lady, I really don't know. Mr. Diogo says that things are better over there. Judging by the trade volume he is conducting, he should be right. At least it is a reality that the lives of Marranos are much better over there. An important fact is that the Inquisition doesn't exist there."

He was honestly sad about our impending departure. He didn't want to be separated from the family. I repeated my offer:

"Lazar, our door is wide open to you. You can come anytime you want to. Your job and place in our family will be ready. You know that, don't you?"

He became emotional:

"Thank you, Dona Gracia. My mum and dad, their mothers and fathers, as a family, we always lived closely in this city. Now, it's my children's turn. I couldn't leave even if I wanted to. My family wouldn't want to leave. Thanks anyway. I will always remember you and Mr. Francisco with very warm feelings."

"We won't forget you, Lazar."

"Don't forget that you are being closely followed, Dona Gracia. They are watching your every move. Act as though you intend to meet with me. We will spread the word that we will meet tomorrow to discuss important business, but your ship will have left the harbor by midnight. I hear that Mr Diogo has a large entourage there and will make sure that you will adapt and that you will quickly be happy."

Escape from Lisbon

It wasn't easy to convince the inspector. He was warned from above that we might be in the process of taking our fortune outside the country. He used every instrument to prevent it. Even if one of our family members remained, I had no doubt they would use it to blackmail us.

"Why are you leaving the city?"

"I have to settle all inheritance issues with my late husband's brother, Mr. Diogo."

"Well, what of your sister Brianda?"

She will marry Mr. Diogo Mendes. We are to discuss marriage preparations."

"Reyna Nasi and Joseph Nasi?"

"They will continue their education, Reyna in a good Christian school and Joseph Nasi, Francisco's nephew, at Louvain University."

"You want to leave next month. Why are you getting your papers ready now?"

"There are things to do for the schools. We need time to prepare."

He surely didn't believe me. He was desperately searching for an excuse to refuse the application. If it were within his power, he would not hesitate to use force to stop us, or at least some of us. We worked out a strong legal case with our lawyers. He couldn't find an excuse. They could prevent us from living our own beliefs, even force us to pretend we were truly converted but they couldn't stop us from being hard workers and being successful. Still, the best traders, businessmen, doctors, engineers, and architects were from Marrano society. The point they missed was that we had to work hard to be successful. If the locals worked for one hour, we worked two. If they worked two hours, we worked four. Otherwise, we would never be able to surmount the inequalities they imposed on us at birth. That was why Marrano kids were sent to the best schools, taking lessons from reputable teachers. Regardless of their sex, they were trained well, and learned they had to work hard. We never had the luxury of lazing about.

～ ～

Alone in our bedroom where Francisco had uttered his last words, I prayed:

> "Dear God, hear our prayers! Don't abandon us. Save us as you did from Egypt and Persia. Don't deliver us into the hands of the treacherous Inquisition, to their mercy. Don't punish us for having pretended to leave our beliefs! Forgive our unintentional sins! Be at our side. Real believers never lose hope in You. Don't let our hope expire in vain."

～ ～

All preparations were nearly finished when Lazar came with news.

"Dona Gracia, the ship sent by Mr. Diogo is ready and waiting for you in the harbor. It anchored as a trade ship, and its cargo was unloaded. In order that they would not know on which boat you were leaving, we registered it as a commercial vessel. It is thought that it would be loaded and then leave."

"Excellent," I exclaimed. "I hope we can leave this country without anyone noticing."

"That's our main purpose, Dona Gracia. The information I am about to share should not even be disclosed to those closest to you, including your sister and daughter. If possible, tell no one at all!"

"What could you tell me that I wouldn't share with my family? I hide nothing from them!"

"It is Mr. Diogo's orders, no one will know!" I said to myself, "Not another secret!"

"I am listening."

"You will be followed by a security ship. The ship on which you travel will be protecting you but the route is full of dangers. Because the French are at war with the Holy Roman Empire, they attack every vessel that comes their way. They attack and pillage.

"For this reason, you will not go to Antwerp but to England. Not even to London but to a more secluded port that is Bristol."

I cringed. "England?"

~ ~

Though many years had passed, the York massacre of 1190 was not forgotten. The number of Jews in England was few. During the preparations for the Third Crusade, Jews were invited to the York Castle where they were forced to become Christians. The Chief Rabbi asked them to die rather than convert.

"Husbands will kill their wives and children. Then I will kill them, and commit suicide."

Escape from Lisbon

The outcome for those who did not take the Rabbi's advice was no different as they were murdered by the excited crowd. It was remembered that, although the king made disapproving speeches, the culprits were never brought to justice.

Moreover, in 1290, similar pogroms occurred against Jews in London. King Edward expelled the Jews and appropriated their goods, which he transferred to his treasury.

We learned the same lesson from England, and then from Spain, and now from Portugal. Welcoming invitations, followed by our reviving the business climate, ended in confiscation.

The wealth that the Marranos created in Antwerp excited the jealousy of the English king. Even if they regretted the atrocities they committed in the past, it would be difficult to convince the Marranos to trust them.

Jews had been tormented for centuries. Many believed that there was a messianic message in the sufferings, and that this could be signaling the arrival of the savior. There was a condition for his arrival and it was that Jews should be present everywhere, and the name of the Lord should be spread all over the world. There were no Jews in England so this condition could not be fulfilled. To take a share of all of the activity in Antwerp, they used this concept to urge Jews to come to England.

To make me feel better, Lazar said:

"Diogo's relations with the English Crown are very good. He sees no security issues for you. In Bristol, there is a small Marrano community. They light Shabbat candles and pray, celebrate Passover in peace, cook their matzo, and live like orthodox Jews. Naturally, they are not fully free to outwardly practice. As it is a small congregation, no one takes notice of them. As time passes, no one can predict how things will develop. But this much we know: these days Bristol is safe."

I waved my hand. "We shall never enjoy full security."

"On the other hand, there won't be the fear of Inquisition tribunals. Their numbers are so small, no one would think of installing the Inquisition in Bristol."

He hoped to make me feel better with these words. I didn't care.

I went to Reyna's room and entered gently to make sure I didn't wake her nanny. My baby was asleep. Luckily, she was in deep sleep. I took her in my arms, trying carefully not to wake her, wrapped her in a blanket, and slipped out of the room.

Brianda and the others were waiting for me.

I whispered: "We are all set."

A carriage was ready at the door with the coachman in his seat. To reduce the sound to a minimum, the horses were stripped of their bells and the coachman had chosen the ones without horseshoes. We had sent away all but two of the most reliable staff members. The coachman was dependable. Our luggage had been sent to the ship and carefully placed in drawers and wardrobe. I knew that Diogo had procured for our comforts and catered fresh fruits and vegetables. We needed only to carry our small bags.

"Come on Brianda! Get in the coach and take Reyna with you."

Brianda took Reyna, making sure she was comfortable and settled in the carriage with the rest of our retinue. Two of our aides waited at the top of the stairs for my instructions.

"We will be out of town for a while. During that time, you will be in charge of the house. We will return as soon as we arrange the wedding and sort out the inheritance. Until then, take care of the house as if it were yours, and make yourselves comfortable."

I wished to be more honest and tell them we could never return, but how could I? If I said a few more words, I would have broken down and cried. Though they never made us feel it, they seemed to sense that this was goodbye forever, and that we were never coming back.

The eldest said: "I knew and served you from your mother's days. I hope that all turns out as you wish it."

The others nodded in agreement. I turned because I didn't want them to see the tears I couldn't prevent. Sounding cross, I said, "Don't be that way! We will see each other again."

Lying is not good behavior but no one would know what could happen next. Let them think we would return.

"Alright. God bless."

As soon as I stepped inside, I heard the whistle of the coachman's whip.

"Slow!"

I nearly fell. Reyna woke at my scream and cried loudly. The coach moved on. As I stretched over to hold her, I noticed Brianda crying too, silently.

If I wasn't in control of the situation, we would all be moaning and crying. I spoke in a low but reprimanding tone:

"Brianda, I am already torn to pieces! Watch it. If you make a blunder and put us at risk, I will make you regret it dearly before anyone else!" She sensed how much I meant it and shushed.

Dona Gracia

I turned and threw a last glance from the small window. I was leaving behind the home where I married, gave birth, and had such happy memories, never to return. It seems that one can be made to run from one's country.

I could hear only the clicking of the horses' trots.

Travel to Bristol

I worried steadily until we crossed the Biscay waters and reached the Atlantic Ocean. I could hear my heart beat with the fear that a vessel of the kingdom would cross our way and attack us. So far, the only ship I could see was our security one.

The sea was chirpy. I had a headache and felt nauseated. The crew knew that we were the owners. Diogo must have instructed them. Without us saying a word, they treated us like royalty. We didn't dare stick our noses out of our cabins.

The worrisome first night came to an end. I felt better in the morning and decided to go out and take some fresh air. I came up to the deck, leaving Reyna and Brianda in the cabin.

In Lisbon during the nights when the sky was clear, I watched the stars, the thousands of lights of the Milky Way but now, the sky overhead was pitch black but decorated with more stars than I'd ever seen—yellow, white, shiny, dwindling, thousands in all sizes.

The cool wind with an odor of iodine flecked my face, relaxing me relax. Already, I felt better. I raised my head and saw a shiny star.

In this wilderness, it seemed that apart from us and the security boat following us there was no one at all. "Good evening

Escape from Lisbon

Dona Gracia!" I turned to see the captain.

"To you too, Captain."

"Couldn't sleep, I guess."

"I came out for some fresh air. In fact, I think I will sleep well today after such long time, finally."

He gave me an understanding smile.

"I am glad."

"They can't follow us anymore, can they?"

"I doubt it. Even if they try, they can't catch us. Our ship is faster!"

"I heard the sound of a goat. Captain, is there one on our ship? Where could that sound be coming from?"

"We have livestock in our warehouse, Dona Gracia. Mr. Diogo wanted all sorts of preparations made for you. If we wish, we can leisurely sail for a long time."

"I want to set foot on land as soon as we can!"

"That's our objective too, Dona Gracia."

After a short chitchat, the captain distanced himself. I was alone on deck. Even if some of the crew was around, they did not disturb me.

I sat calmly. I was still young. Not long ago I left girlhood, and now I am a young mother, a widow left alone with a daughter. I am also a refugee, torn from my home.

I thought:

"No one will inadvertently knock at our door; we won't live in constant worry. Anticipatory anxiety was left behind."

In fact, things wouldn't be as I was hoping. Our being fugitives would continue for a long time. My chest against the wind, on deck, watching the stars, I didn't yet know this.

Bristol Port

Days later, we walked off our ship anchored in Bristol port, and stepped ashore. A member of Diogo's staff was there to greet us.

As we followed his footsteps, thankful for being safe and on stable ground, I had strange premonitions. Thank God, what was left of my family was with me.

I had with me the most precious thing on earth, my only child, Reyna. Finally, I was away, safe from the extreme covetousness and bigotry in Portugal, and in a calm, welcoming land. Still that strange discomforting feeling was with me. I felt left alone in this universe, awkward, exiled from my home and country, weak. If I didn't realize that I was now the master of the family, in charge, and responsible for their future I would collapse into tears, cry my eyes out.

"You have to be upright, Dona Gracia! Stand straight! You don't have the right to despair! If you go, so would the rest of the family!

"No one would extend a helping hand to downcast! Portugal? What remains there?"

I knew what I left behind, and the reason for my deep sadness: my past, my memories, my childhood, and girlish years, and Francisco's body in a sarcophagus underground.

Knowing that he would hear me, I talked silently:

"Francisco, I will definitely save you from there! At all cost, I will take you to Jerusalem. Don't doubt for a moment! Until then, rest in peace."

∾ ∾

Diogo's man gestured: "This way, Dona Gracia."

Escape from Lisbon

The way he was dressed suggested he was English.

"My name is Eric. Mr. Diogo had a mansion readied for you."

"Thank you."

We got into the waiting carriage and left behind the crowded port, damp air, and swearing people.

Bristol, like many other cities, had growing around the port. Most of the activities were centered around the port, and the rest of the city was noticeably quieter. As we moved along, starting from the port, I could see lined up bars and inns. Further up, there were buildings that looked like work places with warehouses by their sides. As we moved on, streets became more deserted. Occasionally you could see a person or two.

After quite some time, Eric started to talk:

"Mrs. Mendes, your..."

"Call me simply Dona Gracia."

"Thank you."

"Mr. Diogo Mendes asked me to warn you. The place where you will be lodged in Bristol belongs to him. You must be informed that, on paper, Jews are not allowed to live in England."

I was surprised. "How come, but we..."

He raised his hand.

"Don't be concerned! Naturally, this prohibition is on paper only. Jews and Marranos, albeit in small numbers, continue their lives in England. In spite of the law, you can even perform religious acts in public places. Anyhow, it is best to be careful."

This time, my foolish sister Brianda, started to talk:

"Can you tell me why we are in Bristol and not in London? I wasn't told that my wedding preparations would be this way!"

I turned with a terse look. She stopped talking but only for a while. Soon she would grumble again.

"I am listening to you, Mr. Eric."

"Yes, Dona Gracia, he asked you to be careful. The English try to get information through the Marranos about their competitors, the Spanish and the Portuguese. So far, we are not a threat. However, he suggests that you should refrain from openly practicing and performing religious acts in private."

I nodded. He went on along the same lines while my mind drifted. Though I was nearly twenty-six, I had the experience of a woman of forty on matters of being Jewish. We were always threatened, always alert, and always careful.

I remembered a game we played as kids. We would tie up the eyes of one of us and leave him in the middle of the garden. Then the rest of us would whirl around, then hit and run. The target couldn't see the insurgent, he could only try to guess from the sounds: the feet or breath. Occasionally we would approach the target with our fingertips, sneaking, acting swiftly, so the target in the center, would be the recipient of the hit. This was so much like us.

We never knew where the danger could be coming from, always a center target.

"Close relations of Mr. Diogo with Cromwell, who started a wave of modernization, served us well. The power and means of the aristocrats and the Catholic Church were drastically reduced which greatly benefited the Crown. The reign of the

Tudors opened new avenues, creating opportunities for business people like us."

"I see."

"I mean the Tudors."

"Yes."

"I know the Tudors. Henry VIII divorced his wife, Kathrine of Aragon, aunt of Charles V, emperor of the Holy Roman Empire, in order to marry the Boleyn girl. He even separated his country from the Catholic Church and founded the Anglican Church, somewhat similar to the Protestant trend. The fact that the Catholics didn't allow the divorce caused them to lose England, which was just as well for us Jews since the reduction of the pope's sphere of influence would create for us a world easier to live in. I am now thankful to the Boleyn girls, Mary and Anne."

"Thomas Cromwell influenced Henry VIII and appropriated all of the wealth of the Catholic Church, topping off the treasury."

"Four years ago. I heard."

"Henry, of course, didn't quit being a Christian. He had both the Old and New Testaments translated into English. From there on, people understood the prayers. Rome was very unhappy; it was more convenient for them that followers didn't understand what was being said. They thought that important messages, which were undecipherable for humble people like themselves, were read, causing spiritual excitement, even awe. After that…

İnternally I repeated, "Wood and stones!"

"They started to understand what they listened to or read.

Rome was so furious that even if Henry VIII was not punished because of the schism and the divorce, he was excommunicated just for the translation, for killing the spiritual aura. You knew that didn't you?"

"I couldn't care less! I want to get to Antwerp as soon as possible?"

He stopped his historical explanations. After a silence, he started again:

"The safe route to Antwerp was through Calais. The safest passage to mainland Europe is through England, Dover, and then over to Calais. Before travelling over land to Dover, you will rest a little. Then from Calais onto Antwerp by a carriage."

"We will forever be on the road."

I sighed. He sensed my hurt.

"I am OK." I said. "We are all well."

Finally in Antwerp

Our stay in Bristol was convenient. Diogo tended to our every need and organized our stay so were comfortable. With branches in many cities, the Mendes House was well thought of all over Europe. This was the consequence of our constant struggle.

Our stay in England was not long and that suited me just fine. Because of the plague epidemic, we cut our stay in London short. After Francisco, I could not stand the thought of losing another close one. Brianda's only concern was to get to Antwerp quickly and to marry Diogo, and have children.

Joseph used Chevalier Rodriguez Pinto's influence with the

result that our passage to Calais was smooth and uneventful. John Husse, an influential name in the palace, was close to the governor of Calais and to his wife, Lady Lisle. In Calais, we were received like royalty and our stay was leisurely.

After a long, tiring journey, traveling over roads torn by incessant war, we advanced from Calais toward Antwerp. War, in the lands where the Flemish lived, never stopped. It was either the French or the Teutons, and occasionally the English, who fought for domination, and the Dutch and Austrians joined in too.

I had enough experience to know that sitting and idly watching was not a good idea. Since I was the leading person in our family, I needed to know, more than at any earlier time, what was happening all over. Along the way, I kept asking, listening and learning.

The Marranos had played a dominant role in Antwerp's becoming one of the major ports of Europe. The inhabitants of this area didn't call us "Marrano" but "Sinjoren, that is, "Esquire." At least Sinjoren wasn't pejorative. Large parts of the population are Protestants who led modest lives. Probably when they saw wealthy, well-dressed Marranos like us, that prompted them to address us in this way.

Since the waters of the Bruges Port were shallow, large cargo ships preferred Antwerp where city administrators kept out of religious and political issues. Here no religion or sect enjoyed a preference while business people and traders were most welcome. The logistics of the Port were good— with large and safe warehousing possibilities along with capable and inexpensive labor. The stable environment gave confidence to entrepreneurs that their goods and wealth were well-protected. The largest European bankers, such as the Foggers, Affaitatis, Welsers, and us, maintained local establishments. At two yearly meetings, people in the finance business met and exchanged goods, valuables, and cashed bills of exchange. A year before Francisco sent Diogo to move to Antwerp, the municipality gave the English a building as an enticement. The city faced one difficulty in coping with the large influx of people. When the population increased to more than one hundred thousand, rents went up.

In the East, the Turks were the greatest threat to Charles V, who was more powerful than the pope. In order to cope with the Turks, he was in constant need of money, and Antwerp was one of the principal places for European kings to borrow the required sums. Moreover, thanks to the finance network, they could get money wherever they needed it. The prestige of bankers and traders was high, as were their profits.

Thanks to Francisco and others in the Mendes ancestry, we had accumulated a large fortune but in order to grow it, we needed to reinvest it. The sums we commanded were so large, they couldn't be deployed in trading operations. We had to find ways to use our excess cash in a profitable way. Diogo had secured the spice monopoly through King Juan and had no competition. In this way, they drove prices high and generated huge profits for themselves and for the king. King Juan secured safe passage from India and, with his powerful fleet, did not allow anyone else to use this route. Our means were multiplying at such an unbelievable rate, we had difficulty finding safe investments. Previously, only aristocrats had access to spices. Now it was entering the kitchens of ordinary people and consumption was widespread.

Before setting foot in Antwerp, I knew this was the richest city in the modern world, and it was bound to get richer. I now saw how far sighted my late husband was. He predicted the future when, years ago, he started investing here. Neither Bruges nor Venice could match Antwerp, which had stolen their future. Spices arriving from India were distributed to the world through this city. Moreover, silver from the New World found its way here through Seville where customers were ready. This is where the textile industry was bound to grow. Its able Marrano population not only knew weaving but was also capable of handling the fabric trade, a great advantage for them. Attire was a way for people to express their status. As the crusaders came across Turkish cloth, and as Turks started invading parts of Europe, the importance of being dressed with fine and expensive clothes started being recognized. Following such developments, new markets appeared for both cloth and apparel.

I hoped to be able to live according to our true beliefs in Antwerp, which was ruled by the Brabant Duchy. I hoped we wouldn't have to pretend we were Christians.

When we finally arrived in Antwerp, I was not surprised that this city was called the Florence of the North. Antwerp was, undoubtedly, livelier than all the cities we passed by. Ships were berthing, unloading their cargo and passengers, and crews worked like bees in a hive creating a similar buzz. Just across the port, soldiers ensured security, with two of them constantly on guard. Nearby, prostitutes in suggestive apparel swore while luring customers to come inside a brothel. All the roads that led to the sea were as bustling and crowded as the port itself. Even at early hours, customers filled the taverns and inns. To see people of all colors and creeds was bewildering. Next to an Arab, still wearing traditional white dress, we saw a tough, ragged seaman from the north and eastern buyers with large belts buckled around their waists. We saw rich business people wearing shirts with wide collars and strange hats that looked like cones. We saw locals torn from the New World, British redheads, pitch-dark Africans, slant-eyed Far Easterners as if brought over by Marco Polo. They were all here as if in an opera setting, thousands, of all ages, everyone, from little kids to old people with sagging skin, from youths to people with graying beards.

If I learned anything about human beings, it is that we have sharp noses. We can smell better than the sharpest greyhound. Our sense of smell is unlike the small noses of rabbits or quail. Human noses have the sense that excites greed. If people don't sense opportunity, they would not gather here. I found Antwerp to be much more bustling and restless than Lisbon.

Diogo gave us a red carpet reception. He made preparations as if a queen were coming, instructing the servants to make sure we didn't have to lift a finger. Passersby that didn't know Diogo must have wondered about these people wearing opulent finery.

We settled in the mansion that he had ready for us. There wasn't a large garden in front. It was a tall building attached on both sides to the others with a pointed roof top. Thank God it was comfortable and spacious enough, for a city where real estate is so expensive.

Escape from Lisbon

I asked the servants to prepare beds for Reyna and for me. My little one was exhausted from the long journey. As a devoted mother, I always wanted to be close to her, and I wanted to be sure that I could shower her with all the love I could give her.

Brianda wanted a separate room for herself. She wanted to start the wedding preparation as soon as possible. The help that came with us settled in rooms one floor below. This way they would be close to the entrance floor and be able to answer the door for guests or others.

After settling in my room, I laid Reyna in her little bed and opened the windows. A beautiful day with crystal clear skies. Canals and rivers behind clean and neat streets, quaint bridges and even some small boats. People seemed happy. I saw well-dressed ladies, and gentlemen who saluted them with their hats.

While it seemed that we would be able to breathe, I still had some doubts. Francisco was still in Lisbon's suffocating atmosphere.

"I hope the Inquisition never comes here!"

Brianda impatient to marry

Brianda asked, "Why are you delaying my wedding? You have to allow me to be independent from now on."

We were seated in the lounge, sipping our delicious port wine. Reyna was making all sorts of funny sounds and from time to time looking with her wide eyes in our direction.

I repositioned myself in the armchair where I was sitting.

"Brianda, what is the hurry? We still haven't finished the

mourning period for Francisco. We came such a long way and haven't even settled properly yet!"

"I think we waited long enough. Anyhow, why the delay?"

The door opened and Diogo walked in.

"Hello ladies, how are you today?"

He came close and kissed Brianda's hand and mine.

I saw a part of Francisco in him. But younger, more handsome, more warm-blooded. In excellent shape, he was one of Europe's most important businessmen, and the dearest of our family. I doubted that Brianda would understand and appreciate him. Had she noticed that although he was meticulous in his dress, and concerned about his outlook, an honest and perfect family member, that he was also an unrepentant workaholic?

"The two of you, chatting sisters."

"Oh, don't ask. Brianda is trying to make me angry."

He sat in the armchair opposite us.

"What has she done this time?"

Brianda threw a stern look at him.

"She is trying to delay our wedding!"

She hoped to gain Diogo's support but it was not forthcoming.

"Brianda, my little darling, if your sister wishes it to be that way, she must be right. No need to hurry. We will belong to each other soon."

Brianda tried to hide her resentment:

"You too, Diogo. You are saying the same thing? Why should we wait? What is there to wait? The whole family is reunited; you are doing well in business. My dowry is ready. So?"

I hated to see her come out in that hysterical way. I raised my voice:

Escape from Lisbon

"Brianda, behave like a lady!"

She turned around and retorted:

"I know what you are up to. You are trying to prevent what is my right. You don't want me to control the family fortune! You want to be in absolute control! For this reason, you are trying to delay my wedding to prevent my appropriating my own fortune! You will fail! You won't be able to manipulate me! I am not your daughter; do you get it? I am your sister. I have the same rights as you. Why should I sit on the sidelines while watching you manage our fortune in any way you choose?"

I was astonished at what I just heard. I always thought Brianda to be a little light headed but she was the daughter of my mother and father. It was unthinkable that she could be so foolish.

"What are you talking about Brianda? What does this have to do with our conversation? You own whatever you want. Why would you think that I am an obstacle?"

"Yes, I own everything. But only the way you see fit and for as much as you approve!"

"Don't be foolish! You don't know what you are saying!"

I was sad. I didn't want Diogo to see the woman he would marry in that light. At the end of the day, he is our uncle, knowing all details of our relationship but now, his role was changing. He will marry Brianda and start a family with her.

"I don't want to live in your shadow anymore!" said Brianda. "I want to make my own decisions. Stop obstructing me!"

Diogo felt the need to intervene.

"My little bird, Brianda, we are not going anywhere. Whether we like it or not, time goes by. We can get married in the shortest possible time, if we so wish."

Brianda faced him:

"Diogo I want you on my side on this issue. Don't object!"

It would have been stupidity not to notice Diogo's infatuation. She really was much prettier than I was. Sister, you are denigrating yourself to no avail. Diogo blushed but did not express his feelings.

"OK, calm down."

I expressed my dismay:

"Brianda, you spoiled our evening! I never imagined you would talk that way!"

Reyna was also restless and crying. I signaled her nanny to take her away. We waited until they left the room.

I said without restraint:

"Sometimes you drive people crazy! Get married whenever you want! Don't even wait at all, do the wedding tomorrow. Since you don't want to consider your elders, act according to your dumb head. It's your choice!"

Having had enough of this conversation, Diogo stood up.

"I will leave you to yourselves. You two sisters can plan all preparations. The company lawyers can work on company management issues."

I stood up.

"Diogo, forgive my sister's behavior. You can arrange everything as you see fit."

Brianda stood up too and took his arm to see him to the door.

"There is nothing to be forgiven. My future husband and I share the same opinion."

Escape from Lisbon

As Diogo was leaving, he saluted me with his hand and threw an ambiguous look toward me.

I knew it. He also understood that I was more capable in business matters than my sister. Even if he didn't show it, I could tell that he trusted me more on such issues. This was inevitable, Diogo was a business man. He was able to discern between destructive and constructive business approaches.

As he walked out, I was left alone with my sister. Again, she sat facing me. At twenty, she was younger than I, but her wants were beyond her capabilities. During my father's time, while he was working on our education, he shared his business experiences as if they were stories. Brianda was bored and her mind wandered. She was not interested in occupying herself with business matters.

I enquired:

"What was your purpose? Diogo was also unhappy with what you have done."

"I doubt it. He kissed me as he left. It's natural for him to side with me. After all, I will soon be his wife."

"Even so, you shouldn't have used words unfit for a lady. Fortune control and all that."

Once again, she raised her voice:

"That is my right!"

"Brianda, my dear sister, you always had your head in the air. But, even you should know: the fortune we control wasn't made easily. My father, husband and many others lost their lives struggling to build this fortune. We need to work hard constantly to protect it. That's really not the main issue. You should know by now that the goods, gold, and money we possess are not for spending for our whims. In our life, we have been endowed with other duties and responsibilities apart from living a life of luxury. We have all we need, anyway. What is it that you need and cannot get? You can tell me whatever it is. Would I withhold anything from my dear sister?"

"That's absurd," she said in an uninterested way. "This is my fortune; why should it be used for other purposes?"

I was really getting mad. I refrained from being harsh, thinking that, after my daughter, she was my closest relative.

"Brianda, get this into your head, once and for all, our ideal is not to make more gold, money or possess more goods in order to live a more sumptuous life. If that were the case, we could have stopped working years ago. Because my dear sister, our earnings were such that we couldn't spend them all in our lifetimes. Our goal is to provide a peaceful living environment for all Marranos and Jews. Like any idealistic Jew, this is our primary aim."

I felt a strong desire to let her into the secret my father shared, but I held back. If I gave in to my urge, I would be as stupid as Brianda. To open up to her where my father hadn't seen fit to do so would be unbecoming. Both my mother and father were believers. Even under difficult circumstances, they had given me a good Torah education, and to Brianda as well.

In the face of new developments, I have to understand that she is completely dizzy.

"Come on! Do you really believe in all that?" she asked, amused. "Why should we be responsible for all the Marranos? There are many rich Marranos. Let them think of the rest. From now on, I want to lead a good life. Didn't we suffer enough in Lisbon, and by leaving too?"

I had difficulty digesting her words.

"You can't be serious! Aren't you genuinely concerned about the welfare of your co-religionists? The difficult times we all are going through, not being able to use our proper names, living our true belief, having to fake our identities? Don't you think that it can happen to us, that the Inquisition can follow us here too?"

"I naturally worry. Of course, I would like to save all the Marranos, but what can we do? The things I can do are so limited."

"Don't talk like that! As the Mendes family, we do have responsibilities. Tables we shared with kings, balls we attended with ministers, and aristocrats and the many other affairs we have engaged in. All is for a purpose, and that is, to ensure that you, me, Diogo, Reyna and even your future children can all live fearlessly and as free individuals, without being forced to hide or to pretend."

I could go on and on. It was as if I were talking to the walls. I felt that whatever I told Brianda, in her present state of mind, would not be enough to convince her of our insecurities. She stared at me half mockingly with an ugly smirk on her lips.

I said to myself:

"Forget it! If she doesn't realize, surely Diogo does. By cooperating, we will be able to keep her checked."

However, her ambitions were uncontrollable. I didn't fathom that she was making plans that could ruin us all.

Unexpected visit

When the news came that Father Fernando wished to dine with us, naturally, I said:

"He will be welcome; I will be happy to receive him."

Father Fernando had come from Portugal. He was known by many Marranos and knew most of them.

Before his arrival, I firmly instructed the staff to put away all objects that had a connection with Judaism and to make certain that no trace remained. We were out of Portugal and not under threat as before. Still, we needed to be cautious.

As soon as he stepped into the house, he crossed himself and blessed the house. We acted as respectful and good Christians, happy for his action. We joined him with a jolly and grateful attitude. He was a man with soft features and he spoke tenderly. An outsider could easily think of him as a good person, full of love and affection.

"Honorable Father, you make us very happy with your visit. We will share with you the yearning we have for our country, the nostalgia."

Diogo also greeted him respectfully.

Father turned to the one who would be the fourth at the table. Her long silence was not appropriate. I quickly stepped in: "My sister Brianda misses our country even more."

Brianda bent and kissed his ring.

"Bless you my child."

As a good hostess, I said:

"Father, the table where you will be our guest of honor is ready. If you wish, we can continue our conversation while eating and drinking so the food does not get cold. You must miss the fabulous Portuguese wines. Tonight, they will be served. Apart from that, we have prepared dishes with vegetables from the New World, where they are called potatoes. You will find the taste interesting."

He made a sound with his lips against his palate.

"Have no doubt!"

We all sat at the table, the Father at my right.

Diogo asked: "Dear Father, how does our country fare? What news did you bring us from Portugal?"

I too, added: "Our country, our home we miss it all. We will be back as soon as we finish the wedding preparations. Would you believe it? I even miss the smell of the fish market!"

Father should be younger than his looks or at least more youthful though his voice was lively.

"As usual, ships, discoveries, new places where the message of God should be taken. Even if our king forgets the duties of the Church, we go wherever our mission takes us, however far. Some choose the New World, others Antwerp where there is an important community of New Christians.

"Which is more worthwhile?"

"If you want my opinion, helping people in the crowded city of Antwerp is more important than trying to educate heathens in faraway lands. But who, except God, would know which is best? Our duty is to carry his message under any circumstances, wherever we may be. Even if we save a lost soul, that's good enough."

While dinner was being served, I noticed the look on his face as he saw fish on the plate.

"Don't you like fish, Father? Perhaps you prefer something else. There are fish in Antwerp, the likes of which we had never seen, delicious, too. We also have tasty pork chops if you prefer. I can have it quickly prepared."

I said this on purpose. I didn't want him to think of us as Jews who don't eat pork.

"No, fish is good. Thanks for all given by God. What is this that you call potatoes? Is it edible?"

We smiled.

He started praying. We joined our hands in respect, and waited. He finished.

"Amen!"

We all repeated: "Amen!"

Diogo:

"Father, in Antwerp you can eat the best fish in the world. Fish is plentiful in Portugal but we can get species here that can only be found in cold waters, tastier than our country and considerably bigger."

"Really?"

Father tasted the white wine and started eating the fish.

We had cleaned our kitchen from all that was not Kosher. The Rabbi had come and checked all cutlery too. Even for Father Fernando, I didn't want to defile our kitchen. I had invited him with the hope that he could help me discover a way to transport Francisco's remains to Jerusalem. From now on, I had no intention of returning to Portugal where the poisonous climate of the Inquisition terrified Marranos. Still, it was wise to maintain good relations.

"Our yearning for our country is ever so strong. Obligations separated us but I look forward to sitting on our balcony and breathing the familiar smells of Lisbon."

"When do you plan to return?"

"After Brianda and Diogo's wedding, I also want our little darling Reyna, this was the name given her during her baptism, to grow a little. It will take her some time. We are lucky to have fellow citizens like you close to us. We can discuss our longings with you."

Brianda smiled.

"Congratulations, my child. You too, Mr. Diogo."

Diogo:

"Father, how did you come to be in this city? Are you responsible for saving these lost souls? If that's the case, it seems that you will have a very difficult time. The population of Antwerp has grown over a hundred thousand."

"You are partly correct. Immigration to Antwerp was much larger than Spain, Portugal, and other regions. Originally the city administrators were happy and welcoming of immigrants but their attitude is changing. Corruption, wickedness, perversion is rampant. Portugal is receiving such reports too. The atmosphere of freedom in the city is creating a convenient climate for the spread of heretical views and actions, Mr. Diogo!"

I curved my lips as if I thought this was an atrocity. I crossed myself piously.

"God forgive our sins!"

Father continued, "My duty is to make observations in the city and report to Rome, to His Eminence, the Pope, and to the Inquisition."

Diogo decided to play more openly:

"Father Fernando, you know full well that the saving of

the lost souls living here is not an easy task. There are so many people of different ethnic origins that it's hard to say who is Christian and who is not."

"Right. This is what attracted us."

"In this case, you have a different and additional duty too."

Father took a large portion of the fish and gobbled it down with the wine.

"Mr. Mendes, I had heard that you are a very clever person. That seems right. The problem stems from the invitation we got from the Antwerp administration. The concern is with those that come over, settle, and then collaborate with our enemies, the Ottomans."

"Ottomans?"

That was me asking.

"Yes, Ottomans."

"Dear Father, what reasonable Christian would wish to associate himself with the Ottomans? They are our enemy!"

Brianda nodded to assure her agreement.

"Dear daughter, not everybody is a sincere believer like you. Many come over to enrich themselves among the true Christians and reap the blessings provided by God. This is their aim. After that, armed with these riches, they go to the Ottoman lands. Recently, complaints about the alarmingly yet increasing number of such people is on the rise. My duty is to investigate particular such cases. More clearly, it is to find out the ones who are either intending or facilitating the making of such moves."

I felt as if I would choke. Did he know that we were one of the principal people helping Marranos who wanted to go to

Ottoman lands? Is he trying to make us talk? Is this an investigation, and not a visit?

"But, dear Father, what would a Christian do in Ottoman lands? It is said that the Ottomans are impounding goods of Christians or decapitating them."

I was saying all that, as I believed them. I was sure he was carefully listening to catch an insinuation, a slip, a lead.

"Yes, that is so. Still, there are many escaping that way."

"Unbelievable!"

Diogo:

"Dona Gracia, there are some that are running to Ottoman lands as Father Fernando explained. I hear such rumors too. Provided they bring their wealth with them, regardless of their religion or creed, Suleiman is opening his doors to them. Luckily, the numbers are small, measures must be taken to keep them here. Isn't that so, Father? It is needed to prevent the immigration of simple and well-intentioned people to the East."

"That's right. The Duchy wants to stop this flow. What is earned in Antwerp should stay in Antwerp!"

Father had no difficulty spotting the weakest link at table. After taking a short sip from his glass, he turned to Brianda:

"My child, what is your opinion on such matters?"

"I have no idea. I wouldn't want to live with Muslims," Brianda replied.

Father nodded approvingly. I was terrified that she would make a blunder. In reality, Brianda had no concept of these issues.

I added: "It is inconceivable to turn a blind eye to people leaving Antwerp and going to the country where the Sultan is the most feared enemy of Christianity. Emperor Charles V can never accept or allow it, Father. Well than, how can that be prevented? Can you tell us? How can they be prevented from transferring their fortunes?"

"It's not definite yet, I hear that all new arrivals will be registered. Then, an investigation will be made, even the inn keepers will have to keep a record of guests who stay in their lodgings. I think it's a good start. Then the permanent residents must be separated from the newcomers! Newcomers should not be allowed to remain longer than a month."

"As New Christians and as an establishment, we are prepared to assist in any way we can, Father Fernando," I said enthusiastically. "Don't you agree Diogo?"

"Of course! We owe it to the Church."

The priest seemed more convinced and continued with his wine.

"How long have you been in this city, Mr. Diogo?"

"With short absences, about 20 years, Father. Though I have been here for so long, we opened our branch before Francisco died. Since I am 52, I must have come in my thirties."

"I heard that your family is exempted from the immigration formalities."

"You are really doing your job well, Father! My family was not treated as an ordinary immigrant, particularly Brianda, my wife-to-be. I am not a foreigner. My partner also should be considered similarly."

He looked lovingly to Brianda who blushed at this unexpected gesture.

"May I ask what you have dedicated your life to?"

"By all means, Father. To whatever a Christian believer would, to be a good Christian. My aim is to assist anyone who has been wronged, suppressed, in need of help, for all to have a better living. I will not stop for as long as I can. I will work constantly."

"You should be meeting heretics too?"

Diogo put down his spoon.

"God forbid, Father! I wouldn't want to even breathe the same air as these people! You can be sure that, if I ever meet a wretched one like that, I will not hesitate to inform you so you can help save his miserable soul."

Father, happy from what he heard, nodded approvingly. His empty glass was refilled. Diogo continued:

"Father, what is your opinion. Do you think that the Inquisition will be established here?"

"He looked pensive and said in a tone as if he was sharing a secret he shouldn't: "Why do you think I am here?"

Longings

We sat together for a while after the priest left. Most of our staff were in their quarters. In the darkness of the night, lit by a few weakened candles, from the open windows of our balcony we were watching aimlessly, sipping our drinks. I felt paralyzed, crushed as if under a ton of bricks. I was breathing but my chest felt static, motionless.

When the priest announced that the Inquisition would soon be established in Antwerp, I pretended I to be happy but at that moment, I had made up my mind:

"If I cannot prevent this, I will not remain in Antwerp!"

Dona Gracia

A fleeting glance at Diogo was enough to see that he was thinking similarly.

"We are paying for our sins, Diogo."

Diogo cleared his mind from dark thoughts and leaned back in an armchair.

"How do you mean, Gracia?"

Brianda was silently listening. From her looks, I saw that she sensed negativity.

"We are paying for the sin and betrayal we committed to our true religion. Apostasy, denial of Judaism, choosing the easy path. These calamities are visiting us because of our real sins. Inquisition is following us. I fear that we will be followed wherever we go!"

"Don't think that way Gracia! The priest doesn't have definite information, only crumbs. If he had credible material, he wouldn't doubt for a moment before sending us to the stake. After this meeting, I think his doubts were dispersed. Even if King Juan and his advisers suspect that we are helping Marranos go to the Ottomans, after Father Fernando's report attesting the opposite, they will not act in any way."

Suddenly I was anxious. Diogo was my partner, we were both responsible. It was true that our ships were helping Marranos go to the Ottomans. If they had any evidence at all, they wouldn't hesitate to ruin him. Competitors also would try to take advantage with the goal of getting rid of us. I had always thought of myself as the prey, and now realized that Diogo shares the danger.

"What if they are after you? They tried once before, didn't

they? What if you are the target of the whole thing?"

Brianda was frightened of this possibility.

"Good God! Can this be true?"

Diogo was comfortable: "No. I doubt it. At least not at this stage. In one way or another, the priest will return to Lisbon and present his report. For us as well as other Marranos, the greatest threat is the Inquisition. We have to maintain our struggle to prevent the Inquisition courts from being established in Antwerp."

Brianda: "I wish we had remained as Jews! The Inquisition is not bothering Jews. They are after crypto Jews like we are."

I scolded her: "Don't say such stupid things. Did you forget that all Jews were converted to Christianity before we were even born?"

She was silent.

Diogo: "Their main objective, these days, is to prevent the ones that are going to the Ottomans. Along with fortunes, dangerous information is also being transferred. They want to put an end to this. If they block the routes to the Ottomans, there are alternative roads through small, liberal Christian Duchies. We can channel refugees through these routes for a while. As a precaution, I will stop all activity until Fernando leaves Antwerp. When things calm down, we can continue to help people travel."

"Brianda: "Can't they find their way on their own?"

"Many are robbed or killed as they try to run. The ones that travel with unreliable captains never reach their destinations. Some are robbed and murdered; others are sold in slave markets, raped and so on. Leaving the land with just any ship, a wise person wouldn't even try!"

"You have to inform other Marranos too, Diogo."

"I will do so. We all agreed to form a common fund. With this fund, we will be able to help many more Marranos." He straightened up in his chair, and said, "It's getting late. Oh, didn't you mention something regarding Joseph?"

He got up.

"His father, who is a doctor, wanted him to be a business man. I thought he could join our company in the future. He has extremely good manners, and is as intelligent and reliable as one can get. He is continuing his education in the same school you attended, Louvain University. He will form invaluable relationships there. Don't forget he is your nephew too."

"I agree and think it's a good idea."

"Diogo, please help him as best you can to get a good business background. Share your experiences. Help him develop himself. He thinks the spice business is a thing of the past and believes the potential for growth is in banking. Moreover, he says risks will be reduced and profits increased considerably."

"Is that so! He doesn't know much about the spice business, that's why. If spices were not available, he would be eating meats and fish that were salted and rancid. There would be no aromas. Does he know that wealthy people offer spices as gifts to each other? And about the aphrodisiac effects?"

"He knows all that, also how we increased our wealth thanks to the new sea trade routes and that you are the spice king of Europe."

"Joseph knew all this, and that apart from spice business, we allocate large credit lines to aristocrats and rulers, conduct a large wine trade, and are active in mining. While our side of the family occupied itself with business, another branch continued as doctors and left Portugal for the Ottoman Empire. Joseph, being the youngest of that branch, joined forces with us."

"So, I have to start him in the spice business. A good test will be to see if he can be successful doing something he doesn't particularly like. In this case, we can be sure that he will enjoy business activities and get good results in other assignments. I wish you a good night."

Diogo turned as if he had forgotten something: "You didn't forget that we are invited tomorrow night by the Consul of Portugal Damião de Goes for dinner? He is a cartographer and a humanist. He helps all Portuguese coming to Antwerp. He is giving the reception in honor of Castel Rodrigues de Castel Branco or Amatus Lusitanus, as he is known to us."

"Surely I know Lusitanus well. He studied in Salamanca, Santarem and Lisbon universities. He was our doctor and close family friend. He had run from Lisbon to come to Antwerp. He was heading for Ancona and was famous for his medical series called Centuria where he would write, in each one, about 100 illnesses and the cures. These became textbooks in medical schools. His dream also was to live as a free man and help patients in need, free of charge. He wanted to use the rest of his life in research, seeing patients and educating future doctors."

"How can we forget. We will come with you."

"Diogo Pires from Evora is also in town. He will be among the guests. If he comes, he will read us poems in Latin. He is also yearning to be able to use his original name, Isaiah Co-hen, and to live openly as a Jew. If we are lucky, the famous Renaissance painter, Albert Dürer, will be there too."

"He will probably ask you whether you will commission a work."

"Dona Gracia, I know your aversion to paintings stems from religious teachings. I respect that but I also like Albert and his works. Have a good night."

Brianda followed saying, "I am going to bed too."

Left alone in the room, I reminisced about my nights in Lis-bon when I would open the door to the balcony, feel the cool air against my face, and listen to the singing of working people. I missed that. At night from the balcony, I could watch passersby walking the streets even in the early hours of the morning. Por-tuguese songs, mainly fados and sad melodies from the guitars mixed with men yelling, and using bad language, so many dia-lects that I couldn't decipher and also foreign languages, people talking loudly without a concern for disturbing others. During the days, the scene was quite different. People dressed more soberly and wandered around considerably, greeting others politely but at night, the streets were left to shouting and yelling by impudent people.

I was thinking about Diogo. If we had met in different circumstances, we would have been perfect matches for each other. We were both equally wealthy, and shared the same religion, attitude toward life, and business approach. In many other ways, we shared so much. He was handsome and, con-sidering his years, quite vigorous. I was the widower of his deceased brother. If it wasn't for Reyna, he would have had to marry me. The Torah commands that the brother of the dead husband should marry his wife in order to maintain perpetuity in the family. Failing to do that, he would be embarrassed in front of the community with an unpleasant ritual.

"Be realistic, Gracia! He loves Brianda. Many Marranos would die to be his wife but he was infatuated with her beauty, her carefree airs. He was set on marrying her."

On business issues, Diogo always asked for my opinion, shared his sincere inner thoughts and consulted me on all major issues but, since we arrived in Antwerp, he could not take his eyes off Brianda.

"Her light minded attitude, taking each day as it comes must have appealed to him. Sure, he enjoys talking to me but it is Brianda that he would sleep with. If he formed another partnership, it would be with a person like me but for marriage, he chose Brianda, seductive and fetching."

I took a deep breath. It felt as if I swallowed the night. I liked it. It was quite some time that I was alone since Francisco's death.

She was in a trance too when he proposed. I understand her. On such issues, we didn't really have much of a choice.

I looked down on the street. A stocky one was walking by; his dress suggested that he was a Spaniard.

However much I liked or even felt emotional about someone, I didn't have the option of marrying him if he didn't adhere to certain precepts. It was the same for Brianda. We had to marry someone similar to us: a Jew, perhaps a Marrano, rich, from an equally reputable family and if possible, a very close relative to ensure that our fortune would not be diluted.

I thought of Reyna. I had to plan her suitor already, while

she is still a baby for the day will come when she will grow into a beautiful young girl. Then she will join her life with someone who meets the same criteria as those who were chosen for me and for her aunt.

I saw the cresset of a ship, in the distance. It seems it was simply rocking where it was. Fresh wind filled my lungs and I felt passion growing in my chest.

"If I didn't have my obligations, commitments, the secret that I was entrusted with, the duty of helping Marranos who suffered because of their beliefs, my life would have been much different, maybe happier. I will never know.

My heart was palpably beating and I felt the need for the warmth and care of a man.

With my colossal wealth, I could marry anyone I wanted and lead a luxurious life to my heart's content. In a city where most women don't even have a private kitchen, I am wealthier than most men and getting richer each day. That cannot be! İmpossible dream.

Who knows, maybe one day the suffering of the Marranos will end. Then, probably, they will enjoy freedoms, not hiding their identity, their Jewishness, with no pressure or threats. Then I might consider getting married.

Who knows? Then I might even marry an ordinary person. Love might be my only drive. I could choose whoever my heart desired from the multitude of courting types, close to my age, a fun guy.

I knew well. The probability of the realization of my dream was not only further than the pole of the ship but even further than the stars above: That would be the case for little Reyna too.

I thought of Joseph. He could be a potential suitor. For Reyna. I always had this hunch. My wish to watch him closely might be the reason I took such a special interest in him. I am his aunt; one day I might be his mother-in-law too.

Ohh Diogo! I so wished that we didn't have to live under the same roof!

That gave me a second reason, though a personal one, to want to leave Antwerp.

I thought of the priest. Last night, he crowed like sinister owl. He had his assignment, and the more he gobbled down the wine, the more he yapped. He wanted to save lost souls but was unaware of his fanatical bigotry. Enemy of the other, he had come to check on us.

Wedding and Arrest

One night, months later, I opened my eyes and the first thing I heard was a terrible noise. It was as if the whole building was shaking with this rumble. I wondered why the maids didn't open the door. Since I was awakened on the top floor, they should have woken up, one floor below, and heard the door.

I put on my robe and rushed to Reyna's room, wanting to be there before she woke up. I was too late. She had already started crying. I wondered why the maids hadn't run to the door. Unable to wait any longer, I yelled:

"Hey! It's midnight, who the heck is this? Why the hell this noise?"

On the one hand, I was hugging and calming Reyna on the other I was shouting: "Why has nobody answered the door? Is this my duty?"

Both Diogo and Brianda were awake. They opened their door and watched in astonishment as they tried to figure out what was happening.

Finally, the door was opened. A maid had come and prevented the door from being smashed.

The rumble was replaced by a murmur.

"What's up Diogo?"

Brianda was holding her tummy, afraid that something could happen to the baby in her belly.

Diogo lifted the lantern in his hand.

"Gracia, we didn't really understand. In an instant, we were alarmed by banging on the door."

Wedding and Arrest

Our curiosity didn't last long. The housemaid came upstairs, grumbling. When she saw the three of us together, she pulled herself together and explained what had happened:

"Mr. Diogo, they are here to arrest you. They are asking for you to come down immediately."

~ ~

Father Fernando's visit gave me an extra reason to rush and it served as a serious warning to me.

"Seeing that we will not stay long in this city, we might as well get the wedding over."

It wasn't difficult to organize the wedding as most of the preparations were complete. A large crowd attended the church wedding. The business community, our family members, most of the Marranos we knew well from Portugal came to the church.

Brianda was so happy she wandered around joyfully as if her feet had been swept off the ground.

I was with her all the time, hurling instructions to workpeople, watching Reyna while at the same time, making sure nothing was missing. Since our parents weren't around, I felt it was my responsibility, as head of the family to keep everything under control. I was happy as it was my sister's wedding, a little disconcerted as it was Diogo's too. I was half-happy as I would not be responsible for Brianda anymore, but not so happy to see the closeness of Diogo and Brianda.

We didn't neglect the clandestine wedding observance with full Jewish ritual in the privacy of our home.

After a few months, Brianda shared the good news: "A new member is joining the family. I am pregnant!"

I was so happy, I could fly. A new Mendes I could love as much as my daughter. From the smile on his face, I understood that Diogo was informed, and I was assured of his happiness too.

"Brianda, that can't be! I am so happy, I could cry!"

She started crying before me, and I joined.

Diogo: "Are you saddened?" he asked half playfully.

Typical men. They can never understand women's tears. They only think they do.

I held Brianda's hand: "I am happy, so happy!"

This was the first that we had news that filled us with joy.

~ ~

This can't be serious. He was standing up, half asleep but dead serious.

Brianda shrieked: "Oh my God."

I asked: "What is that all about?"

Reyna started crying again. I took her in my arms, patted her back, and tried to calm her.

Diogo kept his cool: "Did they give a reason?"

"No Sir."

"OK, tell them that I will get dressed and come down. Ask them not to make too much fuss. Tell them that my dear wife is pregnant, and they shouldn't bother her more!"

Not paying attention to Brianda and my enquiring looks, he went to his room. He started getting dressed to be ready to go.

Brianda was crying: "Diogo, why are they taking you away? How come? When will you be back?"

"I don't know my love. We soon will find out. Send one of

the servants to inform my lawyer. Don't worry and take care of our child."

He caressed Brianda's belly gently. They were expecting shortly. Taking him into custody was most unexpected and untimely."

First thing next morning, I went straight to the police station.

I said, "I want to talk immediately to the captain."

Knowing our relations with higher up officials, they didn't keep me waiting long.

I knew Captain Van der Giel. We had short conversations in our previous encounters.

I said with a voice half offended and half vexed: "Commander, may I ask why you are keeping under custody a well-respected business man?"

I continued: "In the middle of the night! Not even considering his pregnant wife!"

He waited for me to be seated before he sat down. He was careful to show some respect.

"Pray be seated. Calm down. I will explain it all."

I sat down as he bowed and pushed my chair. I grumbled until he sat too: "I didn't expect to be treated this way! You came to our home at midnight to arrest Mr. Diogo as a simple criminal! You nearly smashed our door!"

"First of all, I apologize for the rudeness of my soldiers. It is not for us to decide custody but for the prosecutor. You know well that we are bound to obey and execute orders."

"What are the prosecutors' accusations, I wonder?"

I didn't expect an answer. Everyone knew that Diogo

wouldn't commit an offense, let alone a crime. I asked this to be a little cheeky.

He was thoughtful for a while. Then apparently feeling uneasy in explaining an awkward situation: "Mr. Diogo is being accused of 'continuing Jewish traditions.'"

It was as if the sky closed on me. I was gasping. "I can see your surprise Mrs. Mendes but that's the situation."

"Me. Me. I am lost for words."

My shock was not for the denouncement but for this act to be an offense. How could that be, in Antwerp, far from Inquisition courts, in a supposedly free country?

I said in a rebellious tone:

"You have to let him go immediately. Everyone knows that we are Christians. We attend mass and contribute generously. We are performing all the duties that a good Christian would. This is insane!"

"Only the courts can decide that. Prosecutor's accusations are rather serious. You don't attend services on Sundays, don't eat pork, and even help fugitives going to other countries, Marranos. Even more."

He stopped there.

"Not true. We go to Church on Sundays. When we are not seen there, it is because we pray in the private chapel we have at home. As for pork and things like that, we often have it at our table. Some of our guests could attest to that."

"Then there is nothing to worry about. Your guest will bear witness to that."

He wasn't smiling. He had a mocking attitude, as if saying "I know you are lying."

Wedding and Arrest

I was infuriated. If I couldn't control myself, I could smash everything in sight. I knew this wouldn't help Diogo, and doing so, could cause me to join him in prison.

Trying to keep calm, I said: "If that is all, then there is no cause to worry."

"There is another more serious accusation. I don't know."

"For God's sake, what can be worse?"

"It is said that Mr. Diogo is collaborating with the Turks."

"That's too much," I said, standing up. "I want to talk to Diogo immediately. Put an end to this farce before our lawyers inundate your station. Otherwise I will go straight to the Duke!"

Papen, our lawyer, was already waiting outside with Joseph. He was a good lawyer. I asked him for permission to talk to Diogo for only five minutes.

"OK, I will let you talk to him. Please keep it short."

As I was walking toward his cell, I thought of Brianda. I asked her to come with me but met with an unexpected reply: "I am really sleepy. You go and tell me all about it when you get back. "

While I couldn't blink an eye the whole night, she managed to go to bed and sleep. Surely Diogo would ask about her. I wouldn't know how to explain.

The detention room had ugly iron bars that were thick and rusty. Specks of brown flaked from the iron surface, and the cell was damp.

It was clear that Diogo hadn't slept the whole night. He rushed to the iron grate separating us. As I approached him, the guard stepped back.

"Gracia!"

"Diogo! How did you get through the night? Did they keep you here all the time? Did they treat you properly?"

"No, no. I am OK. They brought me here and left me. They didn't even ask for a deposition. Where is Brianda? Why is she not with you? Is she well?"

I had to be quick. "Thinking of the baby, I asked her not to come. She is really a wreck. If she came here and saw you, she would feel worse. That could harm the baby. She hardly slept at all last night, thinking of you."

"My poor little baby," he said sadly "I think more of them than of myself. You did right."

"Diogo, how do you read the situation? Why do they suspect that you are a secret Jew, that you help fugitives?"

"It's absurd! Of course, this is all false. It is probably the vilification of a competitor. The truth will be known shortly."

"Our lead lawyer, Mr. Papen is here. The rest started work on the case already. He will come to see you, if he can get permission. We will do all we can to get you out as soon as we possibly can."

"Thank you, Gracia."

"I found the document with the pope's seal. Last night, we wanted to come with Joseph. Unfortunately, we had to wait for the morning. Papen will request your release and they will surely let you go immediately."

I could tell Diogo wanting a private word. He came closer. I moved closer too.

"This arrest is an important message. At first, the unwarranted visit of the priest, then the follow up, the chase, and now the arrest. It is not hard to guess what is next. God only knows."

Wedding and Arrest

I chose to ignore the guard standing next to us, trying to make sense of our talk. I dished it out:

"Antwerp is no longer the safe city it used to be. Diogo, this might have been a good opportunity to open our eyes. We are the target of some malevolent people. I fear a forthcoming catastrophe."

We both knew full well who that person was.

While Joseph and Papen worked for his release, I was with them, waiting. The same question kept bugging me: Would Antwerp continue to be the safe haven it used to be for the Marranos?

It didn't take long to understand the underlying issues. Consistent with our mission, Diogo was very generous in helping Marranos and Jews. Naturally, he was cautious but unexpected things did happen from time to time. This was such a case. A Marrano woman who was tormented by her husband, who was a doctor close to the palace in Portugal, escaped to Antwerp with her three sons and a daughter. They came to Diogo asking for help in disappearing to a place the husband could not find them. Diogo suggested that they would be safe in Salonika and he helped them to go there. They reached the city safely and were living there happily.

Ten years later, one of the sons, searching avidly for his roots in Portugal, turned up in Antwerp and continued his inquiry by knocking at every door he could. One of those who heard his sad story realized the potential harm that such a story could do to Diogo, and promised to help on condition that the youth do what was asked of him. He took the young fellow to Diogo's competitor, a man who detested Diogo and, for that, he was compensated generously.

"You are really and genuinely saying that Diogo helped your family to flee to the Ottomans. What a magnanimous and charitable act! I will certainly help you find your father but you must also do something for me."

The fellow was taken to an official in the court of the Duke of Brabant. He told them the whole story of how as a Jew protector, Diogo assisted this family in reaching Salonika, what mechanisms he employed to transfer their fortune, and the names of some of his close friends including Moslems to contact in the Ottoman city. Once the boy signed the official deposition, the evidence needed to convict Diogo was at hand.

Charles V was furious when he learned of Diogo's illegal activities, transferring people and their money to the land of his bitter enemy, the Ottomans. He immediately started an investigation and issued an order for Diogo's detention.

The detention of an important business man like Diogo was the talk of the town. Everybody wondered how this would affect market activities. Friends rushed to our help and competitors worked this opportunity to get rid of us.

At this point, we had Diogo freed on bail but before we could explain our situation, a second warrant for his arrest arrived. We still hadn't had time to explain to Brianda what happened.

"Charles V is acting fast!"

In a few days, they were at our door again. They came and took Diogo away again. Charles V declared that, in view of the seriousness of the charges, the immunity granted regarding possible religious accusations was null and void.

Wedding and Arrest

I felt again as if my eyes were covered. I was in the dark, unable to guess from where the next attack would come. I couldn't guess from where evil would come, behind which corner it was hiding, or when it would show its ugly face? I felt completely defenseless against blows that could come from unanticipated directions.

This time, I listened to the accusations from the prosecutor.

"Mrs. Gracia, the case is based on three possible offenses: Judaizing himself and assisting in such a crime, monopoly in the spice trade, and lending at unacceptable rates."

Ingenious defense saves the day

The certificate that provided immunity from religious matters was no longer valid. Charles V had managed to cancel it. Our defense wouldn't be so easy. Joseph and Papen and the rest of our lawyers worked harder on the case. Charles V wanted it to be taken up at the Brabant courts as they were within his jurisdiction and consequently he could easily use his influence. We objected to this on the ground that this was a civil court that was not authorized to rule on religious matters whereas the courts in Antwerp would be more appropriate. Guarantees were issued by the authorities for all Marranos arriving in Antwerp declaring that they cannot be judged on religious grounds. Now was the time to make good on that commitment, and we should not be judged on charges of being heretics.

The case should be dropped in total.

It was true that we held the spice monopoly but all such

privileges were conducted with the support of the king of Portugal and with the knowledge of the local administration. This was done in order to be able to meet the heavy pecuniary demands placed on the activity. Consortiums with the involvement of many companies were put in place to maintain and fix the high prices needed to reimburse the large sums requested by governments. For prolonged periods of time, there had been no objections to these openly conducted activities, it was reasonable to conclude that these were seen as acceptable. So the accusation was unjust and the motives ill intended.

The easiest charge to defend was lending at high interest rates. The interest rates were established by all the banks active in the market and our rates were in line with these.

Either all bankers should be detained, or Diogo should be acquitted of this accusation!

I knew the forces behind this parody. The case was more political than judiciary. Business in the courts was conducted in a way required by the emperor and efforts were made to reach verdicts that would please Charles V!

We had to fight the case carefully with Joseph. We couldn't leave our destiny in the hands of these courts that can be easily manipulated.

The King of England, Henry VIII and Charles V's sister, Mary, and the main business actors, worried about market destabilization. They all pleaded on our behalf but couldn't convince the Emperor.

I visited Diogo in his cell. Though he had special treatment and we made sure he was well looked after, he looked tired, weakened, and pale. With black rings under his eyes, messy

hair, and unshaven beard, he looked devastated.

"I am OK," he said wanting to comfort us. "Concentrate not on my looks but on how you will get me out of this hole."

Papen: "Our case is solid. If the verdict will be based on judicial norms, we have nothing to worry about."

Joseph was listening carefully. I was exhausted from digging into archives and collecting evidence and information to support our claims.

"The judge in this case is Charles V!"

Diogo: "That's why you have to be even more diligent."

It was time to disclose my inner thoughts: "Diogo, while going through the books I saw a contract you signed with the Fuggers. We have a debt of 200.000 ducats to them.

"Right."

"Then you invested this sum as credits to various people."

"Charles V, these days, needs to borrow money for his military expeditions. He will knock on Fuggers doors as usual, and they will come to us. If we cannot pay the Fuggers, there is nowhere else they can raise this kind of money for him."

Diogo looked at my eyes joyfully: "Gracia, you found the way out!"

Diogo is Released

Diogo was imprisoned for three months. We did all we could so that he would be well looked after. In spite of that, it was a nightmare. These horrible experiences helped make up his mind. He whispered in my ear: "We are leaving Antwerp!"

Anxious anticipations, a restless life, even a palace for us.

Brianda, one hand on her tummy, the other around her husband shed tears of joy.

"That's the end of it!" exclaimed Diogo. "Don't worry darling, we will lead a happy life with our child and never live through such trauma again. I'll start working on it, no later than today."

"Is that so? How will you do it?"

"Be patient. First I need to shave and have a good bath. After that, we will have plenty of time to talk."

"OK. I have already asked the maids to prepare your bath. Enjoy the bath and then I'll have you on my lap."

Diogo left the room for his bath. I warned her: "Brianda, first think of your baby, and then your husband. Stop constantly crying. Let us have some joy in the house. We had three unfortunate and depressing months already. I don't want you to top this off with a miscarriage. This is the last thing we need these days!"

Brianda tried to compose herself.

"OK but I can't help it, Gracia! I cannot stop. Pregnancy made me weaker."

"Sit right here. Don't stand too much."

After she sat down, she came to her senses and started asking: "Well, but how did you save him? How? Let me know."

I took a deep breath and exhaled. I remembered the night when she thought Diogo would be out immediately and was fast asleep. She still was Diogo's wife and had the right to know:

"Diogo owed large sums to the Fuggers, Charles V's bankers. As long as he was kept in jail, there was no way he could have paid them back. Then the Fuggers informed the Emperor that unless Diogo was released, and could pay them, there was no way they could lend the amounts promised to Charles V. Moreover, putting the Mendes House out of business would cause such a disruption in the markets, it would be like an earthquake leading to chaos. There was also some political pressure on him so he had to let go."

Brianda gave an empty look: "I am totally confused."

"Brianda, a rule for the markets to function is that there should be enough money in circulation, and people should trust the system not to be unpredictable or cause them huge losses. No money, and business stops!"

She continued to wonder how he was set free.

"Leave business to me and enjoy having your husband back. Just be happy."

I have been blessed by my Creator for coming into this world as a member of the Mendes family. I was born into a family with doctors, businessmen, diplomats, and many more exceptional people. I have been lucky to possess such riches that many wouldn't dare dream of. I have people who have served me all my life. Whenever I wanted company or advice, I had men, ladies, even rulers of countries around me.

But together with this, God inflicted me with a curse: Every man I love, dies.

Would whoever I love die? Would faith separate me from whichever man I value?

First Francisco, and now Diogo.

Testament and Teo

Diogo was out of jail but to what avail? Was he not well taken care of behind bars? Or was it from sadness, I don't know. He fell ill after coming out of jail and starting working as before. Perhaps he was not well inside and didn't want us to know.

Unable to hide his sorrow, he said, "It is time for me to prepare my will."

I had heard this accursed sentence before! From Francisco.

It shuttered my heart, tearing it to pieces. If, at that moment, I didn't collapse and fall on the floor it was to not further sadden our sick Diogo, our dear Diogo and Brianda with the newly born baby.

Two months after Diogo's release from prison, a new member had joined our family. To honor me, my sister and Diogo gave her my name Gracia. As two Gracias would be confusing, we called her La Chica. Even the joy she brought to our house wasn't enough to reverse the direction of Diogo's worsening health.

My lips were trembling as I spoke: "Of course, there is no hurry, Diogo! You will get better, will live a long life, and take care of our business. We will do much business together. You will live until the day we save all Marranos."

He smiled a sad smile from a distorted face. He didn't believe me, and neither did I.

"Gracia, it's always good to be cautious. I am free today but so long as Charles V is as greedy as he has always been, he will never leave us in peace! If it is not Charles V, there will always be others after our fortune. It's good to be prudent until then."

I had so much I wanted to say but I refrained. From now

on, it was in vain. From now on, my world has become darker, less attractive. If it wasn't for responsibilities with which I was charged, I would wish to follow after him.

A knock at the door. The servant announced the arrival of the person Diogo had asked for.

"Ask him in," he said as he looked into my eyes.

He knew well. He knew how I felt, at least he sensed it. Between me and Brianda, he had made a choice and went for the prettier, more fun, and attractive one.

The notary entered.

Diogo's body was ill, weak, and tired but his head was as sharp as ever. He must have thought carefully of what he would dictate. He was leaving the control of the larger part of his fortune to me and leaving Brianda at my will. It seems that he contemplated this eventuality for quite some time. He prepared a detailed list of all our assets in various countries, had carefully considered commercial and religious issues to the last detail, without leaving a hint of ambiguity. He had worked on preparing the legal basis to protect us, as he was aware of how the Inquisition was weaving its web, spreading like a disease. His machinations were not only to consider the future of the family; he was also worried about the wellbeing of all Marranos.

He poured the wax and sealed the testament that he had his lawyers draft.

"Now my will is done too."

As the notary left the room, he said in a tired voice, "The control of our investments out of Antwerp will be in your control, Gracia. If ever, I am not capable of performing my functions due to illness, imprisonment, or death, Agostino Enrique will replace me. He was also forced in Portugal to change religion at the same time as I was. He left the Benveniste family name that he was so proud of. But the fortune, since you are not married, will be under your direction. Brianda will have the dowry she brought with her when we got married. That is enough. My little angel, La Chica, will be in the custody of you and two others I trust. Should Brianda need something, she will get it only with your consent."

"Brianda will be vexed."

"I know. She will be disappointed. I cannot leave the family fortune and our daughter's future in her hands. When it comes to money, she will understand one day."

He drew closer and held my hand. He moved with difficulty. It wasn't the first time he was holding my hand but it had never felt that way before. I was agitated and prayed that he would not notice my trembling.

"Gracia, as you know too well, Brianda is not wholeheartedly committed to reducing the suffering as well as transporting the Marranos and Jews to a safe haven. It is not that she wouldn't want that; no, it's that she couldn't do it. Brianda likes to live a social life of luxury, wearing expensive jewelry, and showing off. It is hard to expect her to be compassionate about the torture the Marranos are going through because of their beliefs, nails unstitched, stomachs dredged up, Brianda wants to wear glamorous dresses and mingle with the aristocracy while displaying beautiful jewelry. We both know this well, don't we? Gracia, I tried to make her happy. I wanted her to be happy in our family, as a wife and mother. I tried all I could. Our commitments and business objectives are a different story all together."

I couldn't follow his talk; my heart was pounding. If he kept holding my hand a while longer, I felt I would collapse.

A knock at the door came to my recue. "Come in!"

I didn't recognize the person who came in. He was dressed like us and spoke with our accent. He tried to act casually but I could tell there was more to it, a difference in his look that only a close observer would notice. I felt uneasy.

"Come in, Teo."

He looked at me. I didn't know whether to stay or go.

"Dona Gracia, this gentleman is Teo. In reality, he has hundreds of names, one in here, the other in Venice, and another in Ottoman lands. Among us, we call him "Polecat." If he grabs, he never lets go, like a polecat. You can trust him to finalize any commission you would assign!"

He bowed respectfully.

Diogo lowered his voice:

"I wanted you to meet Teo, Gracia. These days he lives in Antwerp as a fur merchant. He often comes to Antwerp with heavily charged ships, our ships, as you would guess. We trade with him. We entrust him with Marranos and Jews that should flee as well as with the information we would send to the Ottomans. In Istanbul, he is known as Tahir Aga."

The man bowed again. I couldn't believe my ears.

"Gracia, it is time for you to know that this is the only place we can live as free people: the Ottomans. Our relations with Istanbul have always been good. Teo is a member of a family that ran from Portugal to be installed there. You could think of him as a relative. Naturally, this is top secret! Ottomans want information on ship building technics from Portugal, cartography from England, and many things like that. They need to know who is close to whom in Antwerp, in detail. On these subjects, our company is very accommodating."

He waited a little for me to assimilate this new information. I guessed at some similar involvement but I didn't expect them to reach such a practical level. Stupefied!

"Gracia, you will continue to cultivate our relationship with the Ottomans. They are the guarantee of our maintaining our livelihood in Europe. With Teo, and others that I will introduce, relations with the Ottomans will continue uninterrupted. The bridge to Istanbul should be strengthened."

I was trembling with excitement. Not knowing how to reason with what I was hearing and desperately but unsuccessfully, I tried to calm the heavy beating of my heart that was ready to leave my chest. I filled a glass of water.

Diogo couldn't stand up anymore. He sat. Teo, still on his feet, maintained his respectful stance. I turned and asked:

"Could you tell me, Sir, in Ottoman lands, are Jews really free to practice openly their religion. Did you experience this yourself?"

Teo spoke for the first time:

"They wander about freely, in all streets and live according to their beliefs openly, wearing kipas, tallits. As long as they pay their taxes, they enjoy identical rights as Muslims. These rights are protected by a religious ruling that even the Sultan must abide; no one is out to harm them."

"Sounds like a dream!"

"I can vouch for it."

"I received similar information, many such reports, always found it hard to believe."

"Have no doubt!"

In a waning voice, Diogo continued:

"Gracia, Ottomans are the only people that accept Jews and their lands are where Jews can live happily. As my brother Francisco, my relations with Istanbul have always been excellent. All our efforts, sufferings, tears, sacrifices are such that our co-religionists can go to such safe havens like the Ottomans and finally, lead a life worthy of a human being."

"I understand, Diogo, I understand really well. But so much of this is hard to swallow, even for me."

Diogo showed the man to a seat. Then, with slow movements, he took out a key that he carried all the time. With it, he opened a hidden flap on his table, and took out a document and put it on the table.

"You will take these to Istanbul. Nasi will deal with them." Teo nodded.

"In your next visit, if I am not around. "

"Don't talk like that," I intervened.

He didn't pay attention.

"If I am not around, you will contact Dona Gracia or Agostino Enrique. As a businessman, you are working with us, and you will continue to collaborate and do business too, in the future! You will reach Venice before me. I want you to take a message to the Mendes House there. Shortly I will visit there. Life has become unbearable in Antwerp. We will transfer our business and household to Venice. Ask them to start preparations."

Diogo's death

The priest, who came to offer his last services, was relating to Diogo the parts of the book about the suffering and death of Jesus Christ. For days, Diogo couldn't leave his bed. Hope for his recovery was remote, nearly nonexistent. I was constantly by his side. Brianda too was with us most of the time, sitting on the couch, crying nonstop, leaving from time to time to check on La Chica, and then returning.

I noticed Diogo's lips move while the priest recited parts of the New Testament. The priest couldn't understand but I knew. Diogo was saying the "Shema" prayer. He didn't want to hear the priest. For one last time, he prayed for the purification of his soul and pronounced his eternal commitment to his true faith.

If the priest was more intelligent or better versed in Jewish traditions, he would know what was going on. But Diogo, who dedicated his life to his co-religionists and family, in his last moments, gave up being prudent, at least when he was dying. He wanted to live his last moments wholeheartedly, in pure honesty, true to himself and to his creator, the way he yearned for all the days of his life.

Two lonely tears came down my cheeks. I prayed silently:

"Oh God, please forgive your wretched soul for having committed apostasy, sin under forced conditions! Forgive us for not being able to resist the threats and having to live with an unbearably guilty conscience all our lives. Forgive Diogo, who spent his last moments with your name on his lips. Accept him into your heaven! I attest that all his life he wanted to live as a Jew; he always strived for that. Do not disown this poor soul who pretended to desert his faith!"

Then I whispered in Diogo's ear, so only he could hear me:

"Diogo, I know. If it were at all possible you wouldn't have committed the sin. If you didn't resist being burned at the stake, being disgraced and dismembered like so many that did so willingly, it was to run to the help of the thousands who were in pain. You sacrificed yourself for them. It was harder for you to remain alive as the hope of the people than to walk into the flames. Diogo, so long, I wish that God will preserve you in the most beautiful gardens in heaven as you fully deserve. Good-bye, my adorable great man, with a giant's heart. Good-bye, my love."

Diogo left us. Expecting to get well and go to Venice, strengthening the foundations of the Mendes House to serve the Marrano's better, the second love of my life left this world too.

"Ohh my God, this must be my punishment. Will all the men I love die?"

After becoming a widow at twenty-five, now at thirty-three, I lost Diogo too.

Diogo's Legacy

Diogo left several small funds to help people in jail, girls without a dowry, and Jews in need. He thought of associations including Marrano, Jewish, and Christian, one by one. During his life, he had formed a special fund that benefited many in that it helped meet the urgent needs of refugees.

Even when dying, he thought of us and acted in such a way to ensure that he avoided attracting the attention of malevolent people. Brianda's interpretation was superficial as usual:

"If he was alive now, I would have killed him with my bare hands!"

"Please don't talk that way, show some respect for his memory!"

"Dear sis, you can show as much respect as you wish. It seems he has already shown you much respect! Leaving me with the mere dowry that I brought myself, he left control of the entire fortune to you! Even my daughter, La Chica's too!"

Her voice was so loud toward the end that it reverberated in the house.

"Calm down! Don't raise your voice! That's most unbecoming of a lady!"

"Well, teaming up with the brother-in-law and appropriating one's sister's fortune—is this becoming of a lady!"

"What is it that you need that you don't have? You have all you need. You have never suffered poverty in all of your life. So long as you don't marry, your fortune is under your control. What else do you want?"

She stood up. It was as if she wanted to show off her superior looks.

"What do I need? I will tell you what I need: I need the jewelry that you never use and don't let me use either! What I don't need is to live like you, an accountant working all her life to accumulate more money."

I was vexed but I took it as coming from a person in mourning.

"Don't say things that you will regret later!"

"Am I not correct? You are an accountant and will always stay that way! You can wear the same clothes for a whole month and you wouldn't care! You wouldn't know how to improve your looks. Whereas me, I can live like a queen. I can be richer than all European queens. Ohh, just wait a minute, I was richer than they were until my sister blocked everything! We own more jewelry than all of them but Dona Gracia doesn't let me wear it!"

In despair, I tried to explain:

"Brianda, queens and other rich people can adorn themselves. They look more attractive by wearing expensive jewelry. Our jewelry is not for looking wealthy. It is to save our skin in case of danger. Never forget this. To stay alive and function actively, our only solution is to make large payments even when they are 'must pay' bribes. We need to have the money at hand. We have nothing else to protect us!"

"Huh!"

She turned and left.

I can try to explain to her from morning to night to no avail. My father tried as did Diogo, and both failed. It was clear that I wouldn't succeed either.

"Why?" I asked myself. "Why? How come I cannot explain these realities to my own sister, to the only sister I have on earth?" She had more money than she could dream of but she wanted what I had too.

I already knew her answers. She hated being in my shadow. She was younger than I was and decisively more beautiful. She'd lived in my shadow all of her life, and always in the background. Finally, as a rich widow, when she could finally be my equal, she found herself again as number two. That was too much for her to tolerate. My understanding of her present mental state was enough to convince me further that I couldn't trust her with new initiatives.

I dressed and left. I had no desire to stay a minute longer in Antwerp but we needed more time, at least until La Chica was ready to travel. After losing her husband and the bewilderment of the inheritance, Brianda had seriously neglected her baby just when she was most in need of care and attention. I was waiting for her to be a little stronger so she could endure the long trip. My darling Reyna was growing too.

~ ~

"What you have just done is mind boggling, shocking," said Robert Smilov.

Recently Russia was growing as a state and playing a role in European affairs. The tsar had realized that, without substantial trading activities, Russia could not be a great nation, so he encouraged the lazy aristocrats and smaller companies to merge and form stronger conglomerates. Smilov was one who benefitted from this trend.

"Thank you, Mr. Smilov."

"I deposited the money at your branch in Venice and picked up the goods here in Antwerp. Am I dreaming? In old times, we would have to load gold coins in bags and carry them to where we would buy the goods. The system you organized has greatly simplified trading. Tell me, Dona Gracia, why don't you marry?"

It wasn't the first I'd be hearing that question. The husband automatically assumed the role of controlling his wife's fortune, if she wasn't a widow, of course.

"I am afraid, Mr. Smilov, I'll have to wait until I meet someone I really love," I replied with a casual tone. "Because most people's motives are the same: to marry me and take control of the Mendes House. I will never know whether he really loves me or is after my fortune."

I didn't tell Smilov this: those in religious congregations had already peppered me with similar questions. The revenue of the congregations stemmed from member contributions. Many such groups were after us and we were often agreeable to their demands. This gave us the opportunity to form relations, in several locations, with many religious leaders who formed an important part of our sources of valuable intelligence.

"All right then, I won't try to convince you!" Smilov said, trying to be funny.

"Good idea."

"Nevertheless it would be good for you to have someone by your side to protect you from evil. I'd heard that you have kings and emperors as customers in France, Portugal, Spain, and other countries. Is all this true?"

"Our operations are carried on with extreme secrecy. We don't share customer secrets with anyone. Would you trust us, if we did?"

"We had many who trusted us and as many who disliked us. We were the targets of our competitors as well as administrators who would not miss an opportunity to ruin us. I felt less secure recently and engaged a bodyguard by the name of Pierre. He is well-built, a strong Christian but I could tell that he was not a stern believer. All he cared about was money and I made sure I paid him handsomely to make sure that others won't get the better of him. I learned well that everyone likes earning as much money as possible. There are a few people who won't be tempted by the dazzling shine of gold. One doesn't need to have been in business for so many years to know that. What people don't try to decipher is the reason for which money is needed, this is more important."

Some liked money to spend their days in dens of vice and others economized and saved gold coins. Some did so to feel more powerful while others did so to feel more confident. Pierre didn't gamble or drink excessively. His relations with women didn't strike me as unnatural. Pierre was hung up from birth. On the left cheek of his face was a long thin scar that he had been born with. Although you could say he was well built and handsome, he felt ugly because of this scar. Who knows? Perhaps he was made to feel that way because of some unfortunate event? He did not look directly at people. He preferred to keep his head bent slightly. He did not tie his long hair, which dropped over his shoulder to hide the scar. Pierre also learned from life experience that as long as his purse was bulging, no one paid attention to the mark on his face. That's why he aimed to keep his purse full all the time and chose jobs where he could make a lot of money. That's how he found me. I had this insight into his character as soon as I met him.

"Look at me!"

His head was still bent forward. "I want you to look at me. Straight into my eyes!"

He did so timidly.

"Yes, Dona Gracia."

"Pierre, from now on I want you to be with me all the time."

"You will always make good money. You will be my shadow, always at my side. Your purse will always be full and people will not pay attention to anything other than your power and your money. But I want you to know something too, about hiding your face."

He seemed slightly put off and seriously embarrassed. I felt he might run.

"Yes, this is about hiding your face. I prefer you not to feel that it's necessary. Look at me! Do you think I am pretty?"

No answer.

"If you were to ask me, I would say I am not. My being beautiful or not was never an issue because people always paid attention to other issues—my wealth, my strength, my mind, my family. This is what I want you to be like. Whoever bothers you because of this scar will see only this and not your intrinsic qualities. They will die of envy. Pierre, we need to understand each other well, because of our shared experience."

A faint smile emerged from his stern face. I felt he would trust me for the rest of his life and I could trust him. I reached out to stroke his cheek without letting him pull back his head where the scar was.

His face was on fire, his heartbeat quickened.

"From now on, there is nothing for you to feel awkward about," I whispered. "I wish for your only concern to be plotting by my enemies."

"Dona Gracia, I am at your command!"

If my enemies want to attack only me, that is not a problem, but if their goal is the establishment, then that's another story all together. They would want to swallow the Mendes Institution. If it were not for our branches spread all over Europe and the system we set up, they would already have been successful in ruining us. But the complicated system that we established was such that if they confiscated our goods in one branch, it would create a domino effect and the economic system of that market would collapse. Trade would come to a halt. It would be impossible for anyone to collect their receivables. The kings, queens, and dukes who lived comfortably would suddenly experience difficulty and discomfort.

I learned their plan to come at me in the shortest way possible: they set Reyna as their objective.

Eyes on Reyna

I was aware of Charles V and Queen Mary's plans. They killed the second man I loved. They killed Diogo themselves. Maybe Charles V didn't issue a direct warrant but the accusations he made and the three months in prison were enough for Diogo's health to deteriorate, killing his wish to go on living. Now that they buried him underground, they thought it would be easier to succeed in their machinations.

I was informed that Charles V's debt was not sustainable. It didn't take long to get this information from our spies at his palace. The letter written on thin silk paper could easily be torn.

"The Emperor Charles V received an indecent proposal regarding the Mendes Institution. Your enemies and their advisers have suggested to Charles V that your daughter Reyna should be married to an elderly Spanish nobleman. I heard that, if this is realized, Charles V would receive two hundred thousand ducats as compensation to be obtained from Reyna's dowry. The Spanish noble, Don Francisco of Aragon had helped Ferdinand of Aragon and his wife Isabella during their difficult times. In a show of appreciation, he was appointed president of the Inquisition courts. Don Francisco has already convinced Charles V of this scheme to marry Reyna. Soon, Dona Gracia, you will be invited by his sister Mary to her palace and she will use all the power she has to persuade you."

While I held the letter to the flame of a candle, I felt my heart pounding for Reyna, my life's most precious asset. They had their eye on her now. I cannot bear it! If Charles V was with me right now, I could have killed him with my bare hands.

"Charles, I know what your greatest fear is!" I mumbled to myself. The Ottomans.

"Sultan Suleiman will prepare your end one day and I will do whatever I can to speed it!"

Charles V, the Holy Roman Emperor, looted Rome, took over Milano, warred with the Papacy, made peace with the pope, and was blessed! Barbarossa Hayrettin Pasha, who attacked the Spanish coast, was counterattacked by the forces of Charles V, and lost Tunisia. Charles V entered Rome the year the Inquisition was established in Portugal. Worried about these developments, the French King, François I, badly needed Suleiman's help, and signed a peace treaty in 1538. Before Diogo died, Charles V shelled Algerian coasts. Wanting to conquer the whole of Europe, he kept Castile and Rome under constant pressure. He managed to have Queen Mary of England marry his son Philip. The Ottomans were his most feared enemies.

I moved to my table and sat down. As anticipated, Mary's fancy letter was already on my desk. She invited me to her palace, mentioning that she would be happy to host me. With a painful smile on my face, I wrote in reply.

"Your Majesty,

Your kind invitation made me very happy like last time and I felt extremely and undeservedly honored as your humble subject, Dona Gracia Mendes.

I will do so at a first opportunity. I cannot

125

wait to visit you in your palace and benefit from your knowledge, your intelligence, and the enjoyment of being around you in your circle.

I would like you to know that, after completing my preparations, I will be on my way to attend at great haste to your kind invitation.

I wish your happiness to be etenal."

I sealed the end of the letter and now, I could send it. The motives behind her occasional letters of invitation sent by private messengers had become clear. I had done well by delaying and stalling. Let her imagine that I am making preparations.

Suleiman was powerful, having become the fear that was terrorizing Europe. Our relations with Suleiman and his state were good. We had mutual interests, but now I, and more importantly, my family was in Europe. A member of Europe's mightiest dynasty had invited me and I was delaying. How much longer could I keep this game going? Obviously, not for long.

"Maybe one night, they will come to take me away, like they did to Diogo, God forbid. Maybe they will come for my daughter too. Urgently, I must find a way out!"

Diogo came to my mind and the last plan we made before he died. I sat down to write letters that would secretly be delivered to their destinations.

Queen Mary's Wishes

At the point when I had exhausted all excuses and could no longer delay, it became inevitable to be on my way to Brussels to accept Queen Mary's invitation. I acted cautiously by not taking Reyna and not succumbing to Brianda's insistence to join me. Brianda wanted to show herself off at the palace. I left them both behind.

Mary knew I was desperate and had accepted the invitation as an obligation. She spoke her mind and without wasting time showing me around her fancy salons. She told me about the marriage arrangement she had in mind for my daughter. Doing away with unnecessary compliments and the customary exchange of gifts, she declared the bitter truth of her intentions. Mary seriously expected me to accept her offer on the spot.

"Your Majesty," I said respectfully, really putting on an act pretending as though I liked her very much. "You know your wishes are like orders to me. However, it is not possible for my daughter to marry at this stage. You will appreciate that, even though she reached the age of marriage, there is a thirty-year difference between the proposed groom and my daughter."

"Dear Dona Gracia, what is the importance of age difference? If we waited to marry someone our age, we would all be left without a husband, would we not?"

"It is so, but…"

"Even you, didn't you marry a man much older?"

Aristocrats and chambermaids gathered around the Queen hoping to hear the expected agreement of Dona Gracia. They wanted to attest to the fact that the engagement was official.

Not cracking under such pressure was really hard. Even harder was saying "no" to a Queen, particularly in her own palace.

"A member of a noble and wealthy family, Reyna Mendes cannot possibly marry an ordinary person, Dona Gracia. We think he is the best candidate for her."

"But it's too early. I do not know if...? I do not know what to say..."

"Come on dear! Say 'Yes' and we will crown this beautiful visit with a very happy event."

"Your Majesty, the last thing I would want is to differ with you, as your humble subject, but my daughter is too young."

"We do not ask for a wedding to be conducted today. Moreover, the Emperor, Charles V wants it too. Refusing his wish would mean to confront his demand..."

"I know but..."

There was a threatening tone in her voice:

"Dona Gracia, you know that you have branches almost everywhere, large trade networks. Would it not be better for you, by this relationship, to provide a strong protection for your business and indeed for your whole enterprise?"

She was publicly threatening me. It is an ugly attitude that would not be expected from a queen let alone even from an ordinary nobleman. A definitive answer was no longer avoidable:

"Your Majesty, sadly, I must respectfully inform you that I cannot agree to this marriage."

Mary looked at Dona Gracia with inquiring eyes. With the powder on her face mixed with perspiration and the crown on her head slightly tipped, she looked heinous. Never had anyone had the courage to say "No!" directly to her.

"What was that?" as if she had difficulty hearing "What did you say?"

"I said 'no,' your Majesty. I cannot accept this proposition!"

The mood in the room turned ice cold. The servants who rushed around serving wine disappeared. The noble women put on faces as if there was a bad odor. I was all alone.

This was my daughter. Even if the world ended, I would not ever say "yes."

"Be brave, Gracia! People that want to hurt you, whatever you give them, will hurt again! Do not give in. Do not give little Reyna to them!" I repeated these words firmly to myself.

"Oh, OK. Fine! You cannot say I didn't warn you what is to come! I was talking for your good. But you, you turned out to be as stubborn as a mule!"

She was being rude. I remained cool.

"When your Majesty calms down, she will see my point."

"See your point? What is there to see? I wrote you several letters, sent messengers, invited you to my palace. I allowed you to trade with all the institutions in my country, to whomever you pleased. I treated you as an equal. I allowed you to sit at the table with me, as royal protocol. You were received like a queen. Is this your way of thanking me, refusing my proposition as if it were too much to ask? 'No!' So your answer is 'no'?"

Staying longer was meaningless.

"If your Majesty has no further instructions, I would like to ask your permission. I'd better get back early tonight and rest."

She stood up. Her coat of several layers, of rare and valuable fabrics, rustled with her every brusque move. She waved her arms around, almost as if she wanted to beat me:

"Very well then, go and rest. I hope, after that, you come to your senses! I hope you realize that by saying 'no,' you have vexed me as well as the Holy Roman Emperor. The maids will show you the way out!"

I respectfully saluted her. I knew the way out.

As soon as I reached my room, I gave the order:

"Get ready! We are leaving the palace early in the morning!"

If possible, I will not see Mary anymore! This is best.

Once again, I felt as though I were in a void. My eyes tired. I felt insecure, not knowing from where the next blow would come. This time, though, I am less afraid as I know I must be brave for my daughter. I have no doubts.

"The emperor or the queen may think whatever they want. They cannot take my daughter away, ever!"

Maybe if they thought of a different way to get the money they needed, they could get it but not this way! I remembered the Jews who killed their children with their own hands rather than allow them to be baptized.

"I now understand them better."

"My dear girl!" I murmured. "I will not allow such things to happen to you. I will surely find a place where you will live, keeping your dignity!"

When I returned to Antwerp, some letters I sent were answered but when I could not be found, they were not delivered, and the senders were kept waiting. I knew well that from now on, there would be no tranquility in Antwerp. Day by day, life was becoming harder. Father Fernando, who visited us and sat as a guest at our table, took his place at the Inquisition court, tracking down Marranos. Detentions started.

The Marranos, who had not been taken into custody in the past without serious proof, were now arrested without any tangible reason. They were jailed, tortured, and forced to sign papers presented to them. The beast with bloody eyes became more and more violent. If it continued that way, even giving them their goods would not save the Marranos from execution or from rotting in dungeons. Maybe we were on the top of the list but we had a wide circle of friends who were as strong as our enemies. Because of our intricate and voluminous involvement, attacking us would send shock waves to the market, causing uneasiness, and disrupting the flow of business. Some other Marranos were not as lucky. They were either arrested, or they fled in small groups, with our support, to safer lands.

Because I rejected Mary and Charles V's proposition, repercussions would follow for sure, but not immediately. In the end, our position was not sustainable. They would definitely find an excuse to harm us.

As before, our way out was to run.

Run to a land where we could live in peace, without authorities meddling in our affairs, where we could be ourselves with dignity and without pretending or hiding.

Planning for the Future

When the thought of fleeing became a priority, another option appeared. At first, there were things to do and places to go. I pondered this for months and planned our departure in the smoothest possible way.

Blockhead Brianda still didn't understand what was going on.

"Stupid! Why leave the comforts we enjoy here and go to a land with an unknown culture and language?"

"Brianda, don't you understand? It's not up to us anymore. If they don't arrest me as they did Diogo, they will cause problems with our children. They will force our girls to marry men whom we do not approve. Did you want La Chica to be married to such a person?"

"Depends on who it is," she said indifferently. "If it is an appropriate person, why not?"

There have been times when I wanted to slap her hard. This was one of them.

Diogo was aware of realities and understood well his wife's weaknesses. He gave not only the administration of the business to me but also left La Chica in my custody. Brianda can go wherever she wants but I will take Reyna and La Chica with me wherever I go.

She went on in other frequency talking about business although she didn't have a clue:

"If we go somewhere else, we cannot follow our business. Remember we're the bosses. How would things work without us?"

"Soon business will come to a halt."

Eyes on Reyna

"No problem. We go to another European country. All kings and princes are inviting us. We go and live our lives in another beautiful city."

"They are inviting us but, usually it goes well for a while, then it is always the same. First pressure, then confiscation, imprisonment, finally forced conversion. Sister, good days are ending quickly. Ugly faces are coming out quicker. Time and again, we are confronted with an unfortunate and invariably vicious cycle. Remind yourself that you are a Mendes, and think as one. People love you not because you are beautiful or sociable but for your wealth. They are agreeable to you for this reason. Without your money, you would be forgotten instantly. We need to be in a place where we can live happily, without fear, and be principles and not dependents."

She sat up in her chair.

"In this case, there is no need to move from where we are! Because sister, there is no such place!"

Despair is such a bad state of mind. Sometimes you can explain things to anyone except those with whom you share a destiny. Brianda really drives me crazy at such times.

What was our purpose in life? Why was Brianda so ignorant? We shared the same belly, were born to the same mother, sat at the same tables. How could she be so indifferent?

"OK! You go get dressed up and go for a ride! I need to figure out how much of our fortune can be transferred, how much of it can be rescued. Agostino Enrique will come. We will work."

"Good luck to you then."

After La Chica's birth, she had shed all the extra weight,

gained her former beauty, and as a rich widow, wandered around social circles hungering for the admiring glances of men. Her beauty placed her at the center of attention at receptions but, luckily we had the same blood and she was smart enough not to give her heart to someone in marriage. She left.

"Reyna is going to marry Joseph," I murmured. "But not in Antwerp."

I had it in mind for a long time. Joseph, my nephew, was on his way to becoming excellent in business. Moreover, we shared the same values and sensitivities. Joseph was well educated in Europe and quite knowledgeable about Ottoman ways. This made him invaluable.

Though I might have been cornered and looked defenseless, I hadn't yet made my last move against Charles V and Mary. Don Francisco, the aristocrat from Aragon, can be angry for not being seen as an acceptable match for the daughter of a Marrano but he learned there still are people upon whom the Holy Roman Emperor and his sister cannot impose their will.

I received the information that he was seen kneeling down in front of Queen Mary and was heard to swear angrily, saying "the Jewess called Dona Gracia will kneel in front of me and beg me to marry her daughter!"

"Their plan was based upon my staying in Antwerp. When they don't find me, they will be helpless."

Before Agostino came, I sat down and wrote a letter to her majesty:

> "Your esteemed Majesty, Queen Mary, the
> personality I admire, respect, and never fail
> to honor.

"I know I have bothered you recently with my own indecisions and doubts. Of course, you are justifiably a little cross with me. You will appreciate that I do not have the opportunity of being as wise as you are. For this reason, and given your carefully considered and open-minded proposal, I might have vexed you.

"I still think, day and night, about your proposal that has honored me highly. I want to go to Aix La Chapelle to talk to aristocrats and wealthy people about this subject and get their ideas too. Doubtless, your views are most important but please appreciate that I have to decide not only as your subject but as a mother too. That's why I ask you for your permission to go to Aix La Chapelle.

"With my deepest respect."

I sealed the letter.

There was a knock on the door. Agostino had come. He saw the letter on my desk.

I explained:

"I wrote Mary asking her permission to go to Aix La Chapelle. If she agrees, we will be closer to Venice. By hiding our intentions, we will buy time to settle all our affairs and concentrate on transferring whatever we can."

Aix La Chapelle

As Mary sent her permission, she must have believed my story.

We spread around the information that we would be holidaying in Aix la Chapelle. Agostino was left behind to execute our plan. He had already transferred a large part of our fortune to our Venetian branch.

We did not neglect to visit the Cathedral of Aix-la-Chapelle that is the pride of Christianity. Charles V had his people following every step we took, and naturally, we were carefully listening to our spies in the palace about their intentions. As we were going about our daily activities, we had to make doubly sure they received their reports in conformity with our wishes.

The cathedral architecture was amazing. The dome, rising as if trying to reach the sky, was adorned with unique glazed glass. Each corner was a beauty in itself. When the visitors entered the cathedral, they were so charmed they believed every word said by the priests waiting to welcome them. Charlemagne was buried there. Kings and queens chose this church for their coronation. We lit the candles, wetted our hands with sacred water, and crossed ourselves. We made a noticeably high donation and prayed in front of the crucified Jesus.

"I only worship God, the Creator of the Universe, with all my being."

The weather in the city was beautiful; the streets were clean. The crowds were different from those in Lisbon and Antwerp. Peaceful people lived in these exceptionally beautiful buildings in this serene city. Soldiers with fancy uniforms paraded through the streets more to show off than as a security measure. As we wandered around, we saw painters painting in the streets, pure waters flowing from fountains and many people who were visitors like us, admiring the city.

I was sorry for not being able to stay there longer. It was a first in a long time that we agreed with Brianda:

"This city and its social life is a blessing not to be found anywhere!"

Man can live here until the end of his life by befriending poets, writers, musicians, nobles and rich people. It is understandable that both Charles V and François claim it. As our plan was set, we couldn't stay much longer and had to move to Lyon.

"Oh, I also wanted to stay longer but our branch in Lyon is experiencing some minor problems. If you only knew how sad we are to have to leave this enchanting city!"

Lyon was a city that produced fabrics and silk. Our business there was voluminous but we had problems with our receivables. Since we were Marranos, our being there after our money would be seen as reasonable, raising no doubts!

Teo was waiting for us in Venice. He explained the situation.

"They did not find anyone in your Lyon estate, except servants to accept the invitation sent by Mary." He chuckled as he spoke. "When there was no one to accept the invitation sent from the palace, it was understood that you had left the city. Don Francisco of Aragon was furious. He pressured Mary to have you arrested immediately and brought back. He acted like an angry fool but when they heard you were in Venice, they realized there was nothing they could do. This city was not in the sovereignty of either Mary or Charles V."

Then he became serious. I expected he would say something bad. Brianda, Reyna, and La Chica were with us. Of course, apart from bedrooms, Pierre, who has always been my shadow followed me everywhere except my bedroom.

I said, "Say it!"

"Unfortunately, Don Francisco of Aragon's disgusting nature didn't know any limits, Dona Gracia. I do not know how to say it."

"Please! My heart will sink. Is it that bad?"

Don Francisco of Aragon

"My God! Will he really do that?"

We pretended to go to Lyon but arrived in Venice instead. This would not be our last stop. Evil knows no boundaries. It could go through any door, climb over any wall. Our only option was to get away, don't know where.

The news that Teo gave shocked us all. I felt pain in my heart.

"Don Francisco of Aragon says that he will have the body of Diogo dragged out of the grave and his skeleton burned as a heretic."

All of a sudden, we all stopped breathing in fear. Brianda seemed to be fainting. Reyna rushed to help her.

"Mary did not seem to accept as her reaction to Don Francisco was: 'This is a disgusting plan!' But."

This was a ray of hope.

"Mary... in spite of all is a noble person. Even under the

influence of Charles V, I hope, she will not be brought around to be part of this disgusting plan. Is it not so?"

"Don Francisco spoke to her for quite a long time. He tried to convince her that this was the only way of bringing you back. Maybe she will not say yes immediately, but I do not know what will happen in the future. Unethical, horrible man, he is trying hard."

I was constantly praying:

"My Lord, what is this! That poor man, beautiful Diogo, he doesn't deserve to be treated that way! Please protect him!"

Brianda cried constantly. La Chica shrunk into a corner in fear. Even if she was little, she knew what they planned to do to her father.

"Is there a limit to their evil doings?" I said, revolting. "Is there not a limit to evil? How does a human being do this to another?"

Teo continued:

"If the man from Aragon succeeds in convincing the Queen, the Inquisition will not hesitate to do whatever is asked. Already Don Francisco is the president of this horrifying court. He will make the judgment and he will seize your property. He will settle down in our mansion in Antwerp and live there all his life. Even if he did not act as the judge himself, he would certainly get the decision he wanted."

Pierre was disturbed.

I said, "Who cares about the mansion? I hope that house will be his grave! As long as he is not allowed to disrespect Diogo!"

"Maybe Agostino's lawyers will find a way to prove that

Eyes on Reyna

Diogo was a good Christian. According to the Bible, it is forbidden to shed Christian blood. Maybe then…"

It was an unfounded hope. It was not realistic. In fact, the court did not specify the mode of execution to be either by spilling blood or by hanging. They simply said "Do the necessary" which lead to execution.

Would Diogo have wanted it proven that he was a good Christian? The man regretted hiding his Judaism even to the last moment.

I have to find another solution.

"Ma'am," said Pierre.

We were all puzzled and looked at him surprised, as he seldom spoke.

"Yes, Pierre."

"Ma'am, leave this issue to me, if you will."

I was confused but hopeful. Brianda stopped crying. We were all ears, listening carefully.

"Give me permission to go. I will be quiet, I will cut Don Francisco's throat and I will come back immediately. No one will even suspect!"

The offer surprised us all. I did not know what to say. I looked into his eyes. He meant it. With time, he was becoming more and more attached, ready to do whatever I wanted.

Brianda: "What do you say?"

"No way! There would be many political and commercial implications. We would attract all the ill will. Even if it were only an accusation, Venice could not let us live here! Let him be cursed and find his misfortune elsewhere."

I lay in bed but no way could I find sleep. I got up and

paced the room from one end to the other, feeling anxious. When troubled, I was attracted to the garden for the fresh air. The weather in Venice was similar to Lisbon. I felt like I was back in my childhood. Damp and hot nights. And then there were hallucinations about Diogo's skeleton with a string round his neck, being placed over a fire. While still awake, this was my worst nightmare. I tried not to think but rather to concentrate on other subjects.

It was not just our family that escaped from Antwerp. Thousands of Marranos and Jews who wanted to save their lives were trying to reach Venice by crossing the Alps. As soon as I was settled in Venice, I tried to solve Diogo's issue and I tried to help them too.

~ ~

"Please Adela! Give me your baby. I know, you don't want to be parted, but she's dead. She went to heaven."

Adela did not want to leave the baby that died from the cold while crossing the Alps. No one was able to separate the dead baby from her arms. Finally, they asked for my help.

I spoke to her. I tried to be gently convincing but she didn't seem to hear me. She was in a dream. Her eyes looked empty. She swayed back and forth, cuddling the lifeless baby.

"You know, Adela, I have a baby too. I understand you very well. You don't want to leave her, but if you don't, your little angel will never reach heaven. And yet, she already started flying toward heaven."

Her eyes looked toward me and she saw me for the first time.

A hope!

Eyes on Reyna

The woman next to her said:

"We tried everything to convince her with no success. The baby died from freezing. When we noticed, it was already too late. She has been holding it from that time on and refused adamantly to let go."

"Adela, I know you are a believer. Though it's hard to accept, she is dead. But, you would know, the body dies but the soul never does. The soul of your little angel will wait for you in heaven. I promise you. I will make sure she gets a proper burial according to Jewish traditions. I will see to it personally!"

Her arms relaxed. The others, as if anticipating, grabbed the child's body immediately. If I hadn't held Adela in my arms, she would have collapsed.

Most of them had no house or even a place to stay. A few Marranos received these poor newcomers with open arms. Some did not want to risk their comforts; others were concerned about being chased from here too. Many that took to the road never made it and the ones who reached Venice were in an exhausted and terrible state. The old, the ones who were ill or pregnant, the children, nearly all of them never saw Venice.

The Venetian harbor was full of people who could not remain there and who wanted to go to other countries, especially to the Ottomans. Some of our vessels were reserved for transporting people only. The hangars were full of food and they were trying to get these miserable people to the Ottoman ports, avoiding corsairs who plundered and sacked ships in the Mediterranean. The destinations of Marranos and Jews escaping from Spain and Portugal were cities like Istanbul, Izmir, Salonica, and Brousse. As the escapees heard that life in these cities was comfortable, their hopes were raised. Everyone wanted to run until they reached a destination where the Inquisition could not function at all.

We received messages from the Duke of Este, ruler of Ferrara, informing us that he knew well of our ordeals and that if, at any time, we felt uncomfortable in Venice, he would be glad to accept all Marranos into his city.

Although many people wanted to go to the Ottomans, they worried about adaptation difficulties that might crop up because of cultural differences and for that reason preferred to go to Ferrara. If the Duke was sincere, as he had always been, would he welcome us at first and then show an ugly face, as had been true in so many places before?

Don Francisco and the Inquisition had come to another conclusion that, behind the migration of the Jews to the Ottomans, lay the aim of the 'infidels' "to strengthen the enemy." It was alleged that the migrations that appeared to be a way to save the lives of Marranos disguised its purpose, and that instead, the migrations were "an organized system against the State and to serve the enemy."

A new danger emerged around Milan. Jean Vuygsting took statements under torture, captured the travelers, confiscated their property, and left them to rot in prison. Through our branch in Milan, we tried to pay the necessary bribes to Vuygsting. As we tried to help the prisoners, we learned that the purpose of the enemy was to prevent Marranos from going to Ferrara. Although the Duke of Este caught Vuygsting's shady dealings, sued him, and succeeded in having him condemned, the danger was still not entirely over.

The sky was full of stars. Years later, I saw for the first time the bright cluster of stars that later came to be known as the Milky Way. Years go by, people come and go. Some are born and others die but the stars alwaysshine. How long is their life compared to ours? Perhaps it is infinite. Does David's shield look like a star because of that? We should have the right to live comfortably in our short lives, under this starry sky. Why are they persecuting us? Why do they try to prevent our God-given right to live?

"Dear Diogo!" I murmured. "Some of us are not free even after death! A beautiful person like you cannot find peace even after death. Your immortal soul, I hope, will always be resting happily in the most beautiful corner of Paradise. Those who try not to give you peace and comfort under these starry skies cannot prevent you from living in the beauty of the eternal Paradise."

I thought of Francisco. I had almost forgotten his face. The few drawings that remained had faded with time. One of his paintings lay on the table in our house in Antwerp but it was left behind in the turmoil. The memories never disappear; they always remain but people don't. The bodies die and vanish but the soul finds its way to our Lord. The only consolation for those of us left behind are the faces we vaguely remember and the frail memories.

I heard a squeak. I didn't have to look back to know who it was: Pierre, of course. Perhaps Pierre was more loyal to me than my sister Brianda.

Dona Gracia

Still, he was like a shadow, silently following, protecting me, without making his presence felt.

"Do you think I'm under threat in this city, Pierre?"

He was silent for a few seconds. Finally, he answered with a clear voice:

"My duty doesn't change with time or place, Dona Gracia."

I continued without turning around.

"Thank you. Sometimes I even forget your presence, but when I look back, you are always there. I feel safe with you."

He did not make a sound. He was silent and nearly invisible. This was what he did best.

He was there for a long time and I could feel his special interest in me. In another life, perhaps in another place, perhaps under different circumstances I might have been interested in him too but not in the present conditions. We both know and never mention it. I did not intend to say it to his face and embarrass him nor did he intend to open up to me one day. If he did, he knew we could never be together again.

I invited Gaspar Lopez, my trustee, working as our staff in London and Antwerp. He would come to Venice, and from there he would go to Milan and deal with the Marranos. Of course, I did not know that this hardworking and successful man was going create a huge problem, as I was watching the stars in the garden and trying to relax.

Confession

Lopez was detained in Milan.

While I was investigating why he was taken into custody, questioned, and how I would be able to save him, news about him arrived.

This man I trusted so much, was forced to confess, God knows by whatever means!

"I was sent to rescue the Marranos under pressure. They wanted to help them materially and spiritually. Dona Gracia and Joseph Nasi are continuing to live as secret Jews. They hired an assassin named Gonzalo Gomez to kill Vuygsting. They asked me to pay this assassin."

This document was more than enough for the Inquisition to accuse all of the Mendes clan of heresy, hostility to Christianity, and helping the enemy.

The arrest warrant instructed that we were to be taken into custody wherever we were seen. Though he watched as though his hand was not in it, Charles V was aware of every fresh development since this saga began. Earlier though, he had given us a document stating that we could not be tried for the crime of heresy.

This was the second time that our 'immunity from religious accusations' was invalidated!

I envy the poor souls who managed to cross the Alps to arrive in Venice, although they encountered all kinds of difficulties on the road. We can get on one of our ships and go to one of the Ottoman cities where we could live comfortably with the Muslims and co-religionists who had previously migrated. Refugees have a chance of saving themselves the humiliation

of being tried without even knowing the accusations, being thrown into the flames alive, or being tortured and killed in other ways. These are my nightmares. I'm not worried about myself but about Reyna, La Chica, Brianda, Joseph, and other Mendes. We are the targets.

Venice was far different from the exuberance of its earlier days. The eastern part of the Mediterranean was dominated now by the Ottoman Empire, and not by the Venetians. Portuguese discoverer Vasco da Gama, who traveled with Marrano money confiscated by the Spanish Crown, discovered the way to go to India by sailing around Africa, and Christopher Columbus found the New World. As Antwerp became the new star of European trade, Venice dropped into the background. The reason was quite clear. During my stay in Venice, I noticed many people lead lives concentrated on having fun. Venice is a city full of people who think and live like Brianda's ideals —like an inheritor, not working at all, having fun, organizing carnivals, looking exclusively at having a good time. The administrative government was corrupt in turning a blind eye to ominous developments. The collapse was fast. They either didn't see it coming or it was not in their interest to take precautions. Although artists flocked in and people from various nations come here for entertainment, business people and investors like us were skeptical. Musicians serenaded beneath magnificent palaces overlooking the Grand Canal. Guests wore colorful dresses and fantastic masks to the many balls and parties. No one seemed to notice the signals of the impending economic collapse!

While living in Venice, which was declining fast economically, we were accused by the Inquisition in both Milan and Antwerp. The fact that we ran away from Antwerp was interpreted as an admission of guilt. Moreover, there were rumors that we followed Jewish customs and religious rites while living outwardly as secret Christians in Venice.

After Gaspar Lopez's statement, we were issued an invitation for us to be tried in the Brabant courts. "Come back and defend yourselves!"

I knew that if we returned to Antwerp to defend ourselves, we would never again have a chance to see daylight. Our attitude was also interpreted as accepting the accusations and confessing to the alleged crimes.

Now it was up to Joseph who was in Antwerp to find a way out. He had to save us from these charges somehow.

Through our lawyers, he answered the court that we would not be able to honor the invitation. It was winter and difficult to cross the Alps. Dona Gracia's health was frail but in the shortest possible delay, we would document that Dona Gracia and the rest of the Mendes family were living in Venice as good Christians.

These explanations didn't satisfy Charles V.

Joseph reminded that in the Brabant Duchy at Antwerp, the administration had made promises and given guarantees to foreign traders of their right to leave the country and take their assets with them.

Joseph kept me informed of developments with letters sent by special messengers:

"The nephew of the emperor, Maximilian is my friend from military school. We had promised each other to act honestly and as gentlemen throughout our lives. Since he would not brush aside this commitment, our defense should be accepted. The emperor also knew that the refusal would be against the feeling of friendship and honesty between the two of them. Though the emperor's only concern was to get money, his unethical behavior would bring into question whether he is a just ruler. I believe that negotiations with the emperor will start again."

The next letter:

"I explained that you only received twenty thousand ducats and Brianda thirty thousand ducats from Diogo's inheritance and consequently I could offer thirty thousand ducats against a settlement. The emperor found this offer ridiculous and was angry. I replied that I would talk with our accountant and find out what the maximum sum that can be presented is. Finally, I offered a loan of a hundred thousand ducats free of interest."

The skeleton plan, efforts to take us to court, the wish to confiscate whatever they could lay hands on. When we left Antwerp, it wasn't just our residence that remained behind. There were also forty cases of jewelry and valuable goods too. Joseph, knowing full well that the queen and emperor were both after our money, played his cards well and took the necessary measures.

Finally, he sent again with a special courier the good news.

"The skeleton burning intention was cancelled."

Joseph, while working hard to solve the Diogo as well as the judgement issues, also managed to get all of our fortune out of the country except for the hundred thousand ducats. He did this by making parallel arrangements with people needing money in Antwerp and having their funds sent abroad.

Dona Gracia

After my refusal of Reyna's hand to the aristocrat of Aragon, Mary was looking to create some mischief. Since she thought me responsible as she had lost face to the groom to be, she reminded Charles V that they also owed another hundred thousand ducats to the Mendes House and the only way would be to confiscate the Mendes fortune.

Joseph shared this information immediately:

"I increased my offer to the emperor to two hundred thousand ducats for one year, interest free. Judging from his urgent needs, I think he will have no other choice but to accept. Mary is writing to the emperor that the war they staged against the Protestants was very costly and that even this sum will not be enough to save them. Their correspondence is continuing."

Finally, Mary and the emperor agreed: They decided to confiscate all our goods and they issued an arrest warrant to catch Joseph and bring him to the palace.

It was too late. Joseph was nowhere to be found. It was supposed that he had run to Venice, to be with us. By the time they were exchanging letters and carried on their greedy discussions, Joseph had managed to get the remaining fortune out of the country. Whatever they could find was of a much less value than what Joseph had proposed. Now there was nothing they could do.

We managed to begin a new life in Venice but I didn't yet share with the family that this could not be our ultimate destination.

Ghetto

There are times I wish I could free myself from the load I carry. From time to time, I feel drained. I wanted to take Reyna with me to wander about and have fun together.

We planned a trip on a gondola in the Grand Canal. Reyna, already a young adult, loved the idea, got ready, and waited at the door. As usual, Pierre would accompany us.

The gondolier rowed us around with gentle strokes of his oar. The sun shone brightly and the air was pleasantly breezy. Reyna laughed out loud from time to time, touching the tip of her toe in the water and playfully yelling. Men in the gondolas passing near us couldn't take their eyes off her. Some whistled and others made inviting comments.

We passed in front of, adjacent to, and under some of old, monumental stone buildings that include churches, residences, palaces of every size, and stone bridges. You could spend your whole day in these canals. From our perch, it was as if the whole city had been built on water. Had I been a young girl living in this city, I would most probably be caught up in the enjoyment, go dancing to music at the balls, join masquerades and have much fun. In reality, life had worn me out and it had made me an indomitable woman constantly fighting and resisting. Resisting the absence of my husband, resisting the loss of loved ones, resisting being a constant target, resisting the stubbornness of my sister, and forcefully resisting those who want to use my child for their own purposes. My life summed up in two words: Working and resisting.

I resist as I need to be strong. To do so, I work hard at it.

Dona Gracia

A Jew never knows when time is up. That being our situation, whether we like it or not, we need to accumulate gold to facilitate our relocation and to cope with insecurity. We must work hard, be very rich, and be ready all the time.

After many hours on the gondola, Reyna said, "Mom, I think I have had enough being on the water. Mosquitoes are stinging me."

In fact, even if I tried to fan them away, the mosquitos had no intention of leaving. They were biting me too.

I signaled to the gondolier to drop us off. He approached the station and stopped the gondola in front of some stairs. As I was getting off, I didn't neglect to push a bundle of money into his hand. He was grateful and asked us to come again.

After walking up stone steps, we reached the road and Pierre called for one of the horse drawn carriages that were waiting in a line. After opening the door for us, he sat next to the driver.

The horseshoes clacked rhythmically over the cobbled stones. From the window, we watched pretty ladies and well-groomed gentlemen taking walks, and soldiers parading in their fancy uniforms. It struck me that there were an excessive number of statues. We passed by ornate squares topped by beautiful marble statues and watched in admiration the unusual splendor of buildings decorated with relief and embossments. Groups of artists worked on new projects.

We had gone quite a long way before the coach stopped. I put my head out and asked:

"Why did we stop, Pierre?"

He didn't answer. I opened the door and stepped down. I understood. I had heard.

Eyes on Reyna

Occasionally, our help came here but this was a first for me. The area grew apart from the rest of the city as if it tried to differentiate itself.

"Ghetto," Pierre murmured.

Reyna:

"What is this mother? Where did we come to?"

"My dear darling, this is a ghetto, the place where the ones who are not New Christians like us live. It is the place where those who insist on remaining Jewish are forced to live."

She stood by me, shocked but not afraid. She appeared upright and self-confident as if she grew several years in one instant, facing the reality before her and aware of it as much as I was.

Jews who refused to convert to Christianity and insisted on remaining Jewish met with this response in nearly all cities, condemned to live in this place called a ghetto, isolated from the rest of the population as a segregated people.

I held Reyna's hand. What we saw weighed on our soul and was enough to take away the day's joyful mood. I felt heartbroken but why? Who was this feeling directed against? Was it against the ones that jailed a whole people? Or, while enriching themselves and having a comfortable life as New Christians, like us, to the Marranos that didn't think or even know about conditions these people lived in.

I was disgruntled without knowing why.

No one questioned our commitment to Christianity or gossiped about it in Venice. Nonetheless, we were considered a group apart. At home, I was free to worship the way I wanted but here, in this quarter, people were forced to pray within these walls. We were not even given this choice. But my co-religionists were living the weight of their beliefs in this segregated environment. We were settled in an enchanting gothic style mansion with balconies overlooking the canal. Called Gritti Palace, it is close to Fundai dei Turchi where Turkish merchants choose to live. We were in close contact with and easily accepted by the aristocrats and top social circles in Venice. At home, we occasionally invited ambassadors of the Holy Roman Emperor, the French and English too.

"Mom, Ghetto in Italian means 'thrown.'"

"I know, my beauty."

"There are two Ghettos in Venice. Scrap metal was dumped in the old one. The new one was built next to the old and Jews are obliged to live there."

"How do you know that?"

"I like listening. The more you listen, the more you learn!"

I wondered. Did my daughter know there were only two doors in and out, and Jews had to use them? Did she know they were not allowed to be outside these doors at night? Or that they had to pay for the Christian guards. While we were buying kosher food from the butcher in the ghetto, it never occurred to me to visit.

"Come on my baby, let's go. We have seen all there is to see, no need to linger longer."

Getting into the coach, I noticed the sad and embarrassed look on Pierre's face. Being our shadow, never letting me out of his sight, Pierre was sad for the treatment we endured. He was embarrassed for what his co-religionists had done to us.

There was no need for him to be embarrassed. In fact, no

Christian should be embarrassed. The ones that did all these abominations did it for specific personal purposes and used religion as a means, to hide their real interest. A person is not good or bad because of his religion but from his personal motives and actions. As there can be really bad ones among us, there can also be some very good Christians too.

"Can't we do something for them, mother?"

I put her head on my shoulder.

"You will, my darling. One day, when my old, worn-out heart stops beating, you will work for your co-religionists, helping the ones in difficulty. You will continue where I leave off. When the time comes, we will talk about these things in detail. If it so happens that my days are not long enough, use all our power, spend all your wealth for this goal. But my dear Reyna, always be cautious! What do I always tell you?"

"We can never anticipate where the danger will come from!"

"Yes. Exactly. For this reason you will always work hard and be cautious. You will earn much money. Always work for more, this is your security, if you have no money you cannot have security!"

She waived her head. She was turning out to be such a beauty.

"Well then, what do they do if they need a doctor at night?"

I really hadn't thought of that. In our family, we always had many excellent doctors and called them as needed. But, how about people that lock up the Jews, with traditionally good doctors and don't allow them into the streets at night by putting guardians at their doors, what if they need the doctors?

I laughed.

"Why did you laugh?"

"What was I to do, I couldn't stop. Start thinking, even the pope's doctor is Jewish. Several kings and queens have Jewish doctors. Perhaps it was because no one else travelled, read and studied as much, stressing in the family the importance of a good education. That's probably why Jewish doctors are successful. They reject them but won't go anywhere without them. How can we not laugh at this absurdity?

She laughed with me.

"Being afraid that we might contaminate their souls, they want us to cure them!"

Our laughter went on for a while longer. Unfortunately it wasn't a funny situation, rather satirical. I learned later that the doctors, for obvious reasons, were not obliged to wear the yellow skullcap and they could go out at night by having a pass signed by the guardians.

On the way back home, I was watching the surroundings and thinking about the ghetto. I was itching to go and visit but I must do that in a way that the Catholics won't know, silently and with no trace.

"A day when Reyna is not with me, alone."

Invitations

My table was full of letters from counts and dukes. Whoever was outside the jurisdiction of Charles V and not threatened by him invited the Mendes House first, and then other Marranos to settle in their domains. They were giving all sort of guarantees and promises for a comfortable and free life mentioning that they would never ever interfere in our affairs.

I saw the seal of Cosimo de Medici among them. The old shark had spent much in his struggle against France. He had the support of his people in Florence where he succeeded in creating an artists' paradise but he also wanted the city to become a financial center.

I was still holding the letter in my hand when Brianda entered the room.

"What are you reading?"

"Cosimo de Medici sent us a letter. He says he would be very happy if we settle in Florence."

"Great! Let's go and settle there immediately! I heard that Florence was a city with rare beauties, full of painters and musicians. They organize amazing parties and entertainment."

I raised my head and looked at her, not hiding my disappointment in her comment. My sister didn't have as much common sense as Reyna.

"Brianda, he is not inviting us to have fun. He is after our money! He hopes we will settle there and put our fortune at his command."

"What's wrong with that? The Mendes fortune can stay in Florence rather than in Venice. I have become bored in this city with water all around. Let's go and live there for some time!"

As if saying something very simple, she threw herself into the bergère. She hadn't had enough sleep, and yawned with both hands outstretched.

I tried to calm down. The closest relative I have left is my sister, Brianda. I had learned to tolerate and accept her strange attitudes and eccentricities. Probably she would not be the one to continue our mission in the family. Perhaps it would be Reyna and La Chica, and of course Joseph. My feelings for Joseph were growing each day. I had long thought that one day, he would marry Reyna, lead the Mendes House, and liberate all Jews and Marranos. It was starting to happen. After skillfully moving nearly all of our valuables out of Antwerp, and leaving safely, he joined us in Venice at the helm of our new headquarters.

I told Brianda, "We cannot trust Cosimo. He is close to Charles V. He is also his financial competitor. Above all, he is a Catholic who will never see us as his equal. Perhaps we can arrange a credit line for him and make him a debtor. That way we might get another person away from Charles V and to our side but we will never settle in Florence."

"Wish we could go! People talk about huge paintings by Leonardo da Vinci. Apparently he is a genius."

"Everyone knows da Vinci."

"Wish he was alive. We could have a family painting made. Dear sister, it means that we will continue to attend the prestigious masquerades."

"Don't get too accustomed to these balls. We will not stay here for long."

She seemed to be on alert.

Eyes on Reyna

"Where to?"

"The Duke of Ferrara insists. Our detailed intelligence research shows that he is dependable."

"You can go without me, then!"

I looked to see if she was serious.

"What then, will you stay behind?"

"I don't know. I might stay here or go to Antwerp."

"Don't be stupid," I said, not wanting to be harsh with her. "If you go to Antwerp, they would take you to court, and then burn you."

"It's you who should not act stupid! You are constantly feeding me these diabolical stories! This is how you get to control us. If we go elsewhere, you fear you will lose your control."

It was now time to have a serious talk. I decided to talk in all openness to Brianda. If she is vexed, she will be vexed.

I sat down. Calmly and without raising my voice, I started explaining.

"Look sister, you are the closest I have with my daughter and niece. If I say that you are my other half, it will be true. Particularly in the absence of mom and dad, I am the senior person in the family. Up until today, I have overlooked your futile expenses, your bankrupt existence and your not assuming any responsibilities. I tried as much as possible to protect and watch out for you. Enough is enough! Stop accusing me. Your father, Francisco, your husband Diogo, all shared the same views: Business cannot be entrusted to you! This is not a shortcoming. Each of us has different attributes. Unfortunately, you are not sensible. God created you to have fun and to get about. You must well understand the situation we all are in; you will not endanger yourself only but all of us too. Sadly, I can see that coming. Even Diogo couldn't trust you and charged me with control of the inheritance and custody of your child."

She interrupted me unexpectedly in a very loud voice:

"It's all your fault! If you didn't act like a man, befriend Diogo, and hadn't followed him like his assistant, you could never have stolen my share."

"Speak quietly!"

I heard a knock on the door. In the next room, Pierre was ready to defend me even against my sister.

"Don't come in!" This time I raised my voice.

I turned to Brianda.

"Listen you blockhead! You are a Marrano, more openly a Jewess. We can pretend to have changed our religion. Since we were chased out of Jerusalem, we lost our freedom and became a people wandering, robbed, tortured, and maltreated. So long as we work and enrich ourselves with an abundance of gold, you will be treated as if you were their equal. If you were poor, you would be in that ghetto, devoid of your freedom, and worried for your life. Get this straight in your head!"

She shrugged, not impressed.

"Huh? If it were so, I would think about it then. Now I am rich and I want you to return what is mine. I am fed up living in your shadow. Dona Gracia knows all! Dona Gracia decides all! Dona Gracia's word is gold! To hell with Dona Gracia." She stood up and raised her voice further. "Even my husband, my real husband gave my proper daughter to you! I could even hate you just for that, do you understand? I can hate you for that till the end of time and you deserve it."

Her eyes were red from fury. Always slick, always coquette Brianda was showing a different face to her sister. This time, I calmed down.

"Whatever I have done was for you, our children, and our co-religionists. Was it a mistake? Would it be better if I didn't take care, so diligently, of our business and we were reduced to shambles, if they judged and condemned us in the courts of Inquisition? If you care about no one else, think of La Chica. Is it a mistake to ensure her security?"

"None of your business. None of your business at all. Don't you think I am able to protect my daughter? Why should she be given to your custody?"

"Instead of constantly looking to have a good time, had you taken better care of your daughter, Diogo wouldn't have needed to decide this way!"

She nearly cursed Diogo but managed to refrain. She directed her fury, again, against me:

"If you allowed me to manage my part of the business, I wouldn't have so much free time for fun! So what happened with you who never had fun? You look like an old bag already. Even the accountants working for us are more attractive and better looking than you. Should you be taking revenge from me because God created you ugly and me beautiful? You didn't even allow me to wear any of the jewelry stacked away in cases! You never wore it and never allowed me to! Damn you, look in the mirror. Should we both have been two ugly old beldames?"

I felt my heart break in two from its depths. My chin

trembled, I couldn't talk. I dropped on the armchair with two drops running down my cheeks.

"Why are you so cruel?"

She intended to continue but restrained. She must have realized that her words had hurt me deeply.

"I want you to leave me alone. So long as you return what is mine, you can go wherever you want! I don't want you to drag me here and there. If the Inquisition catches me and hangs me, so be it. If they want to do this to a woman, let them burn in hell. It's all over! Brianda will never be in Dona Gracia's shadow anymore."

She slammed the door and left.

Pierre peeped through the open door. It was clear he had heard it all. I didn't say a word and tears flowed nonstop. I raised my hand so he wouldn't ask or say anything or come into the room.

He stretched gently and closed the door.

New Rumors

As Marranos and Jews flowed into the Ottomans, we helped as much as we could. Recently our enemies spread a new rumor saying that Jews were mistreated in the Ottomans. My intelligence, from sound sources, was to the contrary. We had a good life in the Ottomans. So long as minorities paid reasonable taxes, Ottomans did not interfere in their livelihood or religious practices. Suleiman wasn't satisfied with making religious laws only. He made sure that laws dealt conveniently and fairly with the daily life of people of every creed. He was nicknamed 'Kanuni' (the Lawgiver). We heard the same information from people around Suleiman and from the rabbis. Jews were free to practice their religion, full stop.

If it were only me, I would go immediately to Istanbul and live there. Leaving Antwerp, I knew the final destination would be Istanbul, but I was not only responsible for myself. I had a family to care for, and I had to plan for the movement of the Marranos for which The Mendes Institution was the umbrella.

And of course, I was responsible for Brianda too.

My dear sister. I thought she realized that she'd hurt me, and that she would apologize. I thought she would try to win me over.

Rather than apologizing, she ignored me. After spewing venom, she felt better. She felt no regret and seemed to be insisting on her views. She exchanged the minimum possible words with me and avoided spending time together. I knew she didn't want to leave Venice. She didn't think she could find the life she had in Venice elsewhere. The unknown that was called Istanbul attracted her not at all.

I too was not so comfortable with the idea of Istanbul since the culture is so very different than what is familiar to us. Even if we were not considered equals in Europe, as New Christians we had much in common with Europeans. We lived and worked and laughed and cried in the same way. Life could be completely different in the land of Muslim Turks where traditions and ways of living are so different. I wasn't so sure we would integrate well. If we succeeded in taking Brianda with us, it was crystal clear she wouldn't find masquerade parties there. The concept of music is also different. Everyone in Europe knows that Suleiman strongly disapproves of men and women dancing close to each other.

Even if we were guaranteed a similar lifestyle in Istanbul, I doubt that Brianda is ready to even try to adapt. She wanted the inheritance from Diogo and her daughter's share. She wanted to spend without being accountable to anyone, and to compete with the rich ladies of Venice by wearing fine jewelry. She wanted to spend time with men who would court her. She wanted to be envied not only for her beauty but also for her massive fortune.

Perhaps, if I shared the secret that father entrusted to me, she would be more responsible and purposeful, and maybe she would think and act differently.

This wasn't an option. She proved me right several times for not trusting her.

While contemplating this issue, I asked myself the question I always asked when in difficulty.

"What would Diogo do?"

The Ghetto

On Yom Kippur, the most sacred day of the year, I will fast from sunset to the next, on this day of atonement. Jews spend the whole day in synagogues, remembering all their sins, the people they wronged, praying in full sincerity, and repenting for their iniquities. Even so, we can only do this secretly, inside our homes. I will remember all the sins I committed during the past year, one by one, I will pray as sincerely as I can and hope to be pardoned.

On Yom Kippur day, I took a broken bracelet with me and

asked for the carriage to be ready.

Pierre wanted to assist me as I stepped into the coach.

"Pierre, today I am going to a place full of Jews. I don't think that any harm can come to me from them. You stay behind. There is a very good repairman in the Ghetto. I will have my bracelet repaired and will be back shortly. Don't leave the girls alone!"

He didn't object. When I said "Don't leave the girls alone," he understood that I trusted him more than I trusted Brianda.

Naturally the repairman wasn't there. His was not the only shop that was closed. All Jewish shops were closed. I said to the coachman:

"I will wait for the repair man. You can leave now and return to fetch me at sunset."

He left.

I guessed where I would find them— at the synagogue, of course.

I appeared as having been forced to change my religion and to hide my true beliefs. In this day when all prayers are heard from above, I want to spend my whole time in sincere atonement. And listening to forbidden melodies inscribed in our hearts— El Nora Alila, Kol Nidre, Shemoneh Esrei— sung by all, and watching the spiritual rituals, listening to the shofar.

I became more agitated as I came closer to the synagogue.

It was dangerous for me to be with the congregation. Some might know or recognize me, perhaps some gossipers, perhaps a spy sent by the Catholics that know of this day. I took a prayer book and hid myself, like a convict, in a dark corner of the building. The scriptures in the book reminded me of my father, teaching us Hebrew secretly and joking about our mistakes. I still read some but couldn't decipher the meaning. I prayed for an absolved conscience and free spirit:

"Oh my King, my Creator! I came to repent for all the sins I committed during the whole year. Forgive your sinful servant. Forgive this soul that has to live her beliefs secretly and appear as a goy. I beg for your forgiveness, Eternal Father."

I recounted all my wrong doings, people I hurt and maltreated, one by one, all my sins one by one. I asked to be pardoned for each one individually. As I prayed I had a warm comforting feeling inside, absolved perhaps, I felt lighter.

As sundown approached, the shofar was sounded announcing the day's end. Everybody was there, even bringing their little children to hear the shofar. The book of life was closed for another year. I had heard so much about it but this was the first I was hearing it played. I felt an excitement, hope for the days to come when I will take my place in the synagogue and pray to my heart's content.

I, Hanna, rather than Dona Gracia had been finally able to spend a whole day praying and being with my Creator as a Jew. This was worth more to me than the world's greatest fortunes. I felt happy with myself, energized, lighthearted, and above all hopeful.

I had crossed to another spiritual dimension realizing how meaningless and empty our lives had been. If, at this instant, the Inquisition arrests me, tears my legs and arms, and threatens to throw me into the flames, I could still scream:

"I am a Jew. I have never been a goy and will never be! I

will never worship anyone but my Creator the one and only God, the God of my forefathers."

The coachman arrived as I had instructed him, at sunset.

I silently stepped into the coach and returned home.

Dinner was ready.

Waiting for a repairman might sound acceptable to Christians who do not know our traditions but not to Brianda.

At table, while eating and not talking, I sensed a cheeky gleam in Brianda's eyes. It seems that, in my day of atonement, she started silently planning my destruction!

Betrayal

The Inquisition was a nightmare not only for Jews and Muslims but also for Christians. Once accused there was no escape. If taken before the court, it would be the end and the person would become useless for the rest of his life.

The terror of the Inquisition was a threat not only to us but also to intelligent administrators. Many did not want to have it in their country. Venice was one of them. Ferrara insisted on our coming to Florence. He renewed the original invitation as did Rome. Even a pope like Cosimo de Medici did not want the Inquisition. As a consequence, trading activities continued to a certain extent in Rome and in Florence. Marranos fleeing Spain, Portugal, and now Antwerp were all rushing into Venice and other Italian cities.

Though the change in attitude in Venice might seem strange, we could understand it.

The Ottomans were also involved in issues like the spread of Protestantism by Martin Luther, and in the animosity between Charles V and François. The Ottomans supported Luther and François against their main enemy, the Holy Roman Empire, whom they hoped to weaken. Suleiman found the popes' extravagances foreign to his understanding and so he felt closer to the Protestants as they preached a more modest way of life, more like the Muslims. Having made his views on this well-known, he sided with the Protestants against the Catholics.

Worried about moves by the Ottomans, and thinking that many of his followers would switch sides, the pope became less tolerant. The Inquisition was one of the instruments available to him. The population of Spain and Portugal was purged of non-Catholics after Jews, Marranos, and even Muslims were expelled. The motto was 'pureza de sangre' or 'purity of blood.' Their ideal was a population was made up solely of Christians in the Catholic Church.

To slow the current of Protestantism spreading in his jurisdictions, the pope ordered to begin the Inquisition in Italy.

Knowing that, I started preparations to move elsewhere. What I ignored was the stupidity of my sister that would endanger the lives of herself, her daughter, and all of us.

When it was announced that two clerics had come to visit me, I didn't know what to say. Even the information coming from the Church was blurred. This visit was completely unwelcome and a surprise.

"Ask them in immediately."

I hid my emotions and tried to act naturally.

"Mrs. Luna," said the older of the two.

"Please come in, dear father, make yourselves comfortable."

They exchanged glances.

"We won't sit. We are here to ask you a few questions.

My curiosity grew bigger.

"Oh, sorry!" I said coming out with my surprise. "I was mused a little."

I rushed to kiss his hand. The other didn't tender his.

"Pray be seated Dona Gracia!" said the priest.

They were hurling orders at me at my own office. There was no need for them to explain they had been sent by the Inquisition.

Dona Gracia

"We are here to question you in the name of the Offices of the Holy Inquisition."

"Question me? Why? What are the charges?"

"Mrs. Luna, is it true that your real name is Dona Gracia?"

The situation I most feared was enfolding in front of my eyes.

"With your permission, I'd better sit," I said. "Well then, will you question me alone or should I call my lawyer? Will I be questioned here or will you arrest me?"

The younger one:

"A few questions for the time being."

"Yes, in the same way as they know me here as Mrs. Luna, where I came from I was called Dona Gracia. I got this name from my father and was baptized in Portugal with his name. In spite of the religious immunity document that Charles V had given us, we the New Christians are always suspect, as you would know. It is for this reason that I use the name of Luna in Venice."

The older one shook his head.

"It is reported that you are Judaizing and a heretic."

"How come Father? I am a good Christian and everybody knows it."

"You were denounced as having spent the whole Yom Kippur day in the Ghetto, praying in the synagogue. You went there with the excuse of finding a repairman but you didn't have such contact in the ghetto. At the same time, we were told that you secretly continue to be a Jew and continue Jewish

rituals at home."

I felt as if hit by a thunderbolt. So my fears were coming true. Someone who knew me, or recognized me or spied on me in the Synagogue had denounced me.

"I am sorry to say that, Father, all this is nonsense! It's true that I went to the New Ghetto. Unfortunately, the only person who could repair my bracelet was there. It's also true that I spent the day there but how can you imagine that a good Christian like myself can pray as a Jew. I was there because the repairman was Jewish.

After I got ready and left the house with them, I noticed several soldiers dressed in fancy dress waiting outside. They imagined that I would resist and would not want to go with them. Pierre was still behind me. The household was taken by surprise. Not knowing what to do, they stood there like frozen ice statues, looking after us as we left.

Father turned and asked:

"Who are you?"

I replied instead.

"He is my assistant, Father. He will testify to my being a good Christian." I turned to Pierre and tried to look in his eyes. "Pierre you better stay here and inform Joseph and Brianda of the developments. Ask them to come with our lawyers."

He nodded.

Before Joseph could bring our lawyers, the priests asked a few more questions, in the small room in the tall stone building. At this point, they were not being impudent but they were trying to corner me with some questions:

Betrayal

"Did you go to the Ghetto on Yom Kippur day?"

"Father, you know I did."

"Why?"

"To repair the bracelet that has been in my family. I was told there was an excellent repairman working there who could fix the bracelet with its valuable stones."

"Well then, why did you go to the synagogue and spend the whole day there?

"I wandered around looking for him and didn't spend the whole day in the synagogue."

"Why did you ask the coachman to pick you up in the afternoon? You knew you would be there the entire day."

"I thought I should have time to find the repair person, respectful Father."

Then the younger one followed with his questions:

"What do you carry in your ships?"

"Father, I am the owner of the company. I don't follow what is loaded on which ship. I don't go to check the ships. We import spices from India, fabrics and cotton from the Mediterranean. Other goods are loaded from here and transported. I know there are some valuable metals. İf necessary you can go through the books; all information is available."

"So far, how many people did you help run to the Ottomans?"

"None. Ottomans are enemies of our Holy Roman Emperor. We don't help people wanting to go there."

The older:

"You know, my dear girl, that we have all the equipment needed to make you talk. I want you to tell us all without causing us to lose time."

He took a letter from his inside pocket. I knew this was the letter of the person who had denounced me. Judging by the quality of the paper and the broken seal, it must have come from a wealthy and well-known person. Rather than a spy, it must be from a commercial competitor.

They stopped questioning me when a knock came on the door and another person, who looked like a cleric, entered. In a short time, they were having quite a conversation. Then two lawyers wearing wigs walked in. They showed documents and declared they were here to defend me.

I had some experience. I don't know how long I could resist under torture though I was well equipped for verbal duellos.

Fundamental rule is 'Answer only what they ask. Never admit any allegations!'

If you accept one of the accusations then, from there on, you cannot stop. I resisted successfully so far not accepting anything.

Luckily, the Venetian Dutch still wanted us around and many unusual facilities were accorded to us. I was released only to be questioned in the future with my lawyers.

"You can go home now but you must remain in Venice. I would advise you not to try otherwise!"

On the way back, Joseph and Pierre were dead silent. I was curious like crazy about all that was happening:

"Joseph, did you talk to our lawyers? What happens next? How should we act? Do we need to run? Can the papal authorities interfere in the case?"

Joseph was silent, as if he did not hear me. İnside the

coach, he was uneasy, listening to the clacks of the horseshoes on the cobblestone road.

"Joseph, is it that bad that you cannot tell? Why all this mystery?"

He drew a deep breath and spoke:

"This time it will be really difficult, Aunt Gracia. It was Brianda that denounced you."

Aftermath

As soon as I entered the house, I yelled: "Where is she?"

I grabbed the big chandelier by the door and ran to the stairs, yelling with all my might:

"Where is that stupid? Where is that brat?"

She saw me coming from the window and had already locked her door. The door was strong and made of ebony, however much I pushed, it wouldn't open. With all my strength, I threw the chandelier at the door. There was a big bang but the door didn't move. I kept on knocking by hand and with the chandelier. The whole house was shaken but she wouldn't open the door.

At the end, my head was spinning from exhaustion. As the chandelier dropped on the floor, I realized I was fainting and I collapsed.

It was all dark.

When I lifted my eyelids a little, I noticed that I was in Pierre's arms. He was taking me to my bed.

"Where is she?" I said, furiously but no sound came out. "Leave me and bring her here!"

I heard Joseph's voice:

Dona Gracia

"Aunt Gracia, the kids are terrified. The girls are crying. Calm down a little and we can discuss it later. Please! You are exhausted by now."

It was all dark again.

I don't know how long I lay that way. When I opened my eyes, I could see Joseph who had pulled a chair and was sitting by my bedside all the while. Reyna and La Chica were sitting on armchairs opposite my bed.

"Do you feel better?" Joseph asked.

I shook my head.

"Some water."

He filled a crystal glass from a Chinese porcelain jug and held it.

I drank a few drops. My throat ached as if it was sanded.

"Where is she?"

"If you calm down, she will come. But please calm down! Otherwise we cannot discuss anything. We have, though, many issues to discuss. First, the Inquisition."

I waved my head.

He turned to Reyna and La Chica:

"You go to your rooms now. We will talk a little."

With damp eyes, the girls left unwillingly. They saluted respectfully and left the room. Pierre opened the door and I saw Brianda.

Strange! By the time she entered the room, my rage was over. I didn't feel like kicking her or tearing her hair or even slapping her. I felt nothing. I don't know if it was because I was exhausted. Perhaps it was and perhaps not. I don't know but undoubtedly, I wasn't like before. I would never be. Deep inside, I felt that Brianda could never be my sister again. The woman who entered showing no sign of regret can be whoever she is but she can never again be my sister! Our direst enemy didn't do what she did to me. They never succeeded in taking me to the court of the Inquisition. I can now feel how uncomfortable the souls of mother, father, Francisco and Diogo are. The very children they tried to protect were under threat from their own wrongdoing, thrown to the mouth of the monster called the Inquisition.

I tried to compose myself and sat up at the corner of the bed.

Brianda still doesn't get it. I will treat her as a stranger. Our relationship is shattered. From now on. I will distance myself from her. She doesn't realize it but from now on she cannot be my confident and she has no chance of being my friend.

"How could you?" I said with my voice, still weak.

"I didn't want it to be that way," she said from the armchair where she sat. "But you left me no alternative."

I shook my head, aching. She still doesn't get it.

"OK, you were angry with me. Didn't you think about the kids? Didn't you think of La Chica and Reyna? Did you think that the Inquisition would be satisfied with punishing me and executing only me?

Her look was glazed as she began to realize.

"What does it have to do with them? Since I am the denouncer, you are alone in this. If we were like you, why should I denounce you?"

Joseph was respectfully listening, careful not to take sides. I was sure he thought as I did.

"You endangered all of us! Their issue is not our beliefs. They are after the Mendes fortune. Now they will do all they can to confiscate everything. For that, they would not hesitate one minute to sit you on a stake, take La Chica's intestines out, or skin her!"

"That's nonsense," she said though slowly understanding.

I felt her fear.

"It would be good if they stop at that. You will suffer the worst tortures. They think you are the one holding the biggest fortune. You can kiss goodbye to all of your jewelry. They will take it all. They will take you to the dungeons instead of to the masquerades. Worms will nibble at your beautiful body. From hunger, you will be forced to eat mice!"

Joseph felt he should interfere:

"Aunt Gracia, please!"

I turned to him:

"Why? Why should I be silent? This dumb girl didn't take any of this into consideration. Now we have to do the thinking. No, I am not worried for myself or for this rattlebrain. We need to save the girls. You have to take them away immediately, somewhere out of this country."

"You can't take away my girl!" Brianda objected with a pathetic voice. "You cannot take her away anywhere! I will decide about what is mine! You can't take my daughter and leave me penniless!"

Joseph was still calm.

"This won't be easy, Aunt Brianda. It is denounced that she intends to take your share of the fortune to the Ottomans."

The damage Brianda caused wouldn't stop at that, it

seemed. Would I see more? Who knows? She reported that I was a heretic and had helped the infidels. She was hoping that she would gain control of the fortune. I could read it in her eyes. This would not be possible. Judgment for the ones who helped the infidels, supplied information about war technologies and shipbuilding techniques to the Ottomans would be taken to court with all their relatives. Consequently, the entire family fortune would be impounded. While roaming from ball to ball, Brianda had thought only of looking ever more attractive. She never learned the details of the laws of the Inquisition and its workings.

"Ottomans are the greatest enemies of Venice. If you told them we helped the Ottomans, Venice would be after you, even if you manage to escape the claws of the Inquisition!"

It was unnecessary to tell her anything else. I couldn't bring myself to look at that woman who once upon a time, used to be my sister.

"Joseph. Send her away, so we can discuss the way out.

Brianda was about to object when Joseph made a sign. She quietly left.

Pierre must have gotten the message too, as he left after she did.

Freedom Lost

Before sundown, there was a knock at our door. I hadn't had time to recover but it was the inquisitors and they would not leave me alone.

Joseph informed me:

"The Inquisition has decided that all your property will be

seized until the end of the case and you will be locked up in a convent. You have to get ready."

"Oh God!" I said, "They will never let me go!"

"No, don't worry. I will run to the lawyers immediately. We will challenge the decision. Better than a jailhouse. This shows they realized the sensitivity and consequences of their actions."

"Joseph, forget about me. Take the girls out of Venice."

With a hopeless expression:

"They decided they will go with you!"

I slapped myself.

"Not possible! Them too?"

"Yes, no need to worry. We will do whatever is possible to get you out, spend until the last ducat of our fortune is gone, if necessary."

Just a thought:

"Is Brianda coming with me too?"

"No, she would be confined to the house."

"To hell with her!"

I got up. While getting ready, I heard Brianda screaming. She must have heard that La Chica was taken into custody with me and would have to go to the convent for a compulsory visit. She should have known that since La Chica is in my custody. Accusing me would affect her too.

"Idiot!"

While I roamed through the room, trying to think of what to take with me, I couldn't stop wondering whether that scream was because La Chica was taken into custody or because Brianda was under house arrest and her social life would be interrupted.

Dona Gracia

Settling in Venice with the de Luna name wasn't enough to save us. Again, our hands were tied. We felt abandoned, not knowing where the next blow would come.

Joseph fed me more information:

"Aunt Brianda has done something more, Aunt Gracia."

"What?"

The girls were listening too.

She engaged a representative in France, a certain Marrano called Fenicio, to get her share of the receivables there. Diogo had shifted an important part of the fortune to France. When troubles started in Antwerp, I did the same, and sent more to France. Aunt Brianda wants to take this fortune into her control. She has seized the opportunity to be able to take control of the fortune in France too. If we are found guilty here, the case in France would be affected. Soon, they might put a hold on the Mendes fortune in France too.

"I wish I had died and never lived to see this!"

Reyna and La Chica made awesome sounds. I looked at them. Like two frail birds in each other's laps, afraid of the destiny the coach is driving toward, watching my mouth, listening to each word, carefully and with unease.

"Don't worry!" I said as if just remembering them. "Don't be afraid! Be courageous! All our lives will be this way. Being a Marrano is such a thing. We need to be ready for threats all the time. We must be able to stand straight all the time. If we act as cowards, they would finish us. The idiot called Brianda has wounded us but we won't allow her to finish us off. Trust me, trust yourselves, and most of all trust your God!"

They shook their heads. I didn't know whether the soldiers

accompanying us were listening.

"Now, listen carefully. From now on, since all our conversations or movements will be monitored closely, we need to apply extra care. As soon as we enter the convent, I want you to cross yourselves and go to Church to pray. Don't neglect to act exactly the way a Christian would. While doing that, also don't forget to repent. We only worship the one God."

Reyna said:

"I got it."

La Chica waved her head.

We were silent. As the coach wobbled along the road, we moved ahead, each with different ideas in her head and without a word for the rest of the way.

Though the people who received us were not overly friendly, I knew that in God's house, things can't be so bad and we would be received reasonably well. When large doors opened, I saw rows in the form of a cross, with blanks in between lined up. There was the altar, the sacred water jug, and the dome with several large windows. I repeated the usual prayer and walked along.

"Let me take you to you cells," said the nun.

"Daughter, allow us to say our prayers first," I said with a confident tone though I still had a sore throat.

She moved aside.

Nunnery

Naturally, we didn't find familiar comforts. We abided by the same rules as the nuns, waking up early, eating a plate of oatmeal after prayers, then helping with daily work. The head nun treated us as like any Christian. Though some others talked loudly to us, she never raised her voice and even spoke softly. I felt that she knew we were crypto Jews.

Unlike Inquisition officials, this elderly and loving lady, didn't make it an issue. It was as if she understood and felt pity for us.

Since the Inquisition left Joseph out of this case, I understood they didn't want to interrupt the flow of business. Joseph was our contact with the rest of the world. With frequent visits, he kept me informed, as much as he could, of all developments.

Though I wasn't in the least bit curious about Brianda, he told me she was being kept under house arrest, and was not permitted to receive visitors. Forbidden from leaving the house, she stayed at home with the maids.

For Brianda who constantly went out, I couldn't imagine a harsher punishment!

Some bad news came from France. Fenicio, the agent that Brianda employed, switched sides, probably dismayed with what he found in France. He accused Brianda of Judaizing and being a crypto Jew.

Everyone wants a piece of our huge fortune. I understood that. What they didn't understand was that I didn't need this fortune and it was for those who were in peril.

"Did you talk to the Duke of Ferrara?"

"Yes, I did, Aunt Gracia. He repeated that he stands behind his word. If we leave Venice, his doors are wide open to us. Duke Ercole promises that if we move to Ferrara, we would never be interrogated, or locked up for religious reasons. He said we would be entirely free to practice our religion, and that no one would meddle in our business. All this would be under his guarantee."

"Well, what do you think? Are you satisfied? Is he sincere?"

"I checked through our agents there. He means what he says. As Ferrara is ranking behind many other cities, he needs to strengthen and enrich his Duchy. He knows that the way to success would be through Marranos. We can move to Ferrara."

I moved over and caressed his cheek. The tradition that started with father, Francisco, and Diogo continued with him. Positioning himself as the man of the family, he is doing whatever he can, unwaveringly.

"I am trying to reach all of the involved judges. We would have to make hefty payments but I will try to save you at whatever cost."

"I don't doubt that at all, my child. Thank God, you are here. If it were not for you we would be defenseless now and at the mercy of the Inquisition. Only you can do this work. Staff could not manage it. I am happy that one day you will be my son in law. I could not trust Reyna to anyone but you."

Embarrassed, he lowered his head.

"Let's first get out of here. We will leave this city immediately. While working on the case, you can start preparations but not a word to Brianda!"

"Are you planning to leave her in Venice?"

I looked him in the eyes. He understood.

"Don't forget, Joseph, you need to look after yourself too! Plan every step carefully. I am sure spies are following you closely. If I learned anything from all these years is that Jews will never have constant friends or constant enemies. They either want to take advantage of us or they want us to vanish. Don't think that the Duke will be much different."

A Good Woman

While at the altar praying, I noticed someone next to me. Her palms were joined in prayer as she also prayed. Wanting to look credible as a good Christian, I closed my eyes as if in deep meditation. I didn't look at her. She finished praying before me but didn't leave.

When she stood there for what seemed like a long time, I understood that she was waiting for me. I finished praying and turned. I came face to face with the head nun, Sofia.

"Good morning, Mrs. Luna," she said. "You were in a trance while praying. God would be very happy for servants like you."

I lowered my head modestly.

"Next to you, who are we? You have committed your life to serve God."

"Come, let's have a hot drink together. Do you like herbal tea?"

"My dear sister I have been deprived of so many things that, I am ready to drink anything you offer me."

"Come on then."

Betrayal

We walked past the pews without noticing others who were praying. She took me to her room. I thought of the girls. They should be sitting quietly in their cells. If I was a bit far from them, there would be no problem. In the end, we were interned in a small church. Where would they go? Who could come from outside to harm them?

The head nun was covered from head to toe in the traditional nun's habit, leaving only her face open to view.

"What were you praying for?" she kindly asked.

We left the Church and reached the section of the convent where her room was. She opened the door and let me in first.

"To be forgiven as a poor, miserable sinner, Sister."

She showed me to a wooden chair that didn't even have a cushion. She sat on a similar chair before going over to the kettle that was boiling water on the stove. She opened the kettle and threw a few leaves into it.

"Should I address you as Mrs. Luna or Gracia, I don't know. Do you have another name?"

"What do you mean?"

Sitting across from me, she raised her hand as if to stop me.

"I will call you Mrs. Gracia. That is best. This is God's house. You need not lie or disguise your beliefs. We are among women. No men are here. We don't have to tolerate their rough, unpleasant, God forgive me, strange habits. We are here for God only and our connection is the love we have for Him."

"Undoubtedly," I said, trying to grasp where she was leading.

Dona Gracia

"My age has advanced, Mrs. Gracia. God only knows how many days I have left."

I was going to compliment her by saying she looked young, but she didn't need that.

"In reality it was love of God that brought me to the convent. I was a young girl, a dreamer. I wanted to find someone, get married and live peacefully in a hut in the country with many kids. God's design for my destiny was different. I never found my loved one nor did I have any children. But God blessed me with many children, many more than I could ask for. The girls here, the nuns and all Christians became my children. God is my witness. My life has been at least as poor as in a country hut!"

We couldn't stop laughing.

She got up and filled the cups, and then she continued.

"I have devoted so many of my years to love, Mrs. Gracia. I didn't waste time with loving a man but I loved our Virgin, Jesus, and God. I even loved the ones who came with no beliefs, the ones starving on the roadside. I loved them all."

She passed one of the cups to me and sat.

I tasted it. Nice. A tea I had not tasted before. Every drop left a pleasant taste on my palate.

"As I approach my last days, the love of God has taught me something."

"What is it, Sister Sofia?"

"That he loves all his creatures."

I kept quiet. What is she getting at? To understand better, I should remain silent.

"Mrs. Gracia, come on then. We are not in the cabin but

you can be open as in a confession. The Inquisition might have locked you up but you are as valuable to me as the priests of the Inquisition. Think of it, half the world is not Christian. Think of the Ottomans, Arabs, and Muslims and people living in faraway lands believing in many different ways, worshipping God and other things in other ways. Well then, aren't these also God's creatures?

"Naturally, sure."

"Well, God does not discriminate among his creatures. He loves them all and since he is keeping them alive without any calumnies, it should be so. How can we say 'I love this one,' 'I don't love the other?' If God values every one of them, do we have the right to single any of them out? Are we as perfect as God to decide for him?"

"Of course we are not, but."

"I mean, Dona Gracia, you don't have to hide your true feelings here. You are naturally afraid that I can testify against you. I watched you pray in front of the altar and could guess at your feelings and thoughts.

She was right. I can never trust a Christian nun for that, which I cannot even trust my own sister.

"It's up to you not to trust me! In fact, I didn't expect you to. The reason I wanted to talk to you is different." She sipped from her cup. "The Inquisition will consult me regarding your case. I want you to know that I will say positive things about you so that you can be acquitted a moment earlier. Perhaps I will even have to lie to this end, God forgive me."

"But."

"No, you won't need to bribe for this. Don't even think of

it! I will give you a piece of advice. When you leave us, I don't know how you can manage. But live your own beliefs. Don't hide anymore. Many can think differently about you. If God gives you this opportunity, it means he is liberating you. No one can judge you because of your beliefs. No one can punish you! Find a place where this is so."

I couldn't trust her. I kept silent and didn't even share meaningful looks with her but in the depths of my heart I knew she was saying the right things. This lovable old lady was saying the right things.

Hanna Nasi

Nearly five years.

We spent nearly five years in Venice, initially leading a happy life. Then we found ourselves in the claws of the Inquisition, judged. We saved our skin with many difficulties. At the first opportunity, we fled to Ferrara.

I came to Ferrara, leaving behind in Venice, The Gritty Palace, part of our business, and a sister. I was lucky to have the girls with me, my real fortune.

The Duke of Ercole received us well and awhile later published an edict:

"I guarantee the rights of all Jews. They can trade, openly live their beliefs, and pray as they wish. All of their rights are under the protection of our Duchy."

I was exactly forty. After so many years of living as a sinner with a guilty conscience, my Creator had given me the greatest gift ever.

From now on, I could live without hiding that I am a Jew,

and I could live to the full extent of my beliefs!

I went to the synagogue and repeated the same prayer as I always did, this time I could hear it:

"I worship the one God, Creator of the universe, with all my might."

Then I made an announcement:

"I am Hanna Nasi. From now on, I am a Jewish woman born from a Jewish mother. From now on and until my last day I will live as a Jew."

It was known that we, as the Mendes family, had returned to our true religion. Many, particularly the Jews, found this a positive development. Many Marranos, like us, were encouraged to declare our conversion back to Judaism. Many living elsewhere wanted to come to Ferrara.

According to those who disapproved, we had committed a big sin by reverting to the religion of our ancestors.

"If we step onto soil where the Inquisition is operative, we would be arrested on the spot!"

I did not care. At my age, I had tried everything I could in Europe and succeeded. Who would have imagined that we would lead a free life in Venice before the Inquisition imposed itself again on our lives? Who could have predicted my sister's stupidity that resulted in our being arrested and confined to a convent? How else would we have met Sister Sofia? I knew that none of this was a coincidence. I knew it was the road my Creator had designed for me, and it gave me what I wanted most: being Jewish.

I was not a Marrano any more but a Jew. The happiness that my mother, father, Francisco and Diogo never tasted was now mine.

Dona Gracia

There were no ghettos here but a district born of necessity. The Jewish quarter was called 'Zuecca.' There was no work or transport on Shabbat and the kosher butchers were all here. The synagogues were within walking distance of the houses. Under these conditions, a Jewish quarter automatically arose.

"What is our next destination, mom?" asked Reyna, who was by then already a young adult.

"We wandered around looking to find a place were Jews could live and work without any hindrance and here it is."

"My experience tells me that nothing is guaranteed forever. We should always work on an alternative. Today we are fine, but no one can say what the future will bring."

There were Jewish people in Ferrara that dealt with money matters before we came. With our support, trade and retail volumes increased. The Duke was meeting his objective and Ferrara was growing fast. The Duke was very close to the family and we enjoyed his attention. Something Reyna said made me think:

"The Duke is very warm toward the family. To me especially."

I felt like warning her.

"Don't forget—you are promised to Joseph! Because you are a young, beautiful, and rich woman, many will want to court you. Take care, my beauty! Try to understand the motives of people who approach you. Protect yourself. My heart beats for you. If something happens to you, my heart stops."

She threw her arms around me.

Our residence was the Magnini Palace, the most impressive building after the cathedral and the duke's palace.

Betrayal

The growth in trading activity didn't only benefit the Marranos but the whole population as this was becoming a common world market. I felt as if I were in Antwerp years ago. Printing was also much developed so people also came for education. Social life was lively. Christian women together with their Jewish friends added an interesting aspect to the texture of the city. The effects of the Renaissance were strongly felt. The city's aristocrats befriended Jews. Rich Marranos came and so did reputable Jewish academicians.

Many artists were contacting us to sell their works but they didn't really know what we hungered for. For us, the real need was religious books, not paintings or statues.

The only negative thought that crossed my mind in this happy environment was Brianda. I couldn't tolerate her memory.

"I don't have such a sister!"

Ferrara Bible

Although we enjoyed our days in Ferrara, this would not be our final stop. Marranos live freely here. Trade is flourishing, all institutions, including ours, were settling down. Now I can go East to fulfill an old dream—to Suleiman's land.

Again, it was up to Joseph to make the preparations. We didn't even think of informing Brianda.

Just before leaving, I received a request for a visit from Abraham Usque. It was a hectic time and I was busy. My mind was set on the trip but Usque was an important printer and one of the city's most valuable Jewish intellectuals.

"Dona Gracia, how are you?"

Dona Gracia

"Pray be seated, master. I am good. How about you?"

"Thanks to a great woman like yourself, we are all good. You helped us so much, I don't know if we could have done all that we have without your support. I don't think so."

It was true that we helped him and others whom we had never met. This was natural.

"Don't mention it. It gives us endless satisfaction to see the number of scholars like you increase."

"It's not so," he said without leaving what he had in his hand. "Your presence, your actions and missions that you accomplished gave us great encouragement not only materially but also morally. With your presence, the city has transformed beautifully. When I heard of your leaving, I finished the present I had planned to give you so I can present it to you before you leave. I don't have the patience to wait for your return."

"Master, there is no need for a present."

He unpacked the high-quality cloth, took out the book, and gave it to me. It was a Tora, a new print with a binding. I could smell the freshness of the paper.

I took it.

"Thank you so much. It will be one of my most prized possessions. I will keep it with me all the days of my life."

"Please open the cover."

I lifted the cover and my eyes widened. I tried to understand if I was seeing right.

The dedication page was for me, for Dona Gracia, a sinner like me who had lived forty years in denial.

Two tears dropped uncontrollably.

"What have you done, maestro? This is too much. I don't deserve such a valuable gift!"

Betrayal

My hands were trembling. I feared dropping the book. He reached over and helped put it on the table. As I wiped away the tears, I thanked my Creator. In Ferrara, good things happen, one after the other.

"You have made me very happy, really!"

"It's nothing. You have done so much for our co-religionists. What could be more natural than to dedicate the Ferrara Bible to Dona Gracia?"

I took the book and pressed it against my heart.

"Thank you! Thank you! Thank you."

"You should know that there is one more dedicated copy and that one is for our Duke Ercole. Needless to say, we hold you in much higher esteem and consideration. Bless you. God be with you."

On the water

Among the books I took with me, the Ferrara Bible had a special place. Others that came with us included one by our friend and family doctor, Amatus Lusitanus; one by a fellow teacher at Salamanca University; Duarte Gomez's book; one by our old family friend, Diogo Pires; and another by Diacus Pyrrus. Finally, I took with me the epic book *Consolations and Tribulations of Israel* by Samuel Usque, no relation to Abraham.

During the long journey, I had occasion to reread *Consolations and Tribulations of Israel*. It was easy to read as it was in Portuguese and written in a literary style. The book treats the period from Abraham until our days. It addresses the adversities Jews went through after being exiled from Jerusalem and Nebuchadnezzar's destruction of the First Temple. Samuel Usque's three biblical characters describe the tribulations of Jews from generation to generation and, in trying to encourage the oppressed people, they hint at messianic salvation. Its objective was to strengthen Marranos so they could endure the terrors in Portugal. It took me back to my childhood, reminding me of what I had tried to forget.

Before leaving Ferrara, we received news that the case in Venice was developing in favor of Brianda. The ruling transferred custody of La Chica to Brianda and held that La Chica's dowry, worth one hundred thousand ducats, should be kept in the treasury until she became eighteen, and then it would be transferred to Brianda. Luckily, all our dealings were in conformity with Venetian laws. I had procured a document from the Duke re-affirming my custody of La Chica.

"She had the cheek to come after us!" I thought as I watched the clear waters of the Mediterranean reflect brilliant rays in all directions.

Apart from urging me to speed our departure, the arrival of Brianda in Ferrara unnerved me.

We were transported by one of the best boats in our fleet. Although the crew had no idea, the captain was well aware of the boss's presence and he tried to make our trip comfortable and safe. He tried to deliver us to the Ottoman land as speedily as he could.

I took advantage of the beautiful weather to stretch my knees and walk from one end of the ship to the other.

"She had the nerve to come after us in Ferrara! As if it wasn't enough that she created hell for us, she was now trying to influence the Duke to sign a document regarding La Chica's dowry and her custody!"

Luckily the Duke sided with us, leaving Brianda once again empty handed.

Was I concerned about her? No. I checked myself to see if it made me sad. That was a no, too. In spite of it all, I did feel an acerbity inside. I had seen her from afar a couple of times and did not like her demeanor. Her beauty had faded and her facial expression had lost its alertness. The hairs that glistened like stars were now neglected and lifeless. She looked thin and weak. She was my sister, though I'd stopped considering her my sister, I couldn't change the reality and I was sure that if mother and father were alive, whatever catastrophe she created, they would want me to forgive and look after her.

I was moved. My eyes moistened.

"What's up with you? You won't start crying now for Brianda? For the woman that had you arrested, and left you at the mercy of the Inquisition."

Another voice from inside answered:

"If it wasn't for the arrest, you wouldn't have dared to declare your return to Judaism!"

I heard footsteps behind me. Reyna and La Chica were coming.

The crew had their eyes set on the girls. The two of them were young and handsome. They talked and giggled happily.

When I saw them, the clouds of gloom over me dissipated.

"You two! What are you up to now?"

Reyna:

"We got bored in our cabin and decided to look for you."

Dona Gracia

La Chica:

"Really! You seem curious. You are here but cannot see your shadow!"

This time the three of us laughed. When I pulled myself together, I said, "Just wondering. It seems that tiger called Pierre also has some weaknesses. The sea is bothering the sire! The man is like a rock on land but at sea, he changes color and is wavering. Last I saw him he was green and vomiting."

Again we started laughing, this time really loudly.

"Come to my side! Let's watch the sea together."

La Chica pointed. "Look! A seagull. We must be near land or an island."

"How did you know?"

"Because seagulls live near land."

I took a look. The number of seagulls increased from one to two, then to three. Joseph had taken care of all our comforts as well as our necessities. The boat was stocked with well-preserved foods and plenty of vegetables. The food was plentiful, and the cook very capable. Everyday we were served tasty dishes. There was no need to step on the ground. As a security measure, another ship followed us with armed guards. Forty of our staff were settled in the cabins and traveling with us. I had sent one lot earlier to Ragusa and Salonika, to prepare for the rest of the journey.

La Chica: "Aunty, what kind of people are the Ottomans? Do you know them?"

I could see that Reyna was curious too, though not as much.

"I don't know my darlings. I met many but the ones I met

were traders, spies or statesmen. The others, I have no idea, particularly the women."

"Muslim women went about all covered!" said Reyna. "As religious obligations."

"I had seen a few Muslim women but they dressed similarly to us."

"Muslims won't abduct us and force us to marry!"

La Chica had said this. They laughed. I was serious:

"Shush! What kind of talk is that! Well-brought up girls don't talk that way!"

"What if they abduct us?"

"Rubbish! The country you are going to is much more civilized than most parts of Europe. Human rights are protected by law and religious regulations. It is already determined who you will marry. Don't forget that you will marry Jewish men and have Jewish children."

They stopped talking. They knew this tradition from a very young age. It was very unusual among Jews to marry non-Jews. It was more acceptable for women to do so as the child born of a Jewish mother is considered Jewish. But it is not approved for men to do likewise. Already we were too few and we feared melting away and disappearing.

"How would things change if I had had a son?" I wondered. "He might have been like his father Francisco, or perhaps even more like his uncle Diogo. Perhaps like Joseph. I would have said in all these cases, 'It is not an issue.' Joseph is like my son anyway and soon, he will be my son-in-law."

The wind was blowing the girls' hair; they were constantly clearing their sights.

Dona Gracia

"I liked it in Ferrara," Reyna said. "I can't remember Portugal but I remember Antwerp a little and Venice too. My favorite was Ferrara. We are wondering constantly, mom. Where are we going? Will it be for long? Will Istanbul be the last stop?"

"Did that make you unhappy my baby? You never said so."

"My saying so or not, what difference would it make, mom? We are Jewish. We learn young. We don't have a country. Until we have one, we could be expelled from anywhere."

I was happy for my dear girl to know that but it also made me feel sad. With this consciousness, she would not err like her aunt Brianda and would always be cautious. I was sad and demoralized to think that each new-born Jewish child would grow up with this fear.

La Chica added that she also thought that way:

"When there is an epidemic, the Jews are the first to blame," she said in one breath.

"They cannot tolerate the Marranos growing rich and defending themselves when poorer Christians couldn't. First thing that comes to their mind is to accuse us. For the first time, I was afraid."

Duke Ercole caught us by surprise on that score. He couldn't resist the pressure of the locals and came out with a ruling that recently arriving Marranos had to leave the city. Moreover, they were asked to leave on very short notice.

It was hard to find people to transport them out of the city. Coachman, afraid they would be contaminated, refused to carry their wares. Contractors refused to work for them.

"More than three hundred families," I said sharing their

Betrayal

sorrow. "We couldn't leave them stranded and we managed to get most of them to Ragusa."

In that instant, I was sure the three of us thought of Brianda. No one could utter her name. When I noticed the girls' silence, I spoke:

"They spread the rumor that I had denounced Brianda to get her out of the city. That was, of course, not true. Because she was a newcomer, they wanted her to leave the city. I set aside her hatred for me and tried to save her. I had to make many concessions to the Duke but Brianda stopped insisting on your custody. I wanted the best for her and still do."

La Chica:

"I know, Aunty. Don't even think about it! What other people say or do has no importance. My mom made her decisions and she chose to be alone."

I turned around and looked at her lovingly:

"La Chica, my dear girl! You are not angry with me? Not vexed?"

She threw her arms around me.

"No, aunty. Perhaps I was a little at first but I fully understood what mother had done, the damage she caused. She shouldn't have acted so thoughtlessly. I know that if she repents, understands all the mistakes she made and comes close to us, you will be the first to open the door. If she is my mother, she is also your sister. She is as close to each of us. Unfortunately, she is still seeking fortune. One day she will understand. We will wait until then, Aunty."

Reyna also embraced us. We three women hugged each other as seagulls flew over our heads. The Mediterranean was beneath us, and blue skies above us. I saw scattered clouds in the distance.

I asked myself: "Will Istanbul be the last?"

Entering Istanbul

Suleiman's city—modern-day Istanbul—was built in one of the most beautiful corners of the world. The Bosphorus Strait passing through it connects the Marmara Sea with the Black Sea, the Golden Horn at its heart. As if this were not enough, forests filled with woods and rivers lay at its four corners. The architectural creations of the Ottomans accompanied the unequalled beauty of the old Byzantine buildings. Elegant mosques with slim minarets, not at all resembling European cathedrals, graced the hilltops.

As our convoy passed the walls leading to the entrance to the city, I smelled the aroma of spices I like so much and I saw surprisingly lively crowds in the streets. Antwerp was crowded, as was Venice and Ferrara but the crowd here was different. We continued by sea from Ragusa to Salonika and then to Istanbul. Forty of our staff joined us in a caravan of coaches. After entering Ottoman territory, we were completely safe and felt totally secure. Joseph had worked hard. As we passed through towns, we met hospitable pashas and governors who not only welcomed us, but even added soldiers to our convoy for extra security. Until we reached Istanbul, people stared at us, perhaps wondering whether we were an ambassador's convoy. In Istanbul, restless crowds filled the roads and squares. I peered constantly from the window of our coach. Goods were sold from sacks at large markets. In the port district, we saw people from so many countries wandering freely while decked out in all styles and colors of national dress.

Soldiers, called janissaries, wore big hats. Sailors, called Levent, wore loose pants called shalwars. 'Ases' patrolled the city, walking through the crowds. Even if one heard a row somewhere, it didn't last long.

"It's like in story books," said Reyna, holding my hand tightly. "Why do they wear such gargantuan hats?"

Mesmerized, La Chica watched the city with wide eyes.

When we heard someone yelling loudly, it startled both of them.

We checked but couldn't see a row or argument. The people coming behind us, coachmen carrying our staff and goods didn't seem surprised and paid no attention. I noticed some within the crowd starting in one direction.

"Mom, its the same noise," said Reyna. Since Salonika, we'd been hearing similar sounds. Isn't it what they call 'Ezan'?"

"Yes, that's called Ezan. Muslims pray five times a day."

La Chica:

"I don't understand a word of what he's saying but I like the sound. I have to learn Turkish immediately!"

I smiled.

"Darling, even if you learn Turkish, you will never understand it because it's in Arabic. Like other Muslims, Turks pray in Arabic. They pray like Muhammed of Medina as they believe it should be so."

Reyna pointed to a woman passerby, walking slowly and holding her child.

"Look, another Ottoman woman!"

She heard us, turned and smiled, and then walked away.

La Chica:

"So there really are beautiful women here. She is so pretty even when covered so."

I stopped listening to their chitchat and looked around. What I wanted to see was not minarets reaching the skies, big markets where goods of every description are stocked, or even mysterious princes and princesses as you might encounter in story books. I wanted to see in the land of the Ottomans, in the Sublime Porte, a flesh-and-blood Jew living freely under his fig tree.

Not even one?

Within the large crowd, I saw someone. Quite far from where we were, he was walking calmly in a street among houses made of wood. I knew immediately that he was Jewish. Two fringes hanging under his jacket moved as he walked. He had a large head cover rather than a small kippah. Seeing that first hand was enough to believe all that I had been told. He branched into one of the alleys and disappeared.

I returned to the world when I saw a person waving at us from the crowd.

"Dona Gracia!" He shouted "Dona Gracia!"

I turned toward him and smiled. When my coach stopped, so did the entire convoy. He came close to us.

"Sorry for my delay. Welcome." He turned to the girls. "You are welcome too. Excuse the delay. I had to tend to a patient. I rushed as much as I could. At least I caught sight of you at the entrance to the City. Moshe Hamon."

Entering Istanbul

I bent my head slightly, saluting him, as did the girls.

"Joseph has made all the preparations!" said Moshe. He has rented a beautiful mansion in Pera, and asked me personally to receive you. I will lead you with my coach. Follow me."

"Moshe Hamon, please come with us. Why don't we continue in the same coaches? I said. "Then you can tell us about Istanbul."

I made a sign to Pierre:

"Pierre, can you get on one of the coaches in the convoy? We can take Moshe Hamon with us. No need to worry about us!"

Pierre didn't like leaving me out of his sight but, nodding his head, he agreed.

I couldn't help noticing the fleeting glance Moshe threw at Reyna as he climbed into the coach.

"Joseph had written to me that you would arrive today," he said as he sat. "I hope you had a comfortable journey."

"Thanks to you, it was perfect. The document that you obtained from Suleiman stating that we are his subjects was a protective shield. We were received like princesses everywhere we stopped."

"The Porte is very satisfied with the support you supplied so far, Dona Gracia. We knew, from letters sent by the Venetian Doge in Istanbul, that you would have issues or even threats from the papal or Venetian authorities. Anyhow, now you are in safety. Your daughter, I take it."

"Yes, this is Reyna, my daughter, and my niece, La Chica."

"We awaited your arrival for a long time."

I was happy that he didn't elaborate on the reason why he

was so anxious about our arrival. In our correspondence, he had said that he would be very happy to assist us, done everything he could so far and had asked for a little favor.

"Finally we are here," I said casually, not following his lead.

"In the palace, it was said that Chavus would pick you up and bring you here."

"You know we have our own fleet. The one that had already transported thousands of our co-religionists, this time brought us over. After stopping over in Ragusa, we moved to Salonika. We preferred to travel by land as we were told it was safer. I heard of the Chavus you mentioned. He helped us a lot. The authorities had a hard time controlling him and he attracted all the attention. Thanks to him, we could find the time to make all of our preparations and leave Ferrara incognito. We really had no alternative than to find refuge with the Ottomans. Moshe, can you tell me; do all Jews live and practice as free men without any pressure in Istanbul? Do the authorities intervene in their beliefs?"

This was enough to put a wide smile on his face.

"But of course, we don't even think otherwise."

"Finally, God has provided us with a new country where we would enjoy more freedom!" I said not hiding my feelings. "Neither in Europe nor in the New World, there is no getting away from the Inquisition. It is like the rust that eats away iron, it renders living a normal life impossible in whichever city it contaminated. Determined to annihilate all Jews from the face of the world! There was nowhere else we could live like human beings."

"Don't worry, Sultan Suleiman is the fairest of all rulers. From religious considerations and by law, he doesn't interfere

Entering Istanbul

in the beliefs of non-Muslims. People of difference religions and even sects pray next door to each other without any problem. Naturally there are some limitations but the safety of the people, their dignity, and their goods are under the strict protection of his laws."

"What kind of limitations?"

That was Reyna's question.

"At the end of the day, this is a Muslim country. No one is allowed to do things that would disturb Muslims, such as drinking wine in public spaces. Muslims don't bother about our Kosher rules. But for Christians to feed or eat pork openly is not allowed!"

"Is that all?" Reyna asked with a smile,

La Chica:

"Since you are his doctor, please enlighten us a little, what sort of a person is Suleiman? Is he as scary as he is made out to be? Is it true he eats humans?"

Moshe couldn't stop laughing.

"Who said such nonsense? He is a truly handsome and well-built person. All the women in the country, including the ones in the harem adore him. He dresses with the finest clothes and wears refined jewelry. Unfortunately, he is constantly at the head of his army, at the front. He is seldom in Istanbul. When he is here, he only spends time with Hürrem."

"Hürrem."

"Hürrem is called 'haseki' meaning that she gave birth to a son of the Sultan, one of his wives if you will, but his favorite by far, a universal beauty of a woman, and very powerful."

At this point, he stopped and turned to me as if giving me

the message with his lifted eyebrows. "She is the real ruler of the palace. Suleiman might be ruling the country but for the palace, she is the one. Thank God that her relations with Esther Handali are excellent. You might have heard Hürrem's name as Roxelana."

I knew well who Hürrem is. She was known as 'La Rossa' in Ferrara. She should be quite old by now. It was my turn to ask.

"Esther Handali."

"Like yourself, she is an honorable lady. We will talk all about these things. You will meet them all." His mannerism was as comfortable as if we had known each other for a long while. "First of all, settle down. You have been on the road for so long. Relax. Rest. Then we will start again. We have important matters to talk about, don't we, Dona Gracia?"

We looked at each other with Reyna.

Joseph had already transferred an important part of our business to Istanbul. We (the staff) had been moving from country to country, changing headquarters frequently. Hearing of the scandals Chavus caused in Venice, I laughed a lot. He beat up the bodyguard that had been provided to him, and shattered every rule and protocol he could. His job was to make sure Dona Gracia and her entourage left comfortably. He had two options. One was to succeed and the alternative was to have his head chopped off in Istanbul. Though I was happy to leave, Venice continued with the court cases and this was a concern since we still had a sizeable part of our business there.

Joseph had briefed me thoroughly about Moshe. He was

influential in the palace and could possibly help us. His father, Joseph Hamon, had also been a palace doctor in the service of the Sultan Selim, nicknamed 'Yavuz.' He had started an academy of medicine with leading doctors for the purpose of training and educating new doctors. This academy set the curriculum and the rules. Jews—who were close to the palace, multi-lingual, and in contact with western capitals—had a good opportunity to improve their medical skills. The Sultans had a soft spot for Jews, not only taking advantage of their advanced knowledge of medicine but also as a source of information about the West. Yavuz Selim had a four-story mansion built for Joseph Hamon in the Jewish quarter, and after his father's death, Moshe continued from where his father had left off. I knew even if he hadn't said it himself. Moshe was as close to Hürrem Sultan as he was close to Suleiman. He had earned the trust of both men and explained the falsity of the "blood libel" accusations to them. Though a small possibility, if not for the opportunity he had of bringing this issue to Suleiman's attention, pogroms as had occurred in Europe might have been carried out in Ottoman lands too.

A mother can tolerate wrongdoing toward herself, but never to her children. A mother does not care if she is ill but if one of her kids has fever, she stays by his bedside. Those who started the 'blood libel' claims exploited people at the level of this most fundamental instinct. In order to portray Jews as demons, they claim that during the Passover feast, the blood of a kidnapped Christian boy is used to make Matzo. Priests whose bigotry is larger than their faith voice this nefarious accusation from time to time. Using imagination and oratorical skill in crowded squares, they mobilize ignorance and hatred among mobs.

"As it gets dark before the Passover feast, Christ haters go out into the streets to search for an unattended Christian child. Finding one, they abduct him, and take him home where they place him in a vessel with a drum fitted with nails. There they bleed him. With his blood, they make bread and eat it. Hey! Lambs of Jesus! God is your shepherd. Save your children from blood-thirsty Jews!"

Since Muslims love their children as much as any parents do, this was the easiest way to create an atmosphere of chaos. Chaos would lead to attacks on Jewish quarters and synagogues, which would bring about the massacre of thousands as happened in Europe. We could not allow the 'blood libel' to stand. Fortunately, the Ottomans were a people with a strong common sense. Moshe's explanation sparked the curiosity of Suleiman who ordered a thorough investigation of the subject by religious and secular people until he thoroughly understood it.

There was one such case in Amasya, a town near the Black Sea in Anatolia where a Christian boy couldn't be found. It was claimed he was killed by Jews, so that the 'Matzo' bread eaten at Passover could be made with his blood. Jewish homes were burned, synagogues desecrated, and a rabbi killed. Crazy as it might sound, thousands were massacred under this pretext. While in Portugal, we had heard that Suleiman intervened after hearing explanations by Dr. Hamon. Suleiman had the Torah inspected and issued a ruling that the story creating the chaos was a lie. The person who killed the rabbi was hanged. The lost boy was found, ending this catastrophe forever in Ottoman lands.

Later when there arose another, similar attempt to create chaos, Suleiman ruled that he was the only person to decide these cases.

The 'blood libel' is the easiest way to demonize Jews. There were also claims of deicide—the claim that Jews killed Jesus—or didn't believe he was the son of God, or that he'd been born to a virgin. Part of it is true. We don't believe that God can have a son, or that a virgin can give birth. As to the killing of Jesus though, it was known that it was the doing of the Romans. However, if the blood libel didn't work, then deicide was handy as an excuse to attack us.

The Muslims also believed that Jesus was not the son of God but a human being, a prophet!

If there were an epidemic in a city, we were accused of causing it. Where there was poverty, fingers pointed at us. If the administration engaged in war and lost, again, it was our fault. Less ominous events were cause enough to trigger actions against us.

Fortunately, for us, the religion of the Ottomans has many commonalities with ours. As Muslims, they are protected by their own powerful empire, which is not losing on the battlefield. Religion dictated hygiene, resulting in fewer epidemics, a factor that lessened the need to accuse scapegoats.

～～

I looked out the coach window, wanting to see more Jews. I wanted to see more self-confident Jewish men and women wandering about, but what I noticed more were people, stopping whatever they were doing, to watch our convoy with curiosity.

"I guess you like Istanbul," Moshe said, "since you couldn't take your eyes from the window."

"Dr. Moshe, I was really looking to see if there were any Jewish people. I wanted to see whether they really felt free and at home."

"For that you need to go to a quarter called Balat. You would see more than you would want. Sultan Bayezid settled most people coming from Spain there. It was named after an old Byzantine ruin. The ones who came from Portugal live mainly outside Istanbul. Of course, there are those who lived here even before the Byzantine period. In time, you will meet them all. Here also you won't need to make alheiras, the Kosher Portuguese sausage. You can comfortably shop wherever the Muslim population does.

"Doctor, my dream has always been to live in a country like that. But it's not enough for me to enjoy this freedom. Naturally, I want the rest in Europe to be free also."

"Don't worry. As long as the Ottomans are strong, Jews will be safe. As for Europe, in the long run, they will stop this atrocious nonsense. What is their goal? They will not try to annihilate all Jews, will they? They will soon understand that it's an impossible task. I am hopeful of the area called Germany. If the Protestants become strong there, then life for Jews will be much better. I think that starting from the Germanic lands, the whole of Europe will understand that they cannot annihilate all Jews and that these stupid policies will end before 1700. Don't you agree?"

Entering Istanbul

I shook my head. Moshe Hamon knew much about Europe but living in Istanbul made him an optimist. When compared with Spain and Portugal, I had hoped that life for Marranos and Jews would have been better in northern European cities.

"Doctor, have you ever experienced the horrors of Auto-da-fe?

"God forbid! No."

I looked into the girls' eyes, undecided whether I should elaborate.

They waited, silently.

"When I was a child, my father took me to Spain where we visited relatives and he sorted out some unfinished business. As Marranos, we needed to be careful but the Inquisition was severely punishing those who did not accept Christianity, nor follow Jesus. There was a square packed with an exhilarated crowd in a trance."

Men, women, and children. The crowd yelled wildly, impatient for the Jew to be punished in the usual way. He had been found guilty by the court of being a 'heretic.' Days before the execution, word spread throughout the city and nearby towns and villages. Turnout was massive. The royal family and aristocrats took their places in the first row to watch the execution close up and also observe the crowd. The rest of the people stood in the back, pushing and shoving each other to have a better view. Some children rode on their parents' shoulders.

The chief Inquisitor stood on an elevated platform and raised the cross to show it to the crowd. Waving smaller crosses, people made vows about their commitment to the Inquisition and shouted promises to protect Christianity, if necessary, with their blood.

"We follow the light of God!"

"Burn the God killers!"

"Start the fire under the heretic!"

"Burn him!"

Outside the square but overlooking it from a large window on the second floor of a building, my father, Alvaro, had me by his side. I was so terrified, I wrapped my arms around his leg. He caressed my hair.

"I know, my little girl! This is affecting you strongly, but keep watching! You should see and never forget this."

He held my hand tightly.

The Jew at the center of the pageantry was in a desperate state from being tortured. He was tied to a stake. Blood oozed from a cut in his stomach and his face bruised from blows. Part of his right knee was blackened. From it dangled a strained or broken limb. His head was bent as if he had fainted.

The Chief Inquisitor read the list of sins the tormented man had committed.

"You have been found guilty of refuting Christianity, of continuing in your old ways, and of money lending!"

I couldn't hear all of the accusations but knew he had committed what the Inquisition considered serious crimes discovered by a court consisting of two legal experts and a notary who supervised the interrogations. After being denounced, instead of confessing his sins, he waited until he was arrested and denied all accusations.

When there was a fire on one side of the square, women shrieked and the crowd moved haphazardly. While uncomfortable, the royal family didn't dare budge.

Entering Istanbul

As the fire approached, the tortured man made a last effort but his words were lost in the crowd's jeering.

Oil was poured on the stake so it would catch fire more easily. Presented with the torch, the Inquisitor moved toward where the nobles were seated.

"The honor is yours, Sire. Please oblige."

The person honored to start the fire under the heretic got up and saluted the royal family. Without paying attention to the cheering crowd, and in a rushed movement, he lit the oiled wood.

The accused tried to move but couldn't. As a last effort, he straightened his neck and pronounced words that were lost in the crackling fire. Flames wrapped the victim's legs.

"Innnggh!"

Flames touched the top of the stake and the accused cried out in pain.

The heat was felt in most parts of the square and the mob listened to the man's moaning. For first timers, the shock of the execution could be seen on their faces, mouths gaping. The ones who'd seen it all before crossed themselves and prayed.

The Chief Inquisitor, worried that the mood of the crowd was changing, spoke from the podium to address the crowd and raised the cross:

"The end of the heretic. No pity for Christ betrayers!"

As if waiting for that message, the mob was agitated again. The terrible sound coming from the man burning at the stake mixed with the crowd's taunts.

~ ~

This wasn't an appropriate scene to remember on our first

day in Istanbul but I wanted Moshe to know, in all crudity, the horrors suffered by his co-religionists in Europe.

"This was the first I experienced the smell of burned flesh, never to be forgotten. The man who was burned alive did not denounce his faith until the end. The Inquisition was less brutal for those who accepted Christianity! They strangled them first and then burned them because they had seen the light."

"No such things can happen here."

We hoped so but remained silent.

～ ～

Moshe said, "You were personally interrogated by the Inquisition. I was worried when news came. I tried to intervene but Suleiman was away from Istanbul. We waited for his return. The Inquisition is too powerful. By the time Suleiman returned, we heard that your case was closed."

"That's true. We were lucky. We were not stripped of our clothes and interrogated in dark dungeons with metal chains. Instead, we were locked away in a convent. If we were not Mendes, we would have suffered torture."

Pain facilitates confession!

Moshe waved his hand. What Brianda had done was known here too.

～ ～

After being tied to a board with head fixed, a cloth was pushed into the torture victim's mouth. Water was poured slowly over the cloth, creating the helpless sensation of choking. The person's arms were chained behind the back, and the chain was lifted high, then dropped, breaking the person's arms. The skull was placed in a clamp, arms and legs stretched with a cylinder, the stomach filled with water and pressure applied, creating unbearable pain. Whipping, nails pulled out, mice in a pail closed in on the stomach. I had heard of so many other forms of torture from people we managed to save from the Inquisition. Although each one was enough to revolt a normal human being, the Inquisition had the power to pass judgement even on kings. No one could talk. Who knows? Perhaps future generations won't even believe the Inquisition tortures. Even today, it sounds unbelievable. The Inquisition objective is to do to the body whatever would save the soul.

In the end, neither the confessor nor the ones who resisted could save themselves.

Some hundred years ago, a Spanish priest by the name of Ferrand Martinez declared that Jews brought all evil into the world.

He said the existence of Jews was an insult to Jesus. He started a fire in Seville called "Ash Wednesday" that led to the massacre of thousands of Jews and echoes to this day. The ashen embers beneath the fire still burn. With a slight wind, it would be ready to burn Jews again. Muslims too, albeit to a lesser extent, shared the suffering while running from Andalusia, leaving all of their belongings behind.

Mass Christianization came after that. The ones who were baptized were called 'New Christians' or popularly Marranos. Converted Muslims were called Moriscos.

The wedding of King Ferdinand of Aragon and Queen Isabella of Castile united their territories, which they called Spain. The Inquisition started in Spain and spread gradually over Europe. The proposition of a small fortune by Isaac

Abravanel to the royal couple couldn't save them from the pressures of Cardinal Tomas de Torquemada who insisted that all non-Christians be sent away. The Andalusia, built by Tariq Bin Ziyad, was reduced to rubbles, his treasure confiscated, and the 'morerias' or Moorish quarter where Muslims and Jews lived, was razed to the ground.

Books were among what was completely destroyed. If people were better educated, they wouldn't follow blindly the Inquisition. When people were oppressed and sent away from Spain and Portugal, the rest wouldn't applaud, watch passively, and believe that something good was being done. My family, The Mendes' or rather with their names in Spain, The Benveniste's wouldn't have to leave their country, and each generation wander and live in a different part of the world. Finally, I am here. I came to settle but what guarantee do we have that Suleiman or one of his heirs wouldn't change their attitude toward us?

How many families ended up at the bottom of the Mediterranean? How many Jews crossing the Alps in harsh conditions died on the way?

It wasn't only us. The Muslims and Protestants were targets of the Inquisition too. Hatred and blind ignorance harmed everyone. If we go further back, the Orthodox also had their share. While living as a free Jew, I would like to work on the education of the people too. Not only of Jews but of all people. If I get the support I hope for, I want to open schools. Let people be educated and saved from ignorance.

Let no nose ever again smell burned flesh.

Undoubtedly, there were many ignorant Jews too. Sometimes we saw rabbis considering Christians as competitors. They should also be trained in modern thinking. In the academies I intend to build, they would be taught to embrace all human beings. I see the need for open-minded religious people.

Would I be able to do all of this?

I have a good feeling but I don't have the answer. I will live my beliefs that I openly declared in Ferrara and achieve at least part of my wishes. Moreover, one never knows, once so near, the way to our old city, Jerusalem might be opened.

The secret my father had whispered into my ear.

I know that many a religious Jew yearns for 'One King one country.' But at my age, I know: Whoever tries to build on stereotypes fails. The ones who tried it did not have sustainable success. There will probably be others who will try and fail.

This is what I had in my mind, as we were passing through the port, getting close to our residence. In this city no one will commit suicide because of forced conversions, no one will be humiliated even if he switched religions. This city will be one where Jews will live and work as a free people with their academies. In this city we will not be forced to change our names and live with a double identity, no one would care if our males are circumcised or not. Family names will not be replaced by strange names of trees or professions.

I turned to Moshe next to me:

"You can use your original family name."

He had never thought of it.

"Naturally, whose name should I ever use?"

Adapting to the Ottomans

The country of the Ottomans is very different from those we have known. Our prominence in business wasn't enough to allow us to talk to ruling people. For a woman to get an appointment to discuss business matters with ministers, called "Pacha," is even more difficult.

Joseph is with us and acting as the Mendes House representative. Transactions were within my control and I was happy about Joseph's role though I had to remain in the background. From the day we set foot in Istanbul, brokers hovered around us, wanting appointments to do business. These demands were spinning in my head from time to time. We found an excellent mansion in Pera that wasn't out for selling. We rented it for one gold ducat a day. Though this was no problem, I preferred to live in a house that belonged to us. Translated from the Greek, Pera means 'beyond' or, in this case, beyond the palace quarters. I'd heard that the famous Venetian Doge, Andrea Gritti's son from a Greek lady, lied in this building for a while. New buildings and mansions were being constructed among vineyards and gardens. I was here in this city to settle. The brokers, Pachas, and others curious about us, and wanting to establish relationships, could wait. We had plenty of time to make their acquaintance.

I learned well of the cost attached to being a refugee. To settle in the land that hosted us, we had to work hard and prove ourselves useful. Locals didn't have to adapt themselves to us. It was just the opposite. We needed to get accustomed to their ways. I experienced this in Lisbon, Lyon, Venice, and

Ferrara. Many wanted to get to know us but I was most interested in the palace crowd.

The world was rapidly changing. Europeans discovered ways to exploit the New World while new styles became popular in architecture and music. Great churches and cathedrals competed with the grandeur of Roman temples while more relaxed tunes replaced formal religious music. Liberated from hymns, lyrical music was replaced by what people wanted to hear. Protestants gained power and found ways into ruling circles. The Renaissance consisted of conceptual changes in art, music, science, and culture while change in religion became known as Reform.

We had the opportunity to experience these novelties in Venice where famous composers like Andrea Gabrieli and his nephew Giovanni were guests at our home. We were also introduced to many visiting artists coming from Florence. Italian and Dutch master painters were commissioned to create works on religious and other subjects for decoration and wall hangings. With the proliferation of statues and sculptures, an old Roman tradition was revived. The printing press gained in popularity with the result that books became substantially cheaper and reached far larger groups of European readers. The New and Old Testaments were within reach; music books were printed in large numbers facilitating the playing of classics. The masses were entertained in theaters and in the streets and piazzas. Plays focused on the biblical Joseph as the central character.

The cultural scene was quite different in the Ottomans. Books were hand-written by scribes and the progress brought about by the printing press was impeded, adamantly, by religious circles. Calligraphy was an important art form. One of the excuses by the clergy was that, with the new printing presses, this art form would be lost. It is conceivable that the success of the Protestants was seen as a dangerous consequence of the novelty of the printing press, creating questions about religious practices. The famous Venetian Marrano family, the Soncinos came to Constantinople. They printed religious Jewish books though they were neither the first nor the only ones.

Impressive mosques, aqueducts and buildings are being built by an awesome architect called Sinan. You could hear all sorts of different types of music from religious sects to military music and popular melodies. When I first heard the Mehter military bands led by an enormous drum with a voluminous bass sound, I felt my body shaking it was so impressive.

Ottomans went to war with this music, as if going to a wedding.

Religious reservations impinged on the creation of the visual arts in the sense that anything resembling a live form was prohibited. Still, there was an interesting form called miniature painting. There were no exhibitions where you could learn more. It was said that one day this missing part of the Renaissance will be recovered and discovered. The Muslim viewpoint for sculpture and painting was similar to Jewish thinking.

"You shall not make for yourself a carved image. You shall not bow down to them nor serve them." (Exodus 20:3-5)

While I was going about the discovery of this new culture and also entertaining friends in Pera, Joseph put the finishing touches on our magnificent mansion to be. Because of its spectacular view, it was called by many The Belvedere palace but my mind was set on that exceptional lady, the favorite wife of Suleiman the Magnificent, still beautiful in spite of her advanced age and called by many in Europe as La Rossa (the Redhead) while here she is known as Roxelana. I wanted to arrange a meeting to talk with this fascinating character. Many people were at our door avidly wishing to do business with us. Luckily Joseph took care of them and I stayed consumed with my curiosity. Having met Mary and other European queens, I wondered whether she was different. What were her interests and world views? What set La Rossa apart?

There were many Jews from old times, ones who ran from the Inquisition in Europe, and others from North Africa. Many were educated under their Christian names. In the coming days, I intended to meet many of them and listen to their stories. In settling down, odd jobs took up so much of my time, I still didn't have the opportunity to get to know this splendid city.

The Bedesten market place greatly impressed me. This was a large area where city residents, both men and women, shopped for necessities. Merchants of all creeds, color, and nations set up shop there to sell their wares. You could enter this area at one end, buy all you needed, and leave at the other end carrying all you wanted to buy.

When Moshe Hamon came to visit, I intended to go out, if possible to see the most interesting parts of town, visit the Jewish quarters and wonder a little about the Bedesten.

We went out together, leaving the girls at home. Naturally,

my shadow Pierre retraced my steps. I was keeping La Chica and Reyna out of his way as much as I could and avoided situations where they would be together.

When Moshe helped us out of Venice and Ferrara, he never hid his intention of connecting our families by having his son marry Reyna. On one occasion, he expressed his wish openly to me. Now that he brought the Mendes House to the capital, his esteem and prestige ws augmented considerably in the Porte. As with Mary, I didn't openly refuse but left some hope on the table. I left things to the developments in time but Moshe interpreted my attitude to be a shy and modest "yes." Moshe was a prominent character at the palace with many close strategic relations. Hurting his feelings and alienating him would not be the cautious thing to do. He was the chief doctor to Suleiman the Magnificent and head of the academy he had initiated. But I had promised Reyna's hand to my nephew Joseph a long time ago and this was the natural course of things, in keeping with family traditions, naturally maintaining in the business only insiders who were strongly committed to certain unshakable ideals.

As our carriage advanced, we saw occasional mounted officers who were called Sipahi. They were palace troops and Ottoman cavalry corps who carefully patrolled area, mercilessly catching mischievous interferers, men sitting on simple stools, drinking their coffees, sorbets, and chatting. The exotic aromas of strange flowers and spices filled my nostrils, I strangely felt already at home even refreshed in this city. There was so much to look forward to, to come.

"Coffee drinking habit is spreading and rapidly replacing

tea. There is much to be gained by trading," said Moshe.

"Joseph is saying the same thing. Important source countries are in the New World and we should benefit, thanks to our established fleet."

"Luckily, my nephew Joseph is my right hand and is taking care of all issues, business and otherwise. Moshe, you have been a great help. We shall always be grateful for your invaluable support."

He didn't seem to care.

We passed by mansions with strange architectural forms and saw unruly men called bashi-bazouk wandering around the shops and ancient columns. Dervishes lazed about near their temples. We saw men called cevlaki—with their shaven or rather scraped heads and eyelashes— wandering around naked from trousers up. When we arrived in front of a construction site with an immense scaffold where laborers busily worked, I asked:

"Isn't that it? The mosque being built by Suleiman."

"That's right. Suleiman has set his mind on building a temple larger than Sta. Sophia. Three thousand people are working on it. He spares no expense. He instructed Sinan to mix all the gold and treasure that the Shah of Iran had sent into the mortar. He is blessed to have a great architect at hand."

"What kind of person is this Sinan?"

I met him on a few occasions. He is an introvert living constantly with plans and projects in his head. He doesn't even notice people close to him. He is a genius comparable to, or even more magnificent than those in Venice. He constructs colossal buildings commissioned by Muslims. Every one is different from the one before. After building the splendid Şehzade Mehmet Mosque, named after Prince Mehmet, Sinan left us in awe, again, with the Süleymaniye Mosque, which will be seen from each quarter in Istanbul."

Even in its unfinished condition, Süleymaniye Mosque was grandiose. I said, "Sinan is near the top of the list of people I must meet. I don't know if it will be permissible to make such a magnificent building, I doubt it. Perhaps a beautiful but more modest synagogue."

"Take me to the synagogues too, Moshe. Which do you attend?"

"The other one in Balat—Yanbol Synagogue. Originally Romaniote Jews used it but after the Sephardim's arrival, it became their place of worship. There is also, close to it, the Ahrida Synagogue built by Jews running from the Balkans, particularly from Ohri in Bulgaria.

"I think it best to also have a yeshiva next to the synagogue. Moshe, what is your opinion?"

"I wish it were possible. As I have said, apart from the cost of obtaining permissions, construction would require a fortune."

"Perhaps, here you never had to—but after the massive sums we were required to pay in Europe, nothing scares me."

As we reached the Golden Horn, we stepped off our carriage and crossed by boat. The Golden Horn is a long, narrow, and deep inlet on the European side of the city. Fed by two small streams, it is a natural harbor where the Ottoman fleet anchored. Its name comes from the color of the water reflecting the sun at sunset.

Entering Istanbul

I looked around.

"Strange! Ottomans construct monumental buildings but did not build a bridge over the Golden Horn!"

Moshe explained as he showed the way:

"It is said there was a bridge resting on barrels chained to each other, made at the time of the Grand Turco. Leonardo later visited the city and began a project during the reign of Bayezid, but the Sultan didn't like it. Then Michelangelo accepted the invitation but never came. Probably they also consider that transport by boat is the way oarsmen earn their daily bread, and so they keep on postponing the bridge."

We got on the small, narrow wooden boat—called a caique—that was waiting for customers. We sat down and before long, the boatman with powerful arms rowed us over the waters of the Golden Horn. Afterward, he took money that Moshe handed him.

Moshe pointed to another coach. We got into it and were enthralled with the views that surrounded us. From the day we left Venice, we were under the protection of the Ottomans, even in Istanbul. Janissaries escorted us everywhere. Later I asked that they should be relieved as I felt safe and comfortable, and Pierre followed me everywhere anyway.

Finally, it appeared.

It was the place I had visited in my dreams, the place where I would meet the most powerful man on earth as he sat on his throne in his new and regal palace.

And yet, when the moment arrived, it seemed so modest! A large square was in front where people probably met on holidays. A few soldiers watched the two towers at the entrance.

Dona Gracia

Nowhere were domes reaching the skies, or walls decorated with ornate, stained glass. The watch towers were built over simple, stone walls. Between them were high, wooden doors. Armed guards stationed at the doors signaled that, without special permission, no one could enter.

"You are very lucky, Moshe. You can go in and out of these doors where the world is ruled. After all, Turks have succeeded in controlling more than half the world."

"It was thought so until recently, that is, before the discoveries. Anyhow the territory the Suleiman controls is quite vast."

"Is he as grand as his reputation says he is?"

He opened his arms.

"It is true—he is handsome and well built. A characteristic of Sultans is that they are praised constantly. He is flattered so much, he might forget he is mortal."

Moshe lowered his voice toward the end of the sentence, as if sharing a secret. "Dona Gracia, I can easily say that compared to Charles V, he is much more humane."

"Please call me Gracia Nasi. That is my name from now on."

"Fine, Gracia."

"How about Roxelana? Can you talk with her? Are you close?"

"What are you asking, Gracia? A Muslim woman wouldn't talk to a man, whether non-Muslim or even Muslim unless she is his wife. A tête à tête, never! Even attempting such a deed can be cause for capital punishment."

"Why?"

"By faith."

"I thought you knew her well."

"Of course, I know her. Don't forget, I am a doctor. Particularly on health issues I can confer even with the Sultans."

So much to be learned. As I tried to go back to Roxelana, he shared this information:

"What do you have in mind for your daughter, Gracia? Since you are already settled, you must have thought of other issues too."

"Moshe, we are not really settled yet. I have also made promises on the subject. First we will put our business in order, be comfortable with our environment. Then I will look into it."

He sensed that I was being evasive but he didn't want to insist for fear of getting a definitive rejection.

"When can I meet Roxelana?"

"I will plead on your behalf. I hope she accepts. These days Joseph Nasi is the talk of the palace, he is claiming a large sum from the French King who has no intention of paying. We are working on getting Suleiman's intervention. There is a word suggesting he would seize ships with French flags in the eastern Mediterranean to pressure the King to make good on his word."

"Would that be possible?"

"Sure but this would be the last recourse. Initially France will be warned to make the payment, which I doubt would have any effect. They have obtained such trading privileges from the Ottomans and Venice that it has gone to their head. These capitulations give them an advantage in the Mediterranean trade, particularly with the Ottomans."

We reached the Bedesten market where we intended to shop for gifts. Here, and for that matter anywhere else, there was little possibility of seeing jewelry as refined as the ones in my coffers. Still, I was curious. I kept looking. If you want to discover a city, the markets are a good starting place. We transported a large part of the textiles from Italy.

Herbalists displayed all sorts of spices. Further along in one row were shops with multicolored fabric and rare silks for sale. We saw jewelry shops with men outside trying to lure customers inside. There were shops selling colorful head scarfs, shoes and strange sandals, crystals and other glass and shiny wedges. Daggers with their hilts decorated with precious stones were on display. My business was trading. By looking at objects, I could guess their worth. Some approached me with curious looks while salesmen guessed from my attire that I was a rich lady. They surrounded me saying things I did not understand.

I had put some gold coins in a small sewn pocket in my belt. I did not intend to buy anything as I was out more to observe and to get acquainted with the scene when I suddenly felt a hand on my waist. When I turned around, I saw two hands. One belonged to an opportunist taking advantage of the hustle and bustle; the other was Pierre's. The shocked, wretched soul tried to release his hand from Pierre's clutches but it was too late. Pierre caught the inopportune hand and landed a solid punch on his nose. I threw a terrified shriek:

"Oh! What's happening?"

Suddenly, we were surrounded by a group of people. Someone yelled: "Call security. There is a thief!"

The broken nose was bleeding. As Pierre moved him away from me, the thief tried to get loose to no avail. Pierre's clamp squeezed him so hard that, rather than thinking of freeing himself, he twisted his hand in search of a position that would inflict less pain. It was quite a spectacle with a mixed audience. Ladies bit their fingers while terrified kids clung to their mums. Shopkeepers rushed to the scene, some kicking the guy, others hammered him with blows. Two guards appeared from nowhere and saw Pierre holding the miserable guy.

"Ayvaz, not you again?"

Blood poured from his nose and tears ran down his cheeks.

"Don't, please masters! I am not to blame; I didn't do anything. I didn't touch anyone's stuff!"

The taller of the guards lifted his wooden club as if to hit his head. Wishing to disappear, Ayvaz ducked and protected his head with the loose hand.

"Shut up, you bum. You should be ashamed of yourself, now also denying!"

The other approached, asking, "Lady, did he try to steal your stuff?"

I looked at the man. I had seen people in anguish before but this was quite different. With blood and tears running down his face, the terrified Ayvaz was obviously wishing he had never existed.

"No. He didn't steal anything."

Pierre, astonished, looked at me enquiringly. Among the exclamations from the crowd, the guard couldn't believe what he heard.

"Lady, didn't he steal something from you? Wasn't he caught thieving?"

"No. I had little money with me and it's all in my purse."

To convince them, I took out my purse and shook it so they could hear the little that was in it.

Pierre had to release him and, in one instant, Ayvaz started kissing my feet.

"Big sister, God bless you forever! May God grant all your wishes. They were nearly taking me away."

Shop owners threw angered looks at him:

"Shameless thief! The cheek to say he is innocent!"

"Typical women must be compassionate!"

"There will come a day when he will steal something else. Should one show mercy to a thief?"

The episode was being prolonged and the thief wouldn't stop trying to lick my feet. I felt uncomfortable.

"Please leave me alone!" I said sternly. "I said nothing is missing, didn't I. What else do you want?"

The tall guard grabbed the thief by his neck and lifted him up in the air.

"You scum! Now go. If I ever see you anywhere near the Bedesten, I won't care who had mercy on you or who didn't, I will crush you under my feet! Send you to Yedikule dungeons and you will never see daylight again! Vanish!"

He slapped him hard on the face and dropped him like a bag of dirt. The guy found himself a few steps ahead, got up with difficulty trying to regain his balance and started running away like mad.

The guard looked at me and said: "Lady, be careful and

don't create distractions in the market."

Moshe was observing all from a distance. I took a brief look at him, then to Pierre.

Pierre still had this enquiring look on his face, not understanding why I let the thief go, unpunished. As the crowd slowly scattered, I turned to the doctor:

"OK, let's go, enough excitement for a day."

We took a few steps.

"You know more than I guessed," he said wanting Pierre to hear too. "You seem to have investigated well the Ottoman ways! Your compassion is not only for Jews but for all people. You let him go so that his hands wouldn't be chopped off, isn't that so?"

Rumors

After we reached Istanbul, rumors circulated in Europe about us. I didn't care much about what was said except for claims that Marranos coming to Istanbul were treated badly—denigrated, their goods impounded and they were sold in slave markets—were dangerous. Many Marranos that see only cruelty could easily believe all that. I was incessantly writing letters to all the communities in Venice, Lyon, Antwerp, Paris, London, and Ferrara, to the rabbis, doctors, diplomats, and opinion leaders asking them to explain to their co-religionists the real situation in Ottoman lands—facts like the freedom of religious belief and practice and trading liberties. I sealed the letters, and sent them through my reliable channels. I even wrote to my contacts in Spain and Portugal. I tried to convince them that, in these lands, people of all creeds and beliefs

Dona Gracia

lived in harmony and enjoy a peaceful life under their fig own trees.

We had much to do to put our things in order. My top priority was to get Reyna and Joseph married. Our panic grew after Joseph learned of Moshe's intentions and aspirations. On one side was Moshe. On the other, my sister, Brianda, was still trying to harm us.

"Hürrem Sultan, that is Roxelana, has agreed to receive you."

"Is that so? Did she say when?"

"Thursday after midday prayers."

"Well then, what should I do? What sort of a person is she, what does she enjoy doing? How do I address her?"

He laughed.

"Cool down. She is one of the many aristocrats you have met. Palaces are palaces and the people who live in palaces are aristocrats. Behave the same way you would with a European queen. That is all."

Two days. Two days left before meeting Hürrem Sultan.

What preparations I should make? Would time be enough?

I knew of the power Hürrem enjoyed in the palace. The world knew Suleiman well but the only person who had power over him was less known: the love of his life, Hürrem.

I had the best materials I had brought from Italy prepared. Gifts of spices were not so well received here but perfumes enchanted people. I had arranged an assortment of beautiful scents from India, the New World, and beyond in small bottles. There was a uniquely valuable one among them that, once smelled, was never forgotten. The reception was with a Sultan,

Entering Istanbul

the most powerful one. Rather than a few pieces of fabric and perfume, I had to give her a piece of jewelry the likes of which she would not have. I rushed to open my jewelry box.

Most pieces were composed of white diamonds, some of the finest works with thin gold. Necklaces, bracelets, earrings—jewelry that would send most women dreaming. Among them were elegant rings of a single annulus, forming jewelry so varied, it could be worn by a woman to cover her neck to her waist, like a robe. But a woman who knows jewelry, particularly one such as Hürrem, could easily distinguish which is valuable or exceptionally rare. I couldn't risk giving the impression that I took her for an ignorant, uncouth person. I chose a neckless circled with clean, pure white, elegantly cut rare diamonds having a massive, deep red ruby the color of the heart of a burning fire. I raised it to take a better look. There was scintillating light of many colors on the walls and ceiling. The light from the window on the ruby refracted its color.

"This is it!"

The darker the ruby the more valuable it is. Before placing it into a velvet pouch, I took one last long look at it. If Brianda knew that this would go to Hürrem Sultan, she would have sued me for that too.

Harem

The entrance to the harem was different from what you might expect. If someone managed to enter by passing the guards, he would be so shocked, he wouldn't know what to do. I'd heard lavish stories about the harem as a place where the Sultan was fortified with doped aphrodisiac elixirs and fine wines so he could be with tens of women in succession. The one single boss was Suleiman the Sultan. The harem was built so he could be with any woman for as long as he wished. The women tended to his pleasures morning or night, as he wished.

"This is even more modest then my home!"

The harem was no different than houses or villas. Here, though, house rules regulated activities. One major difference was its staffing—primarily by women state employees. The exception for eunuchs, or castrated functionaries—also called Aga, was for emergencies.

Apart from women staff and eunuchs responsible for the daily work, the Sultan's wives, daughters, and small children live at the harem. The environment is neither beautiful nor decorated. From the quarters starting near the kitchens, there were many adjacent rooms connected by exceptionally dull and plain corridors. European palaces are much more ornate with wall paintings, small corner objects, decorative chandeliers and torches hanging from the walls. Surprisingly, the new palace was simple and plain. The only difference was that the windows were colorful glass, not transparent so the interiors couldn't be seen from outside. As a result, lights of many colors leaked into the harem, suggestively illuminating it.

White and black eunuchs, in charge of security, stood guard on each end of the corridors. The floor was of stone except that there were long and thin carpets along the way. In past times, I'd heard that the old palace was used as the harem and was called the 'Women's Palace.' Eventually, the women who gave birth to boys were first admitted into the new palace and called 'Haseki.' Naturally they had women staff to assist them. Later the Sultan's mother and sisters joined the harem. I knew the most impressive room in the palace belonged to the Sultan and was called 'Has Oda.' As for the nicest room in the harem, it belonged neither to the Sultan nor to his favorite, called 'Gözde.' This was, by right, the room of the Sultan's mother, who was called 'Valide Sultan.'

Walking through these austere, stone-paved corridors behind the eunuchs, I wondered what kind of a woman Hürrem Sultan was. The eunuch behind me carried my presents. I had previously seen several different paintings of her but each looked different.

Either they paint from imagination or by hearsay, without having seen her.

We stopped at a door with two flaps and inlaid geometric ivory motifs. The black eunuch gently and respectfully knocked at the door before entering. The other showed me in with his hand.

I crossed into the room and saw her—an elderly lady sitting on an elaborate sofa.

I immediately bowed my head and saluted her. At that moment, one of the eunuchs said loudly as if we were deaf:

Dona Gracia

"The stately, magnificent, majestic, excellency Hürrem Haseki Sultan!"

I raised my head to see her surrounded by young servant girls. I could decipher why the harem seemed so interesting to outsiders. Nearly all the girls here are beautifully seductive.

"Come closer."

A slight impediment in her speech.

This time, the eunuch pronounced my name, this time in a softer voice: "Lady Beatrice de Luna, Gracia Nasi."

Though one of the eunuchs remained in the room, the others departed. The presents were left at the feet of Hürrem Sultan.

"Come, come closer, lady! Moshe spoke very highly of you. Come tell me about yourself."

It was clear that we wouldn't sit and chat as equals, sitting opposite each other as it was with Mary. I approached respectfully and set near her feet.

"My respects your majesty, Hürrem Sultan, La Rossa."

She looked closer at me. Yes, she was aging but still lively and very beautiful. She was wearing a shalwar, which I was accustomed to seeing though hers was made of exceptional fabric. She wore a kimono with long sleeves. Her head was not covered with the usual scarf but with a small cape and a hood stylishly decorated with small precious stones.

"So you came from Europe. What did they call me where you came from? La Rossa or Roxelana, which?"

"Both, most excellent Sultan."

She knew anyway but still asked.

"Tell me all about yourself. Who are you? What do you do?"

Harem

"My precious Sultan, I imagine that you know all about me already. Since it is your order, I will tell. Gracia Nasi, daughter of the Portuguese Mendes family. I am a business woman, your highness. After living in Europe for a long time, we threw ourselves to the shadow of Suleiman the Magnificent and Hürrem Sultan. I live in your Empire with my relatives who are my daughter Reyna and La Chica. I am most grateful to you for the honor you bestowed upon me by your acceptance. This is not fitting for you, my Sultan but…"

As I started to open the gift box, she signaled to one of the girls who rushed immediately. Since Sultans don't do anything manual, neither do their guests. This was the maid's job.

The girl unraveled the bundle, timidly spreading the rare fabrics one next to the other, closer to me at the feet of Hürrem. Then she showed each little perfume bottle. She was watching aloofly, nodding her head. I expected a more dressed up lady. This beautiful lady looked quite simple, even too simple.

I took out the purse from my waist.

"The most exquisite jewels in the world fade next to your splendor. The most valuable stones in the world don't shine as brilliantly as your highness, Hürrem Sultan."

I gave the pouch to the girl. She opened it and showed it to Hürrem.

For the first time, she looked interested. She took a closer look and stretched her hand to examine the ruby placed respectfully on her palm.

"It's a rare stone," she said, displaying her expertise on jewelry. "I hadn't seen such a dark one. You are well into valuable stones."

Dona Gracia

"My Sultan, part of our family business is about valuable metals and stones."

As she returned the present to her maid, she asked: "Did you visit many palaces in Europe? Did you meet Sultans over there? What are they like, tell me?"

"I met many Queens and princes but never saw any as beautiful as your highness."

She indicated the armchair next to herself.

"Come on now, stop being so formal and tell me all about them. Come. Sit closer."

I looked around me. The staff was used to sudden gestures like that. I sat respectfully.

"I'll start with Queen Mary, if you wish, my Sultan. Sister of Charles V."

Later as I was leaving the palace, what remained with me more than the sherbets and coffees we consumed was one sentence. She said: "Let's meet again."

She announced to me the news that I would be invited again.

Evening prayers were said as a soft velvet-like night spreading over Istanbul.

"Suleiman was not enchanted for nothing. It was impossible to be close to her and not be impressed. She had a totally exotic infatuating air, enchanting."

Naval Warfare

My old country Portugal is warring with my new country, the Ottomans. Since Vasco de Gama found an alternative trade route to the Silk Road, Ottomans suffered serious losses and were becoming poorer. If this trend continued, the power balance would be tipped against the Ottomans. One didn't need to be a statesman to sense this change. Whoever dominated the seas dominated the world and Portugal had a strong navy with technological superiorities.

As a desperate move, Suleiman sent his admiral, Piri, to Hurmuz Castle in the Basra Bay to challenge the Portuguese fleet with the intention of diverting the Silk Road back to Anatolia. He wanted to channel commerce to pass through Ottoman lands. Admiral Albuquerque and his fleet were in control of the Indian Ocean and no ship could pass by without their permission, consequently having all goods from India and China going straight to Lisbon. The sea route was much shorter than the traditional land one and this caused the sudden increase in its treasury being partly responsible for the creation of the Golden Age of Portugal. The Ottoman fleet suffered a decisive defeat and the fleet was totally lost, all ships sunk. Suleiman was furious. He knew that this would start a serious, irreversible decline in his treasury. It was said that he was so upset, he had his most valuable admiral Piri Reis beheaded in Egypt.

We were meeting with Joseph and contemplating the future of the Ottoman economy.

"The Mediterranean Sea had to be made safe for all ships to pass. We brought maritime laws that would do just that and then the state would collect taxes for providing this service. The Ottomans neglected switching to a system whereby they would provide protection against pirates, Aunt Gracia."

"I have difficulty understanding all this. How can Suleiman the Lawgiver neglect such an action?"

"An explanation could be that most of his powerful admirals were originally pirates. Europe, particularly Spain and Portugal, are extending their trade routes to the east and west and rapidly enriching themselves. If the Ottomans fall behind in this race, it is clear that their economy will suffer irreparably. Precious metals are being brought from the New World. This has inflationary effect. I hear that the value of silver went up by fifty percent already."

"This means that the currency has gone down by fifty percent!"

"Exactly right!"

"It seems they have found the way to enrich themselves again through the Marranos!"

I could understand by his look that he was puzzled.

"Joseph, when Jews were expelled from Spain and ran to save their lives, remember that Christopher Columbus set out to discover the New World. The means to finance this expedition came from the wealth impounded by the Spanish Crown from the Marranos. You must have heard of the insignia 'B'ezrat Hashem' in Hebrew that was inscribed on the top, right-hand corner of the eleven letters that he had written to his son."

"With God's help!"

"Of course, I knew. He had chosen his cartographers and

able navigators from among Jews who had refused conversion. For this reason, they sailed without the usual ceremonies and religious blessings, silently, incognito, from the unimposing port of Los Palos. Although they had planned to leave on the 2nd of August since this date coincides with Tisha B'Av (the day both temples were destroyed) they postponed their journey by one day."

"I had never viewed things this way!"

"Joseph, the New World was discovered with Marranos' money most probably to find a land where Marranos could live happily. He died before I was born. Otherwise we could have asked Columbus personally."

On our prolonged chats, the subject of our being immigrants surfaced, inevitably followed by a meaningful silence. To him, to the Joseph I trust wholeheartedly, I should tell of the mission given to me by my father.

Not yet Gracia! Wait for one more step!

It was time to change the subject.

"Joseph, I feel ready to make good on my promise. " I said hurriedly. "You can start wedding preparations. Finally, as openly practicing Jews, without a need to pretend or hide we can do the wedding."

"I am so happy, Aunt Gracia. I have been looking forward for this for quite some time. Whatever is necessary will be done."

"Presently, you are managing the business. This condition will continue after the wedding too. If possible, I would slowly like to retire and leave the business in your able hands."

"As you wish."

Dona Gracia

"I have devoted forty years of my life to business, Joseph. Isn't that enough? I hunger for spending time on developing further my true beliefs, my faith which I have neglected for so long."

"We have serious differences of opinion with Kara Mustafa Pacha, Suleiman's grand vizier, Aunt Gracia. He keeps on creating difficulties. The Sultan is aging and lets him do as he pleases and he is getting extremely influential in state affairs. If things go like that, he will be the master of the palace without giving such an impression. Thankfully, our relations with Prince Selim are good. Suleiman kept good relations with France as opposed to Spain and the Holy Roman Empire. The French King needs financial support but Suleiman refused since interest is forbidden by religion and he didn't want him to feel indebted. I am trying to collect but they cannot even pay wages of their ambassadors. The Pacha considers my efforts to be detrimental to relations with France. I have information that D'Aramon, the French ambassador with whom we have working relations, will soon be replaced."

I shared what I had in mind. "Arrange for me to meet with Suleiman."

He looked at me with eyes wide open, and then understood that I meant it.

"Well, I can try."

"Joseph, if you are not convinced yourself how can you hope to convince others?"

"OK, I will."

"I want you definitely to set up the meeting. Ask Moshe or other Pacha's than Ahmet. You had said that Rüstem Pacha was his direst competitor. Approach him. Tell him that I wish to meet with him not as a woman but as the head of the Mendes Institution."

"Aunt Gracia, Suleiman is a person who respects the freedoms of people of all convictions, speaks languages fluently but he is a Muslim. Moreover, he carries the title of Calif that he inherited from his father, that is, head of all Muslims. It would be very unusual to agree to meet with a woman, one on one!"

"Try. If he is as bright as I think he is, he will accept."

Wedding

Beginning with Joseph, the whole family asks why I still keep Pierre with me. They say he is old and that I need a younger, more agile bodyguard. Actually, they don't know what I do: Pierre is attached to me by adoration even love. No one can protect me better than he can.

I know he wouldn't think twice about sacrificing his life for me. He came with me from city to city, and stayed by me in the worst circumstances, followed me like a shadow. These are not qualities I would find in another. If he was from a Jewish mother, we could even have been relatives, though we never hinted at that. He dedicated his life to Dona Gracia, as her shadow, and was happy to live this way.

When I took Reyna and La Chica with me on the way to the Bedesten he was with us too. The girls sat in front and he by my side.

La Chica broke the silence: "Pierre, thanks to my aunt, you remained a bachelor all your life!"

I couldn't understand why she would say such a thing.

"La Chica, behave!"

"Aunty, I didn't say anything naughty. It is clear that Pierre chose to be like that willingly. He got old next to you. If our fathers were around, we wouldn't have spent as much time with them as we did with him."

I took a discrete look at Pierre. He was all pink, as if caught red handed. He sat silently.

Reyna was laughing.

"You should be ashamed and laugh at yourselves. You look

like grownups but still didn't learn how to behave like courteous ladies!"

Reyna: "Mother I share the same opinion. I think we should get Pierre married after my wedding. We should get him a Muslim bride. This way we could have people of all beliefs in the family!"

They all laughed.

"I excuse you since you are rather excited before the wedding. Pierre is not to be treated this way. He is not your toy. Be polite and considerate."

Pierre said, "Never mind."

I turned, took one look at him, and felt gratified inside. It is so unusual for a Christian to love me so much. For an instant, this flashed through my mind. Would he want to be married and have a family? Judging by his looks, the faster this subject is closed, the happier he would be.

"Pierre, we never discussed this. What do you think? Do you intend to form a family?"

He looked totally surprised:

"No, Dona Gracia!"

"Well, why not? Since we have settled in Istanbul, you perfectly well have the right to plan your life. Don't worry, you will still live with us. You will always be part of our family for as long as you desire to be."

"I am happy the way I am." Then he turned his face toward the window.

The girls giggled, and I threw a nasty look toward them.

I never wanted to get married again, not even once more. There have been men I liked in all that time but my devotion to life is of a different kind. I had one partner in my life, Francisco. I felt very close to Diogo but to remarry never crossed my mind.

One of the reasons was to be loyal to the memory of my beloved husband, not to oblige my daughter to call someone else father, and the last consists of legal matters. To marry would mean transferring control of my fortune and all legal rights regarding the business to my husband.

Sometimes I feel tired. Having to fight the pope, who unfortunately pretends to talk in the name of God, at least has convinced the larger part of the world that his decisions are divine, is really and truly tiring. They attack with all their followers and their might and we struggle to survive. This is an eye for an eye, a tooth for a tooth fight. They had no mercy on us. They tried hard to grab us by the throat, and if we couldn't escape, fight back from where we were. While engaged in this battle, if I were only responsible for myself, I might have chosen the easy way, gotten married to a suitable person, transferred the business chores to him, and enjoyed life. I felt responsible for my daughter, my niece, my nephew, the Mendes House and all the suffering Marranos. There might be a handful more people who grasp the urgency but they are mostly alone or a widow like me.

I chose the difficult path.

We strolled through the Bedesten and bought all that Reyna and La Chica wanted. I was choosing the best of everything but expertly haggling at the same time. It was Reyna who was to be married. We also planned for Joseph's brother, Samuel, to marry La Chica. It wouldn't be in the very near future but

Wedding

I wouldn't treat my two daughters differently, so I bought all she wanted too.

≈ ≈

"I don't believe you, Joseph! Won't Brianda ever give up?"

He shook his head in despair.

"Unfortunately, Aunt Gracia. It seems so. You shouldn't have sent La Chica."

"But she had missed her mother very much and heard that she was ill. What could I do? She showed a letter. I allowed her so that, at least mother-daughter would be united for once, you never know."

Joseph raised his hands in the air.

"Aunt Brianda is in very good health. The moment she can bring her daughter to Venice, and if these funds are deposited in the treasury, she will have the right to access one hundred thousand ducats.

Infuriated, I burned with rage. The issue wasn't the hundred thousand ducats. It meant that my sister would never send La Chica back.

"Joseph, please hurry to Venice. You are in good terms with Brianda. Visit her. Then explain to La Chica the real situation and bring her back by whatever means."

I guessed that he had the same idea but it wasn't easy at all. He could be caught and taken to court. Recently the pope's guards were an effective power in Venice."

This was a dangerous mission.

"Aunt Gracia, we have to really plan it well. How shall we go about it?"

I paced up and down the room, searching for a plan to

bring back my niece. A plan.

There it is.

"Joseph!"

"I am all ears, Aunt Gracia."

"Go there. Abduct La Chica from Brianda's house and marry her!"

He looked inquiringly to see if I was serious. To have such a proposition before marrying Reyna was naturally shocking to him. I went straight into the details.

"This will not be a real marriage. La Chica is thirteen, will soon have her bat mitzvah and considered grown up. Organize a fake wedding. Once she is your wife, you have the right over her estate. You both return to Istanbul, announce that you have cancelled the wedding, and go on to marry Reyna properly."

My solution seemed reasonable to me but he was hesitating:

"I don't know. Would it work?"

"Joseph, listen to me. We have no alternative. I want you to bring La Chica back. I can't leave her with my sister whose only purpose is having a good time! If it were possible, I would go myself!"

"OK, it's not possible for you to go. The moment you are out of Ottoman lands, they would arrest you and deliver you to Rome. Stay here. I will go and get her back."

Since I came to Istanbul, this is the first time I felt so depressed. Days seem longer. Disturbing news followed worse news. I wasn't sure that La Chica would be brought back and was hoping that I was not endangering Joseph's wellbeing.

Wedding

"Oh God, will this ever be over?"

Before Joseph and La Chica were caught by the pope's guards near Faenza, Joseph managed to arrange a marriage certificate from a small church, just as Dona Gracia had suggested. As La Chica's husband, he had the right to her fortune. In light of the marriage, there was no obligation to deposit any money in the Venetian treasury.

Another piece of news nearly drove me crazy.

"An aristocratic suitor declared his wish to marry La Chica."

An intricate web was woven and they were caught at the center.

"Diogo is in pain in his tomb! Last thing he would wish for his daughter would be for her to marry a Catholic aristocrat. Oh my, this is too much to bear!"

Venice didn't want to let go of La Chica and particularly of her fortune. I was informed that on a freezing cold winter night, they tried to escape by boat, were caught, and Joseph showed the guards their marriage certificate.

Finally, against all of Brianda's efforts, Joseph succeeded in bringing La Chica to Istanbul, back to me. He announced that the fake marriage was null and void.

∾ ∾

I didn't want to shadow the fun the girls were having while shopping. For Reyna's sake, I tried to stop myself from thinking of, and sharing all that had happened.

The Talmud declares that a woman can only be married of her own free will. Finally, La Chica was outside her mother's sphere of influence. I had long had in mind Joseph's brother

Dona Gracia

Samuel as her suitor. If she preferred someone else, I would consent. My main concern was for her to be happy and apart from her mother's intrigues.

The wedding ceremony took place in the synagogue. Joseph signed the Ketubah and presented it to Reyna. In that document, he affirmed his lifelong responsibilities toward his wife, the livelihood of their children, inheritance division in case of his death, and his obligations in case of divorce.

According to our tradition, first Reyna had her mikveh bath of purification after which husband and wife didn't see each other for one week. After the rabbi conducted their wedding, they were married and everybody was jovial. Reyna was showered with sweets and Joseph opened her veil. This was to refer to the biblical incident where Jacob was fooled by Leah's father into marrying her older sister. This was because he couldn't see her because of the veil before committing.

Reyna and Joseph took their places under the Hupa, covered by a tallit. As the doors of the ehal hakodesh (holy ark) were opened, the couple turned toward the Sefer Torahs and prayed. There was a big crowd and, of course, an ample minyan, that is, a quorum for traditional Jewish public worship. The prayers of the seven blessings were sung by the hazzan. After recitation by the hazzan, the shehecheyanu blessing and thanks, the hazzan sipped from the wine glass. Joseph then smashed an empty glass under his foot in commemoration of the darkest event in Jewish history—the destruction of the first temple.

As we came home, they stayed in their room for a while. We then moved to the wedding dinner, danced, and had fun.

Wedding

Although neither the Torah nor the Talmud contained objections to polygamy, I did. I asked for a promise:

"You will not marry other than Reyna!"

Now he was to oversee Reyna's possessions.

We had three thousand guests in the Belvedere palace. The celebration lasted for three days and three nights. We had a mixed crowd ranging from high state administrators to poorer people and we received them all in the best possible way.

After their wedding, the newlyweds were to live in the Belvedere palace. Joseph had built for himself a beautiful library with an extensive selection of books. Carefully selected carpets covered the library floor where he received military and civil officers called pashas, religious leaders, and intellectuals. He also had a printing press installed in the Palace.

Sultan, The Magnificent

Had I been a man going to a formal reception of the highest order, starting from the outer court, I would have been subjected to a series of rituals before coming close to the internal kiosk where the Sultan would receive me.

In reality, Suleiman with his title as "The Magnificent" considered himself at a different level then other kings. If a visiting king was of a large enough nation, Suleiman considered him only at the same level as his leading official, vizier Sadrazam Kara Ahmet Pasha. Whether an ambassador, an important mission, or even a country leader, it did not matter. If he was successful enough to be accepted in the Hasoda where the Sultan would be, he could talk at most with the head vizier. He could not look at the Sultan's eyes, and could only talk in very exceptional cases with him through an interpreter.

Missions coming to Istanbul were not automatically accepted, no matter who they were. They would be kept waiting for a week or two, sometimes even longer in lodgings that were allocated for them, to see if they would be accepted. If they insisted they absolutely needed to be received by the Sultan himself, and if he was away on an expedition, they would wait until he came back. Fortunately for them, the Sultan usually returned home at great speed with his army.

I felt as if I were part of the seraglio (palace). There were no ceremonies for me. Few people inside the palace even turned to look at me. Outside the palace, I was a rich person, perhaps as rich as the Sultan. We all wore clothes weaved from fine fabrics, ate well, and wandered about wearing quality jewels. My uniqueness rested in the fact that I was the only Jewess affiliated with the palace.

We walked behind an agha with Joseph. We passed by eunuchs who were known to be more dangerous with their bare hands than soldiers carrying weapons. Finally, we were shown to the room where we waited.

I don't recall how long we waited. It was truly boring. There was silence. Whispering with Joseph reverberated throughout the room, let alone talking in normal tones. When we did so, we were intimidated by curious and inquiring stares.

Joseph had been here before and was ready for these procedures.

Finally, an official came and said: "Follow me."

I prayed to my creator that I wouldn't err and that we would succeed in achieving our purpose. The presence of Joseph was encouraging and made me feel good. One of the reasons I enjoyed living in the capital of the Ottomans was that here we could anticipate from where the next attack might come. Here Suleiman was in full control and had the last word on all issues. High-ranking officials, called Pashas, near him could deploy only as much authority as he granted. When they were your enemy, they made it very clear to you and didn't plot behind your back. This was a value that was accepted as 'manly.'

When the colossal doors opened, we were summoned. I felt like I could die. I bowed my head and felt my heart wanting to leave its cage, a strange pounding in my ears.

"Calm down, Gracia."

Dona Gracia

A guard announced Suleiman's long names and attributes, followed by ours:

"Subjects of our Grand Sultan, Joseph Nasi and Lady Hanna Nasi."

It was my first encounter with Suleiman. When we raised our heads, I saw him in full. He looked tall or at least much taller than I am. He was standing in front of his throne but not facing us.

I immediately recognized Kara Ahmet Pasha standing next to him. A few more people stood silently in the background. I guessed they were high officials, called viziers. I immediately noticed Rüstem Pasha among them. All had long beards. They wore on their heads quilted turbans, called kavuk. By these, you could decipher their ranks. Their long robes also indicated that they were Pashas.

I was barely hearing the Sultan's word except for this last one:

"Muhibbi." It was Suleiman's pen name, his way of referencing himself in his poems.

Ahmet Pasha: "This gazelle is as excellent as the rest, my Sultan. I will ask them to add this one to your divan series too."

He nodded and repeated the last section, raising his voice, meaningfully. I was curious to understand. Later I heard the translation. He'd said: "You Muhibbi, if you wish to live in peace, be in self-denial. Renounce the world! Is there a better place to reach the state of togetherness with God than a lonely corner?"

I could sense that his ponderous movement was due not only to his nobility but also partly to his age and declining health. I too was feeling pain in my arms, feet, and waist for no apparent reason. Considering that he was much older than I am, it was natural for him to move slowly.

He sat on his throne, ignoring us. Joseph and I continued to stand at attention, respectfully.

"Speak up Pasha, have we sorted out Tahmasp yet?" he inquired about the Shah of Iran.

"Many Tahmasps would succumb to your formidable might, my Sultan. Still we should be vigilant. Iranian tricks never end!"

"What you mean is that so long as the Persians are fidgeting, Europe will be at ease."

He turned to me, I should have avoided looking straight into his eyes but I couldn't. I looked straight into his eyes. My heart was exploding. I had difficulty breathing. If I continued in that way, I would surely faint.

"Careful Gracia. Don't err!"

I repeated those words to myself.

It was clear he was no ordinary character. Imagine people wandering among us, pretending to be like us but that have the depth of oceans within themselves. He was so.

Anyway, an ordinary person couldn't carry the weight of that throne!

"Joseph Nasi, who did you bring to me?"

"My aunt and mother in law, Majestic Sultan. She is the owner of the Mendes House, the elder of our family, Hanna Nasi. She is known in Europe as Dona Gracia and also as Beatrice de Luna."

From his expression, I understood that he'd already known all that.

"She and her institution have been quite instrumental. What do you say, Ahmet Pasha. Am I right?"

Ahmet Pasha's thoughts were indicated by the tone of his voice. "My Sultan knows best."

"You never could bring yourself to like the Nasi's, could you?"

I nearly laughed but didn't. Ahmet Pasha's face was uncomfortable. Outside the presence of the Great Suleiman, he would have answered very differently. In his presence, he did not dare hint as to his true opinion. I saw Damat Rüstem Pasha, Suleiman's son-in-law, smiling under his moustache.

I felt easier. Suleiman was a human being after all. He frightened, made you laugh, surprised you. Turning his attention to me, he said, "Lady Gracia, you are dressed like Frankish women. Quite fancy, aren't you?"

My tongue and palate dried out. Was Suleiman addressing me? Asking me personally? A ruler who didn't deign to talk directly to kings, emperors, viziers or ambassadors? If I didn't have the guts to answer properly now, I might never have another opportunity!

Apart from pearls arranged around my neck, I was dressed simply but compared to Muslim ladies, I did look different.

"I tried to look as best I could, to appear in the presence of the Sultan of the world, Suleiman, The Magnificent. Whatever I did, it was from the highest consideration and respect I have for you."

I could tell from the expression on his face, he was pleased with my reply.

He nodded. "Well then, what is it that you ask of me?"

Death

Good news reached me in Istanbul. Charles V had abdicated his throne. One of my most dangerous enemies was out of the way. I was so happy, I made extra donations to the poor, and said prayers of thanks in the synagogue. I was not alone in rejoicing. The Ottomans, the French, the English, Protestants, Marranos, Jews and many others suffered during the Inquisition.

He was of noble birth but did not behave nobly. He left part of his empire to his son, Philip, and abdicated as Holy Roman Emperor in favor of his brother, Ferdinand. Charles retired to a monastery. It was ironic given that many years earlier, he had confined the girls and me to a convent. The ruin of Ferdinand didn't come from the Marranos that he had tried to obliterate but from the Protestants. The Augsburg Agreement between the Catholic princes and the ones who had accepted Protestantism, the failed expedition to France, and differences with the Pope set the stage for the end of his reign.

The greatest punishment to someone is to be left to lead a life with the power, he held all his life, taken away from him.

The fact that he had clocks hung on the monastery walls was an extra providential punishment from the most powerful. With his power taken away, lonely and deserted, close ones distancing themselves, writing desperate, unanswered letters to whomever he thought might help, passing his days missing his old might, his only occupation was to stare at the clocks and wait for the day he would die. I can't imagine a more deserved punishment that that! I now understand that to attain revenge, it is not necessary to tear one's self to pieces. Sometimes just watching and waiting for time to do that for you is best. Here we are with the good fortune to see the end of the Holy Roman Emperor.

Naturally, when the news about Charles V arrived, we could not have guessed that malaria caused by a mosquito bite would end his days on earth. There were many lessons that we would learn later.

~ ~

Having retired from the presence of Suleiman and after leaving the Hasodası, the splendid reception hall, Joseph couldn't keep himself from wailing.

"Why didn't we share the list of our needs? At least some."

"Joseph, sometimes it is better not to rush. Suleiman is an extraordinary monarch; he took his son's life without hesitation because the son acted too early. Keep your relations with Prince Selim warm. He will be our greatest asset against Sokollu and other enemies."

We picked up Pierre from a waiting room, and left the palace.

Next, news came from Ferrara. My dear sister, Brianda who had delivered us into the claws of the Inquisition, had died.

It was hard to feel happy. Although our roads had definitively parted in Venice and we sort of made up in Ferrara, I had written her off as my sister. All through our childhood, we had lived through similar experiences, were born to the same mother and father but as two sisters, we eventually reached different destinations. I was making every effort to save the Marranos from the claws of the Inquisition, and try-

Death

ing to alleviate the sorrows of our co-religionists, relocating them in different countries and growing our fortune to serve these purposes. All Brianda thought of was to be admired in futile social circles, and to run after ways of having fun. She did not try to understand our purpose. While I was going through a hellish phase of business activities in Venice and Ferrara, Brianda kept her extravagant living going as she spent evenings with the aristocracy, while refusing to let go of her chosen life as a socialite.

"Was she jealous of me?" I asked myself. I knew the answer. "Naturally. At first my father turned over the business to me. Then she saw Francisco and her husband Diogo act in the same way. If she was only after meeting her necessities, there wouldn't have been an issue. We were not cutting back on any of that. I was her target, she wanted to outdo me, her sister, without applying herself, or putting in any hard work, or making effort to grasp the ideals that drove us. I was her golden cage. She wanted to break me and she succeeded to a certain extent."

My dear sister, while struggling with me, never understood how she was so well accepted by society in their grandiose way of living. If we didn't have such a vast fortune, if she couldn't spend so much, and had been an ordinary Jewess, she would never have been welcome in those circles. The fortune I was defending opened doors for her but she never worked that out. Perhaps she couldn't validate herself to our father or to her husband, yet wanted to do the same to La Chica.

She harmed us immensely. At times, I wanted to beat her. At other times, I wished she had never existed. The unchanging reality: she was my sister.

Dona Gracia

How long can one be angry with one's sister?

We all have different natures. She could not see what I could nor grasp what I did. She defined her own motives and fought for them. Even if it seemed that we were the owners of our fortune, it was dedicated to the ones that created it to protect those who were persecuted because of the religion they were born into. As they experienced themselves, the established principle was simply helping oppressed people who were having their goods confiscated by powerful but jealous and iniquitous people using unjustifiable trickeries, tormenting them, and making their lives miserable.

As soon as I heard the news, I sat down and prayed:

"Holy Father, our Lord, our creator. The King of the universe, the one and only."

Then I called the girls.

While waiting for them, I cut part of my undershirt. If I were close to her, I might have helped in the preparation of her body, making sure all rules were correctly observed, and that she was buried in a proper Jewish way. We had staff over there and Agostino sent me a message assuring me that all issues would be tended to. Perhaps my sister was already buried.

As the law states "from earth to earth," we are not buried in coffins. The soul is immortal but the body is not. In this case, I was hoping that she was buried in one so that I could transport her remains, when the right time came, as I intended for Francisco and Diogo.

My greatest concern was that they could do inappropriate things like burning her, I couldn't take that. Who recited her prayers? Were they the correct ones?

I had so many details in my mind that were bugging me. I

Death

thought I was done with her but I wasn't.

"Could I have handled her differently? Wasn't there a way to convince her?"

I knew it was too late for all that and I ached deep inside. My younger sister is leaving this world before me.

Reyna, La Chica, and Joseph entered. I opened my arms wide without a word.

The three of them entered and wrapped their arms around me. La Chica had understood from the cut in my undershirt.

"It's mother, isn't it? Is she dead?"

She was breathless and started crying torrents, as did the others.

I couldn't hold back my tears. While crying, I tried to console La Chica when I could. Her handkerchief was soaked.

"Don't be so sad and sorrowful! God took her to his heaven. Thanks to Him, she died as a Jewess. All of us will, when the time comes."

I had trouble talking. I knew I had to wipe away my tears and be strong. My intention was to strengthen their morale.

The only one who was in charge of himself was Joseph. He was drying his tears.

"My mother! My mother!" cried La Chica. "Mother. Why, why?"

Her wailing continued.

"Be strong," I said.

Following a knock at the door, Samuel entered. He walked in Joseph's steps. I hoped he would marry La Chica.

"Just heard. My condolences."

He went straight to La Chica and hugged her. She cried for a while on his shoulders.

Dona Gracia

We waited in silence for her to calm down.

Quite a while later, she was her normal self again:

"Aunty, should we go? Can we be there before the interment? Can they wait?"

I shook my head to both sides.

"Unfortunately, my child! Perhaps, by the time we heard the news, all this might already have been done. You know that funerals cannot be delayed. Let's mourn properly for our loss."

La Chica, as if waiting to hear that, took hold of her undershirt and made a cut with the scissors on the upper side; Reyna followed, then Joseph and Samuel.

"What are we to do, Aunty?" said La Chica, with swollen red eyes. "You know best. What should we do?"

"We will act as if the interment was here, close to us. For a whole week, we will not take a bath. We will always wear the torn undershirt, no leather shoes, no jewelry. Joseph and Samuel will not shave. We will cover the glasses and sit on the floor, go to the synagogue for morning prayers and have the mourners' Kadish spoken by Joseph and the rabbi. Whatever our duties are, everything will be strictly according to tradition."

We silently cried for some time. I couldn't imagine that I would feel such a burning pain inside for Brianda. Particularly I felt for La Chica, poor girl, losing her mother after her father.

"How stupid of me!" I thought. "I wish I had forced her to come here and kept her with me all along!"

The Doctor

After the week of mourning for Brianda ended, it was time to return to business. After this, each month for a year we were to attend synagogue prayers. After that, each year on the day of her interment, we would light candles and have the kadish said in the presence of a minyan, perhaps with a rabbi, at home. We were alive and had one purpose. We nearly followed Brianda to the grave.

Our butler, Jorge, was agitated when he came to me.

"Dona Gracia, La Senyora, a catastrophe!"

"What happened?" I exclaimed worried.

"Illness! Emilia died!"

Emilia was our maid who had come with us from Venice. She had a weak constitution. She often coughed but never so badly that she had to stay in bed.

"You don't say? Why did she die? When did she fall ill?"

"A few days ago. I thought she would recover. She could rest for a few days, then go on with her work."

"What do you say, Jorge? Why didn't you tell me? Oh, my God! Call the doctor immediately!"

We had a large retinue in the Belvedere palace. Many men and women slept in their respective quarters. The ones who wanted to, or when they married, could use a separate room.

Instead of waiting for the doctor to come, I got dressed and went down to the maids' section. I sensed a strange mood. The air was heavy. This unexpected death caused anxiety all around.

Dona Gracia

Whoever saw me coming stepped aside and saluted me respectfully. To Jorge who was right behind me, I said: "Show me then!"

"Second door on the right, Dona Gracia. Let me open the door!"

He rushed in front of me and opened the door.

In the room with two more beds, Emilia's cooling body was still on the bed. From the silhouette appearing from the sheets that covered her, I could tell how thin she was. The girls sharing the room with her were crying, bending and twisting handkerchiefs in their hands.

"Lift the sheets!"

One of then pulled it open. I was startled.

"Oh, My God!"

Emilia's skin was covered with spots. Her tongue, seen from her open mouth, had turned brown. Blood that leaked from her nose had traced her cheek and dried. She looked as if she'd started to rot, no different from a cadaver brought out of the grave.

I quickly drew the scarf over my mouth and stepped back.

"This is the black death, the plague!"

The girls screamed and pulled back, terrified.

"Everybody out? Is there anyone who is ill?"

Jorge: "A few complained of feeling weak and having some aches but…"

"İmmediately, gather them in a room for the doctor to check. Right now!"

There was no reason for me to stay in the room any longer. I left. I was going up when I saw the doctor arrive. A young

The Doctor

guy, one of the Jewish doctors. I knew him, one of the ones I supported.

"Abraham! Catastrophe!"

Concerned, he drew, close to me: "What happened Dona Gracia? Are you ill? I was told it was one of the maids."

"No, it is not me. She is in her room. Doesn't look good at all. It might be the plague!"

"I'll check immediately."

He went in. I didn't return to my room. I thought I had guessed correctly. That terrified me.

"I hope I am wrong."

A little later he came out, pensive.

He spoke, standing a step or two in front.

"Lady Nasi, it looks bad!"

He threw a glance at Jorge.

"No problem. Jorge is our butler, in charge of the servants."

"Dona Gracia, you seem right. It looks like the plague. I can go further. It is the plague. We must take precautions. She should be interred immediately and her grave covered with lime! Burn all the materials in this room, and starting with this one, walls in all rooms must be white-washed with lime. Is anyone else ill?"

Jorge answered: "A few more."

"Take them into a separate room and let no one else go into that room."

I was more scared for my girls than for myself.

"Son, what should we do?"

"Stay away from all who might be ill. Be in contact only with people you are sure are healthy. Even from others too, for a long time, until the illness leaves the city."

I thought I knew much of what was happening but, it seems, I had no clue about these happenings!

"Is the illness spreading in the city?"

"We had such news for a few days, but they were individual cases. It seems it has become epidemic. I had heard of ill people near the port area. I thought they contracted it from the ships. If possible, stay away from that area for a while. If you have enough food, I would even suggest that no one go out at all.

Luckily our pantry was full. We had enough to keep us going for weeks. So what, we can do without fresh fruits and vegetables.

"Throw lime to toilets and sewers. More attention to cleanliness. That's all that you can do for the time being."

I turned to Jorge: "Did you hear the doctor?"

"I will do it all, Dona Gracia."

The Plague

In the following days, two women and one man were ill. We put them in a larger room and isolated them. Getting close to them was restricted, and strict hygiene regulations were enforced. Everyone had to wash their hands frequently and well. Two years earlier, we had another epidemic but it passed without much harm. With that experience, I knew well what had to be done.

We waited at home, stupefied, and got all street news from Joseph.

"It is said that some neighborhoods were devastated. Cadavers are seen over the Golden Horn and over the Bosphorus. Patrols are liming whatever they find. All movements, including ships, in and out of Istanbul are blocked. Doctors are roving through town, going from home to home separating healthy people from those ones who have contracted the disease. It is not only in Istanbul. The illness was recorded in Damascus and Baghdad. The epidemic spread over Europe and inflicted England the most, causing many casualties. Strict precautions were taken in the palace too. It is said that the harem was transported to Adrianopolis and doors at the palace are locked. I instructed our staff in regions where the illness is dense not to come to work. At home, take care and do not leave home. This will soon pass, I hope."

Reyna was most worried:

"God forbid! I am terrified to think that we might be contaminated too."

La Chica:

"What if we are infected? How would we know? Sometimes I don't feel so good."

I looked at her with fearful eyes.

"Wish for good things!"

Joseph was relaxed.

"This disease spreads in filthy environments. The symptoms are fever, headache, trembling, weakness, stains on the skin, groin, and backaches. If you had any of these, we would have noticed."

Thank God, none had these indicators.

To prevent going to public places, we skipped Shabbat prayers at the synagogue and did it at home.

"When will this black death go away!"

They all looked at me at the same time. It seems I had read their minds.

Aftermath

It took us a full month to see the disease called Black Death subside. In the end, we lost several of our staff, and didn't have the opportunity to bury them with a proper ceremony.

The city population was considerably reduced. Work re-started but we had difficulty finding enough help. While Joseph tried to get business on track, I distributed gifts to the remaining members of our staff and advised them on hygienic precautions.

The harem and Hürrem had been on my mind. Among many rumors circulating during the epidemic, at one stage it was said that the Hürrem Sultan was a victim. Fortunately, this turned out to be false.

Using this as an excuse, I went to visit. Each time I saw her, I grew more and more fond of this lady. I felt love for her as well as respect for the power she commanded. Compared with Christians, Muslims traditions were closer to ours. They were more like us. Hürrem Sultan turned her influence into power by remaining always in the background, managing her activities behind the scenes. She was being accused of the death of Prince Mustafa but her duties were well over her head. The talk of the town was that the siblings, Selim and his younger brother Bayezid were at each other's throats. She was internally worn out by having lost Prince Mehmet and her youngest, Cihangir, who was born crippled.

Dona Gracia

"Struggling with difficulties is our mutual destiny, my Sultan." I said while chatting. "Yours and mine too."

She shook her head, a distant look on her eyes.

"Come, let's walk a little."

"Gracia, I often wonder how my life would have evolved if I lived as a simple peasant girl, going about my ways. What happened after I was torn from my family, I have no clue and don't remember anything about my village. This is the worst part of aging. You relive your memories. I vaguely remember the face of my Mehmet. I go to bed at night hoping to see his face in my dreams. I pray to God not to test us again with our children!"

"Amen, my Sultan. Perhaps you would have had a second chance. You might have had a different life. That was not a possibility for me, my Sultan. Because of our bloodline, be it a peasant girl or member of the Mendes family, it wouldn't matter, we would find ourselves always as the target of some malice. We never felt at home anywhere. I have a recurring feeling that my eyes are so tired, I cannot see or even guess at where the next attack will come."

"Here too?"

"No, my Sultan. Finally, here we found some tranquility. God bless Sultan Suleiman and you."

We were enjoying the lovely weather from under a tent in the garden. I followed her into the garden.

In the region bordering the city walls, the gardens were full of flowers. In the distance we could see the Bosphorus, a massive galley and smaller sailboats moving along the water. Several colorful caiques decorated the shores.

"I hadn't seen such flowers in Europe, my Sultan. They are so beautiful but they fade so fast and don't open up until the next year. Is my information correct?"

"They are called tulips. During the winter, when it is cold, the buds that look like onions are planted and their flowers appear in spring. You can see them everywhere in Istanbul. Except for black, you can find them in all colors. Suleiman sent them to a king in Europe as a gift."

"You are the rarest and most beautiful flower I have known in Istanbul, my Sultan. Please don't think of it as flattery but only a flower like yourself could make Suleiman fall in love so deeply and truly."

She smiled. Her young maids, dressed in colorful clothes, followed us. When I saw another group coming toward us, I slowed. To show respect, I positioned myself a step behind her. I recognized the approaching group. It was Rüstem Pacha and his wife and Hürrem Sultan's daughter, Mihrimah Sultan, and their servants taking advantage of the lovely weather.

As they came close, they respectfully saluted Hürrem. Rüstem kissed his mother-in-law's hand.

"My Sultan, I pray that you are in good health."

"Thank God, Rüstem Pasha. Are you out for a stroll too?"

Mihrimah was silent. An enchanting woman, she reflected her mother's beauty but at first sight you couldn't tell: she didn't possess the qualities that caused her mother to be respected and loved so dearly by Suleiman.

"What to do, my Sultan, we manage to find a little time. Since our dear Sultan commissioned us to perform new duties, we seldom find time for ourselves."

The Doctor

"It is so. We gratify our yearning by spending time with Mihrimah Sultan."

Hürrem Sultan turned to her daughter:

"Mihrimah, how are you doing?"

"I am good, mother. It's like the Pasha said. We are walking a little."

Hürrem shook her head making them know that she grasped the meaning of their words.

I knew that Hürrem was the greatest supporter of the Pashas that helped the Pasha become the head vizier. She had succeeded in the past but, since he was among the group that had Prince Mustafa strangled, he was deposed and replaced by Kara Ahmet Pasha. This didn't last long. When the head vizier was executed, he regained the seal of head vizier. Everyone knew that it was it was thanks to Hürrem.

She pretended as if this was our first meeting.

"My Sultan, you have a guest. Who would she be, I wonder?"

Hürrem Sultan:

"Gracia Nasi, a businesswoman and leader of our Jewish subjects."

Mihrimah:

"Oh, you are the person who sells these rare jewels! I saw some that my mother bought. Really amazing."

"My Sultan, please accept my respects. If you would, I have ones but they are not a match for your beauty. If you send for me to come, I can show them."

"Good."

Rüstem:

"Don't even think about it!" he said. "Stay away from the daughter of Suleiman The Magnificent. She is the most beautiful jewel in the whole world and I have never set eyes on anything comparably beautiful. Naturally, apart from our Sultan."

With these words, he had made his mother-in-law happy too.

"I will send for you," said Mihrimah, not paying attention to him.

Rüstem seemed to be vexed but I knew he couldn't oppose Mihrimah. It was very difficult for Muslim women to obtain a divorce, though the daughters of the Sultan were exempted from that restriction. They could divorce the moment they wanted to. When the lawmaker was the father, there was nothing more natural than to protect his daughter.

Rüstem turned to Hürrem again:

"My Sultan, with your permission. Otherwise I will not be able to meet Mihrimah Sultan's expenses. I need to go and work some more."

Before taking leave, he again kissed his mother-in-law's hand.

"Come, Mihrimah!" she said. "Come with us. We can wander about a little more."

Then she looked my way. "Well then, what flowers are there in the palaces in Europe, Gracia? Tell us about it. How do they smell? Are they as good as ours? What perfumes do women use? Is it true that women put masks over their faces and have fun together with men?"

"That is true, my sultan."

"Well then how do they know who it is they are with?"

The Doctor

"I don't think they want to know, my Sultan. The reason they use the mask is not to know and not be known."

"Wow-ee!"

"My Sultan, what I wish to tell you today is a little different. Whenever you wish, I can tell you all about foreign palaces and the way they had fun but as we were discussing previously, my life is full of obligations. While an extraordinary Sultan like yourself is running the harem of the greatest empire in the world, I am trying to help my co-religionists."

"I know."

"My Sultan. They are in great difficulty in a city called Ancona."

We wandered around the gardens for quite some time and I had the opportunity of relating to her the sufferings of the Jewish people. How we were oppressed in the past, hoping for salvation by prayer, by appealing to the conscience of people, and how all that came to nothing. Even agreeing to apparently change our religion didn't stop the traumas.

Ancona was a port city where people were engaged in business and didn't bother much about religious segregation. People from all countries and of all credence traded here in peace, and lived in harmony. Because of these favorable conditions, many Marranos rushed to settle in large numbers. We had experienced similar conditions previously in Antwerp, Venice, Ferrara, and now it is Ancona. As the population increased, property and rental prices went up. In a short time, Ancona became a better alternative to Venice.

All restrictions for Jews and Muslims were lifted. Religious discrimination did not exist in Ancona and it was purposely overlooked when people reverted to their original religion. In territories controlled by the pope, however, books in Hebrew and the Talmud were collected but, in Ancona, no books were burned. In many other places in Europe, religious books in Hebrew were collectively burned. A few years ago, such burnings were organized in central Rome, Campo dei Fiori Square, and in Piazza San Marco in Venice. While there was an arrest warrant for Joseph, he could freely go in and out of Ancona.

Pope Paul IV ended the freedoms where they had existed. He ordered that all goods of Jews be confiscated to strengthen the treasury for the war in Spain. The Marranos, who lived in Ancona, as well as the ones who came from the Ottoman Empire, were thrown into jails. Some were murdered.

I could tell all that to Hürrem Sultan. She understood and felt my pain.

"If Sultan Suleiman doesn't interfere, Jews as well as Muslims will be massacred!"

She said she would talk to the Sultan and share what I have told her.

I shared these realities to all guests that came to the Belvedere palace, all Ottoman traders as well as members of the parliament and whoever would listen. It was time for a common and serious answer to be given to Paul IV's atrocious machinations.

The Inquisition, Again

The Ottoman palace was getting much valuable information from the Marranos and it was important to keep it flowing. Luckily, Prince Selim and Rüstem Pasha appreciated this activity. Information is more valuable than gold.

The fact that Nurbanu Sultan's origins were Jewish made our operations easier, and Joseph was known to Hürrem Sultan and she liked him.

Rüstem Pasha gave a note to the Consul of Ancona and requested that an end should be given to all that, He also brought the issue to parliament. It was unacceptable that the goods of Ottoman subjects are confiscated by the pope. This caused consecutive bankruptcies that made it difficult for many Ottoman businessmen to pay their taxes and this in turn negatively affected the Ottoman treasury. The Ottoman fiscal system was built on tax collection. When it incurred difficulties, such as this, it made our struggle easier and raised our hopes.

On hearing that Suleiman agreed to receive me, our optimism doubled.

Procedures for the reception of ambassadors were repeated, one by one, except that Joseph was kept waiting in the Sultan's quarters, Enderun.

I will see him by myself!

On this visit, I was not as excited as the first time since I was more experienced. Still, the greatness of the load of my responsibilities kept me on edge. I transferred my presents and spoke after I was asked to. Remembering his comments about

The Inquisition, Again

my attire, I dressed more simply and without pearls. Perhaps because I was a woman or wasn't a state person, the scribes who recorded all conversations were not taking notes. I had eye contact with Rüstem, and for that, I was grateful.

"The Magnificent Sultan Suleiman, our protector, we are in deep sorrow. Unfortunately, the person who occupies the throne of the Papacy, Paul V, is oppressing all people, who are not Catholic, even Christians of different sects, but mainly Jews and Muslims. They torture people who they try in rigged Inquisition courts, confiscating their goods, making a festival out of burning these people savagely at the stake."

I tried to be as explicit as possible, speaking totally from my heart. Rüstem Pasha made supporting comments.

Finally, Sultan Suleiman rose from his throne, I could see that he was infuriated by what he had heard.

"Rüstem Pasha!"

"Yes, my Sultan!"

"I want a letter immediately to be written and sent to the pope. This is an edict!"

The scribes hurried to get their ink jacks ready. Suleiman continued:

"Suleiman who is the Sultan, emperor greater than all other emperors, son of Sultan Selim, an emperor of higher rank then all emperors, may God make victorious till eternity."

In his letter, he stated that he heard that some merchants of Jewish origin, who were in Ancona for the purpose of trading, had their goods confiscated and that this damaged the Ottoman treasury. He asked for this to stop and for detained to be released.

Dona Gracia

Once the edict reached the Pope, Jews were freed but Marranos who were New Christians were not released on the basis that they continued to live as Jews after they had converted to Christianity.

Instead, they were burned alive.

I was kicking the walls in the Belvedere Palace, going crazy. My broken heart was in pieces.

"Still they insistently burn people. Didn't they have enough! Not satisfied with this atrocity!"

Pierre wanted to say something to calm me but to no avail!

I am furious with the Marranos too. They have no foresight. If their business is performing well, they imagine it will always stay that way. How many times do we have to go through the same experience? How often should our trust turn to naught? While we can see the dangers from Istanbul, why couldn't the ones in Ancona see it coming?

"Giovanni Pierre Carafa! Burn in hell!"

I had a lot of information about him—his ancestors were a noble family from Naples. On his mother's side, he was related to Portuguese aristocrats. Given the title Following the Belief, he was raised by Cardinal Oliviero. Pope Paul III invited him to Rome to take part in the papal reforming committee.

In 1536, he was made a cardinal. When he became the Bishop of Naples, he reorganized the Inquisition in Italy. At the age of seventy-nine, he became pope and took the name Paul IV. His first act was to crash the reformist Catholics. He believes there is no salvation outside the church. He uses the Inquisition to try people with whom he is uncomfortable this court. Even cardinals are targets of his anger. He issued a law stating that non-Catholics, Protestants, and heretics cannot become pope. In that way he prevented cardinals, who were his opponents, from becoming pope.

Paul IV had a *Prohibited Books Index* compiled with prohibitions against printing any Protestant books or the Bible's Italian and German translations. He installed his incapable relatives into important positions. He knew nothing but evil and harm.

In the synagogues, the biblical manuscript is kept in a cupboard directed toward Jerusalem. It is called Ehal. These cupboards were broken into and Holy Scriptures defiled by rubbing them with pork. I even heard that pig carcasses were inserted into cupboards. The harassment continued.

Paul IV, who published the famous report called *Both Nonsense and Inappropriate,* created the Roman ghetto obliging Jews to live separately from Christians and in lower quality quarters. The Jews, who were forbidden to go out at night, had to wear clothes indicating their religion. Heavier taxes were imposed on Jews, and Christians were forbidden to address Jews as Sir.

Jews would not be able to trade anything other than second-hand textiles. There could be no more than one synagogue in each city.

The synagogues outside the ghetto were converted into churches. Jewish physicians were forbidden to care for Christian patients and could not acquire property.

"Not only hateful but also stupid! It both impoverishes Ancona and prevents the treatment of Christian patients!"

The Inquisition in Ancona gave the courts the authority to

check if Marranos were heretics or converts. Paul IV claimed that Jews were guilty of "betraying Jesus." Pope Paul IV hated the Marranos and considered them as "heretics and dishonest" advocates who would return to Judaism at the first opportunity.

"As if we were volunteer Christians!"

He sent an apostolic commissioner from Napoli—Giovanni Vicenzo Fallongonio, who hired spies to uncover those who had returned to Judaism. Ignoring several signed commitments and guarantees issued by earlier popes, Pope Paul IV had those who had returned to Judiasm arrested. The fortunes of jailed Marranos were impounded, their property confiscated, and all receivables by the Marranos were transferred to the Papal treasury under the guise that the pope was the intended recipient. The pope was buoyant in taking Marrano property and money.

Around one hundred Marranos of Portuguese origin were thrown into dungeons. A few managed to escape. This time, bribery was not enough to erase accusations. Interrogations took place in the streets—with the public watching. People in chains, in the middle of the city, were forced to confess that they had left Christianity and returned to Judaism.

"It was like that when I was a child. Humanity didn't improve at all!"

I heard that Fallongonio had accepted bribes from about thirty people, appropriated their properties, and then disappeared after the pope discovered what was going on. Fallongonio took refuge in Genoa outside of the reach of Pope Paul IV.

The fifty remaining Marranos were not permitted to

The Inquisition, Again

mount a rigorous defense. Cessare Della Nave, who replaced Fallongonio, was even more unscrupulous than his predecessor. Some of the accused argued that they had not been baptized, and so it was not possible for them to fake Christianity. They claimed that they had always been Jewish. The Pope claimed that all Jews in Portugal sixty years earlier had become Christians and that no Jews remained. Consequently, their defense was rejected outright. Some of the detainees confessed to returning to Judaism and were exiled to Malta to work as oarsman for the rest of their lives. The punishment was so harsh, it was better to be executed immediately rather than work on the ship, chained and flogged constantly. Enough horrible food was supplied while rowing to prevent starvation. If the ship sank, the oarsmen drowned.

The church was doing the judging, but with a twist: civilian authorities carried out the executions.

These executions drove me mad:

In April 1556, under the ritual of Auto da Fé (Act of Faith) in Ancona, civilian authorities burned people in Campo Della Mostra square.

Brought to the square chained to each other, they were Simon Ben Menahem, Samuel Gaskon, Avram Falkon, Joseph Oheb, and the only woman among them: Dona Yayora.

After the charges against the prisoners were read aloud, the "honor" of starting the fire was given to an aristocrat. From Istanbul, I could hear their screams and smell the burned flesh. The savage executions would not leave my mind. My stomach contracted many times. I heaved and vomited many times.

Dona Gracia

Two days later, they burned the second group. After the first day, there were less interest and fewer spectators but still there was quite a crowd. Izak Nahmiyas and Salomon Aguadis were burned alive, tied to a stake with fire lit under their feet.

As was Molho Avram Kirilio, Davit Nahas, and Avram Ispanya one day later.

One of the greatest doctors in Europe, Amatus Lusitanus, was warned and he managed to escape in a flight to Pesaro. He cared not for the goods and property he'd left behind but for his library, which contained volumes of treatment information and experiments.

In June, two groups chained to each other were tied to stakes in front of a crowd and delivered to the flames. I can hear their prayers thanking God for dying as true believers with their unshaken faith in the one Creator. They did not renounce their beliefs in the end. Joseph Barzion, Salomon Yahya, David Sakriaryo, Joseph Vardai, Joseph Pappo, Yakup Kohen, Yakup Montalban, Avram Lobo, Avram Kohen and a child: Davit Reuben.

My spies from Ancona and Yakup Mosso, an old friend, were among those who were burned. I expected him to be among the people that Suleiman saved. Some claimed he was not burned, that he committed suicide. I never learned the truth.

The Inquisition committed an error. They meticulously recorded the names of everyone they executed. I knew these names would not be forgotten for eternity though The Inquisition did not know it.

Our sorrow was so vast, we did not know who to grieve for.

The Inquisition, Again

But this time we would not sit and wait like lambs waiting to be slaughtered.

"Not this time!"

"Ma'am, who are you talking to?"

I turned around. Pierre is still with me.

"Pierre, I am fuming with rage! They burned everyone, including Mosso. Burned alive! I would like to have my hands on the pope, the so-called man of God! I am so sad, so angry! Furious!"

"I can see, Dona Gracia. For nearly two hours, you have been pacing the room from one end to the other."

I stopped. It shouldn't have been this way. I could not sit still. I did not realize the passing time.

"It will not be this way, this time!" I said, looking into Pierre's eyes. "This time we will make them pay for it, Pierre!"

He was quiet, waiting for me to continue. What was I to say? I did not even know how to respond or how we should make them pay. By having the Ottomans on our side, we could save some of our co-religionists and be effective to a certain extent.

"This time, we need to react much harder and give a powerful answer to their wrong doing!"

When did it become dark? I didn't notice? Pierre stepped out of the room. I sat in a chair, watched the outside, but saw nothing. I felt deep sadness and anger. It was not in vain that it was dark so early. I saw lightning over Istanbul and rain. Torrential rain.

I felt relieved inside. The flood was like a divine sign. The rain was not in vain. I felt a premonition that this rain was a sign from the skies that the fires that burned our hearts will be extinguished once and for all, together with our sorrows.

I walked to the balcony oblivious to the thunderous rain. Within seconds I was soaked wet but didn't care.

I now knew the penalty for those who took refuge behind the church.

Fighting Back

Pope Paul IV accepted Sultan Suleiman as the protector of the Jews, even outside his own territory, but continued the Marrano massacre under the cover of the law. The pope's nephew, Duke of Pagliano, replied in a letter to the French Ambassador in Istanbul:

"The pasts of all Marranos have been carefully examined and they are being judged fairly. After proving their crime beyond any doubt in a just court, there was no other option than to enforce local laws."

When I first brought up the subject with Joseph, he couldn't believe his ears:

"How come? Can it be done?"

"Joseph, there has not been a single action by the Jews acting as a single body since the Diaspora. I also know that it will be difficult, but it has to change! If we remain victims, there will be many coming to slaughter us with their knives. It is time you showed them that we are no longer victims!"

"Will everyone agree?"

"Why shouldn't they? We will use religious leaders. All the rabbis, all of them will advise their congregations and the businessmen in their congregations. They will put pressure if

The Inquisition, Again

necessary. They will force them to act together to cease these injustices."

"As Jews, as Marranos we will all boycott Ancona."

"Exactly! Marrano, Jew, or Morisco, it makes no difference. No commercial ship will sail to Ancona. All of us will stop trading with Ancona. So, the wealth they are after will slip through their fingers. It will be a lesson for those who dare try such atrocities again."

He took a deep breath.

"I don't know if it can be? One of the reasons for our sufferings is the greed of some Marranos that have never enough. Their passion for trade and avidity to accumulate wealth is unquenchable. We can all make mistakes."

"True, but now we must act as one, and if it is Goliath that is our enemy, we should still fight. We have seen that forgiveness of cruelty never helped us. It's punishment time now! We have to incapacitate them, hurt them, and make them regret their bad acts. History is full of incidents where first we were invited and welcome into many countries, then robbed and slaughtered. Whenever they need the money or whenever they are in crisis, they check us out first. Isn't this explained in the Torah? Wasn't Joseph the Grand Vizier of Egypt but after the Jewish population increased and they got rich, their properties were confiscated and all were enslaved? Moses took us out of bondage from Egypt and saved our lives. We had the same scenario in Iran, Rome, Spain, Portugal and England. Who knows, maybe in the future we will not have to live through this morbid cycle again. Maybe our action will bring to an end the unjust treatment of Jews in Europe. Bigots targeting us, politicians confiscating our wealth, murdering us, and kicking us out—maybe this will be the last time."

"You're right, Aunty. I agree with you on many issues, but…"

"I know, too. This will not be the final solution but at least it's time to show we are not easy prey."

"OK. I'm with you."

Finally, I smiled.

My plan was simple: all Jewish merchants will embargo Ancona Port.

It was enough for the rabbis to believe in the plan and convince their congregation. I knew it would not be easy, but I was hopeful.

The rabbis were powerful. They had the excommunication tool at hand. The person who was excommunicated was excluded from the congregation. He could not do business with any member of the community, nor could he even speak to, or be seen with them, or with his relatives. Most of the burden that would ensue would be borne by us, anyway. But the Mendes Institution alone would not be enough. It could not be convincing unless it is a decision taken by all. I would begin by talking to the rabbis.

Only one question remained: Which port will take Ancona's place?

There was no way that trade would stop between East and West. When applying a boycott to Ancona, we needed to find a proper substitute. Duke Ercole was ready and made promises reassuring the wellbeing of the Marranos. But Ferrara was not a city on the sea but it was on a river. The second alternative, Pesaro, near the town of Marches, was a port previously

The Inquisition, Again

attached to the Urbino Duke. There were Marranos living here who had escaped from the Ferrara epidemic and also a small Jewish community from past times. The Duke of Urbino, Guido Ubaldo had opened his doors.

I spoke to the rabbis in Istanbul, and sent letters to Salonica, Bursa, and İzmir to explain the situation in great detail. Duke Guido Ubaldo also hoped that this enormous trade would transfer to his city, and to make it happen, he offered many guarantees. Ancona wanted to compete with Venice and was prepared to keep the doors wide open. The Duke invested in the harbor and its surroundings to bring it to an acceptable level, and for this, he spent heavily.

I wove a web like a spider. Slowly, slowly but determined, I wanted to make sure that, in the end, the execution would be spectacular and that it would set a fine example for all concerned.

The Jews living in Pesaro found an effective way to convince other Jewish communities to support the boycott. They commissioned Yuda Faraci, who, with difficulty, had saved lives from the Inquisition. A talented orator with a strong emotional message, Faraci travels to different communities to describe details of atrocities committed in Ancona. He visits many synagogues, graphically describing barbaric practices, including torture, committed by the Inquisition.

"Our purpose, my brethren, is to punish evil and reward the good—to show that Jews are not helpless against their tormentors, and that we are strong when we are unified. They tortured us. They broke our arms and dislocated our legs.

Dona Gracia

They took our intestines from our stomachs and removed our nails. They defiled the Torah with the blood of pigs. They destroyed our synagogues!

"Not a single ship should go to that damned port! No one should do business with blood-stained Ancona! We should not visit or send our goods or allow our ships to go there!

"Do not forget that during the savagery called Auto da Fé, your religionists were burned alive. Don't forget that, even when they knew they were going to die, they went with joy and pride, reciting full heartedly our holy prayers before surrendering to the flames! Their souls see us and wonder what we will do in response. Let us comfort them in their graves!"

The words of Yuda Faraci persuaded most of those who listened.

I invited him to Istanbul.

He came and spoke in Balat.

The campaign, propagated in waves, was successful. Nearly everyone agreed to a trial period of eight months. At the end of this period, the action would continue or be reconsidered.

Ancona Boycott

The boycott showed its effects in a short time and Ancona was quickly overcast with dark clouds. In difficulty, the administrators were in shock. Bankruptcy, declining tax revenues, unpaid civil servant salaries, unfulfilled commitments, disappearing jobs. Those who failed to sustain their families found fault with the leaders. Public order swiftly deteriorated as no new cargo arrived and necessities became scarce. This, in turn, led to an increase in prices. Goods, especially from the

The Inquisition, Again

Ottoman Empire were unaffordable. Prices for textiles, silk, leather, and minerals increased. Goods destined to the Ottomans spilled over into the streets.

Traders in Ancona sent a delegation to the pope. They wanted him to reverse his policy but Paul IV had no such intention as he was living comfortably in luxury. Continuing his extravagant life, he ignored the difficulties of the people of Ancona. News was also coming from Pesaro. They were pleased with the additional commerce and sent a short but clear thank you message:

"You are giving an unforgettable lesson to these ferocious people. The blood of our martyrs is still on their hands…"

When growth was too fast, Pesaro experienced some difficulties. The infrastructure was not ready for trade volume this size. There were problems with getting the ships to approach the port and the port was not safe enough. Storage was limited. I know that trade likes speed. The other merchants would also be unhappy. The only hope was that the Duke would continue to invest, develop the infrastructure quickly.

The Jews in Ancona were again targeted. They were held responsible for the troubles in the city. Some communities, especially Salonika, participated in the boycott on the condition that everyone would commit. While the Ancona community tried to break the pope's resistance, they also communicated with Jewish merchants that were old acquaintances and demanded that they should help to lift the boycott. If the boycott continued, they would be the ones to pay heavily and those who continued the boycott would be responsible for their ills.

While Istanbul and Adrianopolis respected the boycott,

Bursa was the first to grumble. Having a large interest in the silk trade, Bursa merchants claimed they suffered disproportionally and were being used by the Marranos. They argued that all Jews should not be sacrificed for the benefit of the Marranos who were after bigger profits and that a fairer solution was needed.

"The people burned in Ancona did not affect each community in the same way. Aunt Gracia, while some of us were feeling their pain others didn't care as much. Unfortunately, the reality…"

The commercial activities of the Ashkenazi community who escaped from persecutions in Eastern Europe and came to Istanbul were not so important. They couldn't understand the seriousness of the situation as well as did Spanish-born Sephards, Romaniotes who have lived in Istanbul since Byzantine times, and Marranos.

Resistance against boycotts began with passing time. The Jews of Ancona sent letters to the Ottoman rabbis through Rabbi Shosse Bassola. They explained that if the embargo was not terminated, they would go through hell and their lives would be endangered in which case they would hold the Marranos and the Istanbul community responsible.

"I think we're losing the boycott struggle!"

"No Joseph! We will resist until the end. Do not lose hope! If the boycott breaks, this time the Duke of Pesaro will be angry because he has invested all his fortune in the port, trusting us. He will feel deceived. Wouldn't his wrath fall on Jews living in Pesaro?"

The Inquisition, Again

"In that case, we have to be firmer. Otherwise, this opportunity will slip through our fingers. I can see it."

"I will meet Joseph Ibn Leb. He is a powerful rabbi. I will personally explain the importance of the boycott. I will ask him to meet and persuade all rabbis in Istanbul, one by one. Don't they know that switching ports has had the strongest negative impact on the Mendes Institution? If we are accepting these difficulties and not giving up, the others should be with us. Throughout our lifetime, we fought for our lives. If they want to change the destiny of Jews, this is the time to hold on. If they give up so quickly, and are not ready to accept some small losses, they will lose much more. We lost our friends, we lost our relatives. Even though Suleiman came to our aid, that wasn't enough to persuade the pope."

Ibn Leb trusted us. He made contacts and reported the results:

"I have talked to many rabbis. I told them of the importance of saving lives. But it's hard to convince Yosua Sonsino. The fact that Ancona Jews wrote to him about their troubles and lamentations caused him to seriously doubt the outcome of the continuation of the boycott."

"So, the winds have changed…"

I did not want to despair but I was getting negative signals regarding the future.

"There are allegations that Marranos don't come to the Ottomans but remain in Christians lands—where they are not wanted and are persecuted—because they don't want to forgo the profitable businesses they have. This could even be a reason for their excommunication. Many claim that instead of boycotting, it would be wiser for the Marranos in Ancona to come to the Ottoman Empire…"

"Sonsino's head must be quite mixed up."

"So. I guess when he decides which of these theses is correct, he will act accordingly and do what he thinks is right in order not to sin. It will be wise for you to be prepared, Dona Gracia."

"I cannot understand. He is also a man dedicated to religion, and, moreover, a member of the Sonsino family. How can he refuse punishing people who destroyed synagogues and defiled the Ehal with pig's blood?"

He drew a deep breath.

"True, different people can see the same issue from different angles, Dona Gracia… What you see is seen different by some others. While you are uncomfortable because they entered synagogues, others are arguing that 'those who continue to live in a country where synagogues were defiled' are to blame! When you think we should get help from your co-religionists, others ask, 'What are they waiting there? They should come here…' supporting his thesis."

"I understand."

Those opposed to the embargo campaigned stating that the port of Pesaro was not capable of meeting the needs of captains and business man and, on top of that, a disease epidemic was spreading in the city. There was no epidemic but saying there was reduced people's desire to go to Pesaro.

I invited Sonsino to the Belvedere Palace. He came with two respectable people from his synagogue.

The Inquisition, Again

Joseph put in front of Sonsino the document carrying the signatures of various eminent rabbis who supported extending the embargo.

"Reverend Sonsino, I must go to Adrianopolis to meet the Sultan. I ask you to add your signature in support of this text."

Sonsino was surprised. As an experienced and respected rabbi, he did not immediately decide issues presented to him but analyzed them in minute detail first.

"I think you know my views on this subject. You and Dona Gracia, whom I respect very much, know that I consider the Jews of Ancona and don't want them to come to any harm."

This is the aim of all of us. For the first time, as a united people, we have shown our power. Those who destroy this solidarity are responsible for future persecutions!"

"Joseph, you are a merchant. I am a religious man. I don't choose the most profitable way but I have to make a decision where everyone will not suffer. You need to show understanding in this regard."

"Reverend Sonsino, we are the ones who have been most negatively affected and our losses are growing daily... My aunt, Hanna Nasi, Dona Gracia Mendes was tried in the Inquisition. They issued search warrants and arrest instructions. We lost our friends, our comrades, our relatives. Some were tortured, others burned. You need to understand this too! After all, don't we all share the same ideal? For Jews to be free, not oppressed or persecuted... Am I wrong?"

Sonsino looked at me and at Joseph. He was sure that we both thought similarly.

"I am signing this certificate, but adding my comments...

If the Ancona Jews are faced with serious physical danger, my signature will be invalid."

"This will not do!"

Joseph was getting impatient. Sonsino was one of the most respected religious men. He originated from the famous Sonsino family, the printers.

I felt obliged to intervene:

"Joseph! Please. Our rabbi is completely free to act as he pleases. But if Mr. Sonsino puts such a clause in the petitions, if an important person like him acts that way, will the other rabbis sign? Let's say you added your reserve and the Inquisition heard about it. Won't they be encouraged to start threatening the Jews of Ancona? If you add the clause 'If there is a physical attack, the signature is invalid,' the Inquisition will interpret it as, 'If you want to get rid of the boycott, then do physical damage to Jews!' Even if they had no such intention, upon hearing of your objection, they will do it. I do not think the pope will miss this opportunity."

"This is a possibility but I cannot act otherwise!"

The other two men beside him thought similarly. Unable to stand it any longer, Joseph exploded: "Then don't do anything!"

The mood in the room was as cold as ice. Even if I agree with Joseph, I disapproved of the way he put it. I was surprised.

Sonsino had the last word:

"In that case our meeting is over, with your permission."

Before I could open my mouth, they left without even shaking hands.

The Inquisition, Again

Joseph was furious—and struggling not to curse behind them.

Ester

I was offended. Depressed. So, maybe for this reason I gave up my old passions and kept myself busy with trivialities.

The boycott was off. The efforts I made to prolong it did not help. After the meeting with Sonsino, the disagreements became more pronounced. Some of the rabbis were pressured by businessmen in their congregation not to extend the embargo. The Sephardic people knew what it was to lose their country, their homes, what the Inquisition was all about and favored extending the boycott. The Romaniotes supported the local Jews of Ancona. Then, events unfolded like dominoes falling. The ones from Salonika withdrew their support for the embargo. What remained from the struggle was the Jews of Pesaro who feared the pope's revenge.

We were embarrassed for Duke Guido. It was a difficult to collect enough money among communities to meet the Duke's losses.

When some Marranos, defeated by their greed, sent goods to Ancona harbor, others said that was "unfair competition" and immediately wanted to send goods to Ancona too. Similar requests came from Adrianopolis, Avalon, and Mora congregations.

The boycott was lifted.

I invited Ester Handali to Belvedere Palace.

Reyna and La Chica insisted on joining the reception to be close to the woman they'd heard so much about.

Dona Gracia

Ester was more commonly known as Kira. Her husband, Eliyah Handali, was a merchant who provided jewels to the women in the new palace. After his death, Ester took over the business and became close to Hürrem Sultan. Kira is the nickname given to women closely connected to the harem. I knew her main investment was Nurbanu Sultan. But I do not really want to talk business at all.

In order to make her feel very important, I had the table laid with my finest porcelain. Teas made of aromatic plants from China and the finest Cypriot wines where readied for her to drink, if she pleased.

"I heard that the decision to lift the boycott demoralized and saddened you..." she said.

I was happy that Jewish people like me, particularly women, were taking part in the business life but Esther entered directly into the conversation, pushing me to talk about subjects I was trying to forget. I couldn't help wondering whether her intentions were friendly or hostile. I tried to look into her eyes, but what I saw was a veil. Ester was very capable of hiding her inner thoughts. Like a wall... A barren wall.

"Unfortunately, a very important opportunity was wasted, Ester..." I said, not being able to hide my sadness. "We could have shown that once the Jews are united, we can be very powerful. We could have proved they could not crush us, but it didn't work."

"Why?"

This was the word I was to hear from her many times from now on: Why?...

Ester used this word luring me to say more on what she wanted to hear.

The Inquisition, Again

"We suffered the biggest loss but we could not explain well. We invited Yuda Faraci back to Talmud Tora. He talked about the dangers awaiting the Jews of Pesaro. I suggested that a committee be formed but our competitors argued that this committee would be biased. On whose side would they be? I invited Musa Segura, the President of the Mayor Synagogue, and asked him to convince Rabbi Sonsino. A delegation of five people explained the situation again. Sonsino suggested that a delegation be sent to Ancona, as well as to Pesaro to study the conditions in both cities. Even if we said we didn't have enough of time, he was not convinced. I mobilized everyone. I have encouraged the Portuguese and Spanish Jews to insist on the continuation of the embargo. I got a promise from some rabbis about applying excommunication. Boycotts can be successful only with unanimity, not by a majority vote only. Everyone needed to join. In order to persuade the Ashkenazi community, we undertook to compensate Joseph Eskenazi's loses. The group opposing the boycott was also working. A group trading with papal states and Italy asked Sonsino for his opinion in writing. Sonsino, in his written statement, insisted that the declaration we prepared in favor of Pesaro had no religious validity, that while somebody's safety was secured, someone else's life could not be endangered, this being contrary to the principle of equality."

"I know."

"He sent his article to rabbis outside the Ottoman Empire. He endangered the embargo. When two other important rabbis agreed to sign his declaration, many followed. We obtained the support of leading rabbis, like Joseph Karo and Yakup Mitrani, but this was not enough. We could have given the pope a lesson he would not forget but we were soon defeated. The Jewish union disappeared soon after it was formed…"

"Of course, that wasn't the end of your loss."

Maybe Ester couldn't compete with me abroad but I realized she certainly was well aware of everything going on in the city.

"Yeah, so… Two hundred thousand ducats were collected and sent as compensation for his losses to Guido Ubaldo in Pesaro. I warned but they didn't listen. The duke took the money but got close to the pope. He did not surrender the Marranos to the pope but he exiled them. Now there will be no peace for the Marranos until Paul's death! He was doing well before. Now it is as if he won a victory again!"

I felt drowsy as we continued talking. La Chica's question came to my rescue:

"Mrs. Ester, we heard that you sold jewelry to Hürrem and other sultans. How are they? Are they as beautiful as we hear? What are they doing in the harem?"

Ester smiled. She regretted opening the boycott issue and wasn't so interested in continuing that discussion.

"Very… Very beautiful! Nurbanu Sultan is a stunner!"

Reyna: "Is she more beautiful than Hürrem Sultan?"

"Look, I cannot say anything about her. We evaluate each within her own frame. Hürrem Sultan was a woman like the moon, like the sun. But what can you do, at day break the moon disappears. The sun sets when the time comes. A new star rises in the harem. Nurbanu Sultan's turn is coming."

"I heard you were close to Hürrem Sultan," I said. "Everyone says she trusts you."

The Inquisition, Again

She was obviously proud of that, a pride that verged on arrogance!

"She never says no to me! But I don't like to boast. The people are spreading these words around."

La Chica: "Well, how friendly are you? How did you get close?"

Ester did not answer that. Obviously, she didn't want to share her secrets with us. Compared to our endeavors, her stuff is quite unimportant. I didn't intend to compete with her but, if we had the opportunity, I wouldn't hesitate to sell jewelry to the palace.

"Master craftsmen will only share their secrets just before retiring."

"Oh, don't be like that! Obviously you are very connected to the palace…"

Esther was silent. She took a sip from her wine glass.

I knew it, even if she chose not to say. She was well introduced into the palace, especially to the harem. She was a kind of bridge between the harem and the outside world and she was using that access very well. She was successful at what she did, but I did not appreciate her ways very much. She could have used these relations for the benefit of her co-religionists.

"La Chica, I heard you are preparing for a wedding. I want to show you a few pieces."

La Chica looked at me. "No. Thanks. My aunt fixes all that."

Ester didn't know it, but I had unique and valuable jewelry in abundance that was more precious than what she could show me.

"I saw your gift Dona Gracia… The one you presented to

Hürrem Sultan… It is so beautiful. I wish you had sold it! It's got an expensive color."

"Let her wear it joyfully… she also receives us very well even if we are not on as intimate terms as you are. I have received her support on some important issues too."

She was a bit upset. She was jealous of her helping me and not her.

"Is that so?"

Synagogue and Yeshiva

Our relations with the French ambassadors, especially Joseph's, had always been excellent. In 1557, instead of Codignac, Ambassador De La Vigne suddenly began representing France, and for no reason at all, we acquired a new enemy. As if it wasn't enough for him to be rude and unpleasant, he also bore a grudge against Rüstem Pasha and was trying to harm us both by bad mouthing us here and there. Initially we ignored him but when he started insulting Joseph as a usurer, this upset Joseph and provoked him to claim the money he had lent to the king of France.

When we asked for payment of their debt, De La Vigne wrote to Paris saying Joseph is a heretic and payment, therefore, is not required. The French king was in financial trouble and any excuse not to pay suited him. It was further claimed that, as a Jew, Joseph wasn't allowed to lend money in France and it was unlawful for him to engage in financial transactions. Therefore, the French man argued, Joseph did not have the right to a receivable. In various attempts to avoid just debts, these arguments were put forward in countries such as Austria, Belgium, the Netherlands, and Hungary.

As it was traditionally done, Joseph Nasi bought the rights to collect taxes by paying substantial amounts to the treasury up front and committing for the rest. Joseph was an Ottoman citizen, and as such, his rights were protected by the state. The Ottomans had already pressured debtors in favor of the Mendes Institution. Joseph conveyed the situation to Prince Selim and to Rüstem Pasha.

Dona Gracia

The winter was harsh and a surplus of snow that fell on Istanbul brought everything to a stop. Massive ice blocks floated over the Bosphorus. Due to the severe cold, many products in the market were either frozen or sold out. People didn't leave their homes unless they had to, and the mosques, churches, and synagogues could not get their congregation to attend prayers. Poorer Jews around Balat and Galata suffered. I received particularly negative news about the situation of new arrivals.

We spent quite a bit to lessen their burden and we were not alone: the Hamons and Handalis also aided the poor. There were no Jewish beggars, and if some were in difficulty, the community took care of them. In dire situations, people of means made financial efforts to relieve the burden on poor Jews.

"The sacrifices you make for the needy are known by all," the rabbi said. "During these hard times, it is thanks to you that many families can enjoy a hot meal."

"Thank you, dear rabbi, but this is our duty. I didn't invite you to talk about this. I have something else in mind."

His eyes opened wide. "Of course, I am listening."

"I have a problem, and a big one."

His curiosity increased thinking that my question would be on religious matters.

"Before I was born, many Jews were converted by force to Christianity. As a consequence, we had to live like Christians. We were brought up as good Christians and had strict training on matters regarding the Catholic faith. As a consequence, we are ignorant on many issues regarding Judaism. Once I regained my true faith, I felt the need to compensate for this shortcoming. Dear rabbi, in the spring I want to start a new synagogue and a yeshiva. They would be open for services and also serve to cater to religious needs, such as training new rabbis. What do you think?"

"Dona Gracia, that would be great!"

"I am glad you think that way, dear rabbi."

"Well then, where do you plan to build it?"

"In Balat."

The rabbi's joy quickly disappeared.

"But there is a synagogue already in Balat. Establishing a new one would create problems."

"Why?"

"Dona Gracia, there is a principle in Istanbul that each Jew should belong to only one synagogue. This is so that taxes used in many causes can be collected and tracked. I wouldn't know who would want to transfer to your synagogue. They would be afraid of their respective rabbis. Empty synagogues are not desirable by any one of us."

"Would it really be an issue?"

"Unfortunately! As a man of religion, I don't like putting it this way but you must be careful and treat these issues that will come up diligently."

"Let that be your only concern, dear rabbi. We can modify the tax collection system."

He looked blankly into my eyes. There was such a system functioning in Istanbul since Byzantium times and nobody had thought of changing it.

It was not difficult to get permission for the synagogue,

Dona Gracia

but Sinan, architect to Sultan the Magnificent, was commissioned to design an array of projects at the time. He informed me that he couldn't design the synagogue and yeshiva as he was engaged in building mosques, inns, arches, and bridges, which I admire. Fortunately, it was not difficult to find another architect though he isn't the genius that Sinan is. When the academy was finished, I informed everyone that they could come to pray and no tax would be charged. I was thinking that this would please my co-religionists, especially those with lesser means. Nevertheless, objections immediately cropped ups. Those who control synagogues in other districts were disturbed by the appearance of the new synagogue, thinking they would lose their most important source of income. They threatened to punish those who left their synagogue for another.

I didn't care.

"Joseph Ibn Leb, you will be in charge of the synagogue. It will be your responsibility. I cannot think of a more able person for this task."

He smiled.

"It is my honor to accept this assignment, Dona Gracia. But I would first like to congratulate you."

"I did not do anything to deserve congratulations, Mr. Leb."

"You did. The Karaim, Ashkenazim, and Sephardic already had differences of opinion. At least you have got them to agree on one issue! They all agree that you have done wrong by changing the tax system!"

We laughed.

"They think what I'm doing is wrong, but I think I'm doing the right thing. What is your opinion?"

Synagogue and Yeshiva

"By accepting the mission, I have already declared my views."

He was clever and capable person with words and an effective speaker too. He preached in Bursa and Salonika successfully and gained the trust of the congregation. He did not hesitate to support the boycott, and struggled to prolong it.

"It is said that you left Salonika because of the plague epidemic. So the black death offered us at least this benefit…"

He inhaled deeply. "They say whatever they want to believe."

His voice was sad. It is my fault that the mood of the man who laughed a while ago had become so somber. I tried to summarize: "I am sorry. My goal was not to demoralize you. I didn't believe a word of it."

"Dona Gracia, this is not a subject I like talking about but providence is testing me in many ways. One of my sons was murdered by an ordinary killer. The other drowned while swimming. If I stayed in Salonica, believe me, I too would have drowned, I couldn't breathe."

I felt like I was choking. I didn't know the unbearable ordeal the person sitting in front of me had gone through.

I blundered, "I am lost for words; I am sorry."

"Don't be sad. Believers have to be patient during these periods of trial. In your leadership, our crowned lady, we will continue to serve and continue our work. That's what counts from now on."

"Crowned?"

"The crown of love for God and for human beings. This is the crown I see on your head."

"Please don't embarrass me! What is it that people like us can do compared to a scholar of your caliber? A drop in an ocean perhaps."

I didn't want him to compliment me. "I also invited Joseph Caro to take classes. He said he could come only from time to time. He couldn't come as a full-time teacher. He did some valuable work in Safed academy. I think he intends to remain in sacred land from now on."

"I also thought so."

Portrait

While I was busy with plans for the synagogue, one of many artists who came to town to paint and to sell his paintings was at our door. When Giuliani, a Venetian, wanted to visit, I was not in the mood. My interests centered on religious undertakings—which I had involuntarily neglected for so long. If the visit was about that, I would have welcomed him but people with different interests kept arriving. Still if I hadn't wanted to hear news from Venice, I would have refused him.

"Honorable Dona Gracia, thank you so much for seeing me."

"Our door is always open to artists, Mr. Giuliani." I said in a polite tone. "If you are here to paint an old lady like me, you will have difficulty convincing me!"

He was excited and acted as if he possessed important information he wasn't sure he wanted to share.

"My Lady, I would very much like to paint your portrait. In fact, I saw the vast empty spaces on the walls of the Belvedere Palace. If you like, I can remain here for several months and decorate the walls with family paintings. I can even do beautiful scenes for you. They will be paintings that people would admire. Your generosity is known to all."

"No, no. Thank you. I don't need all that. Our house is ornate enough."

He decided to come out with whatever it was he had hesitated to share.

"OK. I was thinking of showing you something quite different."

He took one of the rolls that he'd brought in his hand. "I have a valuable work that you will definitely want and it will serve you well."

"Oh really, and what would that be?"

He opened the 'valuable' piece of work on the table in front of me.

I looked but couldn't make anything of it.

"What is this?"

"Come on, Dona Gracia! I know she was your friend and that you met from time to time."

I looked with a blank stare. The panting was of an ordinary looking woman.

"Really, I don't get it. Who is she? I have many friends."

"Roxelana of course, Hürrem Sultan. Who else"?

I looked closely. The woman on the painting didn't have the faintest resemblance to her.

"Did you paint this after seeing her?"

"Unfortunately I didn't have that possibility! It is so difficult to reach her majesty. I did this after gathering information from people who had seen her. I was told this looks like her."

I smiled.

"Mr. Giuliani, you can be sure it does not look like her. OK, she is red haired and has green eyes but even these are not accurate."

He seemed disappointed.

"Really?" He showed me another.

"This one too, like the previous, does not resemble Roxelana."

Paintings were also sold in Europe as portraits of Roxelana although none of them resembled her. Suleiman, who was known for his affection for her, would never allow her to pose for hours in front of a foreign painter.

"You were well informed that her skin is pure white. The painting is faulty from head to toe! To start off, Hürrem Sultan is not Turkish. You drew from your imagination a typical Turkish lady. Hürrem is a completely different character. I would have difficulty in describing her."

"I really came here to learn from you and ask for your help. I want to paint her correctly. The reason I wanted to make you a present of this one was for you to convince her. I heard that you were one of the few who could make this offer to her."

I was flattered but had no idea why I should do this.

"She wouldn't accept!"

"Please, Dona Gracia. I beg you. If you can convince Hürrem Sultan, I will be obliged to you until the day I die. This way, the lady that ranks with kings would be known to the world as she is."

"And you, as the only painter with this achievement would become very famous!"

Synagogue and Yeshiva

No sound. That was his purpose: to be the only one who had painted her and he would become rich. I could guess that, like many painters, he would secretly make an extra copy, present one to her majesty who would compensate him handsomely and sell the other at an exorbitant price in Europe.

"OK, since you insist, I will try but don't expect that she will accept."

He enthusiastically kissed my hands.

"Thank you. Thank you so much, noble lady! If you do this favor for me, I would never know how to repay you."

Hürrem Sultan looked very tired when she received me. For reasons I ignored, the acceptance of my application to meet her was unusually delayed. Days later, I heard she would receive me. Though it was early in the morning, she looked drained.

"Dona Gracia, I heard there was an important issue you wanted to discuss with me. What is it?"

Mihrimah Sultan, who inherited the beauty of her mother, was present and her maids were with her too. I noticed they were all a little stressed.

"Hürrem Sultan, your majesty, I brought you a gift."

"Is it jewelry, again? If it's so, I don't have much interest in it. You can show it to Mihrimah."

"No, your majesty, it is this."

I took the canvas from my bag and slowly unfolded it.

She looked at the painting by her feet and couldn't make sense of it.

"What is this, Gracia? Is there something I should notice?"

"Your painting, my Sultan!" I said not hiding my smile." To

put it better, this one too is being circulated as your portrait."

Mihrimah Sultan bent to look at this curious painting.

"This ugly woman cannot be my mother. This is plain insolence."

"Mihrimah Sultan, I would guess this was not done out of insolence. Rather it is due to ignorance. All painters, who hear of Hürrem Sultan's beauty but have never seen her, draw the person in their imagination. I have seen many such paintings in Europe but none are as beautiful as our Sultan."

Hürrem: "Thank you, Nasi. That was in my younger days."

All of us objected.

"Not true at all!" we exclaimed.

"My Sultan, the reason I brought you this painting was that a painter begged me to do so. A Venetian painter, who claims he has studied in leading schools, wants to paint you. At first it struck me as inappropriate then, excuse my presumptuousness, I decided to transmit his wish thinking it might interest you. We all know how much Sultan Suleiman is dedicated to you. Perhaps, with his consent, you might accept."

She laughed.

"Dona Gracia, my portrait has already been painted!"

"Really, my Sultan. I didn't know."

"Of course, you wouldn't. No one knows. It was years ago. My face was drawn but, only those within the harem know. People who have never seen couldn't know. One of the miniature masters painted it, and it remains as his secret. Those who saw it thought it was someone else though it was of me."

"Naturally, my Sultan, as you wish."

She held her head in her palm and continued to study the painting.

Synagogue and Yeshiva

"In miniatures, they cannot draw people true to the original. Not like in the mirror. Big head, small mouth, swollen cheeks. Above all, this one has depth. You cannot find that. It doesn't exist in miniatures." She turned to her daughter.

"My Mihrimah, what do you say? Would it be a sin?"

Mihrimah Sultan: "Dear mother, you know that our religion doesn't see in good light the painting of faces. It would be your decision."

She pondered a while longer.

"Why not? If we don't like it, we can throw it into the fire and burn it."

She pointed to the fireplace in the back, ornate with porcelain tiles. Everyone present shook their heads in approval.

"OK, Dona Gracia, send him over and he can make my painting."

"Are you serious, my Sultan?"

"Sure. Since we are still beautiful, at least he can do it now so that all who want to, can see the real thing."

"Your wish is my command, my Sultan."

Shocker

Leaving the palace, I was still under a spell. I had serious doubts that my proposal would have been considered while Hürrem Sultan again proved unpredictable. Hürrem was still the lady who transferred the harem from the old to the new palace. She was active in state affairs with the power of sending any Pasha to the gallows. In Ottoman tradition, it was the first time a Sultan had an official marriage and a woman had written letters to kings. It was Hürrem who succeeded in all that.

Dona Gracia

After Giuliani finished painting her, the world would see what she really looked like. See the kind of woman she is.

I asked for Giuliani. They found him in the inn where he was lodged and brought him to me immediately.

"Signor Giuliani, I have spoken to Hürrem Sultan."

"Is this true? When there was a delay, I despaired. Please tell me. Did she accept?"

I waited for a few seconds to observe his curiosity.

"Please, don't torture me by keeping me waiting!"

I looked at Pierre, who listened intently.

"What would there be in it for me, if she accepted?"

He was surprised: "What can there be, you already are so rich? My profit of a few ducats would be meaningless to you."

"No Giuliani, I am not talking about money."

He relaxed.

"I get it. I will make your painting too. Yours, and if you wish, all of the your family together."

"It is an irresistible offer, and yet you should know how many painters offer to do that already! My demand is of a different kind."

He got closer. "I am listening."

"A second painting."

"Which second painting?"

"Hürrem's second painting. The one you intend to make and keep secretly for yourself."

He panicked as if caught red handed.

"Where do you get this idea? Why should I make another one secretly?"

"Naturally, to take it to Europe and sell. Don't worry this

will remain between the two of us. But you will not take the second to Venice but leave it with me. You will be paid handsomely. Whatever the price, I am ready to pay."

This time he wasn't denying. He was thoughtful.

"OK, I count on your well-known generosity, Dona Gracia."

"Have no doubt!"

The next morning, I was still in bed when there was a loud knock at my door. I panicked and got up. Suddenly I was dizzy. Jumping out of bed so quickly moved my blood pressure. My heart was pounding.

"Who is that?" I said waiting to open my eyes to see more clearly. "What is happening at this hour of morning?"

"Mother, are you awake?"

It was Reyna.

"Yes darling, come in, what happened?"

She entered, I saw Pierre standing in front of the door.

"Catastrophe, mother, Hürrem Sultan!"

"What happened darling? I will have an attack. What happened to the Sultan?"

"She died, mother. Hürrem Sultan has died!"

France

The Sultan was gone, and the whole world was curious, the likes of which had not been known before. When the oldest, Prince of Suleiman, was killed, the children of Hürrem Sultan became heirs to the throne.

She wasn't my relative. It couldn't be said that we were all that close but still, I was shaken.

"It is said that she could have been poisoned," Joseph said.

"Really?"

"If you ask me, that is not so. She, and those near to her, knew it was woman's illness. They kept it secret."

I had a sudden thought.

"So, that's why she accepted!"

"What did she accept?"

"Joseph, Hürrem Sultan had agreed to have her portrait painted by Giuliani. I had suggested it to her."

"Pity, he missed this opportunity. She will be buried in the garden of the mosque that Suleiman had built. He is so sad, it is doubtful he will take care of state affairs. This is not good for us. What is there to do?"

Suleiman grieved for Hürrem Sultan. He was so saddened that he had renamed a city in Iran to Hürremabad to honor her.

We couldn't get the French to pay their debt but Suleiman had his own problems to tend to. On the one hand, he just lost the love of his life, and on the other, his younger son, Bayezid was having problems with his brother, Selim, who had run to Sultan Tahmasp, Suleiman's rival.

We kept our business going. It was decided to send an ambassador to France and explain to them the situation in all openness. A Chavus was assigned for that. I heard that, in spite of all the blockings, Chavus had reached France.

The new king sent someone called Petremol as a representative to Istanbul. We knew the purpose of the visit beforehand. He was to ask the Sultan to withdraw his support for Joseph. Gustiani was to explain that the debt was unfounded in that it had been contracted under unlawful conditions, and that France had the full right to refuse payment.

We enjoyed once again the advantage of having obtained information early on. When he arrived, his purpose was not only uncovered but also defeated before he even had an opportunity to plead his case. All hopes were exhausted.

They would either pay or lose Ottoman friendship.

After Charles signed peace agreements with France's enemies, leaving him less threatened, he desisted from making payments. It was explained to Ambassador Petremol that Suleiman and Prince Selim were sensitive to this subject. Petremol understood the urgency of the matter and suggested to his king that he should make payments. The debt was at one hundred and fifty thousand gold coins. This could be paid in stages, sixty thousand first and the rest during the winter.

Charles had used the same excuse, saying it would be unlawful to make payments to a Jew.

He asked Suleiman to tear up the bills of exchange as unlawful and to annul the debt.

"Christian law allows kings to borrow large sums from Jews, use these funds for their own purposes but don't allow repayment!"

If we were in France, or a city in Europe, an easier way would be chosen. We would be sent to court, which would rule that, as heretics, we did not have rights to repayment of debt.

Ottoman law, called Kanuni—or law-abiding— decreed that just laws ruled this country and brought about harmony. Suleiman, who was also called Kanuni, did not accept such

shallow excuses. Correspondence between the two countries continued. Letters were written and answered. Ambassadors came and went.

Joseph bought wine produced in the Mediterranean and Aegean coasts. He had agreements with wine growers in Chios, Sicily, and Cyprus to produce high quality wines for his trade. Joseph had the world's best wine cellar and continued sending the top vintage to Prince Selim.

"We should swallow Cyprus itself, not just the wine, Aunt Gracia. That's my full purpose!"

"Joseph, what do we need Cyprus for? I heard that it is a hot and complicated island. Moreover, it is said that it is flooded with corsairs."

"Aunt Gracia, what have we sought for all of our lives?"

I thought but never imagined what he was getting at.

"Joseph, you don't mean…"

Cyprus

Like Istanbul, Salonika was a major city with a dense Marrano population. The palace intended to develop the city and make it an active port. Early arrivals settled near the Lisbon Synagogue in quarters where other Marranos, who originated from the same area, lived. In Ortakeuy, eleven Marrano neighborhoods developed. In Salonika too, as immigration continued, several new settlements emerged. The need arose for more synagogues and the Old Lisbon Synagogue was divided into two, with one becoming the New Lisbon Synagogue. Still, that wasn't enough. Moreover, there was competition to attract the wealthier and more capable Marranos.

Dona Gracia

I didn't want a similar struggle in our community. I disclosed my plan to Joseph:

"I want to build a large enough synagogue with a capacity to accommodate all newcomers."

"Another one? Where?"

"No, not in Istanbul. In Salonika."

He thought for a few seconds. "It would be a good idea. You were helping the ones outside Istanbul anyway. This way you would leave a work that would be permanent."

"OK, but I decided you should be in charge of this one."

"It's fine but my other projects..."

I interrupted:

"Your other endeavors are important but don't neglect this one. The name of the synagogue to be constructed will be 'Livyat Hen.' I am thinking of Moses Almonssino to head it. What do you say?"

"Aunt Gracia, when you open a subject for discussion, usually you have planned every detail in your head. I would say that, since you opened this subject to me, you must have seen the finished building in your imagination."

He knew me well.

"There will still be objections. Some are complaining about the large number of synagogues. When each one is trying to enlarge its congregation to increase its revenues, there are many who will be unhappy about your new project."

"We can overcome that, Joseph. What's important is to convince Moses Almonssino. He is intelligent, flexible, and knowledgeable. He is the best candidate we can find in that vicinity."

"So, convincing him will then be my duty."

Synagogue and Yeshiva

"I have full confidence in you."

I trusted him, really and truly. From the day he shared his dreams about Cyprus, I had something else in mind:

"I have to disclose the secret to him and transfer my responsibility!"

I was not rushing but there was no one more appropriate than Joseph around me.

Once the funds were in place, the construction was not an issue. Particularly the fact that the palace had no reserves in providing the necessary permissions, the main handicap was surmounted, since no one had a say over the Sultan's, Muslim, Jewish or Christian, no one could utter a word. There was of course always some who would oppose a project such as this but my experience showed me that, even if you do something good for the community, there would be some grumbling.

"Almonssino put forward some conditions. They were all reasonable and I accepted."

"Great. Further."

He smiled.

"You have another plan in your mind, don't you, Aunt Gracia?

"Yes, we should build an academy so that all who want to improve their religious knowledge will be able to do so."

"Naturally you planned it all meticulously. Who do you think should head it?"

"The Talmud teacher, Samuel de Medina. We will transfer the rent revenues from our properties in Salonika."

Though he had become "persona non grata" in the Christian world, Joseph continues to work, with the support of the palace, to transfer technical and political information from Europe to the Ottomans. An addional reason for the hatred was that he had managed to dodge their plan to confiscate the Mendes House. Suleiman trusted Joseph enough to send large sums to Selim with him.

The fact that the Ancona boycott was circumvented was a serious disappointment for me but I haven't stopped and my life's ambitions are not over. The Ottomans have been kind to us. We are well treated and have a good life. We can work unimpaired but we do not know what might happen in the future.

My eyes tired. I was mid-circle, not knowing where the next attack could come.

After Joseph shared his ideas about Cyprus, what he said reminded me that I had neglected some important issues.

It was time.

"Joseph, sit opposite me."

"Aunt Gracia, why do you want to talk to me at this hour?"

I put my finger to my lips, asking him to be silent.

"I waited for all to go to sleep, even Pierre."

He lowered his voice.

"You are worrying me. Is there something bad?"

"No, Joseph. Your words about Cyprus brought to mind a subject I have been keeping to myself for too long. A secret entrusted to me, an inherited duty. It is time for you to know."

He looked at me, appreciating the seriousness of the matter.

"The subject I will explain should not be shared, even with Reyna. I will know. Act for this purpose but until you find the right person and the right time, you will not disclose it to anyone! If the span of your life is insufficient, you will transfer it appropriately."

Tiberias

While several families had the means, few dedicated themselves to these issues as we have. Our biggest advantage was that we were close to the Ottoman palace. I do not want to be remembered as a saint or as a hero. The Ancona boycott taught me that however hard I tried, there would always be some, among my co-religionists, who would not agree.

We had come a long way but continued to ponder what the final, irreversible solution would be, one that cannot be altered by a change of administrators.

We had seen many who promised the world and then forgot all about it. Our disappointments were so many, I couldn't count them. The land that did not discriminate against Jews was the Ottomans, giving us hope that we had come closer to a sustainable existence.

Our only hope was to work with the Ottomans who were not bigoted and who held all of our sacred cities (Jerusalem, Safed, Hebron, Tiberias) within their territories.

The sacred lands were added to the Ottoman Empire by Selim I in 1516: Jerusalem, Safed, Gaza, and Nablus were the four cities with a military presence. In this area, four places were considered most sacred by Jews for generations: Jerusalem, Safed, Hebron and Tiberias.

Of course, we always had a yearning for Jerusalem. It was sacred and it was our imaginary capital. Asking Suleiman for this city, apart from being most unrealistic would be folly. Jerusalem was sacred not only for Jews but, to a lesser extent, for Muslims and Christians too. Asking for Jerusalem would create many objections and harm our relations with Suleiman.

Hebron, at the heart of the sacred places, held the tombs of Abraham, Jacob, and Isaac. Hebron was small and nearly inside Jerusalem so it wouldn't be wise to ask for Hebron. Jews lived in peace in Safed, an old learning center with many academies and famous cabalists. There too was an Ottoman regimen that formed a bastion of protection against invaders. That made it safer too. The Ottomans already had a well-developed judiciary in Safed.

The remaining possibility was Tiberias, which was in an appalling state.

Despite all difficulties, this was the only option where a Jewish state could be built. The target was set. We proposed to Suleiman a reasonable package that addressed financial and strategic advantages for the Ottomans. A people known to be friendly and had proven reliability to the Ottomans, our forming a state in this no-man's-land would also serve as a defense against threats coming from this flank. Above all, inhabitants would fight for their own lives against intruders.

After having the plan studied, Suleiman accepted the proposal.

"Joseph, I don't believe it! This is a dream come true!" I said pacing the room in excitement. "Can I believe it? Is it a reality? Did Suleiman gIve us Tiberias?"

He was always one step ahead of me and carefully considered the down sides.

Synagogue and Yeshiva

"Aunt Gracia, now we face the most difficult challenge. How do we convince Jews in the diaspora to settle there?"

My joy came to a quick end.

"What if they refuse to come?"

"It is a possibility. Even those who live in Europe have a steady livelihood and a certain level of comfort there. They might not want to uproot their families to go to a place where even animals have difficulty surviving. It would be hard to maintain a livelihood, and it would be insecure. It is not protected against invaders and it lacks even minimal amenities. What would they find when they arrive—no housing and no work?

"You are saying, at first, we have to create reasonable conditions."

"Yes, otherwise the fact that we are given Tiberias would have no consequences."

"Then we should concentrate on this. We have to create an environment where there is a need for tailors, bakers, carpenters. Don't forget that it is sacred land! People who yearn for freedom would come. Suffice it to say that we must create the infrastructure needed and open the route to Palestine. The Jewish people will realize the meaning of this miracle, presenting itself centuries after the dispersion, and they will come."

"Aunt Gracia, you haven't seen Tiberias yourself. But you know its location, east of the Lake of Galilee."

"I know this is where Jews lived in large numbers. Due to its thermal baths, King Herod Antipas built a city there and named it after Tiberius Claudius Nero. Herod Antipas was renowned for inflicting suffering on Jews. I haven't seen the condition Tiberias is in, but I know that when the city grew, the Galilee lake was transformed into the Sea of Tiberias.

The Jews later fought the Romans and lost the war. Joseph, son of Matthias, commanded the Jewish army. When Joseph joined the Roman army to advise Vespasian, founder of the Favius dynasty, he changed his name to Josephus Flavius. Romans sacked the area and leveled all houses and buildings. By presenting the keys of Tiberias to the Romans, Flavius saved it from complete destruction.

Tiberias was the city where important Cabalists and Talmudists dreamed of teaching and studying, and it is where they lived and settled for a while yearning for the privilege of being interred. Even if now, Tiberias is ruined, it was believed that being interred in sacred soil cleansed the soul of all sins. This was especially important to Marranos who had unwillingly denied their religion.

In the year 68, Jerusalem had become an impossible city to live in because of Roman oppression. After many Jewish revolts, the Romans forbade Jews from living there for eternity. With this punishment, chaos ensued, and in 70, the second temple was destroyed by the Roman Emperor Titus.

Rabbi Shimon Ben Yohai wrote a famous compilation, the Zohar, which entailed cabalistic notions—mystical interpretations of Hebrew scripture—that cleansed the city spiritually, and cleared the way for Jews to resettle there. Yohai wrote the Zohar in Tiberias, which had previously been defiled by Romans, remaking it a sacred city.

Until then, the Sanhedrin met in Jerusalem. This was the

highest Jewish court consisting of a president, a Nasi, who was elected on the condition that his origins were in the Judah tribe and his lineage could be traced to King Solomon. Our Joseph Nasi's family were descendants of King Solomon. The Nasi would lead—with eighty reputable people on his board. Important religious decisions could be definitively decided there as well as certifying rabbis, and defining each district of operation. This was like the general assembly of all Jews living everywhere, and its decisions were applied decisively.

In the year 145, the Bar Kokhba revolt began with great hopes of defeating the Romans, It ended in catastrophe. Jews, expelled again from Jerusalem, settled in Tiberias. There, Johann Ben Nafsha played an important role in making it the main learning center. The Mishna, that is, the codification of the Talmud, was realized in Tiberias. Yehuda Nasi compiled the famous Jerusalem Talmud in Tiberias in the year 200.

In 425, after the Byzantium invasion, Tiberias was devastated, and then deserted.

After the Caliphs took over Jerusalem in 636 during Caliph Omar's rule, Bet Shin, an armed security Jewish organization, took over Tiberias as the regional capital. With 70 Jewish families allowed to settle in Jerusalem, Jewish life was nucleated and Tiberias became of lesser importance.

By the 12th Century, 50 Jewish families were living in Tiberias and it is said that the highest quality manuscripts originated there, including the work of Maimonides. The Biblical scrolls kept in synagogues there were meticulously written by authorized and certified scribes.

Rabbi Moshe Ben Maimon, better known as Maimonides,

was a venerable personality whose name is associated with the city. He was a jurist, writer, humanist, doctor and author of the Mishnah Torah, the most famous Jewish liturgical writing. As he directed in his last will and testament, his remains were transported to Tiberias and reinterred there, after his death in Egypt in 1204.

When the Ottomans conquered the area, they found Tiberias devastated with a meager, stagnant, and poor population short of material. Spiritually, they lived in fear and without contact with the rest of the world. Just a few Jewish fishermen tried to keep up their existence.

"Joseph, I have difficulty understanding. Did Suleiman give us this city?"

"No, Aunt Gracia, the land will continue to belong to him. He is ceding tax collection rights and a vast range of liberties, such that the area becomes semi-autonomous."

"And we will create a city where Jews can rule themselves and are politically independent. After hundreds of years of our being exiled from the Promised Land, we will, for the first time enjoy total security. From now on, once our numbers increase, there will be no one to be jealous of because we will have enriched ourselves through hard work."

"Or we will never again be the victims of greedy administrators."

"Sounds like a dream!"

"It is."

"After the last incident, my hopes are rekindled."

End of an Era

We had a peaceful life here but the Europeans' enmity was never ending. They tried to reach whoever they could to defame us. Also, preconceptions of the grand vizier, Sokollu Mehmet Pasha, turned to animosity toward Joseph. On top of that, the marriage of Esmehan Sultan, the granddaughter of Suleiman, and Selim being the unchallenged prince claiming the crown further strengthened Sokollu.

We work with Joseph with all our might. Israel would be born from the diaspora and gather all of the dispersed in Tiberias. Joseph was accorded the title, 'Lord of Tiberias.' I was fifty-one with graying hair. I didn't know if I would live long enough to see the Jewish people in Tiberias, ruling themselves, and settled in freedom. But I knew Joseph's dream target was not Tiberias but Cyprus. He wanted to take Cyprus from Venice and for Cyprus to be given to us as the country for Jews. He thought Cyprus would be safe and also allow him to take revenge on the Venetians.

"He said he will make me king of Cyprus!" said Joseph, fully thrilled.

Reyna was the first to ask: "Who, how?"

I watched with inquiring eyes.

"Selim. He promised that when the day comes and he becomes the Sultan, he will conquer Cyprus and make me king."

Reyna clapped her hands in joy. Pierre and I were in the background, keeping silent.

"What's up, Aunt Gracia? Aren't you happy?"

"Joseph, I understand your excitement. But I don't find the realization credible. Even if the Sultan wants to give you

Cyprus, although he is very powerful, he couldn't do that by himself. There will be many who will interfere. One of them would be the Divan, where all Pashas sit. The next would be the army. There is also the harem. All of these have influence over him. If one of them strongly opposes it, the deal won't go through. They might be able to stop him from forming a kingdom within the Ottoman Empire. For sure, our enemies would work hard against us. You mustn't forget that Cyprus doesn't yet belong to the Ottomans! It is controlled by Venice and all the riches of the New World flow into Europe. Europe will side with Venice in not letting the Ottomans take over Cyprus."

"I know all that. This is why I will throw all my power for Selim to be Sultan and for him to take the Island."

"Can't we concentrate on Tiberias instead?"

"Tiberias is a desert. It has been a no mans' land for a thousand years. On the other hand, Cyprus is a green island, a pearl without equal."

He wasn't hearing my warnings. He believed in Selim, and was already making plans.

"I will contact the Jews in Cyprus. I will need all the information I can get. I will even ask them to set up sabotage teams. Cyprus must belong to the Ottomans."

I nodded. I wanted him to succeed but there were serious obstacles. We should concentrate our fortune and energy on Tiberias instead of Cyprus, which would have many contestants.

Being buried in the sacred places was the dream of every Marrano and Jew. It had been Francisco's desire as well. We succeeded after encountering many difficulties. In particular, the northern flank of Tiberias had a special importance for Jews. Many rabbis were saying that the Messiah would come from this way and start work there. There were many who wanted to be among the first group that would be brought to life.

"So the Messiah will not come to Cyprus! Many think he will come to the sacred lands, to Tiberias."

He looked as if I did not realize the importance of his victory. He was right in thinking so. In a short time, he managed to gain favor with Suleiman for Tiberias and a promise from Selim for Cyprus. These concessions were not even made to sons-in-law who were Pashas.

"People have been believing in this for longer than one thousand years, it seems to me, it gives hope and will keep us going, Aunt Gracia. If the Messiah comes, he would be more than welcome. What the cabalists don't want to see is this: it's not enough to wait and pray only. We need to work very hard! If there would be a Jewish state in the middle of the Mediterranean, the Messiah would not be unhappy at all, rest assured. We will keep working for Cyprus. And for Tiberias too."

Reyna jumped in: "Mom, why do you feel discomfort with my husband becoming king?"

Trouble in Tiberias

I had seen the death of my father, mother, and husband, whom I'd loved, and so many others. At this time in my life, I am grateful that my child is still with me. In that sense, the timing of Hürrem Sultan's death was a blessing to her in light of what came later. Her son Bayezid, whom I knew she loved dearly, was caught in Kazvin and strangled by order of his father.

Tiberias was given to us probably because of the support we provided to his son, Selim. Suleiman was angry at his other son, Bayezid for having run to Iran. With his father's backing, Selim was pretty much guaranteed succession. While hoping his treasury would benefit from the Tiberias agreement, Suleiman willed that this contract would be respected during the reigns of both Selim's and his grandson, Murat's reign.

The rumors that Joseph would declare himself king of Tiberias and gather all the Jews here spread immediately, not only in Istanbul but also in Europe.

The pope and the French king were among those who felt uneasy. They declared that Nasi would be more dangerous than the snakes in Tiberias wandering in the city's ruins. To activate the Christians, it was said that Nasi would convert a church in the city to a synagogue. The Apostolic Nuncio to Palestine, Bonifazio, visited Istanbul to oppose the project with Rüstem Pasha. He strongly protested, not knowing of the strong friendship between Joseph and Rüstem Pasha.

Triggering my imagination, travelers who had seen Tiberias spoke of orange aromas and palm trees.

Living happily away from fears of the Inquisition, I dream

of spending my last years in Tiberias. I dream of bathing in hot spring waters, feeling the afternoon breeze on my cheeks by the lake in calm and serenity. I hoped to be buried next to my Francisco.

I didn't know for sure how I would end my days.

The following year, Joseph sent Rabbi Joseph ben Adut to Tiberias, and asked him to survey and report back about the situation there. He asked him to build a wall using the stones of nearby ruins. Suleiman issued an edict instructing all governors in the area to assist this development and for help in gathering a capable work force.

Joseph briefed me regarding the accounts of current projects.

"Aunt Gracia, we will pay six-fold the tax collected from the region last year. We promised to pay one thousand gold coins this year, and in ten years, bring that up to ten thousand."

The project was both costly and worth it.

"That's good. This will silence the palace opposition."

"Joseph ben Adut was received by the Sultan before leaving for Palestine. A salary was accorded as if he was an official state employee."

"The walls will serve to protect the city but that's not enough. We have to make the city livable."

"I know. That's why I am trying to make Tiberias into a city where silk and wool can be woven. I asked ben Adut to plant as many mulberry trees as possible so that silkworms can reproduce. If wool is imported from Spain and silk produced locally, very profitable apparel can be produced and sold to Venice at lucrative prices. First, the city must be secure. Safed is nearby and better protected. The quality of life is better and many religious scholars function there comfortably. There is an issue with the underground."

I looked into his eyes.

"There are constant earthquakes."

"Then stronger buildings are needed."

"We have an issue with Jews over there."

"What is it?"

"They want us to open religious academies so that Cabala and Talmud studies can take place. I explained to them as best as I could. Our priority at this stage is different. It would cause bureaucratic complications, if we start right now with this. First it has to become a bustling city. Otherwise we cannot convince the Marranos to immigrate."

"Joseph, don't you have any good news at all about Tiberias?"

"I hope I will in the future. For now, you are informed of the issues."

"Any other problem?"

"The Arabs. They are rebelling. Arabs from nearby regions are telling workers that the revival of Tiberias will lead to the end of Islam, causing its destruction. They convinced workers we hired that they are acting against their religion. Many are running away. Rabbi ben Adut has conveyed his difficulties to the governor in Damascus. He explained that this was contrary to the Sultan's orders. He asked him to get the workers to return to the site. The Pasha started an inquiry and had two workers hanged. Then they all came back to work."

Synagogue and Yeshiva

"Within a year the construction of one thousand three hundred meters of the walls were completed. The wall starting at one end of the Lake of Galilee went around the city like a crescent and back to the other end of the lake."

With constant efforts, we were having good results. This created hope among those who were suffering in Europe. When rumors spread that Marranos were carried from Venice and Ancona, preparations in many communities started. Joseph looked for certain qualifications among people who would come to Tiberias. He preferred those who had means and experience in business.

"We can't take everyone, Aunt Gracia. The voluntary ones are all poor, the ones allowed to trade only in secondhand clothes. If we take them, they will be even poorer. They are not aware of that, and that is why they are so enthusiastic.

"They are excited as if the kingdom of Israel were established."

"I guess so. I was surprised to hear of rumors circulating widely. I even heard that I had a mansion built for myself!"

We smiled. I had such an intention for the future but even the foundations were not yet laid.

"They never gave up tracking us, every one of our steps. It's good that we act cautiously."

"We need technical people to set up textile mills and dye shops. We need a young and active crowd, Aunt Gracia. The newcomers are as bad as the previous ones. Pope Pius came instead of Paul but nothing changed. The oppressed ones talk about the Grand Senior and Joseph Nasi as if they were their saviors. We also have applications from whole towns that intend to emigrate all together. Without waiting for a word from us, many are selling what they have and preparing for the exodus."

"What will they do then?"

"They will deliver the goods to us there and we will give them the counter value here. We cannot close our doors. Apart from that we have to provide safe passage."

"Joseph, I notice that your excitement is dwindling. Is there something you prefer not to share?"

"Not really… I guess I am a bit disappointed. The ones I hoped would come, didn't; the ones that come—they dream of living in King Solomon's times. When they encounter difficulties, they become unhappy. All our activities to revitalize the city is considered atheism. Frankly, if you were not so committed to this project, I don't know if I could continue."

"Joseph, never give up! Don't lose hope! We lived through such hardships before. Remember the Ancona boycott. Sometimes you must work for the good of our co-religionists in spite of them."

"Yes but if it goes this way, we will have difficulties paying the promised sums to Suleiman. It could create problems for us in the future. There is no more Rüstem Pasha to protect us."

The much loved daughter of Rüstem Pasha, Ayşe Sultan, was ill and couldn't be saved from the plague that passed through Istanbul. While concentrating fully to protect Mihrimah Sultan when he couldn't save his beloved daughter, he fell ill himself and did not recover. He lost his life. I learned from his doctors that his was a natural death.

"What do you have in mind, Joseph?"

He was silent. He didn't say but after a while we found out.

Secret News

The doorbell rang continuously. Without knowing what had happened I jumped out of bed. As I opened the door, I saw Pierre.

"Joseph is here and insists on seeing you."

Pierre's priority was such that, even for Joseph or Reyna to see me at unusual times, they had to go through him. I felt blessed once again because I had this aging protector by me.

"Ask him to wait."

He closed the door. I put on something and without getting dressed properly, I went downstairs. Joseph was waiting for me in the library, pacing.

"Joseph, what happened at this time of the night?"

He looked at Pierre, standing behind me. It was clear that he didn't want him to hear.

Pierre got the message but since I was his boss and not Joseph, he didn't budge.

"Can we talk alone?"

"Joseph, I have nothing to hide from Pierre."

"I have. Please!"

I turned around and hopelessly, I looked into Pierre's eyes. He was surprised. For so many years, particularly in the past few, he left me alone only to sleep.

He silently left the room, closing the door behind him.

"He was vexed!" I said. "I hope what you will say is worth it."

"Aunt Gracia, before you were more cautious than me. What happened to you?"

"I am the same. Why did you wake me in the middle of the night?"

Dona Gracia

"I have very important news for you. But, you shouldn't share it with anyone for the time being. Don't even repeat it to yourself! If you slip, the consequences would be irreparable."

"Come on. What has come over you? What is it that you will share? You've got my heart beating quickly."

I put my hand on my heart. Really, either because of my interrupted sleep or because of Joseph's secrecy, it was pounding.

"Listen to me now."

He drew closer and whispered into my ear.

When Joseph was finished telling me, my eyes opened wide and my mouth was gaping.

"Did I hear right?" I said, having difficulties believing.

He waved his hand.

"Perfectly correct. Now I am going immediately. I will be in the committee. Don't forget what I said! The first to know that has met death by strangling!"

It was so many years that I lived in Ottoman lands and so close to the palace but Istanbul still succeeded in surprising me.

Joseph left as hastily as he came.

He was on the other side of the door, waiting. Our eyes met. I didn't have the strength to stand up. I sat on a chair and waited.

Keeping a Secret

Joseph's return took quite some time.

Reyna, Samuel, and La Chica pressed me on where he was, trying to find out what I knew. I was certain Joseph would not have spoken to anyone but me on this subject. He was tight-lipped for the reason that sharing the secret could endanger the life of the one who knew it. He only trusted me, his mother-in-law, aunt, and lifelong confidant, who has long been as close to him as his mother.

"No idea. I know as much as you all. Perhaps he went to Venice or Tiberias. The pope is causing problems. For this reason there are several who want to come and others who are about to leave. Perhaps there was a problem. He said nothing. I asked."

As I spoke, I exchanged looks with Pierre, who looked both vexed and curious.

Dear Pierre. If I could I would share it with you but I know that it will be to your detriment. Even if you are vexed.

Reyna: "Mom, my husband leaves home in the middle of the night. I am sure he must have talked with you. If not with you, who can it be? It wouldn't be Pierre that he would have talked to."

"Darling, are you insinuating that I am hiding something from you?"

"No but. It all doesn't seem natural."

"There is something else that you and La Chica should learn about men: They sometimes do secretive things. Some-times they have to go and be by themselves and disappear for a while. If they return, it means they are really attached to their nest. If they don't, then this is the time to take precautions."

"What then? Is my husband with another woman?"

We all laughed.

La Chica turned to Samuel who was to be her husband in the near future.

"I guess my brother is on a business trip. He will explain when he gets back."

"Haa, that's what I was saying too. You know Joseph is a workaholic. He works like crazy, works and works. Let him work some more and turn Tiberias into paradise for the Jews in Tiberias."

Reyna seemed satisfied: "OK, since we are all together and La Chica is nearly a married woman, it's time for new presents. You are spending all your fortune for the co-religionists. Isn't it time to spend for your girls too. I desire a beautiful necklace covered with emeralds and rubies to decorate my jowl, such that, when my husband gets back, his eyes will leave their sockets!"

"I want new dresses made!" said La Chica "The best clothes pass through our enterprise yet look at us!"

"What's wrong with you? You have more dresses than anyone. You wear better fabrics than most."

Samuel fidgeted uncomfortably: "I'd better leave you, mother and daughter to discuss these things at your ease. I have to cover for Joseph's absence."

"OK, you may leave."

Samuel, like his brother, was well-brought up. Not that I wanted it anytime soon, but one day, just as Diogo took over from Francisco, so too Samuel can take over from Joseph. He is well equipped.

"Pierre, you should be bored by now, I can tell. If you don't fear that harm can come to me from the girls, you can go."

Pierre shook his head and slowly left. As he pulled the door, the girls giggled.

"Mother, don't say I didn't tell you. This man has been an old bachelor because of you! The poor chap dried up because of his love for you!"

"Behave yourselves, girls!"

They laughed.

Royal Succession

Nicknamed The Magnificent, the one who offered a dignified living free from embarrassments and, when needed, acted as protector of Jews, Suleiman had died.

It was the news of his death that Joseph whispered in my ear that night. On an expedition to Hungary, in Zigetvar, after a reign of 46 years, at the age of 71, Suleiman's days ended.

The grand vizier, Sokollu Mehmet Pasha, hid the news from the soldiers in order not to demoralize them. As soon as the doctor declared Suleiman dead, Sokollu had the doctor strangled so the news wouldn't leak out. We sent a message to Selim in Kutahya for him to come immediately. The forty-two-year-old Selim, son of Hürrem Sultan, was a close friend of Joseph.

I remember the words Joseph whispered to my ear:

"Selim is going to be crowned as Sultan. He asked me to join in his entourage. Don't share this news with anyone. If the news is heard in Istanbul and a fight for the crown starts, we would all lose our heads!"

Selim took possession of the crown in Belgrade and was on his way to Istanbul as the new Sultan. Only after his arrival did Sokollu announced the new Sultan to the soldiers and asked them to obey him absolutely. I wasn't comfortable with Sokollu Mehmet Pasha. In fact, he didn't think much of us either but his handling of the situation was praiseworthy. If it wasn't for his experience and wisdom, with the news of Suleiman's death, Istanbul would be in chaos. It happened several times before but this time a smooth transition to the throne was made possible.

When announcing the good news, he said:

"I am from now on The Duke of Naxos! The new Sultan even before he settled in his throne, has declared me as the Duke of Naxos. Naxos and the Cyclades Islands."

"But how did Mehmet Pasha receive the news?"

"Not happy at all. He couldn't risk being at odds with the new Sultan. He looked happier when he heard that we will pay forty thousand ducats yearly for the islands."

La Chica: "So you are not a business man anymore but a statesman!"

Reyna was happy too: "A statesman in the Ottomans! What joy!"

Samuel congratulated his brother. I looked at Pierre automatically. He wasn't looking at me, perhaps to avoid eye contact. I thought for a second that he was not so pleased.

"Well than, will you need to live in Naxos?" I asked. "Ottomans don't keep Pashas with a mission in Istanbul."

Secret News

"No, Aunt Gracia, I will stay in Istanbul. But, I'll have to go to Naxos and look the place over."

Selim was a wine connoisseur. Europeans, wanting to belittle him called him 'Selim the Sot.' According to the information I had from Joseph and other sources he didn't interfere too much in government business. He had a team that he trusted and he kept them happy. After his father's death, he kept his successful grand vizier Sokollu and compensated Joseph. It looked as if he will not drop any of them. I knew how he benefitted from this: he asked for both their independent opinions before deciding.

"What issue has he got with us, rather with you?"

"He has a partner called Michael Kantakuzenos, an aristocrat who is a descendent of the Byzantium emperors. They do business together and earn a fortune. He sees us as his competitor."

I have heard of Kantakuzenos. He was nicknamed "The Devil's son." His dealings were rather shady; he would be involved in dishonest deals while relying on support from the vizier.

"So, The Devil's son is in our game too."

"Selim will support us continuously. We also have the support of Piyale Pasha. The rest is up to you."

"I am on good terms with Nurbanu Sultan. I will try and get closer to her. But Ester Handali is even closer. We should ask for Ester's support too."

"Do you think Ester would back us?"

"She would. Her exaggerated self-confidence bothers me from time to time, I believe she would be on our side, particularly on issues regarding our co-religionists."

"You should visit Nurbanu Sultan shortly."

My excuse was ready. I would congratulate her. Her husband's assuming the throne meant that she would be first lady of the empire.

French Debt

One of the sharpest disagreements between Joseph and Sokollu surfaced in the early period of Selim's reign. Sokollu Mehmet Pasha, guided by Dr. Eskenazi, strengthened relations with the French and accelerated a conflict with the Habsburgs, who had Spain in their sphere of influence. Sokollu intended to encourage a revolt of Moriscos in Spain where these Muslims suffered forced conversion. Joseph knew Spain well, especially that the Ottomans were enemies of the Spaniards. It would be good strategy to weaken the Spaniards by supporting the Protestants. Joseph knew that Marranos, who had also been subjected to forced conversion, had joined the Protestants in Antwerp. Religious fanaticism in Spain and Austria was peaking, and actions against Catholics had begun. Losing Holland as the seat of business would be a strong blow to Spain.

Finally, Sokollu came around to agreeing with Joseph. He told leaders of the Dutch revolution to refuse to sign agreements with the Spanish Governor and that the Ottomans would back them in this struggle. When the Spanish offered to make a peace treaty with the Ottomans, Sokollu imposed the condition that the Dutch also be a part of this, knowing full well that it would not be accepted.

Secret News

War with Spain was becoming inevitable.

Joseph's relation with Sultan was admirable but also causing jealousy. Every Friday he sent dishes from the Sephardic
cuisine and rare wines. Since the Venetians had tried to poi-
son Selim, he only trusted wine and food carrying the Nasi
seal.

When we heard the Armenian Patriarch was coming to the
Belvedere Palace, we were quite surprised. We soon understood the reason for that visit. The Patriarch wanted Joseph to
get an edict from Selim guaranteeing the continuation of their
rights and liberties after Suleiman's death. Joseph managed to
get it and conveyed it to the Patriarch.

When the relieved and excited Patriarch held Joseph's
hand, he wanted to kiss it. Joseph quickly pulled away.

"What are you doing, your Eminence! You are a religious
leader. I am just a business man. Please don't embarrass me!"

I could read the affection and respect toward Joseph in the
Patriarch's eyes.

"My son, you are people who suffered much at the hands
of Christians in Europe before coming here. Now, you intervened for the protection of the rights of Christians. I don't
know how to thank you."

"Don't mention it, your Eminence. We know what it is to
be oppressed because of one's religion. I am sure if Jews needed your support, you would willingly give it."

"Naturally!"

Wine was forbidden in the Ottomans though not totally
forbidden in the sense that part of the population enjoyed
it and it was a source of revenue. Selim lifted the ban on the

wine trade for non-Muslims. Since Muslims didn't want to be involved, Joseph enjoyed a lucrative business. He bought the rights to collect taxes for the wine that originated in Egypt, and was re-exported to the Bosphorus. The Janissaries and our staff checked the ships and collected a ten percent tax. Joseph benefitted considerably more than what he had paid and the wines were exported to Poland, Moldovia, and Romania.

These were profitable activities but the French continued to owe us a heavy debt that we couldn't collect for fifteen years. Joseph's debt to the Ottoman treasury was substantial too. Selim, seeing that France had no intention of paying, issued an edict. He ordered that a third of the value of the goods from ships with French flags was to be confiscated and delivered to the Mendes House until payment was made of the total amount.

I was happy for this decision but it also created problems. The Ottomans had given French ships the right to circulate freely in 1535. To take advantage of this, many ships that belonged to companies from Dubrovnik, Egypt, and several other areas sailed under the French flag. The fact that goods belonging to non-Frenchmen were confiscated too, created chaos and many objections.

Business was as active as always but, from going forward, I wanted to dedicate my time to religious issues. The academies I founded were providing religious education and training for students to become rabbis. I concentrated on social projects. My two girls had wonderful weddings and both married excellent men. Francisco's will was executed and his remains transported to the Holy Land. I didn't have much left to do. I delegated all business issues to Joseph and Samuel.

The Deepest Cut

Just as I withdrew from most of my responsibilities, an unexpected thing happened. Pierre, who had been with me for half of my life, was ill.

The strange thing was that, up until that day, I had never seen him in bed as a patient. When I woke up in the morning, not to see him waiting at my bedroom door was strange.

I went to his bedroom, next door to mine, and walked in without knocking.

He was in bed. It was difficult for me to understand what had tied Pierre to his bed. Apart from an occasional cold, he never had any complications. Luckily the best doctors were Jewish. I sent someone immediately to Natan Eskenazi, the doctor the Sultan trusted regarding health issues. I thought he should be the one to check Pierre.

"What is it, Pierre?" I said, putting my hand on his forehead. "Are you ill, then? I thought you never became ill."

He wanted to talk but words didn't come out. Sad, he looked at me with lifeless eyes.

"OK, I get it. Just take it easy. The doctor is coming shortly."

He had fever and was really exhausted. I looked him over. There was nothing else I could see. I pulled up a chair, sat next to his bed. I was in front of him, holding his hand, consoling him.

One of the maids came to say breakfast was ready.

"I won't come down. Today, I don't feel hungry."

He couldn't speak. Two tear drops slid down Pierre's cheeks onto the pillow.

Dona Gracia

I was feeling strange, stuffy. To see that giant of a man, with the scar on his face, crying, sent tremors through my heart. I suddenly realized how much I cared, how much I loved him. How important he was for me. I squeezed his hand.

"I am here, Pierre! I won't let you go that easy. You looked after me and protected me for so many years. Now it is my turn to protect you!"

He closed his eyes. He didn't want me to see him cry any more.

"That's right, go to sleep. Rest some more. The doctor will come and we will get you on your feet."

He was silent and his breathing noticeably slowed, as if it stopped.

I heard some movement in the house but my full concentration was on Pierre. I was worried that I wouldn't hear his breathing.

A gentle knock on the door, and Reyna was there. I didn't turn around but I knew. She sat next to me, with her hand on my shoulder wanting to console me.

"What is it with him?"

"I don't know. He became ill. I sent for the doctor."

We were whispering so as not to wake him up. He should rest and get well quickly.

"Don't worry, Pierre is a strong man. He will get well."

"I hope so."

I couldn't say anything else. I felt I was choking. One more word and I would break down and cry."

"I will wait with you."

Secret News

I shook my head to tell her that there was no need.

"Please. Pierre is a family member. I want to wait."

I pulled myself together.

"Go and take care of the house. Tell La Chica too, I want silence in the house. The cooks should prepare the most fortifying dishes. Bring the doctor up as soon as he comes."

"Sure."

I can't remember how long I held his hand in mine. It seemed like a moment to me but it was longer. It was as if I let go, I would lose him forever.

"My God, please help this Christian. I have no doubt he served you better than many Jews. He was not born to a Jewish mother but he was a good person. He has rendered many valuable services. If we did a few things, his contributions are many. Let him regain his health and don't part us."

I continued praying until the doctor arrived.

Finally, he was there. I stood up. I guess, Pierre never slept. He opened his eyes immediately.

"This way, Mr. Ashkenazi, come. Cure him!"

"Hello, Mrs. Gracia."

"Come closer, please."

He came. I let go of his hand only then, and took a few steps back so the doctor could examine him. While I waited silently, he checked Pierre's temperature, listened to his lungs, and looked under his eyelids. Then the doctor left Pierre, and signaled to me with his head.

I went after him and closed the door, listening carefully to what he had to say.

"I am sad, Dona Gracia! These are Pierre's last days. There

is nothing left that we can do for him!"

The room started spinning. I nearly fell. I looked for something to hold on to. The ground was sliding under my feet.

He noticed and held my arm.

"What are you saying doctor!"

I sat on the nearest chair. "How come? Pierre cannot die. At least not before me. Make him well!"

"He must have kept it to himself." With a sad voice, he said, "He must have been suffering for quite some time. Didn't he ever complain about his pain?"

I looked up in surprise.

"No, even when he had a cold, Pierre carried on with his life as if nothing happened. He has a strong constitution."

"His illness is related to old age. Probably he never mentioned it in order to continue working for you. He must have been suffering for quite some time. Perhaps you can prolong his end by a few days. That is all."

"Is there no hope at all?"

He shook his head in despair.

I wanted to jump on him, tear his cloak. He couldn't tell me that Pierre is dying!

"Not possible!"

"You are a believer. You know the realities of life, Dona Gracia. We go one day as we came. What's important is the soul that lives on."

I am lost for words. He is right but my insides are rebelling! Will Pierre, who always tried to hide his face, who dropped his hair over the scar, who followed me like my shadow, die?"

"You don't look well either. Let me check you."

Secret News

"No, I am OK. Thank you for your visit."

"I will at least prepare a potion for him to spend his last days comfortably, I'll send it to you."

"Thank you, Dr. Askenazi."

The doctor left. I waited a little so Pierre wouldn't see me shattered. I distracted myself, tried to regain my composure. By the time I re-entered Pierre's room, the maids had brought his soup.

"Pierre, come on, try to straighten up a little. If you can sit up, I can give you soup."

He opened his eyes and tried to move. I could see he had difficulty and was in pain. He used up all his energy to sit up. I helped him and put a pillow behind his back.

I took the bowl and spoon. I gently moved a spoonful of soup to his mouth. He opened his mouth and ate half of it. He swallowed, then took one more spoonful.

After a few more spoon's full, he raised his hand asking me to stop. I could hear him:

"My lady, there is something I should tell you, must tell you."

"Pierre, don't tire yourself. Rest!"

"I have no time. I must tell."

Pierre insisted on confiding in me but I didn't want him to make the effort. I convinced him to go back to sleep. Perhaps I didn't want to hear what he had to say. There was between the two us a bond that went beyond a boss-staff relationship, something we didn't articulate. Behind his dedication, was there a reason other than the money he earned or the affection I showered over him, my empathy for him for having a prominent scar? I suspected more intimate feelings though I wasn't ready to hear them.

When I was sure he was asleep, I left the room. Only then did I realize that I was still in my nightgown. Perhaps I should have something to eat and be stronger while tending to him. Eshkenazi had said that the illness wasn't contagious, meaning there were no risks. Anyhow, I wouldn't leave him alone.

I got dressed and ate a little before returning to his room where he was sleeping.

I sank into an armchair, making sure not to wake him.

I was thinking of the years I spent with him. He entered my life after Diogo's death and for a quarter of a century, he never left my side. It was hard to believe I was losing him. If I was a non-believer, perhaps I would revolt but God was trying me again.

Again, another man I loved was leaving me!

I felt a contraction in my chest. Not to be able to help was so painful. I was very rich. Perhaps even European queens couldn't match my fortune but a simple illness was preparing to take away another man I cared so much for.

Toward the evening, he again opened his eyes. He looked a bit better after having rested. I approached him joyfully.

"Pierre, you are better. Ha!"

"Yes," he said with a weakened voice. "I want to ask for your pardon."

"Come on, Pierre! It is not your fault if you are ill. Get well. That is enough."

"It isn't that."

He stopped for a few seconds, uncertain if he wanted to continue. I waited. He could say what he wanted.

"The Pope—Paul III," he said. "He forced me to."

Secret News

I had a strange feeling. What would a pope who died years ago have to do with this situation?

"What are you saying, Pierre? Are you dreaming? Where did you get to the pope?"

"Please don't interrupt, even if you are angry."

Two more tears rolled down his cheeks.

"I am listening," I said, wondering where this would lead.

"I hid it from you, fearing you would send me away."

I was utterly confused. I kept quiet so he could say it all without tiring himself more.

"Paul sent me to you. He thought that with the death of Diogo Mendes, you would be troubled with feelings of emptiness. He wanted me to take advantage and to gain your trust. It went on this way. Paul VI also pushed me. Dona Gracia, I worked as the pope's agent to inform on you. Forgive me!"

He stopped talking.

I looked at him for a confirmation that what I heard was what he said. Tears flowed. The person I trusted with my life, my daughters, the one who was with me day and night was the pope's spy.

"You are lying!"

My tone was more determined and loud.

"My last wish is to ask only for your pardon. If God doesn't forgive me, it's OK. I spent my life serving him. You, please pardon me."

His words came in short bursts as he spoke with difficulty.

"I beg you to say you pardon me!"

I stood up. Not knowing what to do, I couldn't breathe. My cheeks could explode.

"Pierre, please say it's all a lie! I thought that you loved me. Is all that so that I could get easily used to your loss, so that I don't mourn after you? Look, if it's so! Don't wreck me as you go!"

"No. I am really sorry. I spied on you all my life. I protected you always. Most of the information, I kept to myself. I wanted to protect you, not to endanger you. But if you don't forgive me..."

I drew closer, bent over him. I looked him in the eyes. Groggy, looking lifeless, but telling the truth.

My tears rolled onto his cheek.

"Pierre, what have you done? Pierre, how could you have done it? I wish you never, ever told me! How can I live with this?"

He mumbled, "Your pardon!"

Suddenly indignation came over me!

"I wish for you to burn in the hottest part of hell. I hope your soul doesn't enjoy a day of rest! Damn you. Listen, if you are still alive, open your ears and listen! After you damn well die, I will have your body torn apart! You won't even have a grave! You will not sleep in the shadow of your beloved cross! Can you hear me?"

He opened his eyes once more. Then his eyes rolled upward and I could see only the white in his eyes.

Struggling with Betrayal

Jews in Istanbul wore stylish clothes made from expensive fabrics and rings and earrings with valuable stones. We covered our heads as Muslim women do, but from the way we dressed, one could tell the difference.

Ottomans could not collect as much in taxes as before. Once they conquered a territory, they were charged with the responsibility of looking after the soldiers. The cost was deferred against a certain calculated tax to farmers. Called Timar, this system worked well during Suleiman's reign but times changed. The Silk Road was diverted from Ottoman lands. The sea route was much preferred. The New World was discovered with the result that riches flowed to Europe. While progress stopped in the Ottomans, new weapons and modern ships were built to reach the New World. As poverty settled in again, eyes again turned toward our direction. People who complained about the drop in their standard of living focused their complaints on the palace.

Muslim women couldn't keep up with the fashionable dress of non-Muslims. As the number of complaints rose, Selim couldn't resist the pressure. He imposed limits on the attire of Jews and Christians. We were not allowed to wear expensive clothing, high-quality head covers, or turbans. Using the excuse that the price of fabrics, shoes, and turbans was high, Jews and Christians were instructed to dress differently. Jews and Armenians were to wear dark-colored dresses, wrap half-cotton, half-silk fabrics, and the value should not be higher than thirty akches. (A silver coin, the akce is the monetary unit of the Ottoman Empire.) Turbans were to be made from Denizli cloth, cotton from Broussa, and non-Muslimes should not wear light blue. In short, the nicest clothes and brightest colors were forbidden.

$\sim\sim$

Dona Gracia

As a Jewish family, we were the first to go to St. Francois Catholic Church. Previously, I had visited the Orthodox Church in Fener, seat of the Patriarch, but the Catholics in Istanbul were few in number. It might have been strange that we were hosts at St. Francois Church as Pierre had no one but us.

In our tradition, the deceased is not placed in a coffin. The exception is if someone was buried but the plan was to transfer to another site later. Pierre's body was placed in a coffin, in line with Catholic tradition and his head was left uncovered. I should see his face from the first row where I was seated. He had a strange, sad smile on his face.

However furious I was when he told me, he knew I would forgive him in the end.

As New Christians, we were thoroughly trained in religious matters and I had no difficulty understanding the ritual.

We filled the first row. Another row was filled with people I guessed were from their community. I looked for a representative from Rome, Venice, or at least France but there were none. They probably kept Pierre close to us with threats or bribes and when he died, they abandoned him.

Who was he? Where was he from? I don't know. Did he have a family? I knew that they trained kids left at the door of the church and the abler ones were used in the service of the church. They assigned him to spy on me and he did so for twenty years. Same as I was being informed on them, they in turn followed the activities of Mendes. Who knows? Perhaps some of our agents were disclosed to them and Pierre had a hand in their end.

How could he do it?

Secret News

I thought he never left my side. But that was during the day. How about the nights? He would disappear from time to time and I imagined it was to satisfy his manly needs. We all had the same opinion: Pierre was not attached to me as to a boss but more like a lover. It was insinuated many times and in reality, I felt similarly.

Perhaps I was unjust to Pierre. Perhaps I shouldn't be so furious. Perhaps originally he might have played a role in Agostino's capture but later on we didn't go through major incidents. If he wanted to, he could have informed on our running away from Venice or Ferrara. Perhaps he really fell for me, though he started as a spy, eventually he started protecting us by feeding his true bosses either limited or false information. I would have asked him all that but he is not alive anymore.

When the closed coffin was lowered into the grave in the church yard, I stood by. The priest knew, of course, that we were Jewish. I noticed an inquisitive look on his face but didn't bother. I joined in by throwing a shovel full of soil as did Joseph, Reyna, La Chica, and Samuel. The rest would be completed by the church staff.

I should say 'rest in peace' before leaving but couldn't bring myself to open my mouth and say it.

Joseph got the message and took me by the arm.

"Aunt Gracia, we need to leave."

Reyna held his hand.

"Let's leave mother some time with Pierre. She might want to say a few words."

They moved on. I was by the grave. Alone. I looked at the

coffin partly covered with dirt.

"Ohh Pierre! What have you done?"

The hardest blows always come from those who are closest. First my sister, Brianda. Then my co-religionists, who deserted the boycott in Ancona, and now Pierre.

"Dear God, who is next? Would it be one of my daughters, Reyna or La Chica? Would it be Joseph? Please let me go without being betrayed by one of them."

"Bye Pierre! We will meet again. In eternal life."

I turned and walked. Joseph was waiting apart from the rest, closer to me.

He came and gently took me by the arm.

"Joseph! I said. "When did you learn?"

He took a deep breath, then another.

"Aunt Gracia, I knew since we came to Istanbul. Before it was hard for me to check but Istanbul is a city that I know better than he did. It didn't take long to decipher his connections. Don't worry. He didn't send any important information."

"Why didn't you tell me? Why did you allow me to trust him like a stupid woman?"

"You were too attached to him. I didn't want you to be demoralized. He was under control anyway. It was better that he wasn't aware that we knew."

"That's why you asked Pierre to leave before sharing top secret information that Suleiman had died?"

"Yes, I didn't want the Europeans to know before Selim took power. That might have triggered a crusade."

Now, as I walked through the cemetery where people were buried crosses on their heads for eternity, I was reminded, once again, how right it would be to share and deliver the secret to Joseph.

The Medallion

My greatest longing as a Jew, like all Jews, was to live in Jerusalem and enjoy the freedoms and affluence of the time when King Solomon lived there.

The First Temple was built 957 years before the birth of Jesus by King Solomon and the Second Temple 516 years before the birth of Jesus in the same place. The first was destroyed by Babylonians in 597 and the second was destroyed by Romans 70 years after the birth of Jesus. Our dream was that the Third Temple will be rebuilt in the same place.

The Messiah will come one day; the original sin will be forgiven, that is, Adam's eating the forbidden fruit. The world will then be a wonderful place. The dead will be revived; people will not have to work for a living.

Like every Jew, I long for the Messiah. In every Passover, I pray, "This year we celebrate here and next year in Jerusalem." Remains of the deceased were being carried on camels and ships to Jerusalem. Even if I die elsewhere, I dream of being awakened there.

I was feeling more as a sinner probably because of my advanced age. Forty years. For forty years I was forced to hide my Jewishness, my identity, and live, instead, like a Christian.

Will God forgive me for that?

Many Jews under pressure to deny their religion refused to do so. Many committed suicide, or went to the stake singing their beliefs. They became saints. There were many who strangled their children rather than be forced to be baptized. That ensured that their souls went to heaven pure and untainted. Others who couldn't display such bravery became Marranos. Somewhere inside, I always felt a discomfort. Despite that, I never went to live in the dire conditions of Tiberias or Jerusalem. The Holy Land cleanses us of our sins. Not only living there, even walking on that soil would have done me good, though I couldn't do that either.

The year after we settled in Istanbul, I found great satisfaction in transferring Francisco's remains to the Holy Land. He now lies in Jerusalem. We continue to ship spices, herbs, and wine to Europe.

Since Joseph is now a statesman, he is under constant protection of two Janissaries. My bodyguard, though he was my most trusted, betrayed me! I can see one or two white hairs on Joseph's beard. Although this gives him more weight in state affairs, it reminds me of my age.

I sat alone in the garden of the Belvedere palace, at a night hour, watching the stars. I remembered, years ago observing the same stars in Lisbon. This time I wasn't wearing colorful shawls or decorative hairpins though I could still smell the sea and feel the same humidity.

When I heard a crackle behind, I turned round to look.

"My daughter!"

"It is me, mom. What are you up to?"

"Sitting, thinking."

"What are you thinking about, mom? Since you don't have a bodyguard anymore, you must be more cautious. I was so near before you even noticed me."

Secret News

She sat in front of me. As she was growing, she looked more and more like me. Reyna looked as much like me as La Chica looked like Brianda.

"Eee, I am an old lady now, darling. No one would have issues with me anymore. But you should be protected. It is you who should really be careful."

"Don't say that. You are the foundation of the family, the post that holds the roof."

"Thank you, darling, but I am old now. Recently I felt a spasm in my chest. I wonder if we will be forgiven our sins. You were luckier and had to pretend less than I did but forty of my years went by hiding my beliefs."

"Don't say so! At the end of the day, you spent all of your fortune for Jews. Every day you feed in your home forty poor people. You extended a helping hand to people who were on the road, evicted from their homes, and their country. You paid the ransoms for the freedom of so many. You allocated your ships to the ones coming to Istanbul or going elsewhere, helping them to build homes and find work. You built the La Siyora Synagogue and the yeshiva next door. I am not saying this because you are my dear mother but if each Jew worked and was as dedicated as you are, we would have built our kingdom already."

My daughter's kind words made me feel better.

"Do you really think so?"

She came closer and held my hand.

"Of course, I do. You even made it possible for many to be able to use their proper names. This is why you are called La Sinyora. You are remembered always with your beneficence.

Even your enemies respect you. Is that an easy achievement? You are the best example for each one of us."

That was an exaggeration. If she continued in this way, I would cry.

"Enough! Don't praise me anymore. These words coming from you made me very happy. You know what I thought?"

"What?"

"Could you also betray me one day?"

Her face dropped.

"What kind of talk is that?"

"I don't know anymore. I saw the betrayal of my own sister, Pierre's, even my co-religionists, and rabbis. The only loyal ones that remained are you, La Chica and Joseph. I pray to God to live my days without experiencing such a disappointment!"

"Don't say that! Don't be like that! You will neither see any betrayal from us nor end your days so soon! I wish for you to be the head of the family for many years to come."

"Destiny." Then I asked as if it just occurred to me. "Where is Joseph? I didn't see him after dinner."

"You know him. He remembered his younger days! He is practicing the sword with the staff. If I didn't stop him, he would start throwing the lance! Years have gone by, but he still wears medieval attire and jousts in the area reserved for that. He looks like a crusader!"

"Our staff has been with us for many years. I sometimes wonder if we had needed to come over with such a crowd. Did we need to bring forty people with us?"

"You did well. Thanks to you, I lived like a princess."

Secret News

"You would say Pierre surprised you."

She took a deep breath.

"Unfortunately, yes. Still I cannot accept. Did Pierre really tell you he was a papal spy?

"Even if he hadn't said it, Joseph already knew. He didn't say it, thinking I would be sad."

"Strange, I always believed he was in love with you."

"As one grows older, one has such strange experiences. I hope that was the last!"

"I hope so too."

"It's good that you could still forgive him."

"I didn't! I just thought he deserved respect after so many years of service. Since he was in the service of the pope, he deserved a proper Christian burial. Let them not respect even our existence. We will show due respect to their dead."

There was a silence.

"I remember Moshe Hamon, who died just over a year ago. Do you recall he wanted you for his son? It was hard to convince him otherwise, may he rest in peace, but thank God he accepted my decision in the end. It was a great thing that, in this part of the world, there are people like him. He saved us from the Inquisition. As Suleiman's doctor, if he hadn't informed him directly, our transfer and settlement would not have been that smooth."

"Mother, please drop this subject? Look how beautiful the stars shine. We are in Istanbul as free people and our business is flourishing."

"Why, darling?"

"I don't know; I didn't like your being nostalgic. There are many sad memories. Let's enjoy the day a little."

She was right.

I said: "The Bosphorus is so beautiful. The view is always great. Some mornings, I open the windows and linger, watching the Bosphorus. Sometimes I also go for short walks. Did you know that the staff of the palace also lives nearby?"

"I had heard."

"The ones that wanted to annihilate us became poorer, left behind. The ones that invited us and treated us well advanced, and became richer. Whoever tried to destroy the Jews ended up living through catastrophes. Do you think they would learn from this? Would there be others to try again?"

"I hope not."

"The sainted Suleiman appreciated us. As he appreciated the qualities of Moshe Hamon, he also did so of Joseph. He gave him the title of Frenk Bey, friend of the palace. Selim also was close to us. He honored Joseph as the Duke of Naxos."

"He became the Duke of the Cyclades! The Polish wine producers worked to prevent this."

"I know. Joseph keeps me up to date on all happenings. If you ask me, his mind is elsewhere, not in Naxos or Tiberias."

"What is it that he has in mind?"

"He wants the island where he will settle all the Jews: Cyprus."

"That doesn't belong to the Ottomans?"

"He is constantly trying to convince Selim, day and night, to conquer Cyprus. He says that Selim promised to make him King of Cyprus. He won't give up. Look at the upside. If he is successful, the Eastern Mediterranean would be safe for all

Jews. We would also be closer to the Promised Land. I also want Cyprus conquered, my little bird. However many ships we allocate to our co-religionists, many are interrupted by corsairs based in Cyprus. Venice is allowing the corsairs to use Cyprus to keep the Ottomans regularly occupied."

"If the opposition of Mehmet Pasha is surmounted than it will be possible!"

We turned around and saw Joseph behind us.

"Oh, it seems there is a family meeting going on!" said Reyna. "Come on Joseph, sit by my side."

Joseph came and sat. From the sweat on his forehead, I could see he had been training.

"Mother, daughter, are talking about Cyprus?"

He continued without waiting for an answer. "Mehmet Pasha prefers to support the Moriscos. He believes he can start a revolt in Spain if he goes there. This way, by creating trouble in west Mediterranean he believes he can hit Spain with their own weapons. In case Cyprus is occupied, he worries that it can trigger a unification of the Christian powers against the Ottomans."

"He might be right," I said. "Europeans have improved their navy considerably. If they confront the Ottomans in an organized way, they might win."

"Mehmet Pasha trusts the Pasha Müezzinzade but has serious reserves about his ability as a seaman of this pious man. Even if I share the same concerns, taking Cyprus has become inevitable for us. Some fresh news, I bought the rights of the monopole for wax trading with Poland."

This was good news.

"So, you are all excluding me from the family meeting! I am cross with you all!"

I had difficulty not to laugh. It looked as if we had planned a family meeting in the garden. La Chica and Samuel also joined. When they saw us laughing raucously, they joined in the laughter.

They came and sat across us.

"The staff said you were all here," said La Chica. "We decided to join you. It is so warm, we can't sit inside. There is a nice breeze out here."

She turned her face toward the Bosphorus. A pleasantly refreshing wind was blowing.

While watching her pretty face, it was as if I was looking at Brianda. It took me back many, many years and we are with Brianda. One difference, La Chica is not such a frilly pop. Beauty was inherited from her. In our family, wisdom came my way and physical attraction her way. The same continued with our daughters too.

She turned when she noticed I was gazing at her: "Aunty, are you watching me?"

"Yes my dear. God protect you! You are so beautiful! Just like."

I stopped talking.

She smiled. "You were about to say, just like my mother?"

"Yes."

There was a sad silence. I felt strange inside. God had given me a sister but took her away too soon. I wish she were alive and continued pushing me for money. Maybe she would have come to Istanbul with us, and maybe she would have calmed down.

Secret News

Samuel: "You are missing your sister."

"Much. So much! My mindless sister, I hope she is in the most beautiful corner of Paradise. I am still angered with her but I missed her so much, it's hard to explain. I wish she came with us to Istanbul!"

Another silent moment. At a distance, we could hear music played with reeds, like. Probably it was a wedding celebration with people jovially dancing. The sky was clear, a half-moon shining over the waters of the Bosphorus.

La Chica interrupted the silence. Looking inside her purse that she took out of her purse,

"It would be good, if there was a souvenir or a picture, Aunty." She said "Ohh look, what I have here."

I looked at what she held in her hand. A medallion. I brought the chandelier near it, to see better.

"What is that? Let me see."

She passed it to me.

I took and looked at it carefully. The engraved 'Gracia Nasi' words were in Hebrew and the year it was made in strange Roman characters. What was surprising was the relief in the center.

"Oh my God, that's Brianda!"

At that instant, tears flowed down my cheeks. It was as if I had seen my sister.

"No, Aunty. It is true that it looks much like her but that's not her but me."

"Where did you have this made? Why didn't you tell me before?"

My tears failed to obey me and kept flowing.

Samuel answered: "After our wedding, in Ferrara, Pastorino de Pastorini offered to make a painting of La Chica. Since 'making craven images' is a sin, we did not consent. Then he made a mold for this medallion and produced it. The painting would be a single original. As for the medallion, probably he had a few stamped from the same mold."

I caressed the medallion as if it were Brianda and touched it to my wet cheeks.

"Ah! Tonight. I don't know what came over me tonight. I feel strange."

Reyna was worried: "Mom, are you OK? You look tired. Let's get up and you can go to bed. You need to rest!"

"I am OK," I said looking at the medallion.

La Chica: "You can keep this one. I have another."

"Thank you, my love." I kissed the medallion. "It's as if you gave me back my sister tonight. I will always keep it with me."

White Light

I lay in my bed without sleeping. I watched the decorated ceiling for a while. I recalled the past. The live burnings, the smell of burned flesh. My stomach was upset. Then my wedding, my relocations from Portugal, Lyon, Venice, escape from Ferrara.

The secret endowed to me by my father was now safe with Joseph. I had transferred our family ideal of living in our own country to him.

"One day, Israel will be rebuilt. Jews will stop being guests and will live in their own home, a free people. Many families work on this mission. Our duty is to serve this purpose. Keep your secret to yourself until that happy day arrives. Work hard. If you disclose this secret, there will be many that would want to destroy you and your ideal."

I dozed off.

When I woke up, the room was a light white. Then the whiteness spread. It was white all around. The universe was all white.

I didn't get out of my bed.

"Was it time?" I asked myself. It seems that I didn't have enough time to see life in the Promised Land! Oppressed, denigrated, I didn't have enough time to see the absolute end of suffering. What to do? At least we took the first steps. The day will come when all will be free to live openly their beliefs. I had an ideal and worked for it incessantly. I dedicated my life to this cause and finally there I am. It is time to meet my Creator. That is all I could do.

If I had another thousand years to live, I would spend it for this cause!

I couldn't serve as well as Sara, who saved Abraham from the Pharaoh's wrath and gave birth to Isaac to become the mother of all Jews.

I couldn't serve as well as Ester, who saved the nation from the Persian King Ahasuerus's vizier, Haman, by entering the king's harem and making him see Haman's true motives.

I couldn't serve as well as Deborah, who led the army to victory as a Judge.

I couldn't serve as well as Ruth in becoming the symbol of loyalty.

I couldn't serve as well as Judith, who went to bed with the enemies' commander Holophernes, got him drunk, and

Dona Gracia

chopped off his head.

I did what I could, using all my means and power to save every Jew I could. Since this was my assignment, it was accomplished. It is time for me to happily meet my Creator. I am ready and happy.

I felt myself melting within an ocean of white, a pure white light. My last words: "I worship the only God, King of the universe, with all my being."

Acknowledgements

This is a novel where strict efforts have been made to ensure historical accuracy.

I ventured into creative nonfiction after reading historical accounts of the times by Cecil Roth, and the biography by Andrée Aelion Brooks: *The Woman who Defied Kings: the life and times of Dona Gracia Nasi*. Fascinated by her character, I read all I could find about Dona Gracia in the Boston Public Library, university libraries, and works written in French and other languages while realising that little had been written about her in Turkey, a Moslem country. I wanted the Turkish public to know about this wonderful Jewish saint who led a most productive life and, in the end, was both saved by and had a marked impact on the Ottoman Empire.

Internationally renowned Turkish historian Halil Inalcik explains: The 16th century brought with it a closeness in Moslem-Jewish relations during the reign of Suleiman the Magnificent, most aclaimed of all Ottoman sultans. The Ottomans saved Jews from the fires of the Inquisition; Jews helped the Ottomans modernize finance and commerce. Such were the contributions that led to a Jew, Jozef Nasi, son-in-law of Dona Gracia, being named Duke of Naxos by the Sultan and Caliph. A sultan is the equivalent of a European king. A caliph is a religious successor to the Islamic prophet Muhammad and leader of the Muslim world.

Turkish historians know quite a bit about Dona Gracia but did not write what would have done her justice. I mentioned this to Halil Inalcik. Though I had read his work on the Ottomans, I did not see mention of Jews or Dona Gracia. Is it possible they had not existed? He said this was a book for me to write. Me? A business man without a background as an academic or historian. Dr. Inalcik generously introduced me to his erudite assistant, Bulent Arı, who guided me through the research and writing, and then carefully edited the historical content in the final version.

Trouble is, I learned, this was a history book, and I was not a known historian. No one would publish it.

My daughter in law, Ellen, introduced me to a sucessful writer friend, Azra Kohen, who introduced me to Yelda Cumalioglu, her publisher. A delightfully open minded and modern business woman, she shared with me her frank opinion; "Aaron, I will not publish it as it will not sell! It has amazing content and history. Turn it into a good novel and it will be a best seller." She introduced me to Uğur Becerikli, the editor who guided me in turning my history book into a novel. I worked with him and when the book reached daylight, it became a best seller in Turkey. I owe him the world. I had spent 5 years researching the history behind the novel. Ertürk Aksun, general manager at Destek Yayinlari, my publisher in Instanbul, said:

"Aaron, correctness of historical content only adds 4% to sales."

This was a blow from an experienced and well-intentioned industry insider. But my publisher consoled me saying that "what Ertürk said is unfortunately true but your book has a backbone. Unlike light novels, it will sell for decades to come."

Harun Elkıran worked hard in the background, editing,

Acknowledgements

preparing the web site, and directing social media for this novel in Turkey.

The English artist Gordon Napier drew illustrations exclusively for this book. A devoted researcher and such a pleasure to work with, Gordon continuously challenged me in authenticating Ottoman costumes and traditions.

My beloved son, Vedat, who has long made a game of criticizing and challenging my thoughts, got so caught up in the soft copy Turkish-language version of this book that, though it was geting chilly on the beach, I caught him avidly reading it. That's when I realised I had something worth taking seriously. My toughest critic who would never deprive me of his opinion, however harsh, gave me the green light.

I am grateful to friends and to Turkey's most famous contemporary historian, Professor Ilber Ortaylı, who encouraged me along the way, and prompted me to think this story is worthy of international attention.

I shared my plan with my guru, Andrée Aelion Brooks. She not only encouraged me but helped me find my constant motivator and inquisitive editor, Bonnie Britt, who guided me through the complicated maze of gettng a book properly edited and published in the West. Thanks to her, I am the author of a book I am proud of.

My wife, Adel, light of my life, modestly pretends she has no share in the success of this novel. Truth is, she sat by me, always encouraging, never complaining about the many hours I neglected her and stole from our togetherness.